To Bri

FIRE & ICE

Secrets & lies can't stay
buried forever...

Enjoy!

[signature]

ALI CARTER

8-5-2025

The manufacturer's authorised representative in the EU for product safety is Authorised Rep
Compliance Ltd, 71 Lower Baggot Street, Dublin D02 P593 Ireland
(www.arccompliance.com)

This is a work of fiction. Names, characters, businesses, places, events
and incidents are either the products of the author's imagination
or used in a fictitious manner. Any resemblance to actual persons,
living or dead, or actual events is purely coincidental.

Troubador Publishing Ltd
Unit E2 Airfield Business Park,
Harrison Road, Market Harborough,
Leicestershire. LE16 7UL
Tel: 0116 2792299
Email: books@troubador.co.uk
Web: www.troubador.co.uk

ISBN 978 1836283 140

British Library Cataloguing in Publication Data.
A catalogue record for this book is available from the British Library.

Printed and bound by CPI Group (UK) Ltd, Croydon, CR0 4YY
Typeset in 12pt Adobe Garamond Pro by Troubador Publishing Ltd, Leicester, UK

BIOGRAPHY
ALI CARTER

Ali lives in Sutton, a small village up on the Norfolk Broads, with her husband, who as a retired Met. police officer was a great help in assuring legalities in '*Fire & Ice*' and her other books are as accurate as possible. However, she still regularly researches police policy and procedures to keep up to date, and has associated contacts who are also very helpful.

All four books in the DCI Harry Longbridge series are:-

Blood List
Dead Girls Don't Cry
The Delegate
Fire & Ice

A fifth book in the series is currently underway.

Ali loves to hear from her readers and can be contacted below. She also sends out a book-club newsletter every other month for any readers who like to keep in touch, but it's especially useful for those who aren't on social media. Free membership can be found on her website.

Website:- alicarterauthor.com
Facebook:- @alicarterauthor
X:- @alicrimewriter
Instagram:- alicarter.author
TikTok:- @alicartercrimeauthor

'Now she could hear and feel her heart thumping, imagine it crashing against her ribs as the room opened up to her fully, because there in all its glory, albeit dusty as hell, was a full-sized grand piano, ivory notes jumping up and down – with nobody playing them. Charlotte's eyes grew wider and wider, but she wasn't looking at the piano because the stool was not in its usual place. Instead, it was about ten feet to the left, near the window. And hanging above, loosely in mid-air, was a long, thick, corded rope – an empty noose dangling at the end of it…'

*To Bruce, for literally being my roadie for fifty-plus events
a year – oh, and doing all the cooking, too!
Thank you so much... xxx*

MESSAGE FOR
MY READERS ...

Although this fourth book in my DCI Harry Longbridge series, '*Fire & Ice*,' takes place during 2021, as for book three, '*The Delegate*,' I have deliberately chosen not to mention anything associated with the pandemic. I hope you feel as I do that we read fiction for pleasure, to get away from our daily lives, and would prefer not to be reminded of what was for many an exceptionally difficult and upsetting period.

PROLOGUE

RAMPTON HIGH SECURITY HOSPITAL
MAY 2021

The rain had stopped earlier, the sun was just peeping from behind a cloud and a radio could be heard playing Chopin's Nocturne, Opus 9, No. 2, behind them. Charlotte and Annie were amongst a handful of patients allowed a short tea break in the garden that afternoon under the close watch of a warden. Having worked hard weeding some low flowering beds, they now sat with their drinks chatting together on a long bench facing a group of majestic firs. Gardening wasn't exactly Annie's favourite hobby any more than it was Charlotte's, but it was better than being on an enforced lock-in, *and they'd had a couple of those.*

Annie was in a sunnier mood than usual given her long-term situation, for which she most definitely blamed the woman sitting next to her. Yes, unusually, to anyone looking on, Annie looked almost jubilant.

She didn't think he'd actually *do* it, but falling in love, *really* in love, probably for only the second time in his life, had clearly had an effect. It wasn't entirely easy. He'd found them behind a light fitting at the flat, *that* part was simple. The carriage to, and transfer of when visiting was substantially harder. He'd told her that day how satisfying it was to know that finally … *finally* … he would be rid of that woman forever. Everything was her fault. *It had always been her fault.*

Charlotte drained the last drops of her coffee, repeatedly wiping beads of sweat from her forehead, her icy demeanour barely detectable. The cloud eventually revealed the full afternoon sun and was now blazing down, but in the last fifteen or twenty minutes she'd begun to feel distinctly unwell. Strange, given she was so rarely ill.

Opening the folded note Annie had just placed in her lap, her eyes tried hard to focus on the short message so carefully handwritten inside. Then in shock more than anything else, turned to meet her companion's accusing eyes before following their gaze to a familiar but hazy man at the far table. As Chopin reached a crescendo, the cramping increased, her focus now fading fast, she dropped the note along with her cup, and clutching at her stomach slumped forwards onto the dewy grass. Staring vacantly straight ahead, Annie lifted the tea to her lips. She watched unseeing, as a huge flock of ravens scattered noisily, soaring high above the firs into the late afternoon sun. Way below them a breeze caught the note, blowing it into a surf-hopping dance across the lawn until it came to a quivering rest. Annie's gaze dropped to her tightly closed hand. Unfurling her fingers, three empty coffee sachets lay scrunched in her palm for just a second before a breeze quickly whipped them up, causing each one to roll and bounce collaboratively alongside the note.

And at the table further along, with Chopin's now more gentle notes continuing to float on the air, Miles Peterson turned around and dipped his head in complicity. The warden came running, shouting for help as Charlotte remained motionless, arm outstretched, glassy eyes staring directly in line with her failed plans ... and Annie's more successful ones.

The note flickered – then finally blew upright.

'Oh, what a tangled web you weaved when first you practised to deceive, you never planned to pay this price – it all goes back to Fire & Ice.'

ICU BASSETLAW HOSPITAL
KILTON HILL - WORKSOP

SATURDAY 8TH MAY 2021

The light above the bed shone brightly, but her eyes did not. The ventilator's rhythmic shhh... tuk tuk, shhh... tuk tuk... steadily filled her lungs with air, breathing for her, living for her, retaining the status quo as she lay in the stillness and darkness of coma, eyes unseeing, lids down – occasionally twitching.

A feeding tube led directly into her stomach, and was taped securely in place. Another for breathing sat securely in her windpipe, emerging alien style between dry lips. Both were ugly but nevertheless absolutely crucial – *thanks to Annie Longbridge.*

Her hair had grown considerably since the sharp pixie cut that had accompanied her to New York some seventeen months earlier, and the harsh dark colour she'd had on that killing trip as Carla Preston – remained...

partly. Her comparable Cruella de Vil look was now very evident, as the grown-out black and natural fairish auburn tones joined in an unflattering half-and-half curtain, spread messily across the white pillow.

Rampton had never obliged her multiple requests for tint which explained her rather grotesque Cruella/racoon presentation that met every nurse and doctor upon entering the room. Sadly, she'd not been one of the favoured patients at the psychiatric hospital, but none of that mattered anymore because Charlotte was unaware of it, unaware of anything and even if she *were*, the state of her hair would strangely no longer be at the top of her list. Her distinctly *unfinished* list.

No. For the time being, living in another world, one that prevented her consciousness, or any form of reality at all, ex-GP and serial killer Charlotte Peterson had no sense of anything – zilch. So, all her addled brain could do now was rest. *And send her back ...*

ONE

KIRKDALE CUMBRIA
CLAYTON HOUSE GRAMMAR
SCHOOL FOR GIRLS

THURSDAY 31ST OCTOBER 1995 -
HALLOWEEN . . .

For the third time that year, the fire alarm was screeching at full throttle, echoing ear-piercingly loud through the classrooms, ancient halls and corridors of Clayton House. However, it wasn't because of any fire. Nor had a drill been planned for that morning or the caretaker's cat become stranded high in the boughs of the larger of the two oaks flanking the entrance gates. No. For the third time in a few months, something very serious had happened at the once-prestigious school. One pupil had already been found hanging in the music room five months ago, and a teacher had completely vanished the month before. Now the rumour was a second girl was missing. Nobody knew how, and nobody knew why. For the second time, they didn't know when, where or how long she'd been gone. At least, no one was *admitting* to knowing anything about the current whereabouts and health status of the Clayton House pupil, or even if *this* one was still alive.

Beneath the sound of the screaming siren, girls began quickly forming orderly queues outside their classrooms under direction of their teachers. Everyone from year seven up moved methodically and autonomously through the building; a low buzz emitting from most; all meeting outside at designated areas of several large playgrounds. Everyone, that was, *apart from seventeen-year-old Charlotte Krane, and sixteen-year-old Emily Rowlands ...*

* * *

4 YEARS EARLIER - THURSDAY 5TH SEPTEMBER 1991

CHARLOTTE ...

Twelve-year-old second-year student Charlotte Krane watched them all file in from her seat in year two. She recognised the younger girl as soon as she tossed her long flame-red hair over her shoulder and marched confidently into the large airy banqueting hall of Clayton House like she'd done it all her life. It was the first assembly of the school year, and she, Charlotte, was watching carefully as the new girls entered to take their places for the very first time.

It was doubtful red hair was as self-assured as she made out – nobody was on day one, not even Charlotte herself the year before, but it made for interesting observation, especially as they were already friends. At almost thirteen, and therefore one of the eldest in her class, Charlotte exuded a sense of self-imposed importance, one who decided on student selection when it came to who would and wouldn't be accepted – and therefore popular. The rules of the private school game were clear. Stake your claim in year one, and fight to keep your place all the way to the sixth form, or what was rumoured to be changing to years seven to twelve. The numbers were unimportant, and she would call them whatever she wanted. What was clear, key in the order of things, was that a *Krane* would always have the upper hand...

EMILY . . .

Eleven-year-old Emily Rowlands tossed flame-red hair over her left shoulder and walked into the hall for the first assembly of the school year. She was nervous. It was a much bigger school than Kirkdale Primary and only a few of the girls in her form were known to her. Nevertheless, she would alert no one to her anxiety as she held her head high, and walked in line with feigned confidence. She got that stiff upper lip from her mother, Margaret, and right now she was grateful for it. Other students moved along closely in front and behind her, some whispering to, and nudging each other, some giggling, one or two turning back as they walked, and a couple of smaller, slighter girls, eerily silent. Emily could sense their fear, those two, she felt sorry for them.

From its centre, she looked left and right across the huge room at all the other kids, row on row of crisp white shirts and dark brown skirts, all the way to the front where the year sevens were to sit. Where *was* she? As Emily passed the empty chairs yet to be filled, she finally saw the slim girl with shoulder-length fair hair, a little taller than her, sitting with other year-eight students a few rows back from the front. She wasn't chatting to anyone which was *so* typical of her, even though, Emily figured, as a year eight, Charlie would already know those other year-eight kids. She didn't look worried or upset about it – it was almost as if she intended it to be that way, like she was too important for the others to talk to her. She thought she was above them ... above everyone. Well ... *Emily Rowlands would soon see about that...*

Once everyone was in their seats, fifty-two-year-old headmistress Veronica Dean stood up gracefully behind her lectern, and with a thin smile, looked out at the sea of faces that filled the hall. Hers wasn't exactly an unpleasant smile, just one that exuded authority and determination rather than being bright and welcoming. It did, however, challenge *anyone* who might be thinking of poking fun at her initials, something she'd had no choice but to accept and deal with, but had always resented her parents' thoughtlessness for. Veronica tucked a strand of fading auburn hair behind one ear, and tilting her head, gently patted the chignon at the nape of her neck. She then looked down and picked up her notes.

To her right, at a floor-level piano, sat a small, anxious mouse of a woman with a mink bob, fiddling worriedly with some sheet music whilst intermittently pushing ill-fitting metal-rimmed glasses up her nose. She scratched the inside of her left wrist until pinpricks of blood bloomed on her skin. Patricia Dean had long learnt to live with her troubling skin conditions, largely due to the domineering older sister who now began to address the school…

"Good *morning*, girls," she said, eyes sweeping the hall, "and welcome back for the autumn term. I hope you all had an enjoyable summer break."

"Good *morrr* – ning Miss *Deeeean*," chorused the school in a musical trill.

"As usual, before I read out my new-term address, we will sing our Clayton House School song. For all the new girls, you will have found printouts of the words on your chairs – just do your best with the tune!" Emily had already found hers and had it in her lap. "Hopefully you're not now sitting on them," she added, as if knowing some would be doing exactly that. Several near to Emily stood up, red faced, to retrieve their song sheets and others began anxiously looking at each other and under their chairs. It earned them all an eye roll from their new headmistress as she cleared her throat before continuing … "For the rest of the school, you should have it memorised by now, and I shall expect loud and exuberant voices using the *correct* words. Please stand." There was a scraping of chairs as everyone stood up, followed by rippled murmuring and a few sniggers which quickly fell silent as Miss Dean raised an overly arched eyebrow. For some reason it was always the left one…

She looked over at her younger sister, whose hands were now poised above the keys of the baby grand, and inclined her head. "When you're ready, Miss Dean…"

Most of the girls obliged their headmistress with a reasonably good rendition of 'Calling All Ye Clayton Girls,' and banging out the refrain a bit louder than the verses because they all knew that bit. This resulted in a general volume increase as the chorus arrived, followed by a distinct reduction, some mumbling and missed words at the beginning of each verse. This did not go unnoticed by either of the Dean sisters, and piano-playing Patricia exerted extra volume at the vulnerable points to cover up the issue.

Charlotte Krane, however, sang not one word, preferring instead to scan the room whilst mouthing a few lyrics here and there. She noted which teachers had returned for the new term, and those who hadn't, along with their apparent mood and general air of emotional stability. Charlotte was intuitively advanced for her age and made good use of it. During her first year at Clayton House, there had been some strange occurrences regarding one or two of them. She wasn't sure what it *was* exactly, although there was talk of a '*Green Lady*' that haunted the old library behind the banqueting hall they were in at the moment. Mrs Lewis, year 1A (technically now 7A), the history teacher, was often in the library, and right now was looking decidedly iffy standing by the door at the back of the hall. But that could also be down to the fact there were rumours she spent half her time snorting cocaine in the music room when Miss Dean the younger, was at lunch, or had a day off.

Karen Lewis had been a teenager in the sixties and seventies. Her favoured attire back then was flowery smock tops and wide-bottomed brightly checked 'Oxford bags,' (trousers), although not necessarily together. Smoking pot had also become a favoured habit, especially during teacher training college where she'd only just managed to scrape through her first year. She'd had to seriously pull out all the stops in years two and three, to gain her teaching certificate. The cocaine habit had developed somewhat later – apparently after a particularly nasty event in her life she never spoke of. Charlotte had made it her goal to discover exactly what that event was, especially as the narcotics information she'd received had come from a very reliable source. One, however, that either would not, or could not, divulge Mrs Lewis' chequered past.

"… *Clay – ton girls, we're Clay – ton girls for – ev – er strong and truuue…*

We're Clay – ton girls, we're Clay – ton girls we're sis – ters through and throoough."

Turning away from her history teacher, Charlotte

mimed the last refrain with a knowing smile. Karen Lewis had slipped out through the ancient arched door to the stone-flagged walkway which Charlotte knew would take her directly to the staircase leading up to the music room…

Although she'd had the song sheet, Emily had absolutely no idea of the tune, but had done her best all the same. Occasionally looking round to see if Charlie was singing as well, it was no surprise to discover her friend was barely making an effort. She'd also followed her eye-line to somewhere behind them at the back of the room, but with several tall girls in rows behind her, couldn't quite see what or who she was looking at. It was all very strange, but the first chance she got, she would ask her about it. Turning back round, Emily sat up very straight. The headmistress had walked to the centre of the stage, speech in hand, ready to make her new-term address.

"Well, that wasn't too bad at all, girls, well done." She looked down at the front two rows where there was shuffling, much lip biting and heads looking sideways amongst the new pupils. "Don't worry – by next term you'll have it all off pat, think of it as ongoing homework." Veronica Dean looked back up at the main hall. "As you know, at the end of last year we sadly lost two of our most well-loved teachers, our French teacher, Miss Haynes, and Mrs Travers who took biology and was also head of year nine…" There was murmuring and some tight facial expressions in the centre of the room. Clearly, 'well loved' was not how some of the older girls would have described one or both of those ex-teaching staff… "Whilst we are most disappointed at not having them back with us this term, we are very lucky to have found Miss White and Mrs Nightingale who will be joining us in those positions. So please stand and let's give them our traditional welcome to Clayton House." The sound of scraping chairs filled the air for a second time as the whole school stood up, a ripple of applause just about aired, and Miss Dean the younger played a few congratulatory-styled chords on the baby grand.

The rest of the address included information about restricted use of the swimming pool for the first few weeks of term, due to a changing room upgrade. Unfortunately there had been no one available to carry out the work during the holiday. *Groans and sighs all round…*

Emily glanced over at Charlotte to see her finger signing. Charlotte framed an 'L' for '*Library*' followed by 'LT' for '*Lunch Time*'. It was their way of communicating at primary school when wanting to meet up later, but unable to speak at the time. Back then, it was to share sweets they'd swiped from home or to swap the latest collectable toy. *This time, Charlotte had something far more interesting to share with her friend.*

TWO

HM PRISON FRANKLAND
BRASSIDE - COUNTY DURHAM
5.00 A.M. 15TH MAY 2021

Former DC Terry Hackett had been practically shitting himself right from the moment of arrest. After poisoning Jerry Kitson the previous summer to prevent the car salvage man giving evidence against him, he and George Gifford (aka Gunner Gifford, or the Ape, given his size), had been duly processed and were both now on Judges Remand, awaiting sentence. Terry knew the score for cops in prison, *any* prison. To go down for murder meant category 'A' at Her Majesty's pleasure – and Frankland had the catchy little pet name, *'Monster Mansion.'* He'd been under no illusions as to who, or what, could be waiting for him in there. Even though he was with others on remand and not with convicted prisoners, some had been in before and most had stepped up their illegal habits considerably since their last stretch. Some were what Terry Hackett ironically considered to be, 'real' killers. He figured he wasn't one of those because he'd been coerced and blackmailed by the mob. Either way, they all hated cops. The fact the cop they were now banged up with had been charged with killing two of his 'own' would make little difference. It would cut no slack with them. In fact, they'd probably think even less of him for betraying his colleagues.

George had been sent to Belmarsh in South East London. It was no skin off Terry's nose he hadn't been down for Frankland. Gifford wasn't exactly a mate – he'd simply been in the pay of the Zandinis as well, carried a gun, and sent to watch his back nine months ago when everything had kicked off. Or more specifically, George Gifford had been the Zandini's Mafiosi (or Godmother), Dominique du Guarde's right-hand shooter. That was the *Chief Constable of Cumbria Police* du Guarde, who had, as far as Terry was aware, still not been outed. Lucky for him, because up till now, he'd been unharmed and reasonably safe inside Frankland, and knew that was largely down to du Guarde's extended influence. Now, wide awake and reflecting at nearly midnight, as he lay on the bottom bunk in his cell, he realised it might have been better if Gifford *had* been sent to Frankland with him. In reality, though, the authorities would have never put them together.

He looked up at the bowed mattress defining the obese shape of the man lying above him, whose snoring filled the cell and was practically loud enough to reach the governor's office on another wing. Terry made no move to complain – he wasn't about to invoke a death wish. Despite having killed three people himself, two through arson and one with thallium, a tasteless poison, being incarcerated with a toxic mix of brutal and notorious terrorists, gangsters, sex offenders and murderers was seriously stressing him out. *And he hadn't even been sentenced yet …*

There was a stirring above as the bulging mattress squeaked, and the snoring that had been a steady grating irritation suddenly stopped. It was replaced by a couple of backward nasal expulsions and a wet splutter. A silent gap in the apnoeic breathing was short-lived, as six-feet, seventeen-stone, forty-something Dave 'The Blade' Cookson, *Cookie to his mates*, resumed his loud rattling snore. Terry had already learnt Cookson could either play the jolly fat guy with a big smile, who occasionally shared his smokes, or he could be Dave the Blade – and nobody wanted to be around when he took on *that* persona. Cookson was awaiting sentencing for slicing up his own brother who'd apparently had the temerity to beat him in a card game. Dave had felt insulted and humiliated in front of his mates. Men who looked up to him, respected him for being the boss, the kingpin – and in one aggressive and sweeping arch Dave had practically separated Rob Cookson's head from his body. Terry had made a mental note to deny knowledge of any type of card game whilst *The Blade* was on his wing – *and certainly whilst he was in close proximity.* All cells at Frankland were single occupancy and it was highly irregular for Terry to be sharing his. He was due to be moved to a single within days, but space was more than tight and thus sleep rarely enjoyed. He'd have been happier, *a lot happier*, if he'd been stuck in solitary, but here he was, lying beneath a nutter… It was at the end of that thought, the snoring stopped completely. Dave Cookson was awake…

"Ere … you asleep down there, copper?"

Terry stayed quiet, hoping, *praying* the snoring would quickly resume.

"Oi— 'ackett!! I *said* – are – you – *asleep*?"

Below, sweating considerably, Terry took a deep breath and yawned as if he'd just woken up. "Uhh … yeah … yep, I'm awake, just. Whassup?"

"I'm going to need you to do a little job for me. Reckon you could do that Tezzer, and … *still* keep your head?"

The sweat went cold and his mouth went dry. His hesitation in replying didn't go down well …

"Of course," continued Cookson, "I could always ask someone else to do both jobs."

"B-both?" replied Terry, a catch in his throat.

Cookson eased his bulk down gently from the top bunk, and after steadying himself, sat on his chair – amazingly it still held… "Well, there's the job I want *you* to do, but if you refuse, then *you* become job number two – *see*?" He crossed his arms and grinned without smiling, discoloured teeth and several gaps in full view.

Terry swallowed down a very large, very dry golf ball that appeared to have manifested deep in his gullet.

Du Guarde clearly didn't have her eyes everywhere, then. He coughed in an attempt to clear the obstruction, and mumbled in a quiet and compliant tone… "What do you want me to do … ?"

* * *

10.00 A.M. KIRKDALE POLICE STATION
KIRKDALE - KESWICK

Eighty miles away, a new constable was preparing to go out on patrol in Kirkdale, Keswick. Andrew Gale, now Student DC Gale, was in his first year as part student, part frontline officer in the Cumbrian Constabulary. When making enquiries the previous autumn, he'd discovered that as he had a degree, he could take the DHEP (Degree-Holder Entry Programme) route, and still earn whilst he learnt. This was a relief as he and Gina had a mortgage to pay, and not long become parents to little Ellie-Rose. He smiled at a photo of Ellie and Gina stuck to the inside of the door as he pulled out a yellow hi-vis security vest from his locker. Ellena Rose Gale had made an appearance a few months prior to their wedding the previous September and was now eight months old – his pride and joy.

"Hey, Andy, aren't you ready yet? We're going to have to get you up to speed if you're going to cut it as a full-blown copper, you know!" Suzanne Moorcroft was checking her watch leaning up against the door frame of the male locker room. For a fraction of a second Andrew looked visibly pale. Since joining the police, being on point for absolutely everything was massively important to him, and he'd always been known for his excellent time keeping ... *pre* fatherhood.

"Sorry, Sarge, I'll—"

Suzanne gave him a playful punch as he exited the locker room. "Don't be daft, and call me Suze, everyone else does. Well, unless the 'pips' are around anyway – not *Harry* obviously." The pips was Suzanne's nickname for the top brass, and DCI Harry Longbridge had been brought out of retirement a year earlier to fly to the U.S. and track down Rampton-escapee killer, Charlotte Peterson. He'd led the original murder case in 2018 and been drafted back in to work as a consultant advisor with his replacement, and *very* close past London colleague, DI Fran Taylor. She'd transferred from their old station, and during a weak moment in New York they'd more than 'reconnected', resulting in a child – Jamie Ross Taylor. With Harry's mentally challenged wife Annie now also in Rampton, having been manipulated and coerced by Charlotte to continue her kill list, he had a great deal of emotional trauma piled exceedingly high on his plate.

It was Harry who was instrumental in Andrew's application to join the police. Over the last four years they'd become good friends, despite an initial tense crime reporter/senior investigating officer relationship, when Andrew had worked for the *Courier* newspaper. Ironically, it was during that time Harry noticed Andrew had good gut instincts at crime scenes, and thought he had the makings of a good officer. They'd also shared a traumatising time in New York when Andrew, Gina and their friend Molly had been staying with Gina's estranged mother, and managed to become involved with Charlotte's final hours before her capture…

"Suze it is then," smiled Andrew, patting his body vest to make sure he wasn't missing any equipment. "Where are we patrolling this morning, then?"

"Well, I thought we'd head over to the high street in town – there's been increasing levels of shop theft in the centre. They're just picking stuff up and walking out with it, so some police presence is needed. They're lucky to get any at all frankly, we're that stretched, it'll only be us out there."

"Is it Bella's buffet first then, officers? You know, I think they may just have a couple of bacon rolls and a coffee with my name on!" Harry Longbridge had appeared in the corridor behind them – apart from The Carpenters Arms pub, Bella's was his favourite place to eat. Not that he should have been eating bacon rolls in twos given his diabetic diagnosis a few years earlier, something the whole station knew about and tried to help him keep on the straight and narrow with.

"*Two* bacon rolls, is it, sir?" Suzanne's eyebrows lifted in a 'you really think that's a good idea?' expression.

"Well, I didn't get any breakfast, and I've had my jab this morning so don't you worry your concerned little head about it. Much as I appreciate that concern of *course*,

Sergeant." Suzanne rolled her eyes. Harry hadn't actually used the expression '*pretty* little head', but he was old-school and the inference was there. He turned to Andrew then quickly turned back to Suzanne as realisation dropped …

"Sorry – I … I didn't mean anything by … by, you know – I'm —"

"It's o – *kay*, I know you don't mean it disparagingly. To be honest, Har … sir – you've nothing to worry about on that score. At least Terry Hackett's gone for good – one less misogynist to worry about." Remembering exactly *why* DC Hackett had been sent to prison caused all three to briefly look down and shuffle their feet in thought. PC Rob McPhail – their '*Big Mac*' – had been a much-loved and respected colleague. To prevent him giving evidence in an internal drugs case, Terry Hackett had burnt him and his wife to a crisp … in their own cottage.

Looking up and fixing a smile back on his face, Harry rested a hand on Andrew's shoulder. "Anyway, how's it going, lad? This one's not costing you an arm and a leg in shoe leather, is she? Sergeant Moorcroft does love a good walk!"

"Heyyy, excuse *me* – patrolling is all part of the basics, *sir*, just doing my job with the rookie." With hands on hips, Suzanne was now looking quite indignant.

"Come on, let's get over to the best café in town and I'll treat you both to breakfast," said Harry, hoping it would take the heat off. It was a sentence that almost always calmed an awkward moment, and rarely needed to be repeated in any police station in the land. As all three made their way to the stairs down to reception and the exit, Andrew smelt something in the corridor he'd hoped never to have experienced again. It was a strong, heavy, woody-scented aftershave … *and he was walking towards it.* There was someone waiting to be seen at the front counter. As Andrew got closer, the scent increased. His throat dried and his chest tightened. He hadn't seen the man for a very long time and had hoped never to again. Yet here he was, looking hard as nails and twice as ugly. *He hadn't even realised the evil bastard had been released.*

THREE

CLAYTON HOUSE GRAMMAR SCHOOL KIRKDALE CUMBRIA
THURSDAY 5TH SEPTEMBER 1991

"So … who's your form teacher then? As you heard in assembly, there've been a few changes around here since last term." Charlotte dipped her hand back into the crisp bag at the end of the question and stuffed a few in her mouth. She and Emily were sitting on a bench in the main playground, having been to the tuck shop after lunch, and were now finishing off two bags of cheese and onion.

"Mrs Lewis – seems okay. She does seem a bit sort of, *over-excited* and *extra* smiley, though, like she's got loads of energy, especially after this morning's break."

Charlotte spluttered a crispy laugh and gave Emily a playful punch on the arm. "Damn it, I was going to tell *you* about our Mrs Lewis!"

"What do you mean? What *about* her?" Emily wrinkled her nose up in puzzlement. It was something she'd always done if she felt in the dark about something and annoyed someone knew a secret that she didn't. Charlotte remembered it from primary school…

"*Don't* keep doing that with your face, you'll get wrinkles." Quickly reaching to smooth Emily's cheek with her hand, she continued … "She's—" Charlotte looked around them before covertly overly forming her words and with a lowered voice said … "Rumour has it she's doing *drugs*, really bad ones – literally *cocaine* and stuff!" Her eyebrows danced up and down as she related the juicy gossip she'd been dying to tell her friend since assembly that morning.

Emily's eyes widened in shock, her mouth dropping as her hand stopped halfway out of her crisp bag before Charlotte lifted her chin up. "But, but, how can you possibly even *know* that?"

Charlotte waited for three girls to walk past before answering. "There's a girl in the fifth year, *stupidly re-named* year 11 as of this term." She rolled her eyes dramatically… "Not the girl, obviously, the *year*. Her name's Jackie Squires and she knows pretty much everything that goes on here. Don't ask me how, but I overheard her talking in the loos last year. It could be 'cos her older cousin used to be at Clayton though – that would make sense."

Emily tipped the last few crumbs into her mouth and scrunched the bag up. "Why would Mrs Lewis be affected at school, though? Surely you're not saying she's doing it… *here*? I mean … *where*? *Where* would she do it without being caught?"

Charlotte threw her empty crisp bag in the bin next to the bench and held her hand out for Emily to pass hers over… "The music room – I've seen her looking very shifty going up those stairs, and more than once. She slipped out of assembly this morning, and the music room is at the top of the staircase opposite the banqueting hall. You saw young Miss Dean who played the piano for the school song?" Emily nodded. "Well, she couldn't be in two places at once now, could she, and the music room is basically her study stroke office, so it was a guaranteed safe ten minutes for our little Miss Coke Head."

Emily thought for a moment. "Is it just *her*? I mean, are there any other teachers taking drugs? And how come nobody knows about Mrs. Lewis?"

"Well, I'll be honest – that, I *don't* know. It's always possible someone else *does*, and there *are* other crack-heads in this dump."

Emily wore her screwed-up, puzzled face again. "Don't you like it here, Charlie? I thought you did."

Charlotte sighed heavily and rolled her eyes again… "Where do I even *begin*? The food's dire, the—"

"I thought dinner was quite nice, I love macaroni cheese."

"Wait till Friday – Friday's *always* Spaghetti M'Gosh."

"What in God's name is *that*?!"

"Long-form name is 'Spaghetti— *Oh My Gosh*!' It's basically all the leftovers from Monday to Thursday scraped into large baking dishes topped with a greasy skin of grilled cheese. So you'll have chicken, sprouts, carrots, pizza remnants, a bit of pork chop or boiled beef, you name it. Your macaroni will be in there too, if you left any." Emily grimaced as Charlotte continued her list.

"You already know about Mrs Lewis's habits, then there's Miss Phillips, who takes PE and *ghastly* cross-country, for us lower years, *definitely* something odd about old *'Fishy' Phillips*, and Mr Stevens the caretaker is ancient, creepy as hell and looks like that bald bloke out of the Addams family."

"Uncle Fester?"

"That's him. Every time I see the man with a shovel, I think he's off to bury another body."

"*Another* body?!" exclaimed Emily, eyes popping now.

Charlotte grinned. "Well, obviously I can't *prove* anything but …" She looked at her friend's horrified expression, waited a few seconds, then suddenly burst out laughing… "Oh my God, Em— your *face*! Honestly, you're such an easy wind-up!"

"*Very* funny, I *don't* think! Has *anything* you've just said been true, Charlie? Or are you just putting me through some sort of new girl's initiation? *Which*, I might add, is highly unfair given I'm supposed to be your best *friend*."

"It's *all* true, Em. Well, not about Uncle Fester, not that I actually know of, anyway, and you *are* my best friend even if we've been split up this last year, you being younger and still at the primary and all. Look, this school has a lot of history behind it so it's more interesting than most. It was founded in the nineteenth century by Sir Darnley Clayton – hence the name, Clayton House. As you know, Cumbria wasn't actually created until 1974 from the counties of Cumberland and Westmorland, and old Sir Darnley was an exiled nobleman from down south, Surrey or somewhere, I think. For some reason he was paid to leave his home hundreds of years ago, I can't remember why off the top of my head, but it's in one of the history books in the library. *Anyway* ... Darnley made his way north, bought the now ruined old manor house nearby, called it Clayton Hall and built this school on his estate. Keswick was originally in Cumberland, so the school was *also* originally in Cumberland. There's actually a rumour old Darnley was a bit of a lady's man, had affairs with several of the teachers back in the day and one ended up hanging herself. They call her the *Green Lady*, and some even say at certain times of the year she can be seen in either of the music rooms, ours or the manor's ... dangling from a *noose* ..."

"Now I *know* you're making it up!" Emily crossed her arms indignantly. She did not like the idea of her so-called friend making fun of her.

"Honest to God, Em, I'm just telling you what I've been told since I've been here, and what I read in that book in the library. You can check it out yourself, it's called *'Sir Darnley Clayton's Legacy'*, or *'The Legacy of Clayton Hall'*, one or the other, I can't remember. Don't reckon our Mrs Lewis has read it, though, *or* seen any noose-hanging ladies – green or otherwise, because nothing stops her visits to that music room when Miss Dean's otherwise engaged."

"You can't be spending all your time watching Mrs Lewis, Charlie, so how come you see her go up there so often?"

At that very moment, the tall, suited figure of Karen Lewis came striding across the playground. Slim, willowy and fists clenched, her wavy ebony hair blew out behind her, exposing a taut facial expression. She'd emerged from beneath the arches of the nineteenth-century part of the school where the tuck shop stood, but didn't appear to be carrying anything resembling lunch. In fact, what she *was* carrying made both girls gasp – even Charlotte. Swinging from her left hand as she marched determinedly across the playground was a single crow ... a very large, very black, and very *dead*, single crow...

"*One for sorrow* ..." whispered Charlotte, leaning towards Emily, eyes following her form tutor into the science block.

"I thought that was magpies?" replied Emily, staring after her teacher.

"Whatever – *looks pretty sorrowful to me* ..."

* * *

Lying in bed that night, Charlotte swam in and out of the weirdest dream, and it was a very long time since she'd had one of those. She was a reluctant boarder at Clayton House, and during her first year had found it quite hard living away from home. It had caused serious resentment between herself and her parents, especially as plenty of girls didn't live in, but her mum and dad travelled a lot and as they'd always said, '*there was nothing else for it.*' The nightmares had eased after the second term, but now, it seemed, they were back with a vengeance.

She tossed and turned as beneath blood-red skies, gigantic black crows flew around her head, cawing loudly, swooping down and lunging at her face with their pointy oversized beaks, before suddenly dropping dead on her restrained body. She opened her mouth to scream but nothing came out – only intermittent bleeping noises echoed in the distance as she tried her hardest to first move her arms and then legs, but they were held fast. She couldn't see what by, just knew she couldn't move. Everything felt restricted and uncomfortable, she tried to wake herself out of the dream but couldn't. Her throat hurt, her stomach felt weird, and then the whooshing sound started … shhh… tuk tuk… shhh… tuk tuk…

FOUR

ICU BASSETLAW HOSPITAL KILTON HILL - WORKSOP
SATURDAY 15TH MAY 2021

The room was full of specialists. Well, one consultant and those rising medics who were each clamouring for their future senior consultant positions. They stood around her bed humming, hawing and chatting to each other in 'medical speak'. Not that Charlotte could hear anything, lying as she was, comatose, chest rising and falling courtesy of the ventilator.

"How long's it been now, and has there been any improvement?" asked sixty-year-old Mr Shepherd, Bassetlaw's top neurological consultant with thirty years and the beginnings of an ulcer under his belt. He was directing his question to ICU nurse Sofia Torres, as he bent to pick up the OBS chart at the end of the bed…

"A week with no change, Mr Shepherd," replied a considerably younger Sofia. "She twitches occasionally, mostly her face, but no response to touch, sound or—"

"*Mostly?*"

"Well, very occasionally she sort of *shivers* slightly, but nothing apart from that."

"Hmm…. you're using the Glasgow Coma Scale – right? Even though she's intubated." Shepherd looked up at her from under his steel-rimmed glasses, OBS chart still in hand.

"Yes sir, I—"

"So why aren't the scores on here?"

"They are, I put them on mysel—"

The consultant flipped the board round to show her. The specialised Glasgow Coma Scale chart wasn't visible. Nervously, she held out her hand towards Shepherd as everyone began to shuffle their feet awkwardly, some sighing, some rolling their eyes and some making twitchy '*Oh— ohhhh…*' facial expressions themselves.

"May I?" Taking the board from him, she lifted the top paper and then the second and the third. There was no GCS report. *Somebody had removed it.* "I – I don't understand, I've been sitting with the patient and filling it in regularly, several times a day, every day since she was admitted."

"Then where *is* it?" Silver-haired Simon Shepherd stood leaning back slightly with his head on one side and arms crossed, waiting. He fixed cold, stony blue eyes in her direction, lasering metaphysical holes through the young Puerto Rican nurse.

"I – I – someone must have removed it. I'll begin again immediately."

"Yes, Nurse Torres— you *will*. And please ensure it remains on there from now on."

Sofia's cheeks burned as she watched the team troop out, Mike Leyland, Shepherd's star protégé, tutt, tutt, tutting and shaking his head as he passed her.

"*Dick*!" she whispered sharply under her breath as he reached the door.

"It's Mike, actually," he quipped, turning to face her, "but you probably weren't close enough to read my ID badge. We *could* rectify that of course, maybe over a drink one evening?"

Sofia fake smiled. "Frankly … *Mike*, I think Dick suits you better, and I'm busy for the next, what, err … *fifty* years?"

"Only fifty, okay, great! I'll contact you via thought transference in 2071 then." Flashing a sparkly eyed grin, he swept out of the room leaving an indignant Sofia seething, until the smallest movements tugged both sides of her cross mouth and a reluctant smile escaped.

Cheeky git, she thought, grinning now as she went looking for some new GCS charts. Finding a stack in the tall medical cabinet, she sat next to the bed, took her pen from her pocket, and as Charlotte was intubated, immediately struck a line through the verbal response section. *There won't be anything coming from you verbally yet; incomprehensible, confused or otherwise. Not whilst that thing's stuck down your throat.* At the end of that thought, and just as she was going to test Charlotte's pain response, her patient's right arm suddenly jerked, knocking the pen sharply out of Sofia's hand onto the floor...

* * *

170 MILES AWAY - 10.30 A.M. BELLA'S CAFÉ KIRKDALE TOWN CENTRE - KESWICK

Suzanne Moorcroft wasn't at all sure she should be spending any part of her shift eating what amounted to a second breakfast. She'd had a very sensible bowl of porridge mixed with protein powder, and that should have sufficed until lunchtime. It also made her feel a bit guilty timewise. However, the wonderful breakfasty smells that hit them when they walked in were going to be difficult to ignore. She knew Andrew had very likely dashed out of the house with a slice of rye toast between his teeth whilst donning his jacket and unlocking the car, and her DCI ... well, he practically *lived* at Bella's, despite his diabetes condition.

She was sitting opposite Harry looking concerned at the yoke dripping from a bacon and egg bap, as he lifted it to his mouth, not convinced he *had* actually remembered to test his sugar levels, *or* had his insulin jab that morning, despite saying he had. Not that it was any of her business, but he was a much-loved and respected boss, and frankly, there weren't too many of those to the dozen.

Harry stopped just as he was about to take a bite. "DS Moorcroft, I *do* have to eat, you know!"

"Yes, sorry, of course it's just tha—"

"Everybody knows about the diabetes, Guv," volunteered Andrew as he put down his coffee, "and we all want you to stay well. Think of it as a group-care thing, a bit like alcoholics anonymous, only ... well, *not* anonymous, or actually anything to do with alcohol." He grinned, waving away the poor analogy, and resumed drinking. His friendship with Harry Longbridge over the last few years granted him a little leniency with overly familiar comments, even with their obvious rank differences.

Harry wondered if he'd ever get used to Andrew calling him Guv. Sounded decidedly weird... "Well, that's all very nice, and I appreciate it, but I'm afraid I'm never going to be giving up Bella's bacon and egg baps anytime soon, if at all, so you'll just have to get over it. There's far more important stuff to be worried about than my sugar levels, and one of them is the current Charlotte Peterson situation."

Andrew's eyes narrowed over the rim of his mug and he shot a glance at Suzanne, then back at Harry. He was still getting used to Miles, Charlotte Peterson's ex, being his father-in-law, and the somewhat delicate situation of the man's relationship with Harry's wife, Annie.

"You know she's in a coma over at Bassetlaw General in Nottinghamshire, don't you?" Harry continued. Andrew and Suzanne both nodded.

"It was on the news," said Andrew, "more than once, actually."

"I think I saw something on social media as well," added Suzanne. "It's like she's gained some kind of notoriety."

Harry raised his eyebrows. Facebook definitely wasn't his thing… "*Really?*" Dear God, it's like Shipman all over again…"

"Shipman?" asked Suzanne.

"GP in Greater Manchester; got twenty years at Wakefield in 2003 for murdering at least two hundred of his patients, ended up committing suicide in his cell. You'd be too young to remember."

"Wow. Yes, I think I'd have remembered *that* had I been old enough at the time!"

"I was only about thirteen," added Andrew, "but I vaguely remember something about it. I think there was a documentary on him a few years ago."

"I believe so. *Anyway*, as I was saying … Rampton's governor, Mark Randall, promised to keep me updated on Peterson, especially after the deaths of their patient Zoe Zandini and one of their staff, Rita Lemon, both of which he believes was down to Peterson. This was despite Retford CID putting Zoe's death down to Rita, and Rita's herself through misadven—"

Waving away the offer of a second cup of coffee from the waitress who'd suddenly appeared, Suzanne smiled a no thank you, whilst Harry leant back to accept a top-up of Bella's best black brew. Andrew was too engrossed to think about more coffee and had already downed his bacon roll.

"So …" continued Harry, lowering his voice as more customers trooped in, passing their table. "Retford CID put Zoe's death down to Rita, and Rita's herself through a mistake on her own part, but Mark Randall is emphatic it was Charlotte Peterson, and frankly, so am I. Peterson had motive for killing Zoe after the boiling-water incident, and apparently Rita Lemon had monitored their mediation meetings that followed. Randall mentioned in his email to me a few days ago that Rita Lemon was not popular amongst the staff at all, and Charlotte didn't react well during the sessions. That's when he let me know about the coma. She was apparently poisoned, but as yet nobody knows who by. Blood tests found a massive overdose of benzodiazepines in her system, which is the second time at Rampton in only a few weeks that one or more persons has had access to drugs. Randall and his team are stunned to discover this security breach."

"How does this affect things now, though, sir," asked Suzanne.

"Exactly what I was thinking," agreed Andrew. "Peterson can't harm anyone now, so why such continued interest?"

"Good question. Being a Zandini, Zoe was a family member of the gang behind Mac's – PC Rob McPhail's – death, and a whole lot more besides. Mac was a damned fine officer, colleague and friend. Looks like someone got their revenge on Charlotte Peterson for something but didn't finish the job. I'd like to know what that something was, who it was, and if it was linked to the Zandini's, the same as the scalding incident."

Andrew and Suzanne exchanged glances again as Harry bent down to his plate to avoid egg yolk dripping on his tie. She shook her head slightly indicating for Andrew not to mention it. Not to mention Annie Longbridge, Harry's wife, who'd committed murder herself under Charlotte's manipulative control, and who'd also been sent to Rampton. *Andrew ignored the hint...*

"There was ... *someone* at Rampton though, who, with hindsight, *surely* shouldn't have been sent to the same psychiatric hospital as Peterson? Is it possible she was housed in the same wing, or ... could have got to her somehow, and ... ?" His voice faded out when Harry looked up from his plate. Licking his fingers, then wiping them slowly on his paper napkin and taking a mouthful of coffee, he sat back in his chair, looking at them seriously for a moment.

Nobody had spoken about Annie to Harry since the realisation of her connection to Charlotte, and the revelations that had followed her actions, including her relationship with Charlotte's ex-husband, Miles Peterson. Initially sent to prison, she'd been assessed by a psychiatrist and then transferred to Rampton shortly afterwards. Pushing his plate to the side, Harry leant forward and leant both arms on the table, clasping his hands in thought. For a while there was an awkward silence, and for the first time in years, Andrew felt uncomfortable in his presence. Suzanne waited for the fallout...

"I agree. My wife should never have been sent there. It was a massive oversight and I've already been told she'll either be moved, or at the very least kept in a separate wing. More than likely she'll be moved if Peterson survives and returns – and that's a *big if*. However … there was no evidence to connect Annie with Charlotte's poisoning, and yes, it appears she *was* with her at the time, I'm not denying that or saying this out of some kind of estranged loyalty. It's just there's literally been *nothing* to prove she's liable. The cup Charlotte had been drinking from just prior to her collapse completely disappeared – it was therefore more than likely the overdose had been planted in whatever was in that cup. I've been told there were lots of people around them and a great deal of chaos at the time, so it wouldn't have been impossible to temporarily hide and dispose of it later. When Charlotte collapsed, there were patients and staff shouting and running for help and doctors trying to resuscitate her – it was complete mayhem."

Andrew couldn't help thinking it would have been just as easy for Annie as anyone else to have planted drugs in the drink and hidden the cup afterwards, but didn't say so. Neither did he mention what had been on his mind since seeing the man at the station's front desk earlier, on their way out. Andrew had far more stuff to worry about than Harry's diabetes and a killer in a coma. As far as he was concerned, after what she did to Gina, he hoped Charlotte *never* came round. As for Ryan Jacks, the man at the station, he and Jacks went way back, all the way to the children's home before Andrew's adoption. He'd never spoken about what had happened in that place, not with anyone, not even Gina. It had been dead and buried for twenty-three years, and Jacks had been inside for at least ten of those. *Now, though, it looked as if all that was coming home to roost ...*

FIVE

HM PRISON FRANKLAND
BRASSIDE - COUNTY DURHAM
12 NOON SATURDAY 15TH MAY 2021

As he slid his dinner tray along the counter, Terry Hackett could not only feel glistening beads birthing across his forehead but popping out from every sweat gland in his body.

The sharpened toothbrush handle in his pocket made choosing the pizza or chicken pie unusually difficult, particularly as it had a target name on it, and Dave Cookson was only two behind him in the queue—watching, waiting, *expecting*. How the hell that man thought he could do anything in the dining room was beyond him, but then Cookson didn't give a toss whether he was seen, as long as the job was done.

As Terry leant forward and held his plate up for a portion of pie, he glanced down the line to the slim, olive-skinned guy with dark close-cropped hair, hooked nose and a goatee. He guessed he was mid-forties, but had no idea why Cookson wanted him dead, and hadn't asked. The warning on his face was enough to let him know it was none of his business – he merely had a choice to make. Do job number one or become job number two.

The line began to move alarmingly fast. Goatee chose pizza and a mug of something, picked up his tray and moved away to sit at a table in a corner. Terry's throat tightened as he added a tea to his tray and forced adrenaline-filled legs to follow him, aware Cookson's eyes were searing into his back as he walked. Standing in front of the target's table, he hesitated before asking the question.

"Mind if I sit?"

"*Whadever*— there's plenty of space over there," replied goatee, shovelling pizza in his mouth and vaguely indicating the alternative with a flick of his eyes.

Terry sat down, not having the slightest clue what he was going to do or say next, and no longer feeling even vaguely hungry. "I'm Terry. Terry Hackett."

"Marcetti – Tony. Handy Andy to my mates." He picked up his tea with his right hand.

"Handy … *Andy*? How come?"

Marcetti held up his left arm, at the end of which was a false hand. "The other guy came off worst. He's thirteen feet under. It's still a bastard though…"

For a few minutes they ate in silence whilst the sound of scraping cutlery and men's voices filled the air around them. Loud jeering voices, some laughing, most swearing; all checking their food for anything dangerous or unusual…

Suddenly, there was a commotion a few tables away. Cookson was holding his throat and looking very grey, eyes bulging like a bull frog. He was trying to cough but finding it extremely hard. Whistles sounded and guards began running. The hollow tone of empty mugs rhythmically being banged on tables along with cutlery and bowls built to a crescendo – his mates were slapping him on the back in an attempt to help him cough up what appeared to be a piece of food... *or some other kind of obstruction.*

Tony Marcetti calmly carried on eating, barely acknowledging the disturbance at Cookson's table, whilst Terry stared at the unfolding drama, fork in mid-air, before turning back to the man opposite him who was staring at Terry's pocket.

"I knew he'd put a price on my head," said Marcetti, finishing off his last bit of pizza and dabbing his mouth on a paper napkin. He nodded at Terry's hip. "So what's in your pocket, powdered glass or a sharpened toothbrush?"

Terry blanched. "*You're* responsible for what's going on over there?"

"He's allergic to nuts. All it took was one to take his attention and another to sprinkle a few sesame seeds in his food. He might make it, probably will, but it should be enough to give him food for thought." He smirked, sniggering lightly at his unintentional pun, and lifted his tea as Cookson was helped out of the dining room by two warders.

"So why does he want you dead?" asked Terry, aware he'd swerved the question regarding the contents of his pocket.

"We have history. That's all you need to know." Marcetti stood up, and then with hands on it, suddenly leant down to the table, face close to Hackett's. "And I'd appreciate you forgetting about what's happened today *and* Cookson's kill order –for *both* our sakes." He pushed himself up, paused while holding eye contact for a moment, then turned and walked over to the other side of the canteen. There, a very tall, very large bald man with tattooed tree-trunk arms stood leisurely supporting a wall. They had their heads together with their backs to Hackett for a couple of minutes before turning round. Then they were *both* leisurely supporting the wall, arms crossed and staring directly at Terry. *Message sent – message received.*

* * *

That afternoon in the exercise yard, Terry looked up around him as he walked. There was nothing but fences, barbed wire and walls. Lots and lots of walls... A green blade of grass was nowhere in sight, it was pissing with rain, and the thought of spending the next fifteen to twenty in Frankland, probably longer, was killing him. *And he knew that nobody had ever escaped.*

He may have been a police officer once, but he'd never been inside a category 'A' before. The most he'd experienced was when interviewing an inmate on remand at the much lower 'D' security prison, Haverigg, near Millom, just outside the Lake District National Park. Large green spaces had been encouraged to be established by the men themselves, with trees planted and nursery areas created. It was a very different environment from the cold and barren HMP Frankland.

"Hey— Hackett, *over 'ere*!!"

Terry looked round to see one of the officers waving him over to the alcove he was standing in to avoid the rain. It was Eddie Radford. A tall, well-built black guy, arms now crossed; a dead ringer for Idris Elba… "*Guv?*"

"After his very … *unfortunate* incident, Mr Cookson has been admitted to the healthcare centre. He's a very lucky boy."

"He looked pretty rough in the dining room, boss, all hell broke loose when he collapsed. Do you know what happened?"

"Well now, I was wondering if *you* knew anything about that, what with you two temporarily sharing a cell, *which*, I may add, you no longer do. It should never have happened in the first place, not even for those few days."

Terry licked the dryness from his lips before answering… "Nope, no idea, but I'll be glad of the single cell, he snores like a wart hog."

"So I hear. Lucky for him, we've got good medical staff and he'll be able to continue that bad habit." Hackett snorted a response as Radford eyed him suspiciously. He didn't believe for one minute the man was telling the truth; he had to know *some*thing. "Well, if you *do* remember anything, anything at all, you come to me. You used to be a copper once, hopefully some of that's remained."

"In *here*? You *are* kidding, aren't you?" Terry sniffed derisively and glanced up at dark clouds gathering above, rain increasing, then looked back at Radford. He pressed his back against the alcove, rain dripping off his fringe as he watched the other men, wet, sauntering past, and a few looking their way. "I can't let any of it *remain* with me in here, now, *can* I, Guv." It wasn't a question. "I was screwed over by the Zandini's, blackmailed and threatened to do the worst a copper can do, and now I'm hated on both sides of these walls. Best thing for me is to keep my gob shut and my head down— *sir*."

Eddie thought for a moment and then nodded, blowing a long sigh. An ex-officer's life in prison was pretty grim, and he knew Terry's history so couldn't really expect him to show willing with inmate info. "Yeah – probably best." He turned to go inside and then turned back. "Oh, by the way, your solicitor has requested a meeting with you Tuesday morning, eleven o'clock. Be ready."

Terry acknowledged the comment, and the officer went back inside to wait for the men to file back in. The rain was no longer messing about, now coming down sideways. It didn't take long. Terry was at the head of the queue until he felt a tug on his sleeve. Tony Marcetti, '*Goatee*,' yanked him back under the alcove and his bald-headed tattooed mate joined them. He reminded Terry of George Gifford, aka Ape man. Only difference being George would have been his bodyguard, not a potential hit-man. Marcetti opened the conversation…

"So what did Shreddie Eddie want with you, then?"

"Shred … *what*?" Terry looked incredulous at yet *another* cringey nickname.

"Mister … *Radford*," confirmed Tony's mate, his face favouring that of a bulldog chewing the proverbial wasp.

Terry didn't bother to ask what the acronym was for – his first thought was a favourite breakfast cereal, but that was just *too* ludicrous. It could also earn him a long spell in the health-care centre as well, so he kept quiet.

"This is Jack, by the way. Better known as the 'Ripper'," added Marcetti, smiling. "So … what were you two talking about, because if I thought you'd mentioned anything at *all* about Cookie's little sesame seed topping earlier…"

"No— *God*, no … no, of *course* not!" replied Terry, still reeling from the 'Jack the Ripper' quip. "He told me my solicitor was coming in Tuesday, that's all."

"Took a bloody long time imparting that from where we were standing," chipped in Jack, keeping one eye on the door, aware there were very few men left queuing to get back inside.

Marcetti used Jack's bulk to conceal him from view, grabbed Terry's sweat shirt with both hands and first yanked him forwards and then back against the wall. Terry felt his head smack the stone as the heavens opened and even the alcove couldn't keep them dry anymore. His jog pants clung to his legs and his stomach clenched down hard, but he barely felt it with the now searing pain in his skull. *Surely Radford would be out in a minute to check on the last few men – there was always a head count.*

"We're watching you, copper. You may be a bent pig, but a bent pig's even worse than a loyal one. We know you killed your own, and nothing's worse than that. Well, except a stuck pig, from your point of view!" Marcetti laughed at his own joke, and with one last throw against the wall, both men left him and walked over to the door to be counted back inside.

Terry felt across the back of his head. It was wet from the rain, as was the rest of him, but he couldn't see any blood on his hand. Not this time. He turned towards the door as Officer Radford counted him last in and locked it behind them. Several other officers were checking the men in through the corridors and multiple locked gates, back to their individual cells, as a single file of wet squeaking and squishing trainers sounded noisily on the floor.

Terry Hackett had never felt as depressed as he did right then. Cold, wet, with a cracking headache and the knowledge this was just the beginning of his life in Monster Mansion. Even the screws up north were known as the Geordie Mafia by the cons, and he could've sworn he'd seen Radford smirk when he'd marked him in. If he was still alive in five years, it would be a bloody miracle. *And right now, a miracle was exactly what he needed.*

SIX

CLAYTON HOUSE GRAMMAR SCHOOL KIRKDALE CUMBRIA

FRIDAY 6TH SEPTEMBER 1991

The following morning Charlotte was trying to forget about her apparently reinstated nightmares, which wasn't easy, other than the fact she was now on a double cross-country lesson and that was enough to make her forget anything. Charlotte hated cross-country with a vengeance. The first thirty minutes was always spent trying to work out where she could disappear to for the following hour or so, as did the PE teacher who apparently *also* hated cross-country. Each time, old '*Fishy Phillips*' chose a different running path, and each time sat out the majority of it at a favourite picnic clearing – usually with a packet of Benson's and a copy of the *Guardian*. Today was no different. Charlotte and the rest of the girls were left alone to complete the course, but having established Miss Phillips was enjoying her usual break wheezing her way through the paper, Charlotte knew she'd most definitely *not* be running any more either.

Today's route led along through the top end of Kirkdale Woods, where Fishy had brought them on the school bus and parked on the gravelled entrance area, and out the other side to Manor Hall Lane. This ran past the ruins of Clayton Hall and along to where it bent left to the bridge that led to the village. Here they were to turn right, run along the bottom path, then up through the south side of the woods and complete the circuit by returning to where the school bus was parked. In theory, it was about ninety minutes of running and walking, with some bending and stretching back in the playground later. *And Charlotte hated every single second of it.* She let her pace gradually slow, to eventually be positioned at the back of the group in order for the others to round a particularly bushy area along the path, and be quickly out of sight. Checking her watch, she waited a few extra minutes before slowly walking to where the trees began to thin out and the woods opened to the lane. As she'd planned, the others were well along it and nowhere to be seen by the time she arrived. Dawdling along, wishing she'd got some smokes of her own to try, she noticed the entrance to the old manor a few yards down on the opposite side of the road. *Maybe not such a crap morning after all then…*

Looking up at the huge wrought-iron gates hanging on either side of the giant stone arch, Charlotte was surprised to see them fully open. *That's definitely an invitation to anyone walking past*, she thought. Her parents belonged to the National Trust and had walked her around dozens of stately homes – most kids would hate it, but not Charlotte Krane. She ran her hands lovingly over the mixed grey and reddy-brown-coloured stones that were uneven in size and rough to touch. She loved all history, especially old buildings, and this place was already drawing her in. Fishy hadn't routed the run along Manor Hall Lane for the second-year students before, which was odd considering the beauty of the building she was now looking at. Even loopy Lewis hadn't brought them on a history field trip, which was even more surprising.

The muddy, unused drive running up to the enormous bleak manor beckoned in a way she couldn't resist. Her breath caught in her throat as she walked. Charlotte had never seen this place before, only read about it in that book in the school library she'd told Emily about, and there was definitely something enticing about it the closer she got. The shadows behind the windows; the hollow feeling of a life and people long gone – the wind that blew the front doors with a noisy clatter, open and shut, open and shut ... Charlotte shivered. Stopping just short of the entrance, she hesitated, hunching her shoulders and twisting her head from side to side. It wasn't the warmest day, but then it wasn't desperately cold either, yet she could swear she'd felt something icy and wet brush her neck. She whipped round to ... absolutely nothing at all. *Stupid arse*, she thought, laughing at herself, *it's just an empty old building, a very intriguing one, admittedly, but nothing to be scared of. Maybe I could have a quick scout about before*

I need to meet the rest of the class half-way back to the bus? And with that, she pushed at one of the creaking wooden doors and slipped through into the shadows …

It smelt. Everywhere she went. Charlotte wasn't quite sure what it was, apart from the dust, but there was a heavy odour … to *everything*. Having walked through the hall with sheets of old plaster hanging off cracked walls and taking care not to trip on loose and up-turned parquet flooring, she was now standing in what she imagined would have been the dining room a hundred-odd years ago. Mould covered dark wood panelling spread from floor to ceiling all around her, a magnificent marble fireplace set in a wood surround centred the room, and decades of grit scrunched beneath her feet… *I bet … I bet there are secret passages behind some of this old panelling, passages leading to secret rooms where forbidden lovers met against their parents' wishes, and creepy dark cellars and dungeons where badly behaved servants were kept as punishment!*

She was actually finding it quite hard to breathe normally, partly from excitement and partly from the smell which she now assumed was the mould. She turned slowly on the spot, looking up at the flaky ceiling and dirty windows, and then with a glint in her eye, ran over to a panelled wall by the fireplace to see if she could find a secret lever that opened it. How she longed to find a secret passageway!

Suddenly, something soft and warm swooped past her head, brushing heavily against her ear. She gasped in surprise, hand flying back from the wooden panel and up to where whatever had left a fleeting impression on her skin. But looking all around, there was nothing, nothing in the room except her. Hands on hips, she smiled slowly because, although in shock, Charlotte Krane was a teenager with a backbone and a ton more grit than her classmates, *and probably most of her peers*. Besides, she'd seen more ancient mansions over the years than most kids had eaten hot dinners.

Walking out of the dining room, back into the hall, the first thing she noticed was the front doors were now shut tight. *No matter*, she thought, *they're old and weak and I can easily open them when I leave. It must simply have been the wind that blew them closed, although … although I didn't hear anything from the other room…* Charlotte threw off that inconvenient thought, and checking her watch to ensure she wouldn't be late meeting the others for the bus, turned to face the grand staircase that led to the first floor.

It rose up majestically in front of her, splitting off left and right to disappear in different directions at the top. Time allowing, she intended to check where both landings led. The steps appeared to be solid, but she tested each one carefully first before putting her full weight on them. Slowly she climbed, not wanting to touch the handrail, the dank heavy smell still hanging in the air, following her as she got nearer to the top. Once there, the long corridor landings stretched out either side of her. A scuffling noise, low and to her left, had her eyes shooting to the floor. A very large, very thin rat was running along the ground, keeping close to the deep oak skirting board. Charlotte remained completely still. Creepy mansions were one thing, rats quite another. Luckily, it darted into the first room it came to, and once out of sight, she turned in the opposite direction, following the right-hand corridor, counting the rooms as she went.

There were several windows on her left that looked out onto overgrown grounds at the back of the mansion, but all were caked in decades of grime. She fished around in the pockets of her running joggers, pulled a tissue from one and wiped a small area clean. *It seems it's even more of a jungle out back than out front.* She cleaned a little more. *Gravestones.* There were *gravestones* dotted about; many slouching at odd angles. Suddenly something darkish darted in between them and the trees, a figure that *looked* like a person, but … not *quite* a person. Charlotte cleaned the bottom part of the next window, and the next, and the next, to follow the flash of green flitting here and there through the headstones, bushes and undergrowth. Suddenly, it stopped just like that, and stared up at the windows – *at her.* The bottle-green ball gown shimmered in the October sun, and fine strands of long black hair blew across a pale face, a woman's *very* pale face.

Charlotte clenched the tissue into a tight little ball. *That's not a person. That … is definitely not a person.* She pulled back from the window, and let her breath out slowly, not realising she'd been holding it, not hearing the rapid beating of her heart, not accepting the cold fingers of fear that now gripped around it…

She got her breathing under control, threw the dirty tissue on the floor and shook herself down, refusing to acknowledge what she'd just seen. At the back of her mind, however, was the ghost story all Clayton girls knew in detail, the one she'd told Emily about only the day before. The rumour that Sir Darnley Clayton had broken the heart of a teacher a few hundred years ago, and the poor woman had hanged herself in the music room. She was named the '*Green Lady*' because of her bottle-green ball gown, the last thing she'd worn before her death.

Charlotte tried not to think about that story, and certainly didn't look out of anymore windows as she continued on down the hallway. Checking her watch, she saw she wouldn't have time to walk the other corridor, the one where Mr or Mrs Rat had scurried along earlier. *No big loss, I can always do it next time.* Walking past several open doors, she popped her head in each room for a quick look. Some were bedrooms, with beds still in situ, bedding frayed and caked in dropped plaster from the ceiling, one or two resembled studies with heavy wooden desks, leather-backed chairs and drawer units, all caked in dust. There were two bathrooms with ornate free-standing tubs on clawed golden feet, their toilets with long Victorian pipes from bowl to cistern. All were like the rest of the house – damp, dirty, dusty and crumbling, but still inherently fascinating, and Charlotte was in awe, despite the scares – she loved everything about it.

After she left the second bathroom, a far-off sound of tinkling notes filled the air. She stopped dead. Again, she felt that icy wetness across her neck, and hunching her shoulders rolled them from side to side... At the end of the landing, she could see a closed door, and her common sense was telling her to turn around immediately, go back down the staircase to the hall – and *leave*. However ... her sense of adventure and, it had to be said, wish to be the one with a *real* story to tell in class, pushed her on. With each step towards that door, the muffled notes became louder and louder. Standing outside, she could clearly hear classical-style music being played rather beautifully, if soulfully, on a piano. It wouldn't have been her choice of music, but she could tell it was someone very gifted. Her hand rose slowly, seemingly of its own volition, to rest on the brass doorknob as the music kept on playing. She took a deep breath, and with her whole body shaking, (*something she'd deny to her dying day if she had to*), turned the handle and very gently pushed the door inwards, just enough to be able to see something of the room. But it wasn't quite wide enough and needed another tiny push. Now she could hear and feel her heart thumping, imagine it crashing against her ribs as the room opened up to her fully, because there in all its glory, albeit dusty as hell, was a full-sized grand piano, ivory notes jumping up and down – *with nobody playing them*. Charlotte's eyes grew wider and wider, but she wasn't looking at the piano because the stool was not in its usual place. Instead, it was about ten feet to the left, near the window. And hanging above, loosely in mid-air, was a long, thick corded rope – *an empty noose dangling at the end of it...*

SEVEN

ICU BASSETLAW HOSPITAL KILTON HILL - WORKSOP

15TH MAY 2021

Sofia Torres squeezed the cool water into the bowl from the sponge, carefully lifting her patient's head, holding her hair up and gently dabbing it around Charlotte's neck. She'd already given her a bed bath with the help of another colleague, but it was a hot day, and she wanted to know she'd made her as comfortable as possible even if she wasn't consciously aware of it. *She really did care for her patients.* Since her sister's accident five years ago, being an intensive care nurse was all she'd ever wanted to do. Raya had been a concert pianist until the coach she'd been travelling in to a musical event had crashed. Many of her colleagues had died instantly, but Raya had lain in a coma for three months first before her body simply couldn't take any more. Now, Sofia gave it her all, which is why she'd felt particularly upset when Mr Shepherd had lectured her so fiercely about the missing Glasgow Coma

Scale chart. A chart she'd *definitely* completed every day and pinned to her patient's clipboard.

Suddenly, she heard the muffled tinkling of piano music coming from her pocket. Sofia's other passion was Chopin, a favourite composer of her late sister, and at that moment his Nocturne C sharp minor, a piece she'd loved to play, was telling Sofia she had a call. Usually, her phone was turned off in ICU, but she'd forgotten after coming back from her very short, very *late* lunch break. It wasn't a number she recognised…

"Hello, Nurse Torres speaking."

"Sofia? It's Mike. Mike Leyland."

She tensed. He'd only left the ICU that morning with a quip about them going for a drink together. Sofia *really* didn't need a relationship right now, not any kind, certainly not with Mike Leyland, and yet… "Yes, hello, Mike, can I help you?"

"I er … wondered if there was any chance you could forgive my crass behaviour this morning, and … well, um … let me apologise – maybe over dinner?"

Sofia hesitated. Mike was one of the most popular doctors at the hospital, always with friends. After a previous bad relationship, she'd got used to making her own entertainment – read a lot, cooked a bit, and kept herself to herself. With long working hours, there was little time for a social life.

"Sofia? Are you still there?"

"Yes, yes, I'm still here. It's just that I—"

"A drink then, you can't be on shift tonight, you've been on since seven this morning."

It was true, although she'd worked past the end of her shift plenty of times, as she was certain he had, too, but today she *was* finishing at seven. However, all she really wanted to do was go home, strip off and enjoy a long soak, a microwave meal and a large glass of wine. She also wondered why he *really* wanted to take her out. He could just apologise on the phone. "Okay, just a quick one, then. I can't stay long, I really need to get home."

"Great! I'll meet you in the White Lion, Park Street. It's only five minutes from the hospital. Do you know it?"

Did she know it…? Of *course* she knew it. It was where she'd got the phone call about Raya. "Okay, I'll be there about 7.30 p.m. – but just *one* drink, okay?"

"Deal! I'll be at the bar – see you later, bye." And then he was gone.

The car park of the White Lion wasn't that big and luckily tight parking was one of Sofia's skills. She turned off the engine and sat quietly for a moment. It was 7.25 p.m. and she was still wondering if this was a mistake. It was hard to distinguish the butterflies in her tummy between pleasurable anticipation and full-on anxiety. She'd not returned for five years, not since that awful night. At least it was still light, and not raining. *At least there wouldn't be another heartbreaking phone call.* She smoothed down her trousers, checked herself in the rear-view mirror and picked up a lightweight shoulder bag from the passenger seat, double-checking her mobile was in it. Just in case.

Inside, the bar wasn't the same as it was in 2016. It was less noisy for a start, less people, no thumping music. Or maybe it was just early. It still smelt just the same though – beer, roasted meats, burgers, French fries, garlic, pasta sauce, anxiety… She saw Mike on a stool at the bar, and with a deep breath, walked over to him. Half an hour, it was just half an hour, that's all. And then he turned round, smiled that smile, and it became obvious her butterflies had been pleasurable anticipation after all…

* * *

RAMPTON HIGH SECURITY HOSPITAL
RETFORD - NOTTINGHAMSHIRE
5 HOURS EARLIER - 2.30 P.M. 15TH MAY 2021

Harry Longbridge did not want to be in that room. It was like some kind of grotesque first date he couldn't get out of. He'd only visited her once since she'd been sentenced and given a hospital order, and that had been difficult enough, but despite everything, felt he should maintain some kind of contact. How long for was anybody's guess, and at the end of the day it was Annie's choice anyway – if she didn't want to see him, he wouldn't be allowed in. Then there was the six-hour round trip for a two-hour visit. That wasn't exactly encouraging, either. He felt very lucky to have such lovely next-door neighbours who helped out with his Labrador, Baxter. At least he didn't have to worry about him being left too long or not getting his dinner. That dog meant the world to him.

His thoughts and emotions were all over the place. He'd been married to Annie for twenty-seven years, and for the most part it had been a good marriage. He'd tried. He really *had*, especially after her terrible ordeal the previous year. Her kidnap by Kenny Drew had changed her beyond all recognition, quite literally in certain ways, and despite many attempts on his part to encourage her to get help, she'd point blank refused. *That was until she found the newly reborn, bright and shiny Miles Peterson in a glossy magazine – now a fake, untrained, private 'psychologist' Miles Peterson.*

Drew, on the other hand, had been a villain from South London Harry had put away in the nineties, and had coincidentally known Annie in their teens. One night in the grounds of a school disco, he'd raped her – an act he'd always denied, and her parents had forced Annie to have adopted the baby boy she'd conceived that night. Decades later, Michael Morton had searched for his real parents and found his father after Drew's release from jail. Lying that he'd had a consensual relationship with his mother, Kenny convinced Michael she'd abandoned him as a baby and had left *him* as well. Subsequently, he'd joined his father in planning and facilitating Annie's kidnap until the truth was revealed. Then Michael had pulled out all the stops to ensure their escape from a disused lockup.

Harry had not known of any of this until twelve months ago. The ongoing guilt he'd felt about not returning from New York because of tracking escapee Charlotte Peterson regularly reared its ugly head, just like it was right now as he sat waiting for his wife to enter the recreation room…

"Well, well, well, if it isn't my dear, *darling* husband actually come to visit me." Annie Longbridge sauntered into the room, her voice raised as she headed for the chair Harry was sitting on and plonked herself down sullenly on the one opposite, crossing her arms and legs as a psychological barrier. She stared at him, waiting for a response whilst other patients and visitors stared at *her*.

"I take it Miles Peterson's been visiting you?"

"I take it Fran Taylor's been doing a lot more than that for *you*?" She spat back.

Harry winced. He knew he was at fault regarding Fran, but they'd both fought it for so long, and in the end lost the battle over a year ago in a small New York guest house. Jamie Ross was now five months old and the light of his life. *Harry could never regret that.* He leant forward and looked her directly in the eyes…

"Did you do it, Annie?"

"Do what?" she replied, head tilted, eyes questioning in mock confusion.

"You know damned well *what*!" he hit back. "Charlotte bloody *Peterson*. Did you…" He glanced around at the people closest to them who were now looking a little startled, and lowered his voice, "…was it y*ou*?"

"Was it me *what*, Harry? I do wish you'd stop talking in riddles, please be explicit."

He was fast losing patience, something that had happened fairly regularly throughout this life and even more so in the last few years. "Did – you – poison – her?"

Annie let the tension ride on the air *just* long enough. He was about to take a deep breath and push her again, when she spoke in a hissed whisper. "That … *witch* … deserved everything she got. She *made* me kill that solicitor, she *wanted* me to kill the cousin who got her mother's money, and she wanted Miles *and* you, Harry, both dead as well. I became her tool – she *used* me. That's all you need to know."

"So you did then."

"I didn't say that. I said she got what she deserved."

"You were the only person in the vicinity. You were sitting right *next* to her." A silence floated between them. "Look … I couldn't give a damn about the woman. I just need to know if Charlotte Peterson is lying in a coma because of you."

"Why, Harry? Why do you *need* to know?"

He didn't really have an answer for that, other than as a police officer, *not* knowing, was driving him crazy. *And he knew she knew that.* Harry sighed and leant back in the chair, looking down at his hands, fingers lacing and unlacing, difficult thoughts spinning around his head. Should he tell her? The *real* reason he'd come, apart from trying to find out if she'd put Peterson in Bassetlaw's ICU? Would she accept it? Would she kick off? Would she even *care*? He was still living in the house they'd bought when they'd moved up from London. It was time to sell and make a new start, a proper life with Fran and his son in a new home. She sat there, now looking bored and fidgety. Part of him felt a genuine loss for what they *had* meant to each other years ago, part felt a great sadness for what she'd become, and then there was that niggling doubt that would never leave him. Just how much had he contributed to this situation…

"Annie – I need to—"

"It's 4.30 p.m., Harry." She nodded at the clock on the wall and then stood up. "Visiting's over. See you in six months, or not – I really couldn't care less." Of course, it was nowhere near 4.30 p.m. – he'd barely been there ten minutes.

Decision made, then.

EIGHT

ANDREW & GINA'S HOME - KIRKDALE

6.30 P.M. SATURDAY 15TH MAY 2021

Andrew had just pulled up outside the house and now sat tapping his steering wheel, beating tensely in time with his thumping head. His mind had been in turmoil all day – to say he was concerned would be a serious understatement.

Seeing Ryan Jacks at the station's front desk that morning had shaken him considerably, and worse, he had no idea what he was going to do about it. Granted, the man's appearance had changed over the years; he'd gained a few pounds for a start, *more than a few*, and had a sprinkling of grey in his otherwise dark hair and beard. But he would've recognised him, regardless. The sweeping snake scar that ran down the right side of his unusually thick neck was the main giveaway. It had naturally faded over the years, *but it was still ugly, still pretty unique, still Jacks…*

A movement from the house caught his attention. Gina was at the window, smiling happily, holding Ellie-Ro and waving her little arm at him. Andrew smiled weakly back and began gathering his things together. As he picked up his phone, jacket, and a take-away fish supper, his thoughts went back to that day in the *Courier* when he first filled out the application form for the constabulary. Back to the exact moment his finger hovered for what seemed like forever above the enter button. It wasn't just about him changing his career forever ... *it was the knowledge he hadn't declared a serious, unknown criminal event from his past.*

"*Hello, Daddy!*" said Gina as she and Ellie welcomed him at the door. Andrew bent down from his six-foot-five to her much shorter five-feet-nothing, as she stood on tip-toe and leant upwards for a kiss. He planted a warm one on her lips and kissed his baby daughter on her forehead. "Hello, lovely Mummy, and my most gorgeous baby girl!" He held up the take-away with an overly bright grin. "Hot plates needed, and 'b and b' and a cuppa would be good, too."

"Already done, it's Saturday night and you're on day shift so I thought you'd probably pop in the chippy. Missy will be *very* pleased!" At which point their pure white cat appeared from nowhere and attempted a serious ascent of his trousers. The delicious aroma coming from the bag in his arms was just *too* tempting, and rock salmon *was* her favourite, after all. Andrew grinned then, genuinely. He was sure he was the only copper in Kirkdale with a hot-fish-thieving Persian in the house, although he'd no idea if any had omitted critical information from their constabulary application forms...

That night in bed, sleep evaded him at every attempt. Normally he never had any problem dropping off, but he couldn't even concentrate on reading, something that had always, whatever the genre, managed to get him drowsy.

Andrew knew he was going to have to tell someone what had happened all those years ago, but whom? Who'd be able to cope with it? He'd wanted to forget, thought he'd been pretty successful overall, but every now and again those hideous memories had wormed their way back into his subconscious, until *wham*!! There they were, *bang in the forefront of his mind.*

He turned to look at Gina sleeping peacefully beside him, completely unaware she was lying next to a man with a dark secret. An undiscovered and therefore unknown criminal secret he'd kept from her and everyone else…

* * *

KIRKBY CHILDREN'S HOME - CHRISTMAS EVE 2001 KIRKBY-OVER-SANDS A SMALL TOWN OUTSIDE KIRKDALE

He knew he shouldn't be there. He knew if the drunken man with the thick neck and black beard saw him, he'd be in trouble – big trouble. There was a hazy memory of another man like that, who used to drink too much beer and shout at a lady, but it was so far away in his mind he just couldn't grasp it properly. But *this* – this 'event' that had made him feel so confused when he first saw it just a couple of years ago, now at ten, he knew it was wrong, so very, very wrong…

It had all started when the posh biscuit tin had gone missing. It was filled with the extra special ones that were thicker, with different brightly coloured foil wrappers that were only bought at Christmas time. Mrs McCall's husband, her *third*, (but nobody was allowed to mention the others), always picked up several smaller tins from the wholesalers, and emptied them into the extra-special big one – the one that came out every Christmas Eve and disappeared again after New Year's Day. Well, that particular Christmas Eve, just before bedtime, Mrs McCall and her two ladies had come into the large lounge where the tall fir tree stood covered in tinsel and decorations with a present for each child beneath it. (*He knew it wasn't a real tree but didn't let the younger kids know that. Two weeks earlier, he'd seen the man with the thick neck and black beard go upstairs onto the landing, then up into the loft and climb back down the silver ladder with it on his back…*) They'd all been sitting on the floor looking at a very cross-faced Mrs McCall standing there with her large hands on her large round hips…

"Right, children, now I'm not going to get angry over this because it's Christmas Eve and I know you're all excited, so will allow some leeway."

He remembered they'd all been told ten minutes earlier by one of the helpers to sit quietly and cross-legged in a semi-circle because Mrs McCall wanted to speak to them. He had no idea what 'leeway' meant, or what she was going on about, though, and looked around at the others for a clue. Nobody said a thing…

"So … if whoever's stolen the Christmas biscuit tin puts their hand up and tells me where it is, we'll say no more about it."

Silence… One or two of the younger kids looked a bit scared, bottom lips trembling – nothing like this had happened at Christmas before. Sometimes the odd thing went missing during the year, but never at Christmas. Christmas was the one thing they looked forward to, nobody would risk ruining that … and so nobody put their hand up. This resulted in Mrs McCall actually getting *very* frustrated, if not exactly full-on cross, as she tried hard to keep a lid on things. It was Christmas, after all.

"Well, if nobody is going to own up to it right this minute, I'm giving permission for the culprit to come to my office and own up privately. Then I'll be willing to forget all about it. Is that clear?"

He looked around at the others. They were all as confused as he was. The helpers just looked bored – probably wanting to go home. When Mrs McCall left the room, the helpers rounded the children up to get ready for bed, and nobody had any Christmas Eve biscuits for the first time since he could remember the posh tin being there. *Everyone was really miserable.*

Later that night, something had woken him. The clock on the dormitory wall said 2.30 a.m., and the air in the room said it was cold enough to freeze the blood in his veins. It was just as he'd pulled his quilt higher up around his head that he'd heard it. The same sound he'd heard before, the sound of the squeaky rocking chair that echoed along the corridor and belonged to the man with the thick neck and the black beard. And that was why he'd found himself standing in the open doorway to the man's room … watching.

Illuminated by the moon through open curtains, the tin of Christmas biscuits sat on a table next to the rocker, *lid off*. He saw the man's hand reach in, lift up a bright round gold one and hold it out to the quivering boy at his feet. Darren Hayes was not a big chap, and only eight, which was why, he supposed, the man was able to make him do those bad things, the things he now knew, now he was ten, were very … *very* wrong. That's why, for the last few months, he'd been sleeping with a small, curved kitchen knife under his mattress. It was why he'd just retrieved it, crept out of his bed at two-thirty in the morning, tiptoed down the long, dark hallway to the end room, and very quietly, very carefully depressed the handle so it wouldn't click when it opened. Now, as he stood silently in the shadows, he shot his forefinger up to his mouth to immediately warn Darren not to alert the man to his presence. Standing behind the chair, he could see long bare legs and a foot rocking it slowly backwards and forwards. The fear of being discovered rendered him scarcely able to breathe, but the heavy, woody-smelling aftershave still managed to infiltrate deep into his lungs.

Andrew knew what must be done. There would be no point in telling Mrs McCall what the man was making some of the boys do, she'd never believe him because he was only ten, and they were too scared to admit it – *and Mr Jacks was her son...*

The bad man hadn't died that night. He'd only just managed to slice the side of his neck, grab Darren and run. In the shock of the attack, Jacks couldn't run anywhere, and with one hand desperately trying to stem the blood and the other attempting to pull his trousers up, he never saw his face. The circumstances ensured it never got reported, and he remembered the man wearing high roll-neck jumpers throughout the winter months to hide the wound.

A year later he'd been adopted by the Gales, and was really happy for the first time in his short life. One day, when his parents were watching the news, he saw a photo of a man on the screen that had been convicted and imprisoned for abusing boys at Kirkby Children's Home. He recognised Jacks immediately, but never told his new mum and dad about that night in case they were horrified at what he'd done and wouldn't want him anymore. He never told anyone else either – the nightmare, however, had remained buried deep inside him, until today...

"Andy? Andy, wake *up*, wake *up*!" Gina was no longer sleeping. The side light was on, she was leaning up on one elbow, patting his shoulder and looking down worriedly at him. There'd been loud mumbling coming from somewhere, his face felt wet, he felt disorientated, and then, predictably, *thankfully*, there was the sound of crying from Ellie-Ro's room.

"I'll go, you go back to sleep." He wiped his face with the back of his hand and was out of bed before she could protest.

NINE

CLAYTON HOUSE GRAMMAR SCHOOL KIRKDALE CUMBRIA
MONDAY 9TH SEPTEMBER 1991

The bell had gone for the end of lessons, and Charlotte was waiting for Emily under the 'Arches' to meet her outside the tuck shop. She checked her watch yet again to see she was now an infuriating *ten* minutes late. What she saw at Clayton Hall was ricocheting inside her, bursting to get out, to be shared, but only with her best friend, and the frustration at Emily's lateness had already led to a second bag of crisps.

Anxiously, Charlotte looked both ways beneath the linked walkway between the old and new parts of the school, her impatience annoying her given she liked to keep an ultra-cool, ultra-laid-back image. Finally, Emily appeared at the entrance that led out from the staff-room and 'dungeon' dining room, which was also close to where Miss Dean Senior, the headmistress, had her office.

Rumour had it Veronica Dean chose *that* room because it was the largest one next to the staff-room, and she liked to keep an eye on her teachers.

"Where have you *been*, Em? I've been waiting *ages* and absolutely *dying* to tell you my unbelievably exciting *news!*"

"I'm not *that* late," Emily checked her watch, 10.40 a.m., and rolled her eyes... "*and* I've got news of my own as it goes."

Charlotte didn't know whether to rush her own to hear *hers* (not ideal), or let Emily spill first. She decided Emily's couldn't be *that* exciting, not like hers, so she'd obviously be quick and then Charlotte could revel in her top news moment. She also needed to calm her emotions down, reduce the hype and appear more in control. So she encouraged her to share... "*Go on, I'm all ears...*"

"Let's find somewhere to sit first. Did you get me some crisps?"

"Well, I did, but ..."

"You ate them, didn't you? Honestly, Charlie, I'm *starving*, I missed breakfast!"

"Look, you go get something to eat and I'll meet you on the bench by the science block, but don't be long, I'm busting a gut here to share something really *big*, and the bell will go for next lesson in less than twenty minutes."

Once Emily had got her own crisps and passed Charlotte a third packet (she knew she'd only dip into hers if she hadn't), and they were contentedly munching on the bench – in between mouthfuls Emily began her news...

"You know yesterday, when we were sitting on this exact same bench and saw Miss Lewis walking across the playground swinging that crow, or raven … or whatever it was … by its legs?"

"Yes – course."

"Well, this morning we never had a lesson, well, not after the first ten minutes, anyway. Instead, she had the entire class under fire with questions about that dead bird, insisted, *loudly*, that someone had sent it to her house yesterday before she left for school. How weird is *that*?"

Charlotte had to agree it was pretty unusual, definitely worthy of red-letter news. She stuck her hand in the bag of cheese and onion and, lifting some out, paused in mid-air and said, "So, what started it off? She wouldn't have just come out all guns blazing, accusing people" – then crammed them in her mouth.

"Oh, no, she didn't. She started the history lesson as normal. It was about the ravens in the Tower of London. She was holding a bird book and began explaining the differences between ravens, crows and magpies, because they're all fairly similar, like we were saying yesterday. Then … somebody sniggered…" Charlotte's eyebrows shot up as she swallowed. *This sounded interesting…* "and she suddenly slammed the book down on the desk and started yelling; *Who was it?! Come on own up, I know it was one of you! Who sent that crow to my house?!* Over and over again, Charlie, I couldn't believe it, my form teacher literally went on a crazy crow rant on day two of term!"

"Blimey. Not so cool and laid-back today, then. Our Miss Lewis clearly hadn't been up to the music room for a quick snort before first lesson!"

"Honestly, Charlie, it was *awful!* She didn't let up till another teacher heard the shouting as she passed our classroom, opened the door and got us all out. *That's* why I was late."

"A very good reason too, I can't deny it, and I must admit I'm gagging to know who sent her that creepy dead bird and – more to the point – *why?*"

"Me too, heaven knows what's going to happen after break, but what about your news? You sounded like you'd discovered gold or something, I'm surprised you've managed to keep it in so long. Come on, what is it?"

"Well, it's definitely not gold ... but it is *green.*"

Emily frowned, looked at her watch and saw they only had ten minutes before the bell went. "What do you mean, green? And we've not got much time left."

"You remember me telling you about the *Green Lady?* The ghost of a teacher who haunts the music rooms, both here in the school and also at Clayton Hall on the other side of the woods?" Emily nodded, and Charlotte noticed she was looking a little on the pale side... "Well ..." she deliberately paused for effect... "Yesterday – I – *saw* – her!"

"What? *No!!* No, you did *not*, Charlotte Elizabeth Krane – you're just trying to *scare* me!" Emily began folding her empty crisp bag over and over into long thin folds which eventually became a tiny square, and then began unfolding it again.

71

"Oh, but I *did*, Em, I did. I had double cross-country yesterday, and the route was through the woods and out to Manor Hall Lane where, *unsurprisingly*, Clayton Hall is. You've not done cross-country yet, being new – it's utterly vile, so I always skip off somewhere once old Fishy has parked herself off course with her cigs and newspaper. *Any* – way, I took the opportunity to take a look around said hall, and it was … *ohhh* … so *many* things, Emily! Creepy, definitely creepy, old *obviously*, and there was so much broken plaster from loose … you know those arty bits on the ceilings, and crumbling walls crunching beneath my feet. It smelt, too, and there are rats, *big* ones, well I saw *one*, luckily it ran off in the other direction, but—"

"What about this, this *Green Lady*, woman, ghost, apparition, whatever. Was she *really* there, Charlie, or are you just messing? Where exactly did you see her?"

"*Apparition* … ? Bit of a fancy word for you, Em!"

Emily rolled her eyes impatiently, then suddenly sat up straight and used them with raised eyebrows and a nod of her head to indicate a warning. Miss (Fishy) Phillips was heading in their direction…

Felicia Phillips was a hard-looking woman with a high forehead and thin two-tone hairstyle that slid off her head and moulded into her long neck. A large nose and angular chin was joined today by narrow, very suspicious eyes… "Charlotte Krane, I'd like to speak with you please – about your cross-country lesson yesterday."

"Oh, yes, what about it Miss?"

"It's about the fact my sources tell me you weren't actually *on* it, not *actively*, anyway."

And at that very moment, the bell for the end of break rang out long, loud and unmistakably clear.

"Sorry, Miss I need to—"

"You need to explain your whereabouts, Charlotte, that's what you need to do." She turned to Emily, who was looking anxiously at her watch. "Off you go, young lady, no need to miss *your* lesson."

Emily screwed up her eyes as if in pain, stood up, and hesitatingly began to move away. She mouthed 'good luck' behind Miss Phillips' back before reluctantly leaving her friend to face the music. Turning slowly, she finally began walking towards the science block, and with one last look, disappeared through the double swing doors.

Miss Phillips folded her arms and fixed Charlotte with a hard steely glare… "So, Charlotte … enlighten me – what *were* you doing hanging around Clayton Hall?" But before she could think up an answer, Felicia grabbed Charlotte's arm, nails digging through her thin cotton shirt making her wince, and began marching her straight across the playground towards the Arches.

"*Owww… Miss!* That hurts! What are you *doing*? I'll be late for Eng—"

"You're coming with *me*. I'll square your lateness with Mrs Jenkins. I need some answers and *you're* going to supply them – *all* of them."

As she was forcibly escorted back under the Arches and through the door into the older part of the school, other pupils en route to their next lesson couldn't help but notice Charlotte's predicament. Some were from her class, inclining their heads and whispering behind their hands whilst looking quizzically at her, Miss Phillips and each other as they passed across the bottom of the stairs that led to Mrs Jenkins' classroom.

Charlotte tossed her head and stuck her nose skyward, trying to look nonchalant. She was, in reality, racking her brains as to exactly what she was going to say to Fishy, and why the gym teacher was so determined to find out about her visit to Clayton Hall. Accepting a telling-off for skipping cross-country was one thing; maybe even a detention wasn't beyond the bounds of reasonable. Being hunted out and dragged across the playground with talon-like nails stuck in your arm was quite another. It was actually feeling bruised now, so God knows what it must look like.

She was beginning to wonder just where Fishy was actually taking her. They'd now passed the banqueting hall and exited to the outside through the little mediaeval door to where the overflow, but currently empty, chalet classrooms stood on the other side of the main building. This dragging her through the school (*well, practically dragging*) was surely not allowed? It was the 1990s, for heaven's sake, not the 1890s.

Apart from the gravel scrunching beneath their feet, this side of the grounds was quiet due to the chalets not being used, and with nobody around, there was no one to witness anything. *Did she need a witness?* Like many thirteen-year-olds, Charlotte was trying to be sixteen most of the time, but at this point was finding it extremely hard to remain cool, calm and unruffled. Suddenly, Fishy shoved her behind one of the chalets, and before she knew it was pinned up against the back wall of a redundant classroom.

"Now, Charlotte, *now* you will tell me exactly what you were doing at Clayton Hall yesterday – and more to the point, *why*."

Charlotte's heart was racing. She had to admit to feeling anxious, even a little scared. *How did Miss Phillips think she could get away with doing this to her? Did she really think she wouldn't say anything? Why would she think Miss Dean Snr., the head, would allow her to behave like this?* The woman's nails dug in deeper, eyes slicing through hers – face coming closer…

"I'm waiting, Charlotte, and you've got precisely ten seconds…"

TEN

ICU BASSETLAW HOSPITAL KILTON HILL - WORKSOP

MONDAY 17TH MAY 2021

Her arm fell back on the bed, the contents of the syringe having done its job ... again. There had been a little fumbling in trying to find a vein, and had she been conscious would have felt sharp pain at each attempt.

The GCS (Glasgow Coma Scale chart) was also removed – again. Folded into four and pocketed, it awaited its shredding later, away from the hospital. There would be no daily records to check improvement; hopefully, there would be no improvement at all. Dressed in the same blue uniform, the 'medic' had been watching the day-shift nurse since she arrived, waiting for her to take a quick break before slipping into the room and dealing with the business at hand. Then slipping back out again and leaving the hospital as quickly and unobtrusively as possible.

This time though, a brief stay, eyes watching her above the mask, enjoying the power; it was strange to see Charlotte so peaceful and relaxed. Her being relaxed was something that had rarely been experienced by anyone in her vicinity, and that was exactly how the medic intended her to stay. Permanently. She could almost certainly have improved without this intervention, possibly even woken up naturally, in time, but that was not the plan and had never been the plan. As long as the additional meds were able to be regularly administered by one of them, she would remain just as she was – peaceful, relaxed … and deep in coma.

Aware of the need to leave quickly, the medic turned from the patient, confidently opened the door, and left the room to merge with a sea of blue in the corridor. A knowing, unseen smile lay beneath the mask. The ease with which the job could be done would never cease to amaze, but it was time to get out now and return to other work.

* * *

PRIVATE LOUNGE OF THE CARPENTERS ARMS PUB KIRKDALE - KESWICK

Gina Rowlands (now Gina Gale) had been Molly Fields' best friend since primary school. She'd lived in the pub with Molly and her parents from the age of fourteen, after the death of her gran, Margaret Rowlands. Margaret had brought her up from a toddler because her mother, Emily, had been forced to leave the UK when Gina was only two, but Gina had since reconnected with her mother, who had been, and still was, living in the United States married to publisher Gareth Stone. She'd also discovered her father was her old employer, GP Miles Peterson, ex-husband of notorious serial killer and ex-GP Charlotte Peterson. It was Charlotte who'd threatened her mother into leaving the country when Gina was a baby, following Emily's betrayal of their close friendship. By having an affair with Miles when they were all at university, and he and Charlotte engaged, Emily hadn't just betrayed a special bond cemented in childhood, she'd also become pregnant with Gina. That kind of betrayal could never have been forgiven by a woman who through no fault of her own had discovered she'd be remaining childless, even if that betrayer was a close friend. In fact, especially as she *was* a close friend…

Now here they both were, her and Molly, both twenty-three and with children of their own. Their trip to the U.S. to visit Emily and Gareth the previous year had certainly been eventful for all sorts of reasons. Gina, newly pregnant with Ellie-Ro had nearly died at the hands of crazed escapee Charlotte, and Molly had had a fling with a Taekwondo instructor in Brooklyn, resulting in a daughter born on Christmas Day, just a week after Gina and Andrew's wedding. Five-month-old Christie Lianne Fields now sat with her older and first best friend, Ellena Rose Gale, on a large pink and blue blanket, with an abundance of soft toys, a shape sorter and the remnants of some Farley's Rusks. She needed some support compared with Ellie, who at nine months of age was quite able to sit by herself. Molly picked up her coffee from the table, took a sip and nodded towards the girls…

"If you'd told me a couple of years ago we'd be sitting here watching our baby daughters interacting on a play mat, especially *me*, I'd have said you were completely nuts!"

Gina laughed as she picked up a yellow star shape and handed it to Ellie who reached out, took it with a pudgy little hand and tried to fit it into the red and yellow shape sorter. Christie then immediately put the red one she was holding up to her mouth to chew and began dribbling… "It *is* pretty nuts, especially as we're still young compared with most mums these days. I knew I wanted kids early, though, and Andy *is* nine years older than me."

"True – and Danny's thirty, but obviously Christie wasn't exactly planned…"

"What do you think will happen there? I mean, he *did* come over for our wedding and stayed till Christie was born."

"I don't know, to be honest, Gee. There's no way I want to move to New York, and it's not fair to ask him to move here. He *did* make the first move last year, looked me up on Facebook and messaged me after we got back, so I think he's fairly committed. He was adorable with Christie when she was born, too, and regularly phones and Face-Times me."

Nursing her mug of tea, Gina smiled and nodded in acknowledgement before looking thoughtful for a moment.

"Changing the subject completely, have you had any visions lately, Molls? Any sort, not necessarily just the ones relating to death."

"No, thank God. You'd be the first to know if I had. Why?"

"I'm not sure. It's a bit of a weird one, and don't say anything if you see him, but … it's Andy."

"Really? He's not *ill*, is he?"

"No, no … nothing like that, well, not physically anyway. But in the early hours of yesterday morning he was sort of fitful – mumbling something I couldn't make out. When I turned the light on, his face was wet. He'd been *crying*, Molly, in his sleep."

"Wow, well that's … well, it's not like Andy, is it? That's for sure. Do you think it's something to do with work? Did you ask?"

"No, Ellie woke up and started crying herself, so he immediately got up to go and see to her. I think he was avoiding me asking him anything."

"Has this ever happened before, I mean, *ever*?"

"No – never. Not with me, anyway."

"Didn't you try to ask him during the day, yesterday?"

"I wanted to, and I did try a couple of times but … I just couldn't bring myself to mention it. It was like he could tell I was about to broach the subject and started talking about something else, in fact *anything* else in order to stop me mentioning it."

"Maybe just sit back and wait a while. If it happens again, just be firmer and ask him directly what it's about.

It could be an incredibly sad situation he's had to deal with at work for the first time and didn't want to upset you about it as well. He *is* a police officer now, Gee."

"Well, a student officer anyway, but yeah, I suppose it *could* be that, especially if it involved a child. He knows I wouldn't want to hear about anything really awful where children are concerned. Becoming parents changes us, doesn't it; emotionally it can be a minefield."

"Certainly does. Anyway, let's get these two out whilst the weather holds, and then we can grab some lunch later. Mum's cooked a—"

"A batch of spicy shepherd's pies?" finished Gina. They both laughed at the fact Maisie Fields *always* had a batch of spicy shepherd's pies in the oven, and began to get the girls ready for a buggy trip down to the village.

* * *

CUMBRIA POLICE HEADQUARTERS & CONSTABULARY TRAINING CENTRE CARLTON HALL - PENRITH

Andrew sat in the training room with twenty other student officers, all starting on their two-year Detective Pathway Programme. Having a degree enabled enrolment on the PPPD (Professional Policing Practice Diploma) in order to join the constabulary that way, finally passing out as a detective. He'd been thoroughly enjoying the training, been able to concentrate and learn easily – *that was until a few days ago.* When he saw Ryan Jacks standing at the front desk of Kirkdale nick, his brain had wandered off somewhere between anywhere and nowhere.

"… so, what were you doing before you applied for the police?" Trainee detective Hannah Carlin was sitting next to Andrew at one of the individual desks that had been spaced out across the room. They were both sitting at the back…

"Sorry … what?" A short break had occurred when the lecturer had momentarily stepped out of the room, and Andrew hadn't noticed *or* heard the first part of Hannah's sentence.

"I said … '*Hi, I'm Hannah. I decided on a new career after a dire time in the NHS.*' I'd guessed we're of a similar age, so then I asked what *you* were doing before you joined the police."

Andrew rubbed a hand down his face. "Sorry, I didn't get much sleep last night. Got a nine-month-old at home; she's absolutely adorable but … *anyway*… In answer to your question, I was senior crime reporter with a local paper, and my links with some of the team at the Kirkdale station led me to apply. What made you leave medicine?"

Her honey-shaded pony-tail hung in mid-air as she tipped her head to one side, slowly raising her eyebrows. "You mean apart from the crazy hours, lack of staff, terrible pay, and zero respect?"

Andrew looked down at his desk briefly before

answering her. Looking up, he said, "Fair enough, pretty sure we'll have some challenges in this job, too, though."

Hannah suddenly folded her arms, sat up straight and with eyes on the door as the lecturer re-entered the room with someone else. "Oh, I'm sure we will, I've *no* doubts about that."

Andrew turned and followed her eyeline to see a very tall, very chic-looking woman in full uniform; her rich mahogany-coloured hair swept up and back, literally gleaming under the lights. Her nose was aquiline, her movement feline. She looked almost regal … almost, but not quite. It was something about the eyes. They were small and beady like a bird's, darting here and there about the room, alighting on this person and that, like she was checking for something. And then she smiled. Cumbria's chief constable had arrived at HQ for a meeting, and while there, had decided to drop in on this year's PPPD group to welcome them. She seemed pleased with what she saw.

The lecturer opened his arms, and with cupped hands, flicked his fingers upwards several times. "It's customary to stand and greet a high-ranking officer when they enter the room, people. I'm sure you all have no difficulty in recognising Chief Constable du Guarde." There was a scraping of chairs as everyone stood up and chorused, "Morning, ma'am."

Dominique du Guarde gave a crisp smile in acknowledgement. "Good morning, everyone, please sit. As I had a meeting here today, I thought I'd stop by to welcome you and wish you all luck at the beginning of your training. I hope you're finding the course interesting and rewarding. Make no mistake, this job is challenging and there is much to learn – but work hard, focus; be consistent with your studies and practical work, and you'll have a good chance of becoming excellent detectives and a credit to this constabulary." There was a short discussion and a few questions, followed by a general mumble of 'thank you, ma'am', appreciative thanks from the lecturer for sparing the time – and then she was gone.

Shortly afterwards, a drugs training video began playing on a large screen on the left-hand wall. The trainees swivelled their desks and chairs round to watch, learn and take notes. One of them made sure they recorded another set of notes as well, in addition to those required for their course work. *A far more personal set…*

ELEVEN

9.30 A.M. TUESDAY
18TH MAY 2021

Harry could hear banging as he shoved the bread down in the toaster for the second time. He'd decided long ago it must've been a Friday creation, because even on number seven it never toasted properly at the first attempt. Leaving the kitchen, he went through to the hall and opened the front door to see a man ramming in a large *For Sale* sign into his flower bed. The realisation of what it meant hit him with each whack of the hammer – *and the pansies didn't look too impressed either.*

The sky was looking distinctly grey, but the air was quite still. Both seemed to fit his mood exactly as he offered a weak smile to the erector and closed the door. At this point his phone rang…

"Longbridge…"

"Sir, it's DS Moorcroft."

"Hi, what's up?"

"We've just had a call in from the head of Clayton House Grammar, a Mrs Sandra Wainright. It's an all-girls' school in Kirkdale, mine actually, I was there till I left in 2012."

"And …"

"Year nine had an onsite geography field trip first thing this morning. The field's right next to the school, a big one that spreads right over to the woods. They're learning how to use metal detectors, of all things. Never had that opportunity in my day, I'd have—"

"Suze, what's the *story*?"

"Sorry, Guv. Seems one girl detected more than she was bargaining for. Alarm went off; they all start digging deeper and deeper, until a spade hit something hard. Out came the trowels for delicate earth removal and …"

"For God's *sake*, Moorcroft, don't keep me in *suspense*!"

"She found a body, sir. Well, a skull at any rate. They didn't want to continue after that, thought it best to contact us."

"Indeed. Right, what have you done so far?"

"I've sent uniform over to secure the scene, and arranged to go down there after speaking with you, what with DI Taylor still being on maternity leave. I've also organised for the CSI team to meet me there."

"Good. I'm still at home so just got to check my insulin, grab some toast and I'll be out the door. And Suze …"

"Guv?"

"No falling into ex-pupil mode... *and* … I've just done a quick search on Clayton House. There's a couple of cold cases going back to the nineties; before your time of course, both here and at the school, and I was in London then, but Chief Superintendent Hitchings will almost certainly remember. It wouldn't surprise me if he was SIO at the time, so when we get back we'll need to check in with him. I'll meet you in the car park."

"*Guv.*"

CLAYTON HOUSE GRAMMAR SCHOOL FOR GIRLS - KIRKDALE (PRESENT DAY)

When Harry and Suzanne arrived at the school, it was clear a strict routine was being upheld despite the bizarre situation, with no pupils or irrelevant teachers wandering around outside hoping to find out some gory information. On glancing up at the windows, however, quite a few girls lined them, looking out to try and see what was going on.

It was quite a walk over to the crime scene, as the uneven ground wouldn't have made for a comfortable ride, and there was no way Harry was going to risk ruining the suspension (or anything else) on his beloved BMW. He felt he was definitely getting too old for this hiking lark though, as his knees and lower back began to play up *and* he began panting – always a clue… Suzanne, on the other hand, was irritatingly striding across the hugely lumpy terrain with zero effort like it was a gigantic football pitch.

They finally arrived close to the site where the adjoining wood ran the rim of the field. Sporadic uniform were present, the relevant area taped off and statements being taken. CSI had yet to arrive, but Sandra Wainright, the headmistress, was there being interviewed, along with the geography teacher, Leah Khatri. A familiar face from a few years ago, though, was *also* present and talking to DC Andrew Gale like she'd known him all her life. This was because she *had* known him for a good deal of it, as he'd initially been her sports reporter at the *Courier*, and then crime reporter when she'd broken her ankle in 2018. Stella Gray had decided to retire that year, allowing Andrew the space to grow into and take over the area he was really interested in – crime. When he'd decided to sign up for the constabulary a couple of years later, a by now very bored Stella (being an active member of the local crime readers group really wasn't cutting it) had decided to come out of retirement and regain her rightful position as chief crime reporter. It was at the reading group she'd met the head of Clayton House, Sandra Wainright (Sandi) – hence her tip-off to be there that morning. Sandra knew it would end up in the paper anyway, and she wanted to make damned sure it got written up properly.

The wind had kicked up since Harry had left home, toast hanging from his mouth as he'd handed Baxter over to Kate Hoffman. The Lab hadn't been out for his morning run, and his next-door neighbour loved having him, as did her boys. She was also used to Harry's hurried breakfasts since Annie's departure, so he never felt uncomfortable on such days.

Now, as he stood analysing what, in all likelihood, would become a crime scene depending on the age of the bones found, he noticed someone new after Stella had left Andrew to move closer to the 'burial' site. He made a mental note to ask him privately if he'd tipped her off, because if so, it really wasn't on.

"Morning, Gale, and Miss er... ?"

"TDC Carlin, sir. Technically, an ex-*Mrs*, couldn't be ars ... er, bothered, to change back. I'm doing the two-year Detective Pathway Programme on the PPPD with Andrew."

"Ah, right, excellent ... so ... what do you two trainee detectives make of this situation so far then?"

"'scuse me, Guv," interjected Suzanne. "I'm going to give CSI another call, and then speak to Mrs Wainright. I'll catch up with you later."

Harry nodded his assent and looked at his watch. It was only 10.30 a.m. but they should have arrived by now. At the end of that thought, a loud rumbling and revving of a van engine hit the air as an unmarked white Transit appeared from behind, bouncing across the lumpy ground towards the flickering tape. *Better late than never, I suppose*, he thought, rubbing the small of his back. "Well done, Moorcroft, even the chief super couldn't have summoned up CSI that fast!"

Suzanne smiled sarcastically and pocketed her mobile before scanning the area for her old headmistress, Sandra Wainright. She saw her standing with another woman she didn't recognise, but assumed was the geography teacher. Both were talking to an older constable whilst he wrote in his pocketbook. Suze did recognise *him* though, as PC Gabriel Downs had recently transferred from Ambleside. She walked over to the group as the teacher was speaking…

"Yes, my name's Leah, Leah Khatri. I was in charge of the field trip."

"Were all the children using metal detectors, Ms Khatri?" asked the officer.

"No, not all, I had six groups of six children, each group with two detectors. Everyone had a chance to spend some time using one, though."

"Thirty-six pupils, then, was there another adult helping to supervise the trip?"

"Well, it wasn't exactly a *trip*, as we didn't travel anywhere." Leah looked anxiously at her headmistress. "The school has always owned these fields so technically we were still within the school grounds. But, yes, for the first half of the lesson, one of the year-twelve students came along to help out. She took Claire, the girl who found the … the remains … she took her straight back to school. Claire was pretty shook up."

"What about the rest of the pupils? How did they react? I understand they're all year nines so, what, thirteen, fourteen? Who took *them* back to school?" He lifted his head up and slightly to one side, almost accusingly.

Leah Khatri looked a little taken aback at the rapid-fire questioning. "Mainly thirteen, a few are on the older end of the age scale for the year. Some were a bit spooked, but I have to say … some were fascinated, too."

PC Downs raised an eyebrow… "Fascinated? Fascinated *how*?"

"Gabe, can I speak with you a minute? Excuse us a moment please, ladies." Suzanne used her eyes to indicate they should move a few steps away from the two women. "Gabriel, one question at a time will do just fine. Neither of these two women is suspected of anything, and from the initial information received, the skull found is pretty old. Bring it down a notch."

"Sarge…" Gabe Downs flushed a little. He was grateful the dressing-down hadn't happened in front of the two teachers, but his eyes were steely and jaw tense. He didn't like being criticised, and certainly not by a woman.

His visible tone had not gone unnoticed by Suzanne. He appeared to be an officer with a chip on his shoulder – a big one. It wasn't something she'd particularly noticed around the station, but it was her first time actually working with him.

She could feel Harry's eyes burning holes in her back, and turned to see him standing in copper stance, arms crossed, feet apart. He had a good idea of what had just happened, and was waiting to see how she'd handle it.

"PC Downs, I'll take over interviewing Sandra Wainright and Leah Khatri. You're welcome to stay or you can go back to the station – your choice."

Gabriel bristled at basically being dismissed from conducting a simple interview, something he felt perfectly capable of carrying out. At forty-five, he knew he'd been a PC for far too long. The years had slipped by since his thirties when his sergeant's exam had eluded him twice, by a mere two percent on one occasion. *That was the chip.* He blew a heavy and angry sigh, turned sharply and marched back across the field, passing his DCI and the two snotty-nosed degree entree trainees. What kind of experience would *they* have notched up two years down the line, compared to what would be, by then, his thirty? Gabriel Downs hadn't a clue why he was even still *in* the job.

As Suzanne watched him go, she saw Harry walking towards her and waited till he was within hearing distance. "I take it you got the gist of that, sir?"

Harry nodded. "I've seen the same situation too many times not to be able to at least take a wild guess. A forty-something PC likes to play the tough cop, and doesn't like it when a considerably younger team-lead DC tears him off a strip."

"Nailed it in one Guv. I was just about to ask the field-trip teacher some actual relevant questions do you want to—"

"I do, yes, lead on."

Sandra Wainright and Leah Khatri had been surprised to see Constable Downs striding away, presumably back to the car park, and waited patiently for the young female officer to return with an older man wearing a dark grey suit and pale blue open-necked shirt…

"Ms Khatri, Mrs Wainright, I apologise for Officer Downs' somewhat overzealous questioning. My name is DC Suzanne Moorcroft and this is DCI Harry Longbridge."

The two women acknowledged them, and then Sandra spoke directly to Suzanne. "Don't I know you, DC Moorcroft? Are you the same Suzanne Moorcroft who was a pupil at our school and came top in the country for A level Biology? Must be about ten years ago now, but I'll never forget it."

Suzanne blushed, and Harry's mouth dropped, eyes widening… "Yes, Mrs Wainright, that's me, and I did. I think there were ten or fifteen others from around the country as well, we all got ninety-eight per cent. I don't really shout about it, though."

"Well, you should. We were all *very* proud of you!"

She smiled and thanked Sandra whilst Harry beamed at her like a proud father.

Hearing some shouting in the distance, they all glanced over at the white forensic tent that appeared to be billowing wildly in the wind, but after some struggling by the CSI team, was finally erected safely over the burial site.

Suzanne continued… "Could you tell me how your pupil … um – I'm sorry I don't know her name…"

"Claire, Claire Wilson," offered Leah.

"Yes, thank you, Claire Wilson. Can you explain how Claire managed to discover the skull using the metal detector? In your experience, would – if there were amalgam fillings present, for example – would they be enough to trigger the alarm on the machine?"

"Well, I'm not an expert by any means, but I *am* a keen amateur detectorist and have been for about five years. It depends on a few things; the quality and type of the metal detector, the depth the metal is buried at, and the skill of the person using the equipment. That list isn't exhaustive of course, but for the purposes of a year-nine field trip, it's a start."

"Well, I understand that only a skull, or part of a skull, was unearthed, and several feet deep. Do you think the metal detector Claire was using would pick up small metal objects buried so far down?"

Leah looked from Suzanne to Harry, who was listening intently and looking quite intrigued. "It's doubtful, frankly, and suggests there's probably a larger amount of metal down there – exactly what, I have no idea. It could be anything."

"Well, we'll be heading over to the tent in a minute, so will hopefully find out more then."

"Mrs Wainright, are you aware of a case back in the nineties, where two girls and a teacher went missing from this school?" asked Harry.

"Yes, Chief Inspector Longbridge, I *am* aware of that. I was a pupil here back then – *and one of those girls was my best friend.*"

TWELVE

The sky began to darken and rain was threatening as Harry and Suzanne made their way over to the now safely erected forensic tent. Stella Gray was still there, along with Andrew and Hannah, who'd joined her.

"Don't you think the burial position at the edge of the field here is a bit strange?" asked Andrew. "Why wouldn't whoever buried the body go into the woods, and deep into the woods at that?"

"Good point." Harry and Suzanne replied in unison.

"Well … we don't know the age of the remains yet," added Hannah. "What if they're centuries old and the landscape was different back then? Maybe the edge of the field *was* part of the woods at that time and it's been cut back since."

Harry's eyebrows rose in surprise. "*That* … Officer Carlin is a *very* good point, and we won't know the exact age or as near as possible, *when* they were put there, until the remains have been examined by a forensic anthropologist."

"It's *why* and *how* that I'm interested in," added Stella, looking every bit as hawkish as she used to at a crime scene. "This is big news in a village like Kirkdale, we don't get that many bodies, skeletons or otherwise."

"I know you were retired when I took over, Stella, but where've you been the last three years?" added Andrew, incredulously. "There's been multiple body parts found all over the county last year, the local GP's murdered several people, including an attempt on Gina's life, and—"

"That's quite *enough*, Constable Gale!" interrupted Harry. "Mrs Gray may have been a former colleague, indeed, your former boss, but right now she's a member of the public, and here in a *professional* capacity." He pulled him aside and a few feet from the group…lowering his voice he continued… "In fact, I'd assumed it was *you* who'd tipped her off! I was going to make a point of saying that was a big fat zero on the team point front, lad, it's simply not on."

"Sorry, Harr – sir, I'm not myself today, and it wasn't me who invi—"

"Ga – Andrew – look, you can drop the sir stuff when we're out of earshot, we've shared too much in a different capacity on the crime front." He tipped his head behind him. "Not back there, mind."

Andrew half smiled, half looked lost. For the first time ever he wanted to offload what was worrying him, and if Harry hadn't been in the police, he would have. He could see him taking a really good look at him, he saw concern in his eyes, and in that moment wanted more than ever to share what had happened in his childhood at the care home. Ryan Jacks resurfacing was a major deal, especially as it was obvious he was still living in Kirkdale.

Harry rested an arm across Andrew's shoulder. "What's up, lad? You seem edgy and yet quiet. It's not like you."

"Harry I—"

Suzanne had walked over to them and looked hesitantly between the two men. "'scuse me, Guv, the CSI team lead's at the tape. He's got news."

All three walked towards the tape and found Hannah and Stella already there. The CSI stood silently, alien-like in full white hooded coverall, white rubber boots and blue latex gloves. He pulled his mask down to speak…

"So … Davidson, isn't it?" asked Harry, trying to detect some facial recognition inside the man's forensic head-gear.

The CSI pushed the hood back off his head. "Yes, sir, it is."

Harry turned to Suzanne. "Officer Moorcroft, your crime scene today, I believe." He caught Rob Davidson's eye to hopefully imply Suzanne's fledgling status.

This was one of the things Suze loved about her boss. Where possible, he always gave opportunities to those wanting to gain experience, climb the ranks, and never distinguished between male and female officers. She smiled her appreciation as Davidson began to speak directly to *her* after picking up on Harry's hint.

"Right, well, we've got a full skeleton, adult male, around five ten, with what is almost certainly a bullet hole to the back of the skull. Given someone tossed a gun in there with him, a Glock to be exact, and a bullet in the skull cavity, the chances of that hole being anything else is extremely unlikely. We've found the casing and got an AFO (Authorised Firearms Officer) on the way to 'prove' the gun safe, bag it with a green safety label and the magazine separately; then they can be lodged into the station armoury ready to send to the lab and/ or ballistics." Harry nodded approvingly. Davidson was known for a thorough scene report, and Harry was glad he was on today. Apart from the obvious, his very distinct detail would make Suzanne's job easier to learn, too.

"Can you tell the age of the remains, even roughly, at this stage?" Stella Gray had jumped in before Harry or Suzanne had time to draw breath.

"*Thank* you, Mrs Gray. I appreciate your desire to write an exacting piece for the *Courier*, but I'd like questions to be asked from *my* department, if you don't mind."

At sixty, and with looks and personality not unlike Fiona Shaw's intelligence officer in the drama *Killing Eve*, Stella Gray was no shrinking violet. She merely stared pointedly and slowly folded her arms, but nevertheless acquiesced to Harry's authority.

Andrew dropped his head slightly and grinned, remembering how intense Stella could be (although not with him), and how *he'd* got under Harry's skin when first promoted to crime reporter in 2018. *It was seriously crazy the amount of stuff that had happened since.*

"Thank you," said Suzanne, grateful for Harry's intervention. "I was going to ask the same question actually, but in addition, was there anything else found with the remains apart from the gun, bullet and spent cartridge?"

Davidson hesitated. "Actually, yes, and this is really quite strange, but it does date the *burial* of the body as being no earlier than about twenty-five years ago. There's a little leather bag. It's well worn, but must've been good quality at the time because it's still holding a stash of five-pence coins – *thirty*, to be exact. Both the bag and coins will be sent to the regular section of the evidence storage room."

"Thirty pieces of silver…" said a shaky voice from behind.

They all turned to see Sandra Wainright's ashen face, just as the heavens opened…

11.00 A.M. HM PRISON FRANKLAND BRASSIDE - COUNTY DURHAM

Terry Hackett sat at the table in the interview room waiting for his solicitor, right leg involuntarily juddering. He felt nervous. This was born out by the boulder sat in his stomach and the intense squeezing deep in his chest. He also felt it was a pointless exercise given what he knew he was guilty of. No solicitor, no matter how good he or she was, could make charges of corruption, arson endangering life, criminal damage by fire, and three murders just disappear into thin air. Although as a police officer, well, *ex*-police officer, he obviously knew he had to go through the legal motions leading up to his trial. The anxiety came from having those legal facts spoken out loud over and over again, and thrown in his face.

Terry glanced up at the clock. Two minutes to go. He breathed in deeply and out shakily. The prison guard standing by the door hadn't said a word since Terry had sat down, not even when there was obviously something kicking off outside. But now it had dissipated, and he could hear two sets of footsteps … one set continued, and one stopped as the door opened. A sharply dressed woman in her late thirties with cropped asymmetric blonde hair and electric-blue balayage swept inside. Dressed in a black Ralph Lauren suit, white silk shirt, and red-soled black Louboutin heels, she immediately dismissed the prison guard, waving away his protestations, who insisted on at least waiting outside as he reluctantly left the room. Startled at her appearance, Terry automatically stood up and held out his hand, which she shook firmly, before dropping her briefcase on the floor, pulling out the plastic chair and sitting opposite him. She took a file from the case, slapped it on the table and looked up. Terry was still standing, in shock mostly, due to the fact she wasn't a fat, bald, sixty-something bloke, with an ill-fitting suit and egg stains down his tie. She indicated for him to sit.

"Well, Mr Hackett, or may I call you Terry?"

He nodded. "Er ... yeah," and cleared his throat... "Yes, yes, that's ... fine."

"It's not *looking* fine, though is it, Terry, *hmm*? Oh, apologies – my name's Rebecca by the way, Rebecca Weston. I've been assigned to your case. You can call *me* Ms Weston. I understand you're pleading guilty to all charges?"

"Yes."

"Any reason why?"

Hackett looked at her quizzically. *Was she for real? Was that actually his file on the desk?* "Well ... *Ms* Weston, I'm actually guilty, there was a witness to the arson attack, two people died in the fire, so ..."

"Do you know who hired me, Terry?"

"Actually, no, I don't."

"Well, it was someone extremely high up in their job, *think stratospherically high*, with an extensive and very specific type of global reach. Does that give you any clues, even a tiny clue?" She looked him straight in the eyes and grilled his gaze till the penny dropped. "Yes – got it in one. And she's paying me a very great deal of money to get you out of here, or at the very least, a reduced sentence. God knows why you're so important to her, but it appears you are."

"I can't see how you ca—"

"Well now, you just leave that to me. You're the ex-cop, blackmailed under the threat of a very nasty death, including having your wife and parents threatened with the same, resulting in you very reluctantly going horribly and murderously bent. And I … I'm the best criminal defence lawyer in the country. Well, possibly on par with Sebastian Cleaver, but he's slipped up recently so that's debatable."

Terry Hackett couldn't believe what he was hearing. Chief Constable du Guarde wasn't just trying to keep him safe in Frankland; she was actually going to a whole heap of trouble, and let's not forget, vast expense, to help him legally. But *why*? Was George Gifford getting the same help down south in Belmarsh?

"Why, though?" he finally responded, leaning back in his chair and staring hard at his solicitor. The nerves had weirdly gone AWOL, replaced by suspicion.

"Why *what*, Terry?"

"Why would Domin—"

"We don't use *names* here, Mr Hackett. Not now, not *ever*. Is that understood?"

Terry sat for a moment, wanting to ask, desperate to know, deciding what his next move should be. *He paused too long…*

"I'll set up your defence as blackmail with menaces. You were put in an impossible position by an international gang, terrified for your life, and more importantly, the lives of your loved ones. You were *all* under the threat of murder. Until that point, you held an unblemished record in the police service with no reason to go rogue and break the law. We will find character witnesses to support your case, and if we can't …" leaning back then, relaxed, confident, smiling like she'd already won, she whispered … "*we'll buy them.*"

THIRTEEN

CLAYTON HOUSE GRAMMAR SCHOOL KIRKDALE CUMBRIA

MONDAY 9TH SEPTEMBER 1991
BEHIND THE REDUNDANT CLASSROOM

The ten seconds had passed. Her teacher continued to hold her against the wall of the unused classroom, face unnecessarily close, eyes glinting and manner determined. The top of Charlotte's arms felt like a pin cushion from Miss Phillips' nails, and her brain raced from trying to think of a believable answer as to why she'd dodged the cross-country lesson to explore Clayton Hall instead. It wasn't easy, especially only being given ten seconds, but finally, out of absolutely nowhere, the 'right' answer suddenly came to her…

"It was for … for a *history* project!" She blurted out, "I took a look round because I thought I might get extra marks writing about Clayton Hall as it's linked to our school." Miss Phillips continued to hold her, both with eyes and grip. It was feasible, but Charlotte could tell she didn't believe her.

"Where did you go and what did you see? Were you alone?" She squeezed a little tighter and Charlotte winced.

"Just, just in the hall, and a couple of rooms upstairs, that's all. It was falling to bits, plaster dropping off the ceilings, the walls, everywhere. There were rats, it smelt awful, really awful, and yes ... I was alone."

Fishy stared at her for a moment. It was clear she was thinking, summing up something in her head, desperately trying to make a decision.

Charlotte waited, holding her breath. She couldn't do much else under the circumstances. Miss Phillips was a bit of a hard nut for a teacher, and even at a rebellious thirteen, Charlotte wasn't stupid – she wasn't going to risk giving her any cheek. She *was*, however, considering making a run for it the moment Fishy was either distracted in any way, or slightly reduced the pressure on her now quite painful arms. Then, suddenly, there were hurried footsteps that interrupted Fishy's train of thought, and she immediately slapped a hand across Charlotte's mouth, following it with a full-on body lean, pressing her hard against the classroom wall.

"*Not – a – sound ...*"

Fishy's beady eyes shot through hers as hairs prickled on the back of Charlotte's neck. Then the footsteps stopped. The temptation to kick Miss Phillips in the shins was huge, but not so huge as the desire to know who those footsteps belonged to, and now, the whispered voice that went with them. Charlotte strained her ears to try and make out any words from the other side of the unused classroom and recognise that voice. Fishy appeared to be doing exactly the same – leaning back a little, she leant sideways and looked to the right. Charlotte felt less pressure from Fishy's hand and body weight, and it only took that one lapse in the woman's concentration for a chance to push her hard, duck down and spring out under her arm. *She took that chance and ran for her life!* Back across the gravel, over to the little mediaeval door, through it to the outside area of the banqueting hall, Charlotte flew up the stairs to the library, through to the far side and dashed down the other stairs along to year two's cloakroom, and *safety*. Heads shot sideways and girls swivelled in their seats, mouths open, as she raced through the school. *Fishy Phillips didn't follow.*

Charlotte sat at the back of the cloakroom waiting for the lesson she'd missed to end, elbows on knees, and biting her nails. A whole myriad of emotions washed over her; confusion, fear, suspicion, excitement (weirdly) … but most of all, resentment. *How* dare *she pin me up against that wall, digging her nails into my shoulders, and then,* then *to slap her hand across my mouth!* She wanted to share her feelings with Emily, she *needed* her; she needed to speak to her best friend right at that moment.

A loud ringing sounded through all areas of the school announcing the end of the current lesson. Charlotte made her way to the entrance of the cloakroom and watched carefully as girls moved in both directions to their next lesson. She had to get back to her classroom to pick up her book bag before heading off to her own, but was hoping to see Emily cross back from the science block where she'd gone after Fishy had grabbed her in the playground at morning break.

Where are *you?* She stared constantly to the right, lifting her head up and around looking for Emily's flame-red waves amongst a sea of blonde, mouse-brown and chestnut hair, bobbing faces that were laughing, chattering or moaning about an unfavourable next lesson. The crowd finally thinned out to a trailing few, and then she saw her. Walking slowly with an unfamiliar girl, hanging back from the others, smiling; heads together and arm in arm, deep in what appeared to be a secret conversation. Charlotte felt a pang of unease – jealousy, even – deep in her gut. She called her over…

"Em, *Emily!*"

Emily looked up and waved. She whispered something to her new friend and the girl nodded and walked past Charlotte, throwing her a timid smile.

"Who's that?" said Charlotte, following the first year with narrowed eyes.

"Ros Lisle, she's in my class, she's nice."

"*Lisle?* Not *Sandi* Lisle's younger sister?"

"Um … I don't know, I mean she said she's *got* a sister, but …"

"Remember I told you about someone in the lower sixth who knew about Miss Lewis taking drugs?"

"Yes, but that was a Jackie something."

"Jackie Squires, yeah, *and Sandi Lisle's Jackie's best friend*. They're inseparable, a bit like you and me." She gave Emily a long, hard look as she delivered *that* line. All pupil traffic had passed now and it was quiet.

Emily checked her watch. "We're going to be late for our next lesson, and you've already missed your last one. What happened with Miss Phillips?"

"That's what I wanted to talk to you about. She literally *pinned* me up against the back wall of an unused chalet classroom over the other side of the school, one that needs the roof mending, demanded I tell her why I was in Clayton Hall instead of running the cross-country lesson."

Emily's eyes widened in shock, and her mouth gaped in horror. "She did *what*? But ... but that's against the actual *law*, isn't it? I mean, surely she's not allowed to *do* that?"

"Not only that, she dug her bloody talons in my *arms* – *look*!" Charlotte pushed up one sleeve of her blouse to reveal nail indentations and some redness that still remained from Miss Phillips' fierce grip. "It's the same on the other arm; I couldn't believe she was doing it, and she wouldn't let me go, she even leant across me and put her hand over my mouth when we heard voices from the other side of the chalet. God knows who it was, but it got her attention, so I took my chance, gave her a shove and ran for it."

"Look, we're both going to be really late for next lesson at this rate," said Emily, "but we obviously need to talk about this. Are you going to report her to Miss Dean?"

"No, she'd never believe me, and I think Fishy Phillips is hiding something. Let's meet in the library after lunch at 1.30 p.m., this one's going to be a *big* discussion."

"I'll be there – *definitely*."

QUIETEST CORNER OF THE SCHOOL LIBRARY
1.30 P.M. MYSTERY SECTION

Sitting behind a copy of *Scary Stories to Tell In The Dark*, Charlotte pretended to read, foot tapping impatiently as she waited for Emily to arrive. She'd chosen her favourite corner, and nobody was sitting on the other side of the dividing bookcase.

There was a general low-level murmuring from time to time though, even though it was a library, as some girls chose to do their homework there, sharing stationery and picking each other's brains.

At last, Emily appeared, swung her bag off her shoulder onto the floor and sat on the long side near the table's end, where Charlotte was sitting at the top.

Charlotte put her book down and clocked the bag. "How come you didn't take your stuff back to your classroom?"

"Thought I'd go straight to lunch from last lesson, make sure I got a seat with people I know. Well, sort of know at least – we're *all* new."

"Smart. Well, look, here's the thing. Actually, hold on…"

Charlotte got up from her chair and, squeezing between the table and the divider bookcase, poked her head around its end before starting her '*big discussion*'. Luckily, there was still nobody on the other side. Sitting back down, she could see Emily was eagerly waiting to hear what she was about to divulge. What had happened to her felt unbelievably exciting, and yet absolutely horrendous at the same time. It was all very confusing. She desperately wanted to work out exactly *why* Fishy Phillips was so worried about people wandering around Clayton Hall, and she *would* find out eventually, no matter how long it took, but on the other hand, she couldn't deny she'd felt scared at what Miss Phillips had done. She kept her voice low despite the absence of anyone on the other side of the bookcase… "Em, why do *you* think Miss Phillips got so heated about me scouting round the old hall? She was absolutely *livid* I'd been in there, and *somebody* had seen me and told her. That's how she knew."

"God, Charlie, don't ask *me*, I haven't a clue! Are you sure you didn't see anyone when you were in there, inside or out?"

"No, nobody, well … except for that shadowy green figure in the graveyard through the upstairs window I told you about. Whoever, or *whatever*, that was, they didn't see me."

"Well, *someone* did. And if they tipped off Miss Phillips about *you*, *that* might mean they're involved in something with *her*. Something she doesn't want discovered. Something *both* of them don't want discovered."

"Good point, Em, good point…" Charlotte sat and

thought for a moment. She lowered her voice further, whispering even more quietly. "Could it be Mrs Lewis? Do you think they're running some kind of drugs operation, even if it's just a small one?"

"Or *maybe* ..." Emily said quietly, narrowing her eyes and doing her scrunchy thinking face, "maybe, it's money they're hiding, someone raided a bank, or ... or a jewellers ... or a dead body ... or they've been holding weird séancey meetings with those ... those *board* things?!" She held her breath, eyes now like huge gobstoppers...

"Em – breathe. *Ouija* boards, you mean? Well, if she, or *they*, whoever the snitch is ... if they believe in the *Green Lady* and have seen the hanging noose in the music room like I have..."

"Maybe they're trying to find *out* something ... from the other side!" Emily's eyes widened as she shivered.

"Adults don't generally believe in all that stuff though, *do* they?" said Charlotte, staring straight ahead and chewing her lip. "I know what I saw but ..."

"That was totally the creepiest story I've ever heard, Charlie, are you *sure* you saw that rope just, just *hanging* in mid-air?"

"On my horse's life," she answered, looking her dead in the eyes.

"You've got a *horse*, since *when*?!"

"Well, not actually got one *yet* ... but if I *did*, I'd swear on its—"

Emily sighed impatiently. "Look, let's be serious here. A teacher from this school held you up against the wall of a classroom, physically hurting you until you gave her some sort of answer to her questions, and you only got away because she got distracted. And she didn't get the answer she wanted either, which probably means she'll try it again."

Charlotte's mouth dropped significantly before replying. "I never thought of that. I *must* find out what Fishy's hiding at the hall. My gut instinct is drugs – and maybe Jackie Squires and Sandi Lisle know more about *that* subject than I first thought."

FOURTEEN

2.30 P.M. ICU BASSETLAW HOSPITAL

KILTON HILL - WORKSOP

Sofia picked up the OBS chart and flipped the top sheet showing the patient's basic checks, the next page for her own notes and then … nothing. She turned the board over and back again, but it was empty. They should have been on the top where she left it, but for a second time, the Glasgow Coma Scale charts were missing. Her stomach lurched and she swallowed hard. This wasn't just a case of forgetfulness or being careless, *somebody* was deliberately removing them. She bobbed down to look under the bed in case the night staff had not secured them properly to the clipboard, but there was nothing there.

In ten minutes, consultant Simon Shepherd would be doing his rounds, and the first thing he'd be asking for was those charts, especially after the other day when they'd also mysteriously disappeared. She didn't have time to wrestle with the impropriety of her next move.

The decision to falsify Charlotte's records didn't come easily, but there was no way Sofia could explain their absence a second time. Moving swiftly, she used her keys to open the meds cabinet, took a few blank GCS sheets from the drawer, a pen from her pocket, and leant on the counter-top to invent recordings of her patient's responses for the last seventy-two hours. She had one eye on the large window out to the corridor as she quickly filled in the boxes. It was totally against her character, but she rationalised the fact they were mostly the same every day anyway, so there'd be no real harm done. Shepherd would never remember any details, he'd got far too many patients under him, and judging by the wincing she'd noticed lately, his ulcer wasn't getting any easier either. However, if she were discovered, it would likely mean being struck off for falsifying records. At the very least, she'd be sacked.

Suddenly, the door opened. In the second her attention was off that window, Shepherd had walked past it and entered the room as she completed the last box. She turned round to smile at him with more confidence than she felt. Today, he was on his own.

"Nurse…" he greeted her in a clipped tone, almost dismissively, and then grimaced, placing a hand on his stomach.

Sofia stepped forward. "Good afternoon, Mr Shepherd, can I—"

"I hope you have *all* your reports today, Nurse," he replied curtly, waving her concern away.

"Yes, of course." She picked the clip-board up from behind her and handed it to him.

The freshly completed GCS sheets were still on top. He flipped each one back and forth quickly, almost impatiently, before handing it back to her. "Still no change then, nothing at all?"

"Well, there was a sudden arm movement on one occasion, I did note it on the—"

"Yes, yes, I can see that, but given there was no physical trauma, no brain damage, I would have thought Mrs Peterson would have responded a little more regularly by now."

"I agree. Initial blood test results showed toxicity due to overdose of benzodiazepines, specifically diazepam and alprazolam, and there's damage to the kidneys and liver."

"Order a full set of bloods. I want to know *exactly* what's going on, and tell pathology it's urgent. Contact me the moment they're back from the lab, which hopefully won't be more than twenty-four hours." With that, he handed the clipboard back to her and left the room, whereupon Sofia Torres' breathing eased considerably.

She blew out slowly … "That was close," she said under her breath, watching him through the window as he continued down the corridor. "*Far, far, too close.*"

Having recovered from her first medical malpractice, Sofia fetched two bowls of warm water containing a sponge and flannel, a towel and soap, and set them on a stand beside Charlotte's bed. Picking up her left arm, she began gently bathing her, and as she did so, pondered

114

on this patient in the bed who was still a murderer, albeit sectioned through a personality disorder. She wondered what their interaction would be like if Charlotte was conscious, how she would relate, and what was behind and beneath her disorder. Like everyone else, Sofia had seen the news about Charlotte's rampage, read the gory details online, including the wide-ranging and probably exaggerated contributions from social media trolls who seemed to delight in regurgitating that kind of stuff. From the first day she'd arrived it had felt strange nursing her under those conditions. A woman apparently devoid of emotion, who'd been so entirely in control of other people, threatening and murdering them, and yet was now so wholly dependent on her and her colleagues for her every need … for her very existence.

She dropped the sponge into the soapy water, and picking the flannel out of the clean bowl, rung it out and rinsed Charlotte's arm. After repeating the same on her other arm, legs and rest of her body, intermittently patting each part dry, she began massaging her limbs with a warm moisturising cream to help prevent her muscles from atrophying and joints seizing up. Once she'd suctioned her mouth and attended to her catheter and bag, Sofia stood over her, arms crossed, thinking hard. *Where are you, Charlotte Peterson? What world are you in now – and why haven't you come back to us yet?*

Moments later, with her back to the bed, Sofia began gathering the used personal hygiene equipment, intending to remove it from the room as soon as possible to reduce the risk of viral and bacterial activity. As she did so, the sound of high erratic bleeping filled the room. She swung round to see the monitor recording Charlotte's vital signs bleeping and spiking erratically, peaks and troughs scratching wildly across the screen in a luminous yellow. She walked over to it to see rapid, uneven brainwave activity. Looking at her patient, it was obvious from her face she was experiencing some kind of traumatic event. It twitched. It had happened before and she'd noted it on the GCS sheet, but this wasn't the same, it was much stronger than that, almost, *and she could hardly believe she was thinking this but* … it was almost like a look of horror had flashed across Charlotte Peterson's face. Then, as suddenly as it started, it just stopped dead and returned to normal. *Nurse Torres recorded it very clearly in her personal observation notes.*

At the end of her shift, Sofia pulled the band from her pony-tail, shook out her hair and made her way down to the ground floor and out to the car park. Luckily, she managed to avoid any long conversations with colleagues by walking quickly and purposefully through the hospital. Today wasn't a day for coffee or drinks after work.

She knew it would still be open till 8.00 p.m., and be quieter then, too. It was why she visited weekday evenings in the spring and summer, rather than at weekends, and had already bought flowers on the way to work. With no florist close by, it was easier to leave them in the car, stems carefully wrapped in wet tissue and bound in a plastic bag to keep them from drying out. On very hot days she used a cool box, but today it was mild and overcast and they just lay on the back seat of her little Fiesta, waiting to be delivered.

Exiting the car park, her mind was barely on the detail of a ten-minute journey she knew off by heart. She practically drove there on autopilot every month and was doing exactly that today, which was why the sleek black Audi snaking the route several cars behind her went unnoticed.

She approached the huge tree-filled roundabout, took her exit, and after driving a short way, indicated right to turn off Netherton Road and drive thoughtfully towards the huge iron gates that loomed up in front of her. She'd been here so many times in the past five years, since that awful day, since the arrival of the news that had broken her heart … the news she'd lost her precious little sister.

Driving through the open gated entrance and round to the car park, she noticed, as expected, only a few other vehicles there, and drove easily into a wide vacant space. Pulling up the handbrake, Sofia sat for a few moments before making the familiar and emotional walk. Closing her eyes, she could feel Raya all around her, even sitting there in the car. Taking a deep breath, she reached behind with her left hand to lift the flower bag from the back seat, not forgetting the water bottle beside her, and with a bit of jostling, finally managed to open the door.

Immediately she got out, a stiff breeze pulled violently at her hair, whipping it sharply across her face as dark skies threatened rain … and the black electric Audi slipped in silently alongside a seven-seater SUV.

Completely unaware, Sofia locked the car, and carefully carrying a beautiful bouquet of Raya's favourite lilies, walked slowly between other peoples' memories, row on row, some recent, some going back years, all a sad reminder for those visiting their loved ones. She was used to death in her job, but the reality of it in her personal life, the finality of her loss, would never leave her. Raya had been her best friend as well as her sister, five years or fifty – she knew she'd never get over losing her.

The sky had turned from slightly overcast to a mottled hash of dark moody greys, and the wind had already picked up from the light breeze that had met her when she'd exited the hospital. Sofia forced the water bottle into her pocket, and now having a spare hand, awkwardly drew her jacket closer in an attempt to button it in the middle. Her long hair flew this way and that, hampering her vision and she wished she'd left it tied up, but nothing could be done about that now. With the button finally fastened, her main concern was that the flowers wouldn't lose their blooms in the wind.

After turning a couple of corners, Raya's grave came into view. She always knew which one it was, even though the headstones were in strict lines set at right angles to the path. Number six on the left-hand side, black marble with piano keys etched deeply across the base end. It bore lilies from the previous month, now wilted and dead, but no matter, they would soon be replaced with the beautiful, fresh white blooms she carried in her arms.

On reaching Raya's resting place, as if her sister knew,

the wind dropped instantly, and looking up, Sofia smiled. She temporarily laid the bag of new flowers across the base so her hands were free to remove the old ones from the vase on the plinth. Taking the water bottle from her pocket, she poured it into the vase, removed the lilies from the bag, and crouching in front of the gravestone, arranged them as best she could.

"Five years, Raya ... five unbearable years, however have I got through it without you, little sister? I say this to you all the time, I know, but it never gets any easier. I miss you *meu querido amigo...*"

Out of nowhere the wind had picked up again, whistling eerily around the graveyard as lightening split the sky, then rumbling followed with a gigantic thunder crash, cracking it as if an automatic rifle had peppered the air.

Sofia flipped up her hood, quickly buttoning the rest of her coat in readiness for the inevitable sheet rain that was about to descend ... *not ready enough though, for what was about to happen next...*

The driver of the black Audi was no longer sitting in their car.

FIFTEEN

She couldn't explain it but suddenly, in the pit of her stomach, Sofia Torres had a deep feeling of impending doom.

As the skies roared above, the very second she turned from Raya's grave, a tight grip squeezed her shoulder causing her breath to catch. Flinching, she held back her overly large hood slightly in order to see better, and there in front of her stood Mike Leyland battling with a large black umbrella buffeting in the wind. A second violent crash of thunder hit louder as he pulled her under it to shield them both from the now falling rain. She didn't resist, and *Raya had done all she could…*

"Wh – what are you *doing* here?!" she shouted against the elements as he held her tight against him whilst another flash triple-forked the sky.

"My *grandmother!*" he shouted back. "*She's buried – over there!*" With no hands free, he lunged his head forward to indicate somewhere across the way. "*I'll have to come back tomorrow, let's get back to the cars!*"

Together they half walked, half ran back to the car park, the umbrella having blown inside out and its use abandoned – they were both soaked by the time they reached their cars, but at least the thunder and lightning had relented and the rain lessened.

Mike steered Sofia towards his white Ford Puma, arm extended to unlock it to be ready. After opening the door, he threw the battered brolly onto the back seat. "Jump in, we can chat about our respective family members, that's if … you want to?"

"Yes … I guess … okay – anything to get out of this rain."

And as they settled into Mike's car, the black Audi reversed out of its parking spot, drove slowly past them and out through the cemetery gates.

* * *

2.30 P.M. FRAN TAYLOR'S HOME
STANGER LANE - KESWICK

Driving back from the burial site at Clayton House School, Harry climbed the stairs from the front door of Fran's house to drop in to see her and baby Jamie on his way back to work. Walking into the open-plan kitchen/diner/lounge from the first-floor hall, he threw his keys into the dish on the countertop and turned to put the kettle on. Fran wasn't in the room…

"*Fran!*" he called out, "it's me, are you in? Do you want tea?"

A noise from a bedroom set round to the left of the kitchen was followed by Fran walking through to the open-plan area carrying a changing mat and nappy bag.

"Harry … your son is lying on a play mat on the lounge rug, shaking a by now very dribbly giraffe. I'm hardly likely to be in *town*, am I?"

He looked over the wide counter-top to see Jamie kicking his legs and waving an orange animal toy at the ceiling whilst intermittently chewing its tail. It did indeed look like a giraffe… "Ah … yes, didn't see him there, sorry, love."

"Yes, to the tea, though, and bring the biscuit barrel with you."

Stirring in the sugar, he eyed her carefully. "You okay, Fran? You seem a little … *tense*."

"Harry, what happened when you went to Rampton? It was three days ago and you've not said a thing. What did she say?"

He carried the drinks and biscuit barrel on a tray over to the lounge area. "Not a lot, to be honest. I was there all of ten minutes before she announced visiting was over."

"So, you didn't discuss anything at all then, not the house, the divorce … *us*?"

He sat down heavily beside her on the couch. "I asked her if she poisoned Charlotte Peterson."

Fran's eyebrows shot up and she turned to face him. "You *are* kidding me – *seriously?*"

"Fran, I *had* to know, you of all people should understand that."

She picked a digestive out of the barrel and dipped it in her tea. "Yeah ... okay, I do to be fair. What did she say then? I can't see her admitting to it."

"She danced around the question and wouldn't answer, just said she got what she deserved. She's insisting Charlotte used her as a tool and made her kill her mother's solicitor, Christopher Mogg. It was after that I was just about to broach the subject about the house and the divorce, and ..."

"She sensed what was coming and terminated the visit," interjected Fran.

"Something like that. She certainly made it very clear she couldn't care less whether I returned or not, so..."

"Well, at least she's not clinging to something that isn't there anymore?"

Harry took a large gulp of tea and stared at Jamie over the rim of the mug. This child who'd given him a new lease of life, the boy he'd longed for and now loved more than life itself... "Pretty sure that's the case," he replied, quietly. "It certainly is as far as I'm concerned. Miles Peterson's still sniffing around too, so she's not exactly being abandoned, although he needs to be very careful if he wants to keep Gina on side. They're still in the early throws of trying to make their father-daughter relationship work." He rummaged in the biscuit barrel for a custard cream, popped a whole one in his mouth and crunched contentedly.

"Well, that's not really our business, is it, Harry? We can't interfere with that."

He swallowed the biscuit and fished for another... "I'm not so sure. Andrew's not himself at the moment. No idea what's up but that lad isn't right. He's edgy, almost snappy at times, vacant at others, and he and Gina are new parents, too. It's not like him. There's a lot going on for both of them at the moment, what with him starting his detective training as well."

"Did you see him today, then?"

"Yeah, we got a call out to Clayton House Grammar, you know, the girls' school?"

"Aha, near the old hall in Manor Lane?"

"That's the one. It was Suzanne's crime scene and Andrew was there with another new trainee detective – a Hannah something. Anyway, their grounds are extensive. They extend to the woods that run along the length of the school's estate, and a group of girls in the third year had a field trip this morning, learning how to use metal detectors, of all things."

"Wow! Kids today, eh? Don't know how lucky they are!"

Harry drank some more of his tea before answering. "Well, I'm not sure they'd agree with you after this morning's session."

"*Really* . . ? Why?"

"One young lady detected a full-on skeleton with her unit. Found it buried at the perimeter of the field where the woods literally run alongside. Before you ask, there was a gun with it – and get this … a little leather bag containing thirty five-pence coins. That's how the detector thing went off."

"Thirty pieces of silver …" breathed Fran, both eyes widening as her hand found its way absentmindedly back inside the biscuit barrel. She was really intrigued with the story now, and for the first time since having the baby – was missing her job.

"Funny you should say that, the head, Sandra Wainright? She said exactly the same thing. It was very quiet, and she was standing a few yards behind me, but I definitely heard her say it."

"First thing I thought of, no idea why, but I wonder if *she* knows why?"

"Good point. I'll get Suzanne to interview her privately this week."

"Can CSI tell how long it's been there, whether it's male or female, or the age?"

"It's male, but we've got to wait for the forensic anthropology lab to give us the rest. The fact the coins were modern means it can't be pre-sixties. I googled when the five pence piece was introduced, it was '68, so that's the absolute earliest that poor guy got shot and dumped in that hole."

Fran munched on her biscuit in thought. It was good to hear about a case again, and this one sounded really intriguing – could either be a cold case, or a missing person that was never reported. She adored their son, and well aware she was lucky to be able to have this precious time with him, but mentally, the challenge of a new case would always pull at her.

From the couch they watched Jamie as he lay on his back shaking his giraffe teething-ring rattle and dribbling profusely. Fran leant forward to pull some tissues from a box on the coffee table, left the couch to kneel on the floor beside him and gently dab him dry. "Ayyy, but you're a dribbly bibbly today, aren't you my little Taybri?" She tickled his stomach and he smiled and giggled at her as he waved his pudgy little arms.

Harry leant forward to kiss the top of Fran's head. "You're going to have to stop calling him that, you know," he said softly, their previous discussion temporarily on a back-burner. "Lad's had a perfectly good name since he was born."

She turned round to look up at him. "Taybridge was such a special name when I was carrying him and his twin brother – after I shortened it when he was born, it kind of stuck. Do you think he knows, Harry? About his brother … does he miss him?"

Harry stroked her cheek and swallowing hard, mentally begged his eyes not to betray him. She put up her hand to hold his, and then got off the floor to join him back on the couch. "You know…" he started slowly… "That day we lost him … I thought the whole world had broken, you were in another place, one I couldn't reach. I felt utterly useless."

Fran leant into his neck. "It was heartbreaking for

both of us, and I just couldn't find a way to disentangle my feelings. It felt guilty to be happy Jamie survived when his brother didn't, then equally guilty being sad because I had Jamie. I still can't … I don't *want* to forget our Taybridge twin, Harry."

He stroked her hair and kissed the side of her head. "We won't forget, not ever. Maybe it's why you've been calling this little lad Taybri for the last five months, so you still feel close to his twin."

"Yes, probably, I'd not thought of that."

"We could make a memory shelf in Jamie's bedroom, if you like?" said Harry quietly.

Fran turned to him smiling, eyes glistening. "Yes, I'd like that."

And at that moment, right on cue, Jamie held out his giraffe rattle, smiling happily, and babbling something seemingly very important towards the lounge window …

SIXTEEN

INCIDENT ROOM - KIRKDALE POLICE STATION

9.00 A.M. WEDNESDAY 19TH MAY 2021

Suzanne Moorcroft stood facing the whiteboard, pointing to several pictures of the skeleton discovered at Clayton House Grammar School. In Fran's absence, Harry had decided to let her take the briefing for good experience. He was technically the SIO, and therefore overseeing the case, certainly as far as Chief Superintendent Hitchings was concerned. However, he was also known for encouraging lower-ranking, capable officers in their careers, and Suzanne Moorcroft sat squarely in the capable category. It was why she'd run the crime scene at Clayton House.

"Okay every—"

"Apologies for the interruption, Sarge, but the chief super wants to see you."

Suzanne turned towards the owner of the rich Irish brogue that had just filled the room and sauntered to the front to take a seat. Even before turning from the board, she knew immediately it belonged to Ambleside transferee Gabriel Downs, who, unusually for him, was not in uniform. This fact was disturbing enough, as it suggested he'd been attached to their team as plain clothes, something Suzanne would definitely *not* appreciate. The fact Hitchings wanted to see her was something else entirely. Could it have something to do with her and Gabe's friction at the Clayton House skeleton site?

Harry stood up and walked over to her. Arms crossed, and wearing a knowing smirk, Downs was looking far too smug for his liking.

He turned her towards the board and whispered… "Stay cool, it'll be fine, I'll fill in till you get back."

"And … er, Guv … the chief asked for *you* to follow the sarge in ten minutes."

Harry swung round to see Gabe Downs slouched in the chair, with his arm thrown across the back of the one next to him, right foot casually lying across his left knee, and full-on grinning back at them. The last thing Harry felt was calm, but quick as a flash, replied, "Yes, *thank* you, PC Downs, I requested a meeting first thing this morning." It was all he could come up with to flatten the Irish officer's insufferable overstep. He was also wondering what Hitchings wanted with *him*. In that moment he made the decision to hand over to Joe Walker, also a fine officer. He'd taken a bullet for him nine months ago and a medal was on its way – Harry knew full well he could manage a morning briefing.

"Walker, could you take over here, please? We'll be back shortly."

"*I wouldn't bank on it...*" murmured Downs into his chest.

As he walked to the front of the room, Joe eyed Gabe suspiciously. He'd had enough of Terry Hackett's obnoxious behaviour when he was there, turned out he was more than obnoxious which was why he was currently on remand in HMP Frankland. Now it looked as though he'd been replaced with another tosser... "Yes, boss – will do."

Andrew Gale and Hannah Carlin exchanged surprised glances. Both remembered the heated exchange between Downs and Suzanne Moorcroft at the skeleton site – they also knew he was uniform, not CID, so what was he doing there?

CHIEF SUPERINTENDENT CHRIS HITCHINGS' OFFICE 3RD FLOOR

Harry and Suzanne arrived outside Hitchings' office and agreed he should go in first, even though Gabriel Downs had said Harry was to follow her ten minutes later. As his new office was within an open-plan room with copious amounts of glass (not particularly to his liking but he was getting used to it), he could see Harry and Suzanne waiting outside and beckoned them both to come in together.

"Morning, Harry, Suzanne, take a seat, I won't keep you too long, I know I'm delaying your briefing for which I apologise, but this is important."

Suzanne felt her guts tighten and clasped her hands in her lap, waiting for the fallout of reprimanding an officer in front of members of the public, and at a crime scene to boot. Harry was a little laxer about such things if he thought they were genuinely necessary, Hitchings … *not* so relaxed…

"You're obviously aware that PC Downs, Gabriel, has joined you this morning in the CID briefing, as I asked him to pass on the message about coming to see *me*."

"Yes, sir, we *were* a little surprised at that, if I'm honest," replied Harry.

"Understandably so, Longbridge, understandably so, but there *is* a good reason I assure you."

Harry certainly couldn't think of one, and had a distinct feeling it *wasn't* going to be good. Suzanne flicked him a glance before looking back at their senior officer.

"What you may not know, mainly because it hasn't been made common knowledge yet, is that Gabriel Downs is my wife's sister's husband, and therefore my brother-in-law."

Harry released a kind of involuntary strangled cough, which was far louder than he'd hoped it would be when it practically choked him on the way up.

"Yes, Longbridge, I realise this is all a bit … *unusual*. However, the reason I've got you two up here in DI Taylor's absence is that he was originally a Garda in

Ireland before he and my sister-in-law came across to the mainland six months ago with their children and moved to Ambleside."

"Any particular reason he's not *still* at Ambleside, sir, or is that off limits?"

Suzanne looked even tenser at that comment, although she was *very* keen to know herself.

"That's a private matter, Harry, for the moment at least. My intention is that he's attached to your team as plain clothes for a few months and … well, not to put too fine a point on it, I'd like you to keep an eye on him. He's been a bit … *unpredictable* of late, shall we say, at the very least a bit curt, sometimes extremely short-tempered."

Suzanne felt she was being given an opener here to speak about the incident at Clayton House's crime scene…
"Sir, there was actually a bit of friction between PC Downs and myself yesterday as it happens, but I felt that—"

"Yes, I know, he's already spoken to me."

Suze felt her throat suddenly constrict and her face flush. She looked at Harry for support.

"I'm sorry, but Sergeant Moorcroft was well within her remit over that, sir. PC Downs was practically bullying one of the teachers with his line of questioning – it was way out of order. Suzanne pulled him aside and reprimanded him, which he obviously didn't like much, in fact he storm—"

"Yes, yes, look, I know *all* this from Gabe. It's not an easy situation, and I'm not blaming you at all, Sergeant. What happened yesterday at Clayton House School …

well, it's exactly the sort of thing I'm referring to. For the most part he's a good officer, *but* … just at the moment he needs a friendly eye kept on him – okay?"

Harry hesitated before mentioning what had been on his mind since entering Hitchings' office. He knew it would go either way, an explosion, or an acceptance of what he was trying to say.

"Sir, I seem to remember not so long ago having to assure you I wouldn't repeat the idea of bringing uniform into CID, after I did exactly that with PC McPhail last year."

"Indeed, Harry, you did. But Rob McPhail, *God rest his soul*, was an entirely different situation."

"Because . . ?" prompted Harry, pointedly…

Hitchings began to adopt his stony-eyed, flushed-neck look… "*Because*, Longbridge, on *this* occasion *I'm* giving the order. *That's* why."

Harry took a deep breath… "It would help if we had some idea of why he's—"

"Look, just bear with me on this, both of you, *please.*" The two men held each other's gaze whilst Suzanne looked from one to the other, waiting for she wasn't quite sure what.

"Right then, thank you for coming in, and by the way, keep me informed about the Clayton House case. I remember there were missing pupils from that school in the nineties and a teacher too, I believe. This skeleton find could very well be one of them, so keep me in the loop."

"Sir," they replied in unison.

"Right, off you go, get back to your briefing, and if there's any real problem … with *anything*, just let me know."

"Will do, sir," replied Harry, before they both stood up and walked to the door. Holding it open for Suzanne, he turned back to see Hitchings looking decidedly concerned. Something was bothering him, Harry didn't know what, but it wasn't only a skeleton – specifically a *male* one at that. No. *There was also Gabe Downs lying at the heart of it.*

"… and I'll clear it with DCI Longbridge, but once we hear from forensics on an age as near as possible on the skeleton, tracking down and interviewing as many past pupils, and also if there are any retired teachers still living from that year, and maybe one or two years either side it, will be required. It's going to mean a lot of tracking and a lot of interviewing."

"Yes, it will. Good job, Walker," said Harry, letting the door shut behind them as he and Suzanne re-entered the briefing room. "And we'll start with the headmistress, Sandra Wainright. She mentioned that one of the two girls, who went missing years ago, was a friend of hers. Now, that skeleton has already been confirmed as male, so we know it's not one of those missing girls or the teacher as it was an all-female-led school back then. But, there's going to be a connection there somewhere, not a random kill, I can feel it."

"I'll go and see Mrs Wainright tomorrow, Guv," offered Suzanne. "We're going to need that forensics report ASAP, though, and as soon as we have it, at least three of you will be tracking down as many of those ex-pupils as possible. It's likely to be around the nineties or early two thousands, but that report is going to be crucial."

A hand went up. It was Gabriel Downs… "They'd have still needed a groundsman or some form of caretaker. All schools have one of those, we certainly did in Ireland, and it would definitely have been a man."

He had a point. Suzanne's eyes switched from Gabe's to Harry's.

"That's a good call, PC Downs," replied Harry, albeit a little stiffly. "When you're going through the cold-case files for the two girls and the teacher, check out if the caretaker's mentioned. I was a young DS in London back then, so not familiar with the details." It was then Harry remembered he'd meant to ask Hitchings if he'd been the SIO on the nineties school case, and for some reason at that very moment a cold chill slithered across the back of his neck… He hunched his shoulders, adjusted his shirt collar and went to sit down. "Carry on, sergeants – you can work together on this one."

CARPENTERS ARMS PUB - KIRKDALE
AROUND 3.30 P.M.

Molly awoke with a start. She'd been having a doze on the bed whilst Christie had her afternoon nap. The window was on the latch to let in a little breeze as she didn't like her room getting stuffy, but it had suddenly blown wide open and there was a right hoolie blowing through her curtains. Not only that, there was a damp smell and a shadowy figure opposite her bed... She slowly propped herself up onto her elbow to concentrate more fully on it, trying to figure out what it was, at the same time praying it wasn't what she thought it might be. Of course in the end, she knew there was no point in denying it. Those familiar unwanted feelings swam through her, wanting her to accept, wanting her to 'see'. *Shit.*

A young girl, about seventeen or eighteen, with long chestnut hair and dressed in school uniform, was floating upright against the middle of the opposite wall. She was desperately mouthing the same two words over and over, in a haunted, throaty whisper...

"*Help ... me.*"

SEVENTEEN

CLAYTON HOUSE GRAMMAR SCHOOL KIRKDALE CUMBRIA

10.30 A.M. SATURDAY 14TH SEPTEMBER 1991

Charlotte hated being a boarder at Clayton House, especially as Emily wasn't. She'd always harboured resentment against her parents for making her live in whilst they swanned off around the world travelling to interesting places. However, sometimes boarding proved useful. Especially as Jackie Squires was *also* a boarder, and right at that moment, Charlotte was learning something extremely useful about that particular fifth-former.

All the live-in girls had their own large communal social room to hang out in after school and at weekends. It was open-plan, but split in half by various pieces of furniture so the older girls from years four, five and six were separate from years one, two and three. Other than the library, it was where they did homework, could relax with a coffee, read, make breakfast and a light lunch, or in Jackie's case as Charlotte was a witness to, have secret conflabs with her best friend, Sandi Lisle.

On that Saturday, from across the top of the brown-weave sofas that divided the room, Charlotte watched them get up, walk round to the door and disappear into the hallway at the top of the social room's staircase. She immediately got up to follow them, wondering if her suspicions were about to pan out. Charlotte may have yet to see her thirteenth birthday, but she was thirteen going on sixteen, as sharp as a tack and with hunches that were rarely wrong.

As she suspected, the journey was a long walk through the woods and out to Manor Lane. The gates to Clayton Hall appeared opposite the woods this time, as Jackie and Sandi had picked a slightly different path from the one Fishy Phillips used for cross-country lessons. Charlotte had made sure she'd kept well back so she wouldn't be seen. What happened next, though, *wasn't* entirely what she'd expected. The two fifth-formers crossed the road and walked through the gates which were still fully open, just like they'd been only eight days before when Charlotte had skipped cross-country.

She remained hidden in the woods until they were so far up the path to the entrance they were out of sight. Her heart was thumping a bit which annoyed her. Charlotte did *not* want to feel nervous; she *refused* to feel nervous, and so taking a deep breath, broke cover from the trees to begin crossing the road, before suddenly having to jump back into her hiding place. A large silver estate car approached smoothly from her left and swung brazenly into the grounds of Clayton Hall. She watched as it crunched slowly up the drive, following Jackie and Sandi to the entrance. And then her mouth dropped in shock as a second car appeared, this time from her right. Black as tar, it swept through the gates behind the big silver one, and she was pretty sure druggy teacher, Karen Lewis, was driving that.

Boy, do I wish you were here, Em, this is something else. With Karen Lewis here, looks like I was right and there is *a drugs ring at Clayton Hall.* She waited until both cars had parked at the top of the drive in front of the manor and then left the woods, crossed the road, and made her way quickly through the gates.

Hiding behind some bushes, Charlotte made sure there was nobody outside the entrance before approaching the steps. She couldn't hear any voices, but then the walls of that place were really thick and the occupants could be anywhere inside. Breathing steadily, she took one step at a time up to the heavy double doors. As on her previous visit, they were unlocked, which she found surprising this time given what was likely to be going on inside, but then Mrs Lewis and friends would probably assume nobody would come to a place as rundown and uninviting as Clayton Hall.

Leaning her shoulder against one of the doors to open it, just enough to listen for any voices, she strained to hear before pushing a little harder to create enough room to squeeze through into the hallway.

Her feet scrunched on the fallen ceiling plaster, and the familiar musty smell filled her nostrils as it did on her first visit. She could hear their footsteps and low voices from above as they walked along the first-floor landing. Walking as softly as possible, she crossed the hall to the staircase and crept up each step to the top. No Mr Rat today, thank goodness, although she had a distinct feeling he was the least of her worries. At the top, stretching her neck slightly forward to look each way, Charlotte saw the backs of Jackie and Sandi creeping along the right-hand corridor, sometimes darting inside a room as if to make sure they weren't seen. *So ... they're not actually with Mrs Lewis and whoever was driving the sliver car, then, which means they must be spying on them. That would make sense and must be how Jackie's had the inside info on Karen Lewis's drug habit.*

Suddenly there was a commotion further down the corridor – she could hear raised voices, and *that's* when she knew Fishy Phillips was there too. *No wonder Fishy was going off on one when she realised I'd been scouting round here the other day instead of running her stinking cross-country route!* Once Jackie and Sandi had emerged from the last room they'd dipped into, and walked gingerly to the end, disappearing round the corner, Charlotte half walked, half ran to where they'd turned left and stopped, peeping carefully round it. As she did so, she noticed flaky, old white paint had smudged all down the left arm of her jacket, and left leg of her jeans where she'd leant against the peeling wall. Sighing, she brushed it off as best she could and then followed them along the next corridor where the voices became louder, and words became clearer…

"You *know* that's not the right money, so why are you even *here*!"

"Please … it's only temporary. I can't manage any more till the end of the month. *Please* Felicia, I really need it, things are just so, so—"

"You *know* who half this payment goes to, Karen, and it's not *my* other half! Your marital problems are none of my concern."

There was silence for a moment. Gritty footsteps could be heard walking impatiently up and down. Charlotte held her breath, heart annoyingly thumping and tense excitement building in her chest as she waited to hear what came next. She wondered what Jackie and Sandi were making of it all, and wondered why *they* were there, surely not to attempt blackmail? And then it happened. Somebody screamed, *very loudly*. There was scrabbling, pushing, a hideous wailing noise, and the sound of running footsteps coming her way. Charlotte looked around anxiously for the closest room to dive into, which was luckily only a few feet behind her. She flew into it just as Jackie Squires and Sandi Lisle tore past her at a rate of knots, their faces suggesting they'd seen or heard something *extremely* scary. Images of the hanging noose rope she'd seen in the music room first time round flashed into her mind, along with Mr Rat from the top of the stairs, and of course the legend of the *Green Lady*… The

Green Lady's music room, however, was *not* where Jackie and Sandi had been hiding. She knew that because it was not in their corridor.

Charlotte remained hidden behind the oak door of a long-ago-used study, squinting through the long gap on the hinge side, to see Karen Lewis and Fishy Phillips also running back up her corridor, albeit not quite as effectively – *or* fast. Considering Jackie and Sandi were both school sprint champions, Charlotte knew they'd be down those stairs, out the door and long gone before those two teachers could catch up to anywhere near them.

After about two seconds thought, she left her hiding place and made her way to where the others had run from, left at the top of the corridor she was in, and down to where she could now see two more rooms. On checking both, it was abundantly clear there was no Mr (or Mrs) Rat, no hanging noose, and no green lady. What she *was* confronted with, however, was, if it were possible, *far* more disturbing. In the centre of the first room, lying at waist height on a wooden stand, was a full-size coffin. It was black, ancient, and hideously dusty with corroded brass handles … and an open lid. In fact, there was no lid. Charlotte hesitated on the threshold… *This must have been the last room Jackie and Sandi slipped into, so they weren't seen by Fishy and Karen, because they ran past me first. The other one must have been where the drugs deal was taking place because it was empty apart from some ghastly old bedroom furniture.*

It took all of her 'thirteen going on sixteen' guts to walk over to the coffin, one small step at a time. *Jackie and*

Sandi, you just wait till I spread the goss you're both just little old scaredy ca— She clapped a hand over her mouth to try and stop the scream from coming out but wasn't quite quick enough. Inside the coffin was a full-size skeleton – a note resting at its head end …

WHOEVER YOU ARE –
IF YOU KNOW WHAT'S GOOD FOR YOU,
YOU'LL STAY AWAY FROM CLAYTON HALL

Backing away from the coffin and its occupant, Charlotte repeatedly tried to swallow the lump in her throat but it wouldn't go down. She was moving faster now and nearly tripped over her own feet as she neared the doorway, except they weren't her own feet at all. It was then she felt the firm pressure of the wet pad over her face with its horribly sweet smell invading her nostrils, rushing upwards to send her head spinning. She tried to pull it off but felt too groggy and weak – her arms fell away from her mouth, her legs wobbled then disappeared completely from under her as she fell further and further into darkness and eventual oblivion…

Later, much later because her bedside clock showed 4.00 p.m., Charlotte woke up on her bed. She was on top of it, not in it, and could vaguely make out someone standing over her, arms crossed.

"So you've woken up at *last*, Krane. That'll teach you to stash a secret supply of vodka in your wardrobe for a weekend's drinking session! No doubt you've got a stinking headache!"

Charlotte could barely make out Felicia Phillips' facial features, but would have recognised that caustic voice anywhere. Her head *was* killing her, and all she wanted was to go back to sleep, but now she didn't feel safe. Now, she knew something was definitely going on at Clayton Hall, something very bad and very dangerous – *and Fishy Phillips was at the heart of it.* Who else, though? Who else was involved or possibly even controlling the drugs racket? Back at the hall she'd implied to Mrs Lewis half the money went to someone else – but *who*?

When she finally managed to open her eyes fully, she looked straight into the piercing ones of her gym teacher and bravely replied, "*I can still smell that sickly-sweet pad.*"

EIGHTEEN

MIKE LEYLAND'S HOUSE
KILTON HILL - WORKSOP
6.30 A.M. WEDNESDAY 19TH MAY 2021

His arm was slung heavily across her waist, breath gently warming the nape of her neck. The retro clock on his bedside table met her sleepy eyes as they slowly opened, before closing mega fast after meeting the sight of their hastily scattered clothes on the bedroom floor. She waited a moment and then lifted one lid to see if things still looked the same. Nothing had changed and the scene reflected *exactly* what had happened the night before. It had been a long time since she'd been with anyone, let alone someone as good-looking, popular, hugely in demand, and it had to be said … *as shit hot as Mike Leyland.* Sofia still couldn't believe he was interested in her, but then she'd been used to living in her sister's shadow for so many years. Her musical talent and beauty had meant Raya was always the one who'd got the attention, won the boys, and went out on the dates. But Sofia had never minded about any of that. Raya had been her little sister, and she still loved and missed her terribly.

Only living a ten-minute drive away from work meant there was no need to rush to get out of Mike's bed, and she *really* didn't want to get out. After they'd left the cemetery in the pouring rain the day before, he'd suggested an early dinner at the White Lion where they'd had their first date four days earlier. Last night's meal had extended to several coffees, followed by another bottle of wine back at the house, and like millions of couples before them, one thing had led to another and … here they were the following morning, snuggled up under a duvet…

"Coffee Miss Torres…? Or are you a PG Tips kinda girl?" Mike whispered in her ear as he squeezed her waist.

She giggled and turned over to face him, rolling her eyes. Faking a straight face, she replied, "I maybe British born, Mike, but I'm still *Spanish*. Tea doesn't really feature. We drink loads of coffee and like it hot, strong and rich, *so* … half milk, half espresso. We call it *café con leche*. It's a bit like latte, only twice as good."

He was quietly stumped for a moment before slowly smiling and then kissing her nose… "I've got Douwe Egberts and semi-skimmed – I'll put in three heaped teaspoons and add some cream…"

ICU BASSETLAW HOSPITAL
KILTON HILL - WORKSOP

Sofia's mood was light all the way to work; she'd even been humming to the radio in the car. A grin gradually spread over her face as she remembered where she'd driven in from, and whose bed she'd got out of that morning. She laughed to herself and shook her head on recalling Mike's coffee, which was truly *terrible*, and made a mental note to teach him how to make a decent cup – *Spanish style*. It was a very small negative – he was a catch and she knew she was punching. She also knew it would take a miracle to get her confidence up to, and over, what she'd always felt was an impossibly high bar.

The ten-minute run was a bonus though – her little flat in Pitsmoor, Sheffield, was about a half-hour drive, not bad, but ten minutes was infinitely preferable. She pulled into the car park, even managing to get her usual space fairly close to the entrance. It was definitely going to be a good day.

The automatic glass doors slid back for her and she walked through reception to head for the lifts. Bingo! One arrived as she approached, and she walked straight in, hit her floor number and leant against the back wall with a soppy grin on her face. She couldn't help it, she was still thinking about Mike – he definitely had attributes even if his coffee tasted like mud!

Reaching her floor, the lift pinged, the doors opened and Sofia made her way to the ICU department to start her day. On the way down the corridor, a lady in heavily tinted glasses was walking hesitantly in her direction, stopping, turning and looking confused.

"Can I help at all? You seem to have lost your bearings, and that's not difficult in here, believe me, I can *still* manage it!" Sofia ended the question with a smile, whilst trying not to breathe in too much of the lady's overpowering perfume.

"Actually yes, er … thank you. I was looking for the bathroom?"

"No problem, just continue on down here and turn sharp left. They're opposite the lifts."

"Thanks, you have a nice day."

"And you, bye now." Sofia carried on down the corridor, wrinkled her nose and coughed. *Maybe it's time the visitors got advised about the no-perfume requirement as well – that was hideous!*

She paused by the water cooler and chatted with a few passing colleagues as she waited for her drink, then quickly checked her phone before turning it off. Carrying her water, she noticed a commotion further up the corridor and quickened her pace. There were raised voices and several staff running in and out of one of the ICU rooms. As she got closer, she realised it was the one she was responsible for.

When she reached it, Charlotte's room smelt overwhelmingly of a sickly-sweet perfume – *the one she'd experienced ten minutes earlier*. Machines were going off and the night-shift nurse was looking worried…

"Sofia, thank *God!* I only stepped out for a few minutes, I knew you'd be on time, you always are and I was dying for the loo. We must have passed each other in the corridor without realising it. I just got back, and …" She trailed off, wringing her hands in disbelief that something had gone so badly wrong on her watch, and in her absence.

"Okay, Debs, *calm* down, just let the emergency team do their stuff."

They both looked on intensely as the specialists worked on Charlotte Peterson, and people were ushered past the room if they slowed down to see what was going on. Debbie Anderson remained as white as a sheet, and Sofia comforted the younger nurse, insisting she'd done nothing wrong, and everyone got caught short for the loo sometimes. After ten excruciating minutes, the machines returned to a steady, reassuring beep, the patient was stable again and everyone gradually went back to their usual work-stations and wards.

Meanwhile, as all the melodrama was going on in ICU, way below in the front of the hospital, a woman with an overly pungent perfume and tight schedule pulled out of the car park – *in a sleek black Audi…*

4.00 P.M. KIRKDALE POLICE STATION KESWICK

Harry was in his office when his mobile rang, and when he answered, was surprised to find it was Kelly Novak,

Kirkdale General's forensic pathologist. If he was honest, he was glad he didn't have to deal with Penrith on this one. He'd had enough of Marcus Ventnor to last him a lifetime. Every time the man's name came up, he heard that quip in his head, '*Marcus Ventnor, Ventnor as in the Isle of Wight*' – it drove him nuts. Then there'd been his incessant hovering around Fran when they were on the 'Body Parts' case and needed to check out a leg in Penrith morgue. That had made his blood boil.

"Hi, Kelly, how's things? Surely you're not ringing with the forensic report on the Clayton House skeleton already?"

"Yes, good, thanks, Harry, and yes again re the skeleton. It's my old school so I made it a priority for you. I started there in '97 when stories about those missing older girls and the teacher were rife, so I'm drawn to anything connected to that cold case."

"You were there as well? One of our sergeants went there and came top in the entire country for Biology A level – *Suzanne Moorcroft*?"

"I know of Suzanne *now* of course, but we weren't there together. She must have joined after me, but I vaguely remember the local papers carrying the story. We'd have welcomed her in forensic anthropology with results like that!"

"I'm sure, but I'm very glad she's in *my* team – damned fine officer, I'll bring her in to the lab with me if there's a need for police to attend."

"Great, I'd love to meet her. Now, back to my report… Without going into too much forensic jargon—"

"Oh God, yes, *please* keep it short and simple," replied Harry, relieved he wouldn't need to pull a book on ancient bones from the library.

"I thought you'd say that, your chief super used to say exactly the same when he was more involved on the ground."

"Who's that? Chris Hitchings?"

"The very same, I've been qualified for nine years now, but I remember when I started, he used to moan at my then boss, Marcus Vent—"

"Okay, I believe you, no need to bring up Ventnor, I won't go into why…"

"Yes, I heard you'd had a bit of friction last year when I was off and he covered me from Penrith. A body-parts case, wasn't it?"

"It was. Sorry, I interrupted you. Please, do go on with your report…"

"Well, of course you know about the bullet hole in the back of the skull from CSI at the scene, and from the size of the overall skeleton, pubic bones, the length of the long bones and the presence of third molars – that's wisdom teeth – all these help to determine it's definitely an adult male. Add to that the absence of growth plates, some signs of osteoarthritis and other degenerative conditions such as osteophytosis – they're bone spurs – on both his knee and hip joints, it's likely he was an older very mature male, at least over sixty. Luckily, with the gun CSI found alongside, and the pouch of five pence coins, we can be sure the man was placed in the ground about twenty-five years ago, so no need for carbon-14 – that's radiocarbon dating of the bones. The highest-yielding DNA will be from the metacarpal and metatarsal bones, I'll have that for you sometime next week – hopefully you'll be able to find out who he was."

Harry was *very* glad he'd not been given the complicated version… "I don't s'pose with your personal connection in forensics you'd know if there was any chance of fingerprints on those two items?" he asked with zero hope in his voice.

"Actually, I've learnt quite a lot in that regard. According to past conversations with my friend, fingerprints last pretty much forever on most things if left undisturbed without exposure to the elements, good or bad. They should be able to obtain some prints off the gun for you, probably won't be absolutely *perfect* but you should be able to …"

"Brilliant, thanks for that info Kelly!"

"You're welcome, I'm sure they'll be in touch with a report soon. At least it wasn't a youngster, but everyone is a loss to someone. It never ceases to amaze me when nobody comes forward to report a missing person."

"Agreed, although I believe the two girls and the teacher from that school *did* have parents and families who came forward, and naturally, they've never given up hope, they're still waiting to know what happened to them. Of course, back then I was in London, so not around when it was a current investigation. Let's hope pursuing this case, and re-opening the three cold cases of 1995 leads us to finally finding those missing students and their teacher – one way or, sadly and far more likely, the other."

"Absolutely, and I'd really love to be kept in the loop if possible, Harry, it's been far too long for everyone concerned."

"Indeed and yes, of course." Something suddenly occurred to him… "Kelly, do you remember if Chief Superintendent Hitchings was involved with that investigation when you were a pupil at Clayton House? He'd probably have been a DI then."

"Gosh, no, sorry, I really can't remember, I'm afraid, it's a long time ago."

"Yes, yes, of course. I meant to ask him myself this morning, but completely forgot." Rocking back on his swing chair, Harry narrowed his eyes and rhythmically tapped his desk in thought. Flashes of unfavourable and crazy possibilities kept poking at his brain. *He didn't like it.*

"If anything comes back to me I'll be sure to let you know."

"That's great, thanks again, Kelly, bye now." He was still tapping his desk, mind in an uncomfortable place, when his phone rang again, and this time it had a different ring-tone…

"Harry? It's Molly. I hate to tell you this but …"

"Tell me wha— oh God not *again*?"

"Afraid so, I was absolutely *gutted*, I can tell you."

"So … what hap—"

"I was just having a ten-minute shut eye as Christie had her afternoon nap, luckily in *her* room, not mine. This time it was a teenage girl, I'd say about … *fifteen*? Long reddish hair, dressed in school uniform and just … floating in mid-air against the wall…"

Harry had always referred to Molly's visions as '*that thing you do*', and even after everything that had happened in the last three years, still found it difficult to accept. The fact she was always right, though … it meant he'd had to acknowledge her abilities, regardless. He just made damned sure she and Hitchings were kept well away from each other. "I don't suppose it – *she* … *said* anything?" As soon as the words were out of his mouth he winced and shook his head. What the hell was he thinking? "Sorry, I just—"

"Actually, yes she did."

Harry's eyebrows lifted. There was a brief silence from Molly's end. He could feel his heart begin to speed up and thump erratically and felt sure it couldn't be good for him, diabetes or not. He heard her take a deep breath…

"She whispered, Harry, but I heard her quite clearly, she said it over and over again … '*Help me*'."

NINETEEN

CLAYTON HOUSE GRAMMAR SCHOOL KIRKDALE CUMBRIA

11.30 A.M. THURSDAY 20TH MAY 2021

Suzanne Moorcroft sat in the school reception area, having been given an ID badge attached to a navy-blue police lanyard. She thought it slightly over the top since she'd only been on-site two days previously, albeit in the fields, especially as Sandra Wainright used to be her headmistress and they'd spoken for a while. However, given a skeleton had just been dug up in their grounds, and she was there to interview her on decades-old cases of a missing teacher and two pupils, maybe their strict ID code wasn't so unreasonable. It also felt ultra strange waiting to see her old headmistress *inside* her old school, watching pupils coming and going, their excited chatter and laughter echoing off the walls, sounds she used to be a part of. Lifting her head slightly, Suzanne wrinkled her nose. She was also convinced there was the faint aroma of a very familiar and *ghastly* dinner being cooked…

Sandra Wainright didn't keep her waiting more than a few minutes. Suzanne stood up when she saw her approaching, and when they shook hands noticed the woman looked a little edgy.

"Good morning, Suzanne. Actually, I suppose I should call you Sergeant Moorcroft, now, shouldn't I?"

Suze smiled – it sounded so *weird*!

"Let's go to my office, shall we? It's just through here."

Unless it had moved, of course Suzanne knew *exactly* where her office was, and walking through the school as a police officer carrying a bag of cold-case files, instead of a pupil carrying her homework, felt *extremely* weird.

She turned to Sandra as they walked. "Is that … Spaghetti M'Gosh I can smell?"

The headmistress laughed. "God, no, I stopped that hideous concoction being served up years ago. I remember it from being a pupil in the nineties – it was *vile*! So was the dungeon restaurant, and that's gone, too! Well, not exactly *gone*, clearly, it's out of bounds and we just don't eat down there anymore. Just wish I could have got rid of the awful McGosh sooner, but unbelievably, the previous head had a liking for it." She smiled, holding her arm out for Suzanne to go through the arched door to the next passageway. "As today's Thursday, you can probably smell cheese and broccoli flan!"

"Oh, I remember the cheese flan, that was lovely!" Suzanne replied automatically. They both laughed as they walked past the staffroom, and Sandra opened a door on the left to her office. Once seated, Suzanne had to mentally rein herself back from already slipping into 'ex-pupil mode', as Harry referred to it. She needed to find out some background to Sandra's missing best friend, and if possible, the other missing girl *and* the teacher, Karen Lewis.

"So, Mrs Wain—"

"It's Sandra, please, that's fine."

She hesitated. To be calling her old headmistress by her first name was taking weird to a whole new level – and what would the Guv say? With the extended silence, she went with it anyway… "Sandra, so, as you know a skeleton was removed from the grounds of the school a couple of days ago, and I'm here regarding that, and the opening of three cold cases of two missing pupils, and a teacher from 1995."

"Yes, I understand, but it was a very long time ago, of course. I was in the sixth-form college then and ten years younger than you must be now. Trying to remember details won't be easy, and frankly, it was just a case of one day they were there, and the next …" She briefly looked down into her lap before raising her head again.

"I understand, maybe if we take each person, one at a time?"

Sandra nodded; a sad but also an anxious look crossing her face.

Suzanne pulled three files, a pocketbook and pen from her bag, and placed them on her side of Sandra

Wainright's desk. She opened the top file. "Okay, firstly, the other day at the skeleton site, you mentioned one of the missing students was your best friend. We know the skeleton is that of a male, so as this is an all-girls' school with female-only staff, it's clearly not that of one of the missing girls or the teacher. So, firstly, do you have any idea who that male skeleton may have belonged to?"

Sandra held Suzanne's eyes for a fraction of a second before answering. "No, no idea at all. As you said, Clayton was an all-female environment, still is to this day. It could be anyone."

Suzanne thought for a moment, hand hovering over her notebook before making a note of her answer. "Secondly, can you tell me if you've seen or heard from your friend at any time, no matter how short, since her disappearance?"

"No, not at all – not once, I would have notified the police immediately if I had. We were very close."

"Of course. Can you confirm the name of that best friend for me, please?" Suzanne waited, pen poised.

Sandra held her eyeline. "It's Jacqueline … Jacqueline Squires."

"And the other girl's name?"

"Debra something, I think, either Debra or … *Denise*, maybe? I can't remember."

Suzanne picked up the next file and opened it. "It's a Denise Fraser, according to the records she was younger than Jacqueline and they went missing within a few months of each other."

Sandra swallowed down a lump that had formed in her throat. A very slight sheen glistened across her forehead. This was bringing back all sorts of memories, unpleasant memories, things she wanted to forget. "Oh yes … Denise, that's right. She was in my younger sister's class."

"Oh? You had a *sister* here at Clayton?"

"Yes, her name was Rosalyn. Rosalyn Lisle – Lisle was my maiden name."

"You say your sister's name *was* Rosalyn, did she change—"

"She died. Ros died. Took her life in May 1995… At least, that's what they *said* happened."

"I'm so sorry Mrs … Sandra – that's … *terrible*. I don't have anything about it in my files of course as it wasn't part of the three MISPA cases. What exactly happened? I mean, you don't have to—"

Sandra pursed her lips, thinking for a moment, and then took a deep breath… "Ros had been terrified out of her life by two girls around her own age, Charlotte Krane and Emily Rowlands. Those two names I'll *never* forget. Emily was in her class and they'd initially been friends. Ros really liked her, but something very bad developed between them all, I don't know *what*, but it ended with Ros *supposedly* hanging herself in the music room. She was barely fifteen."

Suzanne had not been expecting to hear any of this. Sandra had suddenly gabbled it all out really fast, and it resulted in having virtually nothing written in her pocketbook. She quickly scribbled a few notes regarding Rosalyn Lisle, with a view to investigating records on her death later.

Sandra watched her write, and when Suzanne looked up, knew exactly what her next question would be. She was right.

"Sandra, forgive me for pursuing this but … who told you Rosalyn had taken her own life?"

"Veronica Dean, the headmistress at the time. The police were obviously called in and there was a full investigation, but overall evidence showed she'd been depressed, taken an overdose first, and had even left a note saying she couldn't cope with school, or any part of her life, anymore. It was presented as an open and shut case."

"Were you ever consulted or questioned about the state of your sister's mental health? What about your parents' views on it all, were they questioned?"

"We both boarded here, but I was in such a state of shock I was sent home, and my parents and I were visited by the police there. My parents couldn't shed any light on it either. There was no reason for Ros to kill herself, Suzanne, none at all. It never made any sense then and it still doesn't all these years later." Her eyes began to glaze and she looked quickly away, taking a deep breath to control threatening tears. "I've never talked about it since."

"Can you think of *anything, anything* at all, that might have led to your sister's death? Something you felt you couldn't reveal at the time for some reason, for fear of getting into trouble, maybe?"

Sandra shifted uneasily in her high-backed leather swing chair. It was quite plush and luxurious for a headmistress's office, but at that moment didn't appear to be easing her discomfort at all. She hesitated, rolling her lips as she glanced up at the wall clock above the door, willing the hands to meet at the top of the hour in order for the first lunch bell to sound. Hopefully, it would aid her escape from this stripping back of the years, this peeling away of everything she'd tried to forget. The clock still sat firmly at 11.45 a.m. No escape then…"The teacher, Karen Lewis – the one that went missing. She was always a bit … *stressed*, that was until one day she did something about it."

"*Did* something? How do you mean, *did* something?"

"She taught history, but her nickname was 'Little Miss Coke Head', and I'm not referring to her lessons on the 1960s Clean Air Act, or her love of a well-known fizzy drink."

Suzanne's jaw fell. "Are you suggesting she was—"

"Snorting cocaine at school? Yes, and most days, too. I've no idea how she managed to keep upright, let alone teach us, but somehow she did."

"Why do you feel there was a connection between this teacher and your sister's death? And if you felt you couldn't say anything at the time, why *was* that?"

"It's complicated. I couldn't *prove* anything so there didn't seem any point in speaking up. It was easier to just be sent home, grieve and stay quiet. But there were two things. One, Karen Lewis used to do her drugs in the music room where Ros was found – and two…." Sandra ran her tongue over her lips. Her mouth was dry and her heart was pounding – things were about to get *very* detailed…"There was this one time my friend Jackie and I followed Karen and Fishy Phill – that's Felicia Phillips, the gym teacher – we followed them out to Clayton Hall. It's a manor house in—"

"Yes, I remember. We learnt about Lord Clayton being exiled from Surrey and starting the school. He built Clayton Hall in Manor Lane."

"That's right. Well, Miss Phillips was nicknamed Fishy, partly because of her first name, Felicia, partly because she used to have the faint odour of raw fish around her. Never did find out why, although I think her partner might have been in the trade. *Anyway* … that day, when Jackie and I were exploring Clayton Hall, we saw and heard things that would've got us into a great deal of trouble. Very *serious* trouble had we told anyone."

Suzanne was now totally gripped by a story that was either a complete fabrication, or a truth buried as deep as that skeleton and finally brought to the surface. "Well, you know it's perfectly safe to speak now, don't you? Do you think a crime may have been committed at the hall that day?"

Sandra glanced up at the clock again. There were only a couple of minutes to go till the bell, but she'd already said so much…"They arrived after us and when we heard voices on the landing, we hid in one of the upstairs rooms. In another one, Phillips was dealing drugs, and

Karen Lewis was begging her for them but she didn't have enough money. Turned out Jackie and I were hiding in the room *next* to the one they were in, but we saw something really creepy in ours that made us scream, and knew we had to get out fast as they'd definitely have heard us. Luckily, both Jackie and I were excellent sprinters, school champions in fact, so although they *had* heard and followed us, they could never catch us up. Fishy was in her late forties or early fifties anyway, Karen about thirty-ish and hated any form of exercise – they never stood a chance."

"What was it that made you scream?" asked Suzanne, now dashing off notes in her pocketbook.

"Would you believe another skeleton? It was in an open coffin with a warning note telling anyone who found it to stay away from Clayton Hall."

"It was probably just a fake to scare people off because they were using it as a drugs den."

"Probably, but that wasn't the worst of it. Jackie and I hid in the bushes outside to get our breath. Sprint champions or not, it was a long way from that room, that place is *enormous*."

"And ...?"

"For some reason Fishy and Karen didn't come out for ages. I mean a good ten, fifteen minutes. It didn't add up. We were just about to break cover and make a run for it down to the entrance to get away when we saw them coming out. Karen had her back to us, sort of bent over and moving awkwardly, unsteadily down the steps to their cars. Fishy was opposite her but Karen's body mostly blocked hers. Then when they reached the bottom, we saw why they were moving so oddly. *They were carrying what looked like a dead body.*"

Suzanne's eyes popped wide and her mouth fell open. All those years Sandra Wainright had kept this under wraps, some of the time when Suze was a pupil at Clayton House. If it was true, and she'd got no reason to disbelieve her, this information was massive…"Was it? A dead body, I mean."

"At the time we were convinced it was, but we briefly saw the girl's face as they carried her past the bushes we were hiding behind. It was Charlotte Krane. We had no idea she'd followed all of us into that manor, but clearly she'd got caught, and they wouldn't have liked that one bit. However, the next day my sister said she'd seen her with her friend, Emily Rowlands, so clearly she wasn't dead, definitely drugged somehow though, because she was totally out of it when they carried her down those steps and bundled her in one of the cars. But from that day, things were never the same for my sister, Ros."

"Why do you say that, Sandra, what makes you so convinced and how was Ros connected to what you'd seen at Clayton Manor?"

Sandra hesitated for a moment…"I don't know. But for whatever reason, my sister was told in no uncertain terms to stay away from Emily Rowlands after that day."

Suzanne's eyes narrowed in expectation…"By *whom*?"

A sudden and very loud alarm sounded as ringing filled

the room and the corridors outside. Sandra Wainright stood up.

"By the most evil person I've ever had the misfortune to meet … *Charlotte Krane.*"

TWENTY

HARRY'S OFFICE - KIRKDALE POLICE STATION

Suzanne pulled into the station car park a little after 12.30 p.m. and realised she'd discovered next to nothing about the teacher and two girls who went missing in 1995, but a whole lot more than she'd bargained for, nevertheless. Including the fact that despite her old headmistress initially stating she wouldn't be able to remember much, she had in fact told her a considerable amount about an unknown crime or crimes, and in quite a lot of detail. There was also something rattling around in her head connected to Sandra Wainright's damning revelation that Suzanne needed to check with her boss. She needed to report to Harry – *and quickly.*

"You're telling *me* your old headmistress just spilled her guts about a drugs ring in the nineties, with pupils and teachers threatening each other, and none of this was uncovered by police at the time?" Harry leant forwards, elbows on his desk and hands clasped. He was stunned at what his sergeant had just told him.

"Looks that way, Guv, and I must have looked pretty much the way you do now, nearly forgot to take notes."

His eyebrows flew. "I sincerely hope you *did* take notes, Moorcroft?"

Suzanne reached into her bag, pulled out the files and her pocketbook, and spread them on the desk. "Yes sir, of course don't worry, and I did at least discover Sandra Wainright's best friend who went missing was this girl, Jacqueline Squires." She tapped the file and slid it across to Harry. He opened it and saw in the top right-hand corner the case photo supplied at the time. It was of a girl about fifteen or sixteen with long chestnut-brown hair, the name Jacqueline Squires and her date of birth typed underneath it. His lips parted, eyes locking on the page – *and then he froze.*

"Guv?"

Harry came to slowly… "Suzanne … I can't believe I'm saying this without verification, *but* …" he looked up at her with a stern gaze, then dropped his head, and pointing to the photo, blew a resigned sigh. "This girl … she's almost certainly dead. I don't know where she's lying, or if we'll ever find her, probably never will frankly, so …"

"How can you possibly *know* that, sir?"

Harry didn't want to say it because he knew it sounded crazy. It *always* sounded crazy, but then again, so far, she'd always been right…"Our resident village psychic, Molly Fields; she rang me yesterday after I'd spoken to Kelly

Novak re the forensic analysis on the skeleton – told me she'd had another vision. This time it was a teenage girl around fifteen, in school uniform, floating against the middle of her bedroom wall. Hoolie blowing through the window, curtains blowing, funny damp smell, the whole damned shebang, said she was mouthing the words '*Help me*'." Harry stabbed at the profile picture with his forefinger. "*And that's her.*"

Suzanne thought for a moment. "In that case, shouldn't we set up a search of the land attached to Clayton House?"

Harry sat back in his chair. "To get the go-ahead for that, we'd need some kind of evidence to justify it to get the manpower and expenditure, or at the very least, have an exceptionally strong conviction Jackie Squires' remains are out there somewhere. We simply don't have that proof."

"Maybe Molly will come up with some further psychic information on that front then," replied Suzanne, more than a little sceptically…

Harry fully understood her reticence. He had, after all, initially felt exactly the same. "Suzanne, set up a briefing for 3.00 p.m. today. We need to relay details of your conversation with Sandra Wainright to the team, and I think we need an extensive county or countrywide search for Karen Lewis and Felicia Phillips. At least we have *some* kind of proof for that, or at least a witness. Ring Mrs Wainright and ask her how old she thinks they'd be now, and if she has any idea of where they were living at the time. She probably won't know but we have to start somewhere. Failing that, it might need a call to the local council. I'll update Chief Superintendent Hitchings – omitting Miss Fields' input, obviously."

"Right, Guv, will do. There's just one other thing I thought of when I got back. It suddenly hit me about the name Sandra Wainright mentioned, Charlotte Krane, wasn't that Charlotte—"

"Charlotte Peterson's *maiden* name? Yes, God damn it, it was! I knew I'd heard it somewhere. Not only that, the Rowlands girl – Emily. Wasn't Rowlands that *American* woman's maiden name – Gina Gale's mother? God, I'm getting too old for this job, Moorcroft, I should've spotted both of those first off. If it *was* Emily Stone, formerly Rowlands, at that school, it's not going to make it easy for our latest recruit either. Andrew and Gina have had a rough time of it the last few years, especially Gina."

"There could be *other* people with those names. And you'll never be too old, sir, you'll still be here, officially or unofficially, retired well after we've all moved on or up!!"

Harry gave a weak smile, "Possibly so, Sergeant, although the 'Magpie' will have to fly the nest at *some* point."

Suzanne laughed – he'd had *that* nickname ever since his relocation from London.

"I do have a very strong feeling we're right on the money with it being Peterson and Stone, though. Unfortunately, one's in a coma and the other one's in New York – for now, anyway. That being the case, we need to find out if either or both of them went to Clayton House School."

EARLIER THAT DAY IN
KESWICK TOWN CENTRE ...

Although a sergeant, with no PCs spare again and Suzanne involved at Clayton House, Joe had paired up with Andrew as his 'Tutor Constable' for the day, just as Suzanne had the previous week. It was hot walking down Keswick High Street and he'd noticed Andy wasn't only yawning a lot (understandable given he was a new dad), but he also seemed quieter than usual and a bit tense. He was just going to ask him about it when the station's favourite café came up on their left. Joe checked his watch. No reason they shouldn't pop in for a bacon roll and a cuppa, he thought, then he could find out what was bothering him. But he didn't get the chance.

When Andrew's face suddenly morphed into someone who'd spent the previous night in a haunted house, Joe followed his sight line directly through Bella's window to see absolutely nothing out of the ordinary. Turning back to Andrew to question his fearful expression, he found himself talking to fresh air. His trainee constable was now already several yards down the street, walking fast and with no signs of slowing. Joe quickly scanned Bella's window once more in case he'd missed something, before hotfooting it after him.

"Hey, Andy, hold on!! Slow down, mate!!"

Andrew dropped his pace and finally let Joe catch up with him, turning round to wait till he was within speaking distance, glancing anxiously over his right shoulder. "Sorry, Joe, I just couldn't go in, not today."

"I gathered, but why? You looked like you'd seen a *ghost* back there!"

The two of them fell into a slow walk as Andrew stared ahead, looking tense, occasionally checking the street behind him. He was torn between not answering Joe's question, continuing to keep a lifetime's secret bottled up, and telling him everything. Yet if he did open up, he'd be living with the ramifications of what had happened being out in the open, maybe even losing his job, or worse. Then there was Gina and little Ellie-Ro, *what if ...?*

Joe placed a hand on his shoulder causing him to stop. "Andy, let's find somewhere else to sit down, have a coffee and a bite to eat. I think you need to get something off your chest. And if you don't feel like talking, well ... that's fine, too, but I'm parched and could also do with a bacon roll." His caring, steady manner was always ready, probably helped by being a church minister's son. It worked.

Andrew smiled hesitantly and nodded.

Sitting opposite each other with coffees and bacon rolls in the back of a non-high-street Costa, Joe ate as he watched Andrew gazing into his cup, stirring coffee until the spoon had done a tenth lap. Gently, he rested his hand on top of Andy's until he looked up, stopped stirring and placed the spoon in the saucer. "So ... what's going on? Bella didn't poison you with a burger, did she? Or worse, serve you up a weak cappuccino?"

Andrew looked up and managed a hint of a smile followed by an '*as if*' look, before taking a deep breath… "Did you know I was adopted?"

"I'd heard, yes. I think a couple of others at the nick are too."

"Really, I didn't know that? Anyway – my parents adopted me at ten and a half – nearly eleven. Before that I was living at the Kirkby Children's Home because my birth mother wasn't able to look after me. I did meet her later, actually, before she died, three years ago, in fact."

"Oh wow, well, that was good, wasn't it … hopefully?"

"Yeah, yes, it's not that, not why …" He bit his lip, wondering if this was the right thing to do, to tell Joe what had happened twenty-odd years ago in the early hours of the morning, with Ryan Jacks and a kitchen knife…

"Take your time, Andy, it's okay."

"Things weren't … good in that home. It was a difficult time and some of us, *not me* … some of us were …" He picked up his coffee and drank deeply, wrapping his hands around the cup before carrying on… "There was abuse. Only carried out by one person, but it was regular, and always in the early hours."

Joe kept his voice low. "Is this sexual abuse we're talking about here, Andy?"

"Yes. It was always the boys, and always the weaker, more sensitive ones."

Joe flinched. As a gay man, he'd experienced a little of that at school. Although not from adults, it had been bad enough. He stopped eating and sat up a little straighter to give his entire attention to Andrew.

"I was ten. One night, I heard that damned rocking chair squeaking again. He always sat in that chair when …" Andrew blinked heavily and turned to look out the window… "I knew what was about to happen or what was *already* happening. So, this time I—"

He broke off whilst a family of four squeezed past them between the tables, and then tentatively carried on.

"It was Christmas Eve and so cold that night. A tin of those special Christmas biscuits had gone missing, and the woman who ran the home, Mrs McCall, she'd been mad at us kids accusing us of stealing it. Well, we hadn't, but her son, Ryan Jacks, *had*. I'd followed the sound of the squeaking rocking chair to his room and stood in the doorway. Whilst eight-year-old Darren Hayes was kneeling at his feet, he was rocking himself backwards and forwards, dipping his hand into that bloody tin."

Joe's next question was spoken both seriously and sympathetically… "Were you in time?"

"Yes, thank God. I'd started sleeping with a little knife under my pillow. I crept up and …" Andrew dropped his head and started chewing the inside of his mouth. This was crazy. Could he get into serious trouble over what he did? Lose his job? Even though he was only ten at the time? He didn't think so, but wasn't ten the age of legal responsibility? He wasn't absolutely certain… he'd never been certain, and that's why he'd never told anyone.

"… and?" Joe pressed, gently…

Andy made a decision. He looked back up at Joe. "I crept up and slashed that bastard's neck. He didn't die, but he's still got the scar, and little Darren Hayes got away that night."

"You saw him back there in Bella's, didn't you." It was a statement not a question, and Joe now completely understood what Andrew was going through. It didn't answer why he'd been so quiet before that morning, though. *He was just about to find out…*

"Yes, but that was the second time I'd seen him recently. He was at the front desk of the nick five days ago. I don't know why he was there, but in 2006 he was eventually caught for multiple child abuse and got fifteen years. It was in the local paper and on the news. He's obviously just been released."

"You know you need to tell the Guv about this, don't you? It's clearly worrying you – hell, it would *definitely* worry *me!*"

"I've been thinking of nothing else since I saw Jacks. I can't sleep, I can barely eat … I'm worried sick, Joe. If he's come looking for me, he's likely to find Gina and Ellie, too. I'm six feet five, I can handle myself, but how can I tell Gee she could be in danger all over again? She'll never cope with another psycho. All these years…" He sighed heavily… "I honestly thought he never saw me that night."

Joe stood up. "Well, maybe he didn't, and it's just a coincidence he's in Kirkdale at the moment. Come on, we need to see Harry about this, and *now*."

They left Costa and the dozen or so shops in the little courtyard setting, and walked back to the high street. As they continued up towards the car park, sat on a bench opposite them, wearing instantly forgettable, drab clothing, was a stocky scruffy-haired man in his early fifties. From there, he watched the two officers intently whilst rolling a distinctive and carefully bagged button through his fingers. As they passed, he dropped his head to ensure anonymity, angrily scratching at the side of his neck – *where the sun was making his scar itch.*

TWENTY-ONE

KIRKDALE POLICE STATION

Joe put down the phone to Harry and walked over to Andrew's desk where he was waiting to hear if the boss had time to see him immediately, or if he'd have to wait. Apparently, right *now* was the time Harry had indicated would be ideal.

"Do you want me to come up with you, or …"

"No, no, I'm good, thanks. How much did you tell him?"

"Not much, just that a very unsavoury character from your past had shown up and could cause a whole heap of trouble for you and your family."

"Right, okay. Good. I'd better go up then."

"I, er … might've mentioned a knife was involved – in self-defence, obviously." He winced.

Andrew's sharp intake of breath, wide eyes and open mouth followed Joe's additional disclosure…

"It'll be *fine*, Andy. You're going to have to tell him anyway, and you know Harry – he'll *sort* this."

Andrew got up and made his way out to the corridor for a lift to the next floor. Thoughts ran around his head as he waited for the light to drop to his level and the doors to open. *Could Harry sort it out, though? Really? What the hell was he going to say?* The lift arrived and Andrew got in. He was about to find out.

Harry looked up from an open file on his desk where Ryan Jacks' photo was clearly displayed – as was his scar. He called Andrew in and Harry's stern expression met him as he walked through the door.

"Take a seat, Gale."

Andrew pulled the chair out and sat, not sure what his boss was going to do, or say, next. At this moment their relationship was on a purely professional footing and his boss didn't look happy, in fact, he looked anything but.

"I hear you're responsible – for *that*." He swivelled the file round and prodded Ryan Jacks' scar several times with his forefinger, face darkening. He looked thunderous.

"I – Har – sir, I was only—"

An image of Harry's baby son, Jamie, floated across his mind, and he knew he'd instantly remove the breath from anyone that tried to hurt him… "Now you listen to me, son. What I say now will never leave this office, ever— *understand?*"

Andrew nodded.

"To do what you did must've taken a hell of a lot of guts at only ten, and I don't want you worrying yourself about anything, *that's … anything*, remotely official. Do you hear me? Forget about it. It's past. *That nasty little*

177

shit got exactly what was coming to him and you saved an innocent little lad from vile sexual abuse. In my book that makes you a bloody hero. As far as I'm concerned *it was a job well done!*"

At this point Andrew's face resembled a freshly gasping trout. He couldn't believe what he'd just heard. Clearly Joe had filled Harry in on *all* the relevant points, just hadn't told *him* he had.

Harry's expression relaxed a little. "Yes, Gale, I made Sergeant Walker give me the *whole* story. As an analogy, he's not very good at sleight of hand when it comes to information on a need-to-know basis. But I *am* very good at spotting withheld details, so please don't blame him. He tried his level best not to reveal everything, but Joe's strengths lie in being what I call a 'gentle copper', and we need those, too."

"Thank you, sir, I won't. He's been more than a tutor sergeant to me today –he's been a very good friend."

"Indeed, he has, he's a good man and a fine officer. More than that, he took a bullet for me last year, saved my life – I'll never forget it. There'll be a medal coming his way in the next few months." Harry's eyes glazed for a moment before he picked up Ryan Jacks' file and busily banged it down on the desk several times as if levelling its contents.

"There's just one thing I'm really worried about," added Andrew. "I saw him through Bella's window when we passed this morning and also here at the front desk a few days ago. What if Jacks *did* see me that night, has tracked me down and returned to take revenge? I'm worried sick about Gina and the baby."

"Yes, Joe mentioned that, too, so I looked into it more thoroughly before you came up. Apparently, we received info from the probation office a few weeks ago to say he was being released. Jacks is obviously now on the RSO (Registered Sex Offenders) register, and will have to report regularly to his probation officer, but also to a police station if he's changed his address. That could be why he was in here a few days ago. It also says in his file that Chief Superintendent Hitchings was the SIO on his case in 2005. The boss wants Gabe Downs to be kept busy, so I'll be asking PC Downs *to pay special attention to Mr Jacks.*"

"Thank you, sir, I appreciate that."

"Oh, and Gale – make sure you sit down with your wife tonight and tell her everything, because I've a sneaking suspicion Gina's very much in the dark over this, and worrying herself silly over your *almost certainly* anxious mood at home."

3.00 P.M. - BRIEFING ROOM

It was overly warm, so Harry opened a couple of windows before leaning up against a side wall as Suzanne took the front spot and faced the team. Two or three were balancing chairs on their back legs, some were laughing, some checking their mobiles, others chatting about weekend plans. One idiot actually risked lobbing a pen at Gabe Downs – but thankfully missed. She wasn't happy about it, especially given what she knew about Downs' temper, but luckily, Gabe merely scowled at the thrower. She *was* pleased to see Andrew looking a lot brighter and more attentive than he had of late.

"Okay, everyone, can we all settle down and have some hush please, this isn't a junior playground – and Thompson … for God's sake, *ditch* the pasty." Some sniggering followed before the room gradually reduced to a couple of lone whispers, after which a second pen took flight, this time actually hitting Gabe, who shot out of his seat, seething. He reluctantly sat back down when Harry pushed himself off the wall, and a death glare from Suzanne hit the right spot. Finally, she had everyone's attention…

"Right … this morning I went over to Clayton House School to interview the headmistress, Sandra Wainright. She was a pupil there in the nineties, and it's now been established Jackie Squires, one of the missing girls at the time, was her best friend. It appears the other missing girl, Denise Fraser, wasn't especially known to her, but *was* in her younger sister's class. More on her sister later. Both remain missing as is the teacher, Karen Lewis, who unfortunately, because of what came next in our conversation, I didn't get to question her about. That will need another interview, or possibly a phone call."

Gabe Downs raised his hand and Suzanne indicated for him to speak… "You asked me to find out if there *was* a caretaker there in the nineties? Well, there was." Gabe flipped open his pocketbook… "A male by the name of Ron Stevens, he was single, coming up for retirement, vague rumours of an estranged son, can't be sure. Bit of an oddball by all accounts – lived on-site. Could be our skeleton?"

"Okay, where did you get this intel from, Gabe?" asked Suzanne.

"Well, it's a bit of a stroke of luck, to be honest. I rang the school yesterday and asked to speak to Mrs Wainright, but she wasn't available. However, some admin lady was *very* helpful. A Mrs…." He checked his pocketbook again… "Bancroft – Amy Bancroft. Turns out her mother used to run the local newsagents back in the day, and this guy used to get his morning paper from her regular as clockwork. Amy used to see him sometimes, said he looked like that Fester bloke from the Addams family. Well, one day he never turned up, nor the next, or the day after that. She literally never saw him again." He closed his pocketbook.

"Looks like that's our Mr Bones, then, eh?" chipped in Thompson, quickly brushing off sprayed crumbs from surreptitiously finishing his pasty.

Suzanne rolled her eyes. Ricky Thompson, nicknamed *Tricky Ricky* due to his love of Poker, was never without some form of snack on the go, preferably a *pasty*. It was rumoured he regularly lost due to being notoriously bad at the game – luckily, he only played for snacks.

A hand went up in reply to Ricky's comment… "Not if Uncle Fester was responsible for Boney's death and skipped the country, though," added new girl Hannah Carlin, with a satisfied smile.

Harry raised his eyebrows, tipping his head towards her – "Good point, DC Carlin." He left the wall and joined Suzanne at the front. "I hope you're all making notes, it seems the newer members of the team have the edge today."

Hannah sat back, arms folded, looking very confident. She liked receiving praise. She always had. Her mother had ingrained in her to do whatever was necessary to always ensure top-notch position, and to be at the centre of everything. *'Aim high, play higher, achieve highest.'* APA – it was practically etched across her heart.

"Although, Carlin," added Harry, looking at her pointedly, "using *correct* interviewee, witness and possible victim names are the usual form of address in an inquiry."

There was a low-level jeer around the room until Suzanne brought both arms downwards through the air to indicate quiet. "There's a good deal more that came out from my conversation with Sandra Wainright this morning, so listen up. It appears a cocaine drugs ring was being run in the nineties, from the old, ruined building Clayton Hall in Manor Lane, by at least one teacher. *Her* name was Felicia Phillips. Another teacher, Karen Lewis, was a regular user, including on-site at the nearby school. As I said just now, Lewis is our missing teacher. Sandra told me that on one occasion she and Jacqueline Squires followed Phillips and Lewis to the hall, and witnessed the two women exchange money for drugs. However, that's not all. Apparently, the two girls legged it out of there after they saw, would you believe, a *skeleton*, complete with warning note, in a coffin in the room they were hiding in. They both screamed which obviously alerted the teachers of their proximity. They were hiding outside behind a bush to catch their breath from running away, when they realised despite initially being chased, ten to fifteen minutes later, their teachers had still not exited the building."

"Did the skelly jump out the coffin and scare 'em to death, then, Sarge?" Thompson was now standing holding his hands either side of an overly frightened facial expression. He looked ridiculous, but it caused a ripple of amusement and earned him a few paper balls to be bounced off his head.

"Sit down, Ricky, for God's sake, before the *Ghostbusters* whistling starts ..." Suzanne crossed her arms expectantly, as a few bars of the theme tune faintly filled the room... "*This is serious!* Sandra and her friend Jackie witnessed those teachers carrying another pupil out of that dilapidated manor, and at the time they thought she was *dead*! None of them knew she was in there. It was only because she was seen alive and well with no injuries the following day they realised she'd almost certainly been drugged and had been unconscious."

Suzanne stopped for a moment to pour a glass of water from the drinks station. The room had warmed up considerably, and talking always made her thirsty. Whilst she had a quick break, Harry took over.

"Given what Sergeant Moorcroft has said so far, the whereabouts of Felicia Phillips has now been added to these cold cases. We believe Mrs Phillips was late forties, early fifties at the time, so will clearly be quite elderly now, or may even not still be alive. Karen Lewis, one of the three cold cases, was in her thirties so likely now around mid-sixties. We need to locate these two women if possible, not only because of their own illegal activities, but because they may have information regarding the whereabouts of Jacqueline Squires and Denise Fraser. Not forgetting, of course, the sudden absence of the caretaker, Ron Stevens. With no family to ask questions, it appears his disappearance has slipped through the cracks of the original investigation."

Suzanne handed Harry a glass of water, which he took, and then sat back down to let her continue.

"Right, back to Sandra Wainright... Her maiden name was Lisle and as I mentioned earlier, she had a younger sister, Ros. According to Sandra, she was told Ros had hung herself at thirteen, but Sandra doesn't believe she *did* take her own life. She's got no real evidence, but the big news is this. It's possible, just *possible* that the two pupils that may have had something to do with her death, were Charlotte Krane and—" she looked tensely at Harry, they'd yet to say anything to Andrew about the possibility Gina's mother was an ex-Clayton House pupil... Suzanne hesitated, wondering what to do. Harry nodded his assent. It was too late to stop now – they were all waiting for her to carry on... "It's just possible that the two pupils were Charlotte Peterson and Emily Stone, maiden names, Krane and Rowlands. We need to make enquiries to see if they attended Clayton House between 1990 and '95."

The room erupted into a loud rumbling of voices and incredulous looks. Not all knew of Emily Stone, but *everyone* knew who Charlotte Peterson was – *the whole county knew, probably the whole country.* One officer stood up slowly and faced Harry and Suzanne. He looked shocked. He also seemed bewildered at not being given a prior warning.

"No need to check on Emily Stone. I can assure everyone she definitely attended Clayton House between those dates." Ashen-faced, Andrew Gale was standing awkwardly and alone in the middle of the room…

TWENTY-TWO

CLAYTON HOUSE GRAMMAR SCHOOL KIRKDALE CUMBRIA

MONDAY 16TH SEPTEMBER 1991

Charlotte didn't know if what she'd been drugged with was still affecting her, but she felt giddy. Her whole body felt like she was swaying from one side to the other. Strangely, it hadn't started when she'd first woken up but *mid*-morning, after she saw Emily with that Ros Lisle again. That relationship was making her feel *really* uncomfortable. Things were bad enough with Fishy Phillips and Karen Lewis dealing drugs, and Fishy sticking a pad over her face with God knows what on it, causing her to pass out. To lose her best friend to someone as insipid as Ros Lisle, or anyone for that matter – was simply intolerable.

She hated the weekends because Emily wasn't a boarder. Em was lucky and got to go home every day, but now it was Monday again, break time, and she was waiting for her best friend under the arches by the tuck shop. She desperately wanted to tell her what had happened at Clayton Hall, how Fishy and Karen were dealing drugs and had drugged *her* with some evil-smelling something on a pad... And yet, there was that Lisle girl ... *again*. Trickles of sweat glistened on her forehead, ran down her neck – she could feel warm moisture everywhere. Could she possibly have a fever? *Or just be boiling mad!*

"Charlie, hi, this is Ros. She's in my form."

Ros looked anxious as Charlotte's eyes bored into hers. "Hi, how's things?" she asked nervously.

"Fine, would you like some crisps?"

"Oh ... yes, *thank* you!" replied a surprised Ros, overly grateful and beginning to relax a little at the seemingly friendly offer.

"Great. Here's a pound, get three bags of cheese and onion and bring me the change."

Ros looked anxious, head switching back and forth between the two girls. "Um ... I don't actually like chee—"

Charlotte glared at her coldly before Emily stepped in.

"Just get a packet of your Bovril ones, Ros, that's fine." Emily gently ushered her friend towards the tuck shop queue.

"Bovril?! *Eww* ... some people have absolutely *no* taste." Charlotte leant back against the old stone wall, hands clasping the ancient bulbous stones for support whilst fixing Emily's new friend with an icy stare. *At least the overwhelming hot and wet feeling had miraculously vanished.*

"Charlie … take it *easy*, she's a really nice girl, and not that strong health-wise, so play nice. My being friends with her doesn't affect us, you do know that, *right*?"

Charlotte remained sullenly silent, dropping her head briefly before Ros returned with a smile, their crisps and some change. She looked up and held a hand out. Her mouth smiled back, but her eyes remained cold. There was no warmth there at all, and she sensed a nervous twitch at the corner of the left one that she'd never noticed before. Ros deposited a packet of cheese and onion, plus the change in her hand, and gave Emily hers.

Sitting on the playground bench, the three of them ate in awkward silence. On top of her woozy head, Charlotte was experiencing feelings she'd never had before. Resentment, jealousy, cold bubbling rage… How could she tell Emily about what had happened yesterday with *her* there – that *Ros*? Charlotte was used to it being just her and Emily, even when she'd had to go through the first year without her, before Em had joined Clayton House. There had never been anyone she'd really wanted to hang out with, nobody she really trusted with her secrets, or wanted to bond with. Oh, there were always the hangers-on, the girls who knew her parents were wealthy, who feigned their friendship and pretended to look up to her. But a Krane knew the difference between fake and genuine whatever age they were, even at twelve. Charlotte had merely used their company until Em had arrived.

The bell went. One by one, they all got up resignedly

and walked over to the bin. Break times just never seemed long enough.

"Right, I'll see you later, Em." As Ros threw her bag in the bin, Charlotte pulled Emily to one side and whispered in her ear… "Be on your own at lunchtime, I have something *mega* to tell you."

Emily nodded just as Ros turned round. She knew when Charlotte was serious about something, and from her facial expression, whatever she had to tell her, it was definitely serious.

HEADMISTRESS VERONICA DEAN'S OFFICE

Charlotte was due to go into the science block, as her next lesson was chemistry. She'd got as far as the heavy double swing doors when she stopped. Her head had suddenly cleared, and she instinctively felt the need to go and see Miss Dean about the incident at Clayton Hall. Although she was pretty grown-up for her age, sometimes there was a time and place when help from a *real* grown-up was needed. She would rather have talked to Emily about it first, they always shared their secrets with each other, but that bloody Ros girl had been with her so it hadn't been possible, and waiting didn't feel like an option.

Charlotte didn't want to admit it to herself, the *main* reason she didn't want to wait … was fear… fear of Fishy Phillips and Miss Lewis, although she knew it was also likely she'd get into trouble for being at Clayton Hall in the first place. It was such a dilemma, which was why she'd especially wanted to confide in Emily. With her parents touring Asia, or wherever they currently were, who *could* she tell? Grandma and Grandpa Hetherington were with them, and Granny and Granddad Krane were on holiday in America. She had very little choice, Miss Dean it had to be.

She was just about to knock on the door when a phone began ringing from inside. So she waited politely. And listened…

"Felicia? Thank *God*! What's the news? When's the next delivery? Things are getting *horrendously* difficult. I've got to pay the builders for the swimming pool repairs, the down payment on the new computer system's due end of October, not to mention the teachers' salaries – which includes *yours* by the way! That's on top of everything else. The school fees just aren't covering costs." Her voice then lowered considerably as she literally spat down the phone… "*I – need – those – drugs!*"

Charlotte shoved a fist in her mouth to stop her from making shocked screechy noises at what she'd just heard. There was quiet from inside for a moment as Fishy was obviously responding from down the line to Miss Dean's outpouring. That was – until someone else spoke…

"*Nurse Torres, have we got the blood test results back for Mrs Peterson yet?*"

What? Who said *that*? Charlotte turned round. There was nobody there. Who is that man speaking in Miss Dean's office, then, and when did a *nurse* go in there? Are there *two* phones?

"*Yes sir, they came back this morning.*"

"No, Felicia, three weeks is *not* acceptable, not by a *long* way!"

Charlotte checked the area outside Miss Dean's office, including round both corners. Nobody. She then pressed an ear against the door…

"*And…? So what's going on with Mrs Peterson, then? Why isn't she responding more actively?*"

Who *on earth* is Mrs Peterson? Surely she's not in there as *well*?!

"No, Felicia, you tell him, it's two weeks *max*, or we change suppliers. *Yes*, I *am* serious, no … *no* … now you listen to—"

"*Propofol, Mr Shepherd. There's an extraordinarily high amount in her bloodstream, enough to keep her from responding to anything much. That's why our recordings on the Glasgow Coma Scale have reported little change.*"

Charlotte shook her head. It was spinning with what she'd just heard, and although she'd initially felt better than at break, the other side of that door appeared to be full of people holding different conversations, and all at the same time. She shook her head from side to side again, this was far too weird, and *scary – really* scary.

"*Sir, sir … she just moved her head, did you see?*"

"*No, I didn't. Are you sure? I'll stay a few minutes longer, maybe she'll do it again.*"

At this last comment, Charlotte's legs nearly gave way. Feeling extremely unwell, she knew she needed to lie down – and now. There was no point in her listening outside Miss Dean's office any longer anyway. Not only were horribly mixed-up crazy conversations going on in there, but it was abundantly clear her headmistress was running an actual *drugs* business! And as she was clearly running it with Fishy Phillips, she'd obviously never help *her* – which meant there was absolutely no one to turn to. *She was completely alone.*

TWENTY-THREE

ICU BASSETLAW HOSPITAL KILTON HILL - WORKSOP

10.15 A.M. FRIDAY 21ST MAY 2021

With the help of a colleague, Sofia Torres had just given Charlotte a bed bath, turning her gently one way and then the other, washing her the best way they could with warm flannels, bowls of soapy and rinsing water and soft towels to dry her. It was naturally a very intimate part of nursing care when a patient was unable to do anything, and both nurses completed the job respectfully by making sure the window blinds were closed and nobody else allowed in. Once everything was cleared away and blinds open again, Simon Shepherd, Charlotte's consultant, entered the room…

"Nurse Torres, have we got the blood test results back for Mrs Peterson yet?"

"Yes, sir, they came back this morning."

"And…? So what's going on with our patient? Why isn't she responding more actively?"

Sofia picked up the OBS chart with the newly added blood test. "Propofol, Mr Shepherd. There's an extraordinarily high amount in her bloodstream, enough to keep her from responding to anything much. That's why our recordings on the Glasgow Coma Scale have reported little change."

Simon Shepherd held out his hand for her to pass him the OBS chart to read the report for himself. He frowned with concern, puzzled at what he was seeing.

"Sir, sir … she just moved her head, did you *see*?"

Shepherd turned to face the bed. "No, I didn't. Are you *sure*?" He checked his watch… "I'll stay a few minutes longer, maybe she'll do it again."

They were now both staring expectantly at their patient. Ten minutes later, there was still no repetition of movement. Shepherd was already well behind schedule, and with a busy morning list, could not remain there any longer.

"I must get on, but we need to get a handle on this propofol business. There's no reason why there should be propofol in her system. I take it as read it's not you that's injecting it down the line so—"

"No, it is *not*! I would *never* do such a thing!"

"That's what I was *saying*, Nurse, calm *down*. Look, I need to get back on my rounds. Make sure that *every* staff member on this ICU knows to keep a strict watch on this patient. If it gets out there's been any possible medical abuse or attempt on her life – we'll *all* be for the high jump."

Sofia watched him leave the room, flabbergasted the only thing he was really concerned about was his reputation. Charlotte's health, and possibly her actual life being in jeopardy, didn't appear to feature at all. Their patient may have been sectioned in a psychiatric institution for multiple murders, but their job was to care for her and provide every opportunity for recovery.

* * *

11.30 A.M KIRKDALE POLICE STATION
KESWICK

Suzanne Moorcroft had just finished speaking with CSI team leader, Rob Davidson. She and Harry had left the skeleton site on Tuesday whilst investigations were ongoing, and had since been awaiting his call. He'd just told her the gun's serial number, the firearms officer had revealed, was *police issue*. Suzanne had automatically scanned the open-plan office whilst he'd delivered that information, everyone tapping away on their keyboards or talking on the phone, the general hubbub of a police incident room totally oblivious to what she'd just learnt. The thought that any colleague could have been responsible for...

Putting her mug down, she brought up the message giving the info needed to input to the PED (Police Elimination Database) and CED (Contamination

Elimination Database), where the DNA of all serving officers was stored. She also needed to try and find some form of old nineties database, to see if there was still a record of who signed the gun out, and more importantly, *who signed receipt of it.* That was proving more difficult, and her heart was pounding with the very anticipation of it.

After another twenty minutes, she decided the search for a nineties database would have to wait – it was imperative to get what she had to Harry, right now. She was still reeling from the police-issue serial number, and felt her stomach tighten as she pushed the final key on the CED to bring up the name associated with the DNA result. It was the first time she'd led a case and things were beginning to feel horribly close to home. When the officer's name came up for those October '95 DNA markers, she gasped, *eyes frozen to the screen.*

Harry had just left Hitchings' office to update him with Suzanne Moorcroft's interview of Clayton House head, Sandra Wainright. Also, with Emily Stone's confirmed connection (through PC Gale) to Clayton House, the strong likelihood of Charlotte Peterson's and their possible joint involvement in the revived cold cases from the nineties. There was the additional factor of a not improbable chance they'd at least had knowledge of a pupil's suspected suicide, if not some or complete involvement, but with no evidence this was currently a hypothetical theory. Not in Sandra Wainright's mind, however, given the girl who took her life was her own sister.

On top of that, there was Andrew's possible situation regarding the release of Ryan Jacks, but Harry had made sure his boss knew he was getting Gabe Downs to keep a close eye on the man given he'd been seen at the front desk since leaving prison. He'd ensured checks had been made of where he was released to, and any recent home address changes reported, as would normally be the case. Basically, he'd made Gabe Downs responsible for Jacks keeping his nose clean and where he went, just not given his boss (or Gabe Downs) any details about Andrew's connection to the man. Hitchings had clearly been pleased at his brother-in-law being given something to do under Harry's direction and watchful eye, and for Harry's part it made a change to be in Hitchings' good books. Usually, *he* was the one his boss was keeping an eye on.

As he followed the corridor back to his own office, it occurred to him he probably still was. That thought, along with a more than brief breakfast, had made him feel quite tired and foggy-headed. On reaching it, he immediately sat down at his desk and opened all the drawers, one by one, only to discover he was completely out of barley sugars. This resulted in him irritably slamming them all shut again – two at a time. Despite being a diagnosed diabetic and having to carry out blood sugar checks, which he did for the most part, Harry still fell back on the reliance of his favourite barley sugar cubes from time to time. Denise, his original PA, who'd regularly badgered him to get a test when he'd first come up from London, had since moved on to pastures new. This was a damned shame. In fact, it was extremely inconvenient, because despite the odd moan, she would still pop out to Donaldson's to pick him up a large bag of the sweets on a fairly regular basis. He was just debating on whether to pick up the internal phone to ring his current PA, or just go out and get them himself (via the pub for lunch), when the muffled theme tune to his latest old favourite ring-tone, 'Life on Mars', sprang loudly from the depths of his trouser pocket.

"*Longbridge!*"

"Guv? It's Moorcroft. I need to speak to you urgently. Can I come up to your office, please?"

"What's up, Moorcroft? I was just about to go out. I take it this is to do with the Clayton House case?"

"Yes, sir. I've heard from CSI and forensics, just waiting for the ballistics report."

"So what's the urgency? I was just about to head out for a bite to eat."

Aware of several turned heads, Suzanne lowered her voice… "I think you'll want to hear this *now*, Guv, and when you do, you'll be glad I didn't use the phone."

Harry winced, brain now racing. He'd had some very uncomfortable thoughts knocking around his head the last few days, and a horrible feeling Suzanne was about to illuminate them in giant headlights. He yawned involuntarily, massaging his temples. "Okay, Suze, come on up."

Five minutes later, Suzanne was sitting in Harry's office looking as white as a sheet. He poured her a coffee from his machine and passed it to her. She cradled the mug with both hands and took a deep breath...

"Rob Davidson from CSI rang me just now. The AFO spent time at the site carefully cleaning mud off the gun after we'd gone. He revealed the serial number, got it checked, and ..." She paused, biting her lip.

"*And...?* Don't keep me hanging, Moorcroft!"

"It's police issue, sir."

Harry could feel the colour drain from his face as his gut tightened. *She was right to come to him privately with this. He instinctively sensed there were only moments before all hell...*

"I checked the old database for serial numbers of pre-2000 police-issue weapons, and also fed the DNA markers into the PED and CED that forensics emailed just now."

"Who is it?" Harry's voice was barely audible.

She avoided the question and kept going... "They didn't attempt to lift any prints. Apparently, the chemicals used would make a right mess for ballistics to do their checks, and on the balance of probably not getting a great result, decided—"

"Who *is* it, *dammit?*" Harry leant forward and thumped his desk, holding her eyes with an expression Suzanne had never seen before.

She hesitated for a moment, knowing what she was about to tell him was going to light a touchpaper...

"It's Chief Superintendent Hitchings – *sir*."

1.30 P.M. CARPENTERS ARMS PUB - KIRKDALE

Harry was not feeling good. Without any barley sugars, his head had gone from foggy to banging, and he still needed something to eat. Suzanne's news had shocked him rigid. Although Hitchings had only been his boss for a few years, rather than a mentor from the early days, Harry had always believed him to be totally honest, by the book, and straight down the line. So straight, in fact, he'd often wondered if *his* superiors secretly thought him a little 'OTT'.

At the end of that thought, Molly's mother, Maisie Fields, put a particularly inviting steak pie in front of him, cradled by a large portion of chips and a lake of baked beans. No, it wasn't ideal health-wise. Yes, it was what his stomach was craving right now. So he decided to just enjoy it, think positively and mull over the shit show Suzanne had just landed in his lap.

As he sloshed brown sauce over his pie, the guy next to him got up to leave and Harry noticed a copy of the *Courier* on the now vacant table. The headline caught his eye…

Cold Case Re-opened At Clayton House School
Male skeleton found by pupil with metal detector

BY STELLA GRAY – CHIEF CRIME REPORTER FOR KIRKDALE COURIER
PUBLISHED 21 MAY 2021

With a mouthful of pie, he picked up the paper and began to read as he ate. It was clear Stella Gray had got some quite detailed information from her friend, headmistress Sandra Wainright, with regard to suggestions as to who the remains might have been. The implication it might possibly be the then school caretaker, Ron Stevens, was strongly made, and as Sandra was a pupil there herself twenty-odd years ago, she would obviously have some insight on that. Although … Harry racked his brains for a moment, he could swear Suzanne hadn't said anything about a caretaker being mentioned in her interview with Sandra Wainright. It was Gabe Downs who'd mentioned he'd spoken to an admin assistant at Clayton House whose newsagent mother had sold a daily paper to the caretaker until one day he never turned up and she never saw him again.

Harry put the paper down. He needed a drink. It would have to be a soft one as he was working, but he was parched. As if by magic, at the end of that thought, Molly appeared with a coffee and set it down on the table.

"On the house, you looked like you needed it, and I know you can't drink on duty."

"How did you know I was on—"

She smiled, tapping her nose.

"Never mind," said Harry, picking it up, "and … thank you."

She didn't let on Gina was out the back where they'd been talking about her latest vision, and *she'd* just had a chat with Andrew on the phone. But far more importantly,

Molly knew she should mention the red car boot that had swum across her eyes before they'd opened that morning, the panic she'd felt, and how she couldn't breathe. First things first, though…

"Have you done anything about the—" Molly glanced around, leant forward slightly and lowered her voice – "floating vision I had the other day – the student with the long red hair?"

Harry shifted uncomfortably and took another gulp of coffee. He always felt slightly ridiculous discussing Molly's visions, but equally knew he had to accept them as viable. Like it or not, they always, rather annoyingly, proved to be accurate. However, the fact remained he couldn't extend *his* 'acceptance' to having Chief Superintendent Hitchings included in the picture. This made things very difficult when it came to operational procedure. "No, not yet, I can't just start digging up random pieces of woodland on the say so of the local … sorry, Molly, *your* unusual experiences. I know you have a track record of accuracy, but I do need *some* kind of traditionally produced evidence to justify costs. *And keep my boss happy.*"

Molly tapped the paper on the table. "You haven't read as far as the bottom paragraph of Stella Gray's piece, then?"

Harry hadn't. He held her gaze for a moment before turning to the paper and running his finger down to the last few lines on the skeleton report…

...and with regard to the missing girls from the nineties, this paper has received several anonymous emails and calls in the last few days, recommending police excavate certain areas of Kirkdale Woods lying inside the field border of Clayton House School.

He looked up to see Molly standing with crossed arms and a 'knowing' expression. "I'll give Mrs Gray a ring. On second thoughts, I'll get young Gale to do it. He'll probably get a better reaction and a more illuminating answer."

"Good idea. Oh, and er … there's something else I need to tell you before I take Christie out to the park."

Harry put his phone down. He had a distinct feeling he wasn't going to like this… "If you're going to tell me you've had anoth—"

"I'm not sure. It wasn't the same as usual. It was like a flash photo when I opened up this morning."

"A photo of *what*, exactly?"

"It was weird, to be honest. I saw what looked like a red car boot, water, and I felt really panicky in my chest. *Right before I couldn't breathe.*"

TWENTY-FOUR

CLAYTON HOUSE GRAMMAR SCHOOL KIRKDALE CUMBRIA

TUESDAY 17TH SEPTEMBER 1991

Charlotte was not in a good place. She was now looking over her shoulder and trusting nobody – other than Emily of course. But Emily wasn't in her class, and had clearly made friends with that Ros which was something Charlotte would never accept. She knew she was being silly, *really* silly, but she just couldn't help it. It had always been Em and Charlie, Charlie and Em – *always*, right from nursery school. Now things felt different, and she didn't like it one bit.

Having discovered the previous day her headmistress was running a drugs business in order to be able to keep the school running, and that at least two of the teachers were heavily involved, she knew school was no longer a safe place, particularly as she had to live in. Emily had been on some kind of field trip the previous afternoon, and Charlotte hadn't met up with her for lunch because of feeling unwell after the incident outside Miss Dean's office. This meant she'd still not had a chance to speak to her about being drugged by Fishy Phillips on Saturday, after following Jackie and Sandi to Clayton Hall. She couldn't even approach *them* given Em's new classmate, Ros, was Sandi's younger sister. It was all such a nightmare – and *so unfair*.

Of course there were other teachers in her year she could approach. Mrs Dennison and Mrs Ashman, who taught biology and art, both of which looked older than Fishy Phillips and Karen Lewis, so she couldn't imagine they'd approve of drugs, although Miss Phillips must be in her late forties or early fifties. Mrs Ashman was actually really lovely and her favourite teacher, despite Charlotte being terrible at art, but sadly she was in a wheelchair so in no position to protect her. Charlotte couldn't go to her for help anyway, as she most definitely wouldn't want anything bad to happen to her. There was her English teacher, Mrs Jenkins, but she'd never rock the boat where the head was concerned. Charlotte had noticed her clothes had become less smart and a little more worn lately, something that would never happen in Charlotte's own family. Mrs Jenkins was clearly not very well off and wouldn't want to risk losing her job.

So, as she sat in front of her easel in Mrs Ashman's art class, painting a not very good picture of a bowl filled with oranges, apples and bananas, her teacher beaming at and encouraging every girl present, Charlotte's mood was definitely one of deep and resentful concern.

The bell suddenly announced the end of the lesson and everyone began to take off their overalls and started to clear up. Charlotte tidied her area as Mrs Ashman deftly steered her wheelchair around the room to have a last look at everyone's paintings.

"Well done, Charlotte, you're really coming along with your structure, colours and shading now, *so* much better than last year." She smiled her big, appreciative smile, and Charlotte smiled back. It was nice to have *someone* who praised her, especially when she knew her painting was awful and Mrs Ashman was just being kind. *It's a pity there aren't more teachers like you*, she thought, *but there aren't, and that's that.*

LUNCH IN THE DUNGEON DINING ROOM

It was Spaghetti McGosh. She couldn't believe it, that vile plateful of hell was only ever served up on a Friday. It was Tuesday. That meant there must have been more leftovers from the previous week's '*dinners*' than usual. Charlotte wrinkled her nose in disgust and thought seriously about dodging lunch altogether.

Three of her class hangers-on were queuing up with her for this, the worst meal of the week. Charlotte quite liked *one* girl, but knew deep down they were *all* only with her because her parents were filthy rich. To be fair, she used them when she needed to – for homework, to fetch and carry, to keep someone in line … In return, Charlotte allowed them to associate with her. It was a kind of unspoken understanding, a two-way thing that even at thirteen everyone knew exactly where they stood. It was generally accepted that if your background was slightly different, in whatever way, the need to establish one-upmanship from day one was *paramount* in order to survive well. And Charlotte Krane had done, and continued to do, *exactly* that.

When she spotted Emily a few places behind, Charlotte slipped out of line to join her. Amazingly, Ros Lisle was elsewhere for a change, which meant if she and Em could get a corner table they might be able to talk. They certainly wouldn't be doing much eating – not until pudding anyway. Strangely, the puddings were quite nice, sometimes excellent, and as it was Tuesday, chocolate sponge and chocolate sauce was on the menu. She'd decided long ago that good puds were served up to take the taste away from the God-awful first course.

"Em, let's sit together, I've been desperate to talk to you," she whispered in her ear.

Emily nodded. "I know," she whispered back, "sorry, it's been so awkward, it's just that I didn't want to cause a problem with Ros, what with her older sister being in year twelve and everything. She's really okay, you know – *honestly.*" Charlotte snorted, pretending to exaggeratingly blow her nose and sneezing, taking the mickey out of Ros for her many colds. Emily just gave her customary eye roll…

The line moved along as each plate received a large spoonful of the dreaded McGosh (*Spaghetti? Oh My Gosh!*). Soon they were sitting at a corner table (luckily on their own), and Charlotte watched knowingly as Emily lifted a small portion of the mixture to her mouth. It was her first experience of the dish that was rumoured to be made up from the week's leftovers, covered in a grilled cheese topping, and baked in a large, deep silver tray.

"It's ... not *so* bad," she said, eyes looking quizzically at her friend, "not as bad as you made out the other day anyway. Spaghetti and cheese is actually nice."

Charlotte smiled expectantly. She held her breath as she watched Emily take another, *larger* mouthful, whilst prodding aimlessly but not looking at her own lunch. Suddenly, the face opposite took on a look of sheer horror. Emily's eyes widened, shoulders lifted and face paled as a hand came up in front of her mouth...

"Fishcake? Liver? Boiled-to-death spinach? Or, heaven forbid, the unholy trinity?"

After frantically searching, Emily finally produced a big enough tissue from her dress pocket, and swivelling round, furtively emptied the contents of her mouth into it. "That was absolutely *foul*!! How can anyone *eat* this stuff?" She turned back to the table and drank a half glass of water straight down to help get rid of the ghastly taste.

Charlotte couldn't stop giggling, as did some of the other girls on nearby tables. Very few actually *did* eat Spaghetti McGosh, and those who did were considered very odd indeed. "I warned you, Em, *never* eat the McGosh!!" She wagged a finger of mock disapproval in front of her face. "Don't worry, I can faithfully promise the chocolate pudding and chocolate sauce is absolute *heaven*."

Still grimacing, Emily put her knife and fork together and pushed her plate away. "What did you want to tell me, anyway? You still haven't said."

Charlotte also slid her untouched food up the table and leant forward. The next ten or fifteen minutes were spent updating Emily with everything she'd seen and heard at Clayton Hall the previous Saturday. From the moment of following PE teacher Fishy Phillips, history teacher Karen Lewis, and fifth-formers Sandi Lisle and Jackie Squires into the mansion, to the time she woke up after being drugged.

Emily was rooted to the bench, mouth hanging open, occasionally babbling '*buts*', '*noos*', and '*surely nots*' throughout Charlotte's story. They very nearly missed pudding… "What are you going to *do* though, Charlie?" she hissed. "I can't believe how much *danger* you're in, how can anything like this have happened at our school, at *any* school? It's crazy!"

"Well, you're not wrong there. It's the nights that'll be the worst, at least during the day there are lots of people about. I'm just hoping I can dodge any more trouble with Fishy till the end of term. There's er … one *more* thing too …"

"Charlotte? *Charlotte*, don't miss the dessert queue, there's chocolate sponge today – it'll all be gone. Do you want me to get you a bowl?" One of her hangers-on from the next table had called over and now smiled adoringly as she waited for an answer.

"Get us one each, Becks, will you? Thanks."

"Will they give three bowls of pudding to one girl?" asked Emily, looking surprised.

"She'll divide them out amongst her friends, there's a couple who can't eat chocolate. One's allergic and the other gets headaches. It'll be fine."

Ten minutes later they were all done and dusted... "You're right, this chocolate concoction is absolutely to die for!" said Emily, scraping the bottom of the bowl with her spoon. She was about to lift it up to lick it clean when she just managed to stop herself. Charlotte smiled and gave a little laugh.

"It is, isn't it? Thank heavens for puddings, I say." Charlotte finished her last mouthful and, dropping her spoon back in the bowl, crossed her arms to lean on the table again. "Em, there's something else I need to tell you … that happened yesterday."

"Oh God – not *more*?"

"It was after morning break. Do you remember I said I'd meet you at lunchtime?"

"Yes, I wondered where you were."

"Well, I felt so rough after what happened I had to go and lie down, missed lunch altogether." Charlotte poured herself a large glass of water and drank deeply. "I decided to tell Miss Dean Senior about what had happened at Clayton Hall, what Fishy did to me – everything. So there I am, just about to knock on her office door when I hear her talking on the phone. So I stand patiently outside and wait till she's finished. Only she doesn't. She's talking to Miss Phillips about *drugs*. Not only is she talking about drugs, she's sort of *yelling softly down the phone* at her under her breath, making threats; saying the drugs must come immediately because she can't pay the teachers' salaries or the school bills!"

By this time Emily's eyes were on stalks, she was clutching Charlotte's arms across the dining table, and they were both getting funny looks from Becky and her crew.

"But then something *really* weird happened. I don't understand it and it's this that made me feel unwell." She looked sideways at Becky's table who were now craning their necks in their direction…

"Becks, Donna, Lynne, Jess … *do one* – I'll catch up with you all later." Charlotte glared at the four girls who got up and stalked off sulkily through the ancient dining room, up the stone steps and out to the area where the head's office and staffroom sat between the old and new parts of the school. She wouldn't have long before the dinner ladies told *them* to leave as well, most already had.

"As I was saying… something really weird happened then, because more voices were coming out of Miss Dean's office. A nurse and doctor started talking to each other about some kind of medical reports. They were getting all uptight about a woman called Peterson at the same time as Miss Dean was continuing to argue with Fishy Phillips about the drugs, but …"

"But *what* Charlie, *what* happened next?" Emily's breath caught in her throat in anticipation as she squeezed Charlotte's arms harder…

"They didn't know Miss Dean was there, and it was obvious she had no idea they were there either. I shook my head to try and get the nurse and doctor's voices out, and then …"

"And *then*? And *then*?" whispered Emily, urgently, shaking her arms now…

"The nurse said, '*Sir, sir … she just moved her head, did you see?*' And he replied, '*No I didn't. Are you sure? I'll stay a few minutes longer, maybe she'll do it again.*'"

Emily's whole body jerked back as she let go of Charlotte's arms, and they stared at each other, both in shock, Charlotte hardly believing what she'd just re-lived and said out loud, and Emily at what she'd just heard. She tried desperately to rationalise it, for both their sakes…

"It must've been that stuff on the pad Miss Phillips put over your face. I think it's called chlorryfor or something?"

"Chloroform – I looked it up."

"Yes, well, whatever it is, it must've made you woozy at the time and made you hear things that weren't there. Not Miss Dean's phone conversation of course, but the hospital people talking about the other person. Maybe you heard something on the radio in the social room on Saturday? Or just somebody's conversation and it all got mixed up when you were outside Miss Dean's office because of the chloroform."

"Maybe," replied Charlotte, not at all convinced, "but either way, I'm still in what my mother would call 'a terrible predicament…'"

TWENTY-FIVE

ICU BASSETLAW HOSPITAL
KILTON HILL - WORKSOP
1.00 P.M. FRIDAY 21ST MAY 2021

Sofia sat beside the bed, OBS clipboard resting on her knee, hand tapping a ballpoint pen on the Glasgow Coma Scale chart that lay on top. Again, there was nothing positive to write on it. She'd been massaging her patient's hands and arms, but it all seemed so futile, day after day, with rarely any change. Except for Tuesday when something very odd had happened. The monitor recording Charlotte's vital signs had begun bleeping and spiking erratically across the screen, displaying seriously rapid, uneven brainwave activity. At the same time, just for a moment, Sofia had witnessed a horrified expression on Charlotte's face. Even with the intubation tube, there was no mistaking it, but as soon as it was there, it was gone again. Apart from this one occasion, which to be realistic wasn't really a positive occurrence, there'd been no real progress since her arrival.

Sofia couldn't help but think of her sister Raya in 2016, lying in a coma for three months before they switched off the machines that had kept her body alive. At the time she'd believed Raya would come out of it, come back to her, but it wasn't to be and now Sofia was here.

She nearly missed it. In that moment her mind was so full of Raya, and then of all things, something made her sneeze. As her head shook, a movement at the corner of her eye caused her to turn and she saw it. Charlotte smiled. She *smiled*! Even though she was intubated, Sofia could see the corners of her mouth either side of the tube, a full-on smile, even her eyes joined in! She put her clipboard on the bed. It was almost as though Charlotte was responding in gratitude to someone or *something*. Was she dreaming? Either way, Sofia could hardly believe it, and began smiling herself as she picked the clipboard off the bed and recorded it in the motor-response section on the chart. She finished with a flourishingly dramatic full stop. "Well *done* – that smile's just scored you a five!"

Of course Sofia knew Charlotte's history, she was well aware of her crimes. However, in here, in ICU, she was a patient just like any other and they *all* tried not to think about what she'd done. Instead of dwelling on her horrific actions, everyone tried to concentrate on the fact she was the victim of poisoning.

At the end of that thought, Mike Leyland popped his head round the door. Sofia got up from the bed and walked over to beckon him in.

"She just smiled, literally just a minute ago, that's a first. Up till now it's just been the odd twitch."

"A big improvement then, at least Shepherd will have something to look at on the GCS."

"Yes, and this time I'm making a copy of it because I've no idea where it keeps disappearing to, but it def—"

"She wrinkled her nose!"

"*What?!*" Sofia whipped round to face the bed.

"Just now, I swear she sort of ... grimaced and screwed up her nose!"

Sofia walked swiftly back to Charlotte's bedside and looked down at her now, if anything, vaguely tense face. "I wish I'd seen it, but I can still log it as a motor response if you're certain you saw it."

"Log it. I definitely saw her scrunch up her nose. She must be in some kind of dream state, and I know from previous coma patients, it's entirely possible."

"It's strange though, because only this morning I got results back saying she had propofol in her system which was obviously the reason she'd not been responding."

"Well, presumably you ordered the tests a few days ago? Some time has elapsed since then, and the effects will have reduced. But *why*, who would do that?"

"When she first arrived almost two weeks ago, propofol was of course used to keep her in an induced coma to help her organs heal from the poisoning. In the last week it's been reduced to try and encourage responses, see if she can begin to come round, but for some reason the blood tests showed an *increase* of propofol again."

Mike thought for a moment. "It's like it's going up and down, sometimes low in her system and sometimes higher. That implies—"

"Someone's delivering propofol into her bloodstream to deliberately keep her sedated."

"Exactly." He thought for a moment… "Do you think we should request some security in ICU?"

"Can't imagine they'll stretch to that, can you? Who'd want to keep her sedated anyway?"

Mike raised an eyebrow… "Well, I'd have thought that was obvious. *Anyone related to one of her victims…*"

* * *

2.30 P.M. CARPENTERS ARMS - KIRKDALE, KESWICK

Harry had cleared his plate, downed two cups of coffee and was now wearing an imaginary halo for resisting the apple crumble and custard. He wanted to drop home before going back to work so he could take Baxter for a walk anyway, so time was against him, but first he needed to ring Andrew about Stella Gray's skeleton piece in the *Courier*. He was just about to bring up his name when his new and rather appropriate *X-Files* ringtone played, which meant it could only be Molly. He answered it to hear excited children's voices in the background and remembered she'd said she was going out to the park with her little one…

"Miss Fields, *please* don't tell me you've—"

"I've told you, Harry, call me Molly – and yes, sorry but yes, and it was another teenage girl, shortish brown hair, that's all I got."

"Where is it this time?"

"I think it's a wooded area again, but not the same woods close to the school, somewhere else … somewhere … *urggghhh*… so frustrating! Big gates, I think, huge, but I can't—"

"How close?"

"I can't be specific, a few roads away, maybe? I didn't just feel wet and clammy like usual, though, I felt restricted, like there was a solid wall all around me, really close but with a gap, and a horrible musty smell."

"Like a *well*, maybe…?"

"Yes! Now you mention it – that would fit *perfectly*."

"I think it could be the crumbling old manor, Clayton Hall in Manor Road. That's quite close by but it has its own wooded grounds. Did she say anything?"

"This is the kicker. She didn't plead for help or say anything relative to being helped. She said… '"It's time, but what *is* the time, where *is* the time?"'"

"Stranger than usual then… Okay, Molly, thanks for calling. I have to ring Andrew on something that's quite urgent, but thank you, I'll be in touch." He ended the call and rang Andrew, who picked up immediately.

"Gale? It's Harry."

"Hello, sir, everything okay?"

"Well, the pub grub I've just put away was, as usual,

more than okay, and I've just had another vision call from Molly, which isn't so great, frankly, but there's something I need you to do for me."

"*Another* one, she won't like that, Molly hates getting those visions."

"Yes, I can imagine, or rather I can't, but … well, you know what I mean."

"Sure, and *I'd* hate it, too. What's the job then, sir? DS Moorcroft had me making enquiries tracking down the nineties headmistress and two teachers re the Clayton House drugs thing."

"Don't worry, I'll square that with Suzanne. I need you to pay a visit to your old boss, sooner rather than later, if you can."

"Stella Gray?"

"The very same… Mrs Gray has written a long piece in the *Courier* about the Clayton skeleton, but not *only* that. Apparently, the paper has had several calls suggesting we dig up certain areas of Kirkdale Woods that border the fields belonging to the school."

"Blimey, that sounds like a *lead*, sir."

"It could be. Are you in the office? It always sounds weird when you call me sir."

Andrew laughed. "Yes, thought it best – *sir*."

"Right, okay, yes, absolutely. So … it *could* be a lead, on the other hand it could just be a load of nut jobs wanting a bit of attention. That happens a lot. And by the way, if anyone asks, I didn't refer to our helpful, information-supplying public as nut jobs – *got it?*"

Andrew stifled a laugh, "Got it!"

"Stella Gray still thinks the sun shines out of your shiny new copper's backside – never wanted to let you go as senior crime reporter. If her contacts want to remain anonymous to the authorities, she's more likely to open up to you than me, or anyone else, for that matter. I want you to get over there now and see if you can get any useful info. Names, numbers, email addresses, where they live – anything that could help this case, or in fact, cases, plural."

"On it, Guv, I'll get back to you later."

"Thanks. Oh, and Andrew…"

"Guv?"

"Guv sits better with me – stick with that."

* * *

Harry was throwing KONGS for Baxter across the park in the middle of a weekday afternoon. That hadn't happened a lot lately, so Baxter was in his element. There was no end to the number of times he'd run after the rubber toy and, bounding joyfully, bring it back to his dad. Well, mostly he'd bring it back. Sometimes he'd sniff things out in the denser areas, like last year when he emerged from the trees of the local woods with an arm dangling from his mouth. But … *not today*! Today it was purely playtime, and for that Harry was grateful.

After about twenty minutes of KONG chucking, Harry's shoulder began to complain in response to repeated lobbing. He walked to the bench he'd been aiming for since he'd entered the park, and sat down as Baxter returned, dropping the KONG at his feet. With no continuation of his favourite toy sailing through the air, he looked up at him quizzically, then jumped backwards, ran a tight circle, and with an expectant snort, jumped again on the spot, nodding his head sharply.

"No more for the moment, lad, my arm's given up the ghost for this afternoon." He reached into his jacket and pulled out a small bag of gravy bones. The Lab was at his side in an instant, a paw on his knee before Harry even opened his mouth. He dropped a few on the grass by his feet. "Yes, I thought they might ease your disappointment somewhat; typical Lab, always thinking of your stomach." He laughed, patted him on the head and, pocketing the bag, leant back on the bench. All things considered, it had been a very revealing day. To learn that on the face of it, his boss was in the frame for a twenty-five-year-old murder of a man who could well be connected to their 1990s cold cases was one hell of a shock. On top of that, Stella Gray had multiple people contacting her to strongly suggest certain areas of Kirkdale Woods be excavated, presumably because they believed a body, or *bodies*, were buried there. Were they crackpots wanting a few minutes of fame in the media? Or did they actually *know* something? And if they did – *why* did they? He leant forward to ruffle Baxter's ear. The gravy bones had been finished super quickly and he was now resting his head in Harry's lap.

"It's been one helluva day, son, it really has." He sighed heavily. Baxter lifted his head and, tipping it to one side, looked up at him intently, flexing his eyebrows one after the other before dropping his head back down and sighing in sympathy. "You understand every bloody word, don't you? Every *bloody* word…"

OFFICES OF THE *COURIER* NEWSPAPER - KIRKDALE

Andrew remembered to duck his head as he depressed the iron latch on the oak door to walk inside. It felt strange yet comfortably familiar to be back, but only for a moment as 2018 swam through his mind and he swallowed down the burgeoning lump in his throat. As he hovered on the threshold, Jenny Flood rose mentally before his eyes. All that long, shimmering, dark hair, squaw-like, and an overly slim frame displaying her fragility from anorexia so poignantly. And Rachel… dear, sweet Rachel, a typical ditsy blonde who'd been repeatedly hurt by men, and leant on all the *Courier* staff for comfort and support, *particularly him.* Both were vulnerable in their own way, both suppressing dark secrets – *both murdered by Charlotte Peterson…*

Inside, it was like nothing had changed. No surprise there really given the *Courier*'s owners, Peter and Stella Gray, followed an 'If it ain't broke, don't fix it' policy for just about everything. There was *one* new thing, though, and she was sitting at Andrew's old desk. Before he could think or say anything about it, Stella came out of the kitchen, fresh brew in hand.

"Well, to what do we owe this pleasure? Peter will be sad to have missed you; he's got a well-earned day off. Please tell me you're leaving the bobby job and coming back to us?"

Andrew grinned and then raised both eyebrows. He was expecting a comment from her along those lines when Harry had asked him to pay a visit. "'fraid not, Stella, that's permanent, although I'll admit to feeling a tad nostalgic as I got out of the car. On the threshold as I reached for the latch, however … well … Rachy and, er … Jenny… you don't forget people like that."

"No, of course not, it's been a bad couple of years for sure." A brief silence fell between them as one or two office staff began looking at each other questioningly. "Anyway, let's go to my office. *Poppy*, bring Officer Gale a coffee if you're not too busy, please – you'll probably find his old mug in the kitchen somewhere."

"Which one would that be?" asked a confused-looking twenty-something with blue hair and a nose ring sitting at Andrew's old desk.

"*Crime Journalists Hit Better Deadlines!*" they chorused together. Andrew called out, "Milk and two—" as Poppy waved an arm above her head in acknowledgement, disappearing down to the kitchen whilst they made their way to Stella's office at the top of the room.

"So … what brings you back to our world of local news media then, Andy? Or …" she looked at him quizzically over the rim of her mug… "maybe you've read my piece in the paper?"

He leant back in the chair and took a deep breath. "You mentioned in your article that the paper's had some calls and emails; people stating certain parts of the woods alongside the Clayton House School fields should be excavated."

"I did, yes. Are you going to dig up some of it, then?"

"We can't, not without justification – real evidence, basically. Were any of those calls specific? About where or *why* the woods should be dug up?"

"No, they just mentioned a stretch along the west perimeter. It passes the area where the skeleton grave was found."

"They? Did *all* of the informants suggest exactly the same—"

There was a knock at the door. Stella called out for the person to enter and a blue bob looked round, followed by the rest of Poppy Lee carrying Andrew's coffee. She placed it on the table and turned to him. "I couldn't help overhearing. About those calls, I had another one just now. A man. He insists someone's buried out there."

"Did he say *who*?" asked Stella excitedly.

"Did you get his name and contact details?" asked Andrew hopefully.

Poppy looked from one to the other and they both looked back at her, waiting – mouths open. "Jack. *He said his name was Jack, and something about a button.*"

TWENTY-SIX

POLICE INCIDENT ROOM KIRKDALE

1.00 P.M. MONDAY 24TH MAY 2021

DC Ricky Thompson threw down the computer mouse in frustration. He'd been on it all day Friday, since ten that morning, and despite his best efforts, had still come up with absolutely nothing. An outside chance had so far not borne fruit, and he was down two pasties, a second Snickers bar was taking a beating and a third looked to be going the same way. The old sugar devil always raised its ugly head when Tricky Ricky got stressed.

Suddenly a ping announced an incoming email and he snatched back the mouse to click on it. A slow and excited smile crept across his face as his eyes skimmed through its contents, and at the end he thumped the desk triumphantly! "Yes! Yes, yes and … *yes*!"

"Rick? What you got?" Joe had been heading up the office to the coffee machine, situated just behind Rick, so had to pass his desk to get there. He stopped to brush off the pasty crumbs into his bin, made a couple of coffees, adding three sugars to Ricky's, and passed his mug to him.

"Thanks." He took a sip and continued… "I've been trying to track down those two druggy teachers from the nineties who worked at Clayton House; the ones it's come out *were* actually running a drugs ring back in the day. The boss sent newbie one, Andy Gale, out on another job, and newbie two, Hannah Carlin, has a few days off, so it's been down to me. *Anyway* … after wading through some old *Herald* newspaper archives, I found some reports on the two girls, Jackie Squires and Denise Fraser, who went missing at the time. They both literally disappeared into thin air within a few months of each other in 1995, and as far as we know have never been seen since."

Joe nodded thoughtfully. "So … did you find anything on the two teachers then?"

"Not in the actual news reports, no, *but* … there's a piece written by someone called *Roberta* Phillips. It was a long shot, after all, Phillips is a common name, but I thought I'd email her. See if—"

"I don't see what the—"

"*Phillips?* The gym teacher *Felicia Phillips*? Nicknamed Fishy on account of her partner being a fishmonger?"

"Ah – yes, yes, of *course*, sorry, go on …"

"Well, because I'd got absolutely nowhere trying for *likely* leads after phoning a list of current teachers and admin staff, in case anyone else had been a pupil in the nineties, like Sandra Wainright, I thought I'd try looking at the *unlikely* instead. So … I scrutinised *around* the news reports of the missing girls, literally looked outside the box. Clearly nobody made the link in '95." He turned and pointed to his computer screen… "This just came in. Roberta Phillips. She's Felicia Phillips' apparently much younger sister. Not only that, she was *very* friendly with Karen Lewis, the other teacher we're looking for – so … a double whammy." He turned back with a smug grin on his face and rewarded himself by unwrapping Snickers number three.

"Wow, well done, Rick, nice work! What's your next move?"

"Well, when I've finished this, I'm going to call Ms Phillips the younger, and ask her if we can have a little chat, *ASAP.*"

* * *

Andrew had popped home to pick his phone up. He'd left it on the kitchen worktop when he'd rushed out that morning and felt lost without it. As he put the key in the door and walked into the hall, the sickeningly familiar smell hit him, and it wasn't the nappy bin.

His stomach lurched and a wave of adrenaline flooded his body. He could hear Gina talking to someone in the lounge, but from the hall couldn't tell if Ellie-Ro was with her. He placed his keys very quietly on the hall table and crept up to the lounge door, not having any idea how he would react if the man was on the other side.

"Every Monday? Yes, that would be fine, yes, any time, thanks for letting me know, bye … bye…"

Andrew marched into the lounge, heart pounding and temples pulsing. Gina was facing the French window looking out on the little garden – Ellie-Ro wasn't there… "*Who* was that on the phone, Gina, and *who's* been here in the last hour?"

She flew round, jumping in shock at his sudden appearance. "*Andy!* Don't *do* that, I nearly had a heart attack!"

"Who was it, Gee, who was here earlier, and where's Ellie?"

"She's upstairs having a nap. It was just some window cleaner guy doing the rounds for more business, he just rang after checking his schedule, to say he could do us on a … anyway, *how* did—"

"What was his *name*, Gina?" Andrew hadn't realised he'd balled his hands into fists, wore a facial expression taught, like steel. Gina narrowed her eyes, turned her head slightly in confused thought as she walked slowly towards him.

"Ryan … I think he said it was Ryan. Why? Hold on, he gave me a—"

"Ryan Jacks, it *must've* been Ryan Jacks, and now he's got your *number!*" Andrew slumped onto the sofa with his head bent down, running agitated hands through his hair.

Gina sat down next to him. She was starting to feel scared now. Past experiences with Charlotte Peterson had taught her totally normal things could turn into totally abnormal ones pretty quickly, and when one least expects it… "What's going on Andy? I want to know, and I want to know *now*."

Andrew looked up at her with haunted eyes. "You better make a brew; this is going to take a while."

An hour later and Gina was up to speed on the Ryan Jacks situation. Andrew left nothing out, including Jacks' noxious aftershave, recent release from prison, and his own detailed discussions with Joe Walker and Harry Longbridge. When Andy was describing what had happened at the children's home, what he saw, what he had to do – Gina swallowed back tears and immediately picked up his hand to cradle it between her own.

"So what's our next move, then?" she asked quietly. "He knows where we live, and as you pointed out, has my mobile number, too."

"One of our team was supposed to be keeping an eye on him. He obviously isn't doing a very good job."

"How did he find you, Andy, after all these years? You were only *ten* the last time he saw you."

"No idea … although—" he rolled his eyes, "yes, of *course*…"

"What?"

"The *Courier*. He could've seen one of my sports reports from when I was working there; made a few enquiries. He turned up at the station a few days ago, it was assumed as he'd just been released he was reporting a change of address or something. They have to do that when they come out. He could still have been doing that, maybe he overheard someone mention my name while he was there."

This was her chance to bring it up. The worry she'd shared with Molly a week ago in the pub lounge... "Is that the night you woke up disorientated and in a sweat? You'd even been crying in your sleep, I've been so worried, but..." She put her arm around him and pulled him towards her... "You avoided discussing it every time I tried to say anything."

"Yes, I know. I'm sorry about that; I just couldn't believe he was back. I felt sick. I didn't want to involve you, worry you after all you've been through with the Peterson woman." He hugged her close and stroked her hair. "Forgive me? I know we promised to always tell each other everything."

"Of course. As long as telling me *everything* doesn't include informing me when my lardy backside has finally achieved the size of Wales!"

"You have a perfectly lovely backside, Mrs Gale, and don't you ever forget it." He gave her a long kiss and smoothed her hair away from her face.

"Seriously though, Andy, you need to report this to Longbridge, and I'll have to ring Jacks back to can—"

"No – don't. *I'll* ring him to cancel the window cleaning. I doubt he's even doing any – he's just made that up. In fact, I'll get someone to pay him a visit to warn him off, give him a lecture on the fact he's already on the sex offenders register and only just been released. Hopefully that'll be enough."

"And if it isn't?"

At that very moment, a loud protesting wail came from upstairs as Ellie-Ro woke up from her nap.

Andrew looked up. "It had better be, because I won't be responsible for my actions if not."

* * *

2.30 P.M. HARRY'S OFFICE

Harry was mulling over the intel that Andrew Gale's Friday afternoon visit to the *Courier* newspaper had produced. He'd rung in before heading home, and on the face of it, after thoroughly questioning the young reporter, it looked like Ryan Jacks was one of the public contacts who'd called the paper. The young girl, Poppy, who'd taken the call, had either not been given his name correctly by Jacks when she'd told Andrew and Stella a man called 'Jack' had called, or she'd not noted it correctly herself. The others were all anonymous, although one was from a woman who'd sounded very upset and quite urgent an excavation should take place in Kirkdale Woods, where it bordered the field side of Clayton House School grounds.

It was all very interesting, but Harry knew he needed more than just reports of phone calls. When a cold case investigation was re-examined, or indeed when *any* investigation hit the media, it naturally attracted attention. This led to phone calls to the press and to themselves. Sometimes they were helpful, often they weren't, and those that weren't were officially known as '*those who yearned for attention*', unofficially as the nutters and time-wasters. However… Ryan Jacks was a recently released sex offender known to the constabulary. Not a case Harry had been involved with as he'd not been in Cumbria when that little toad was locked up. Gabe Downs had been allotted to keep an eye on Mr Jacks – he needed to pay him a home visit. At the end of that thought, his phone rang.

"Longbridge."

"Sir – er… *Guv*, it's Andrew, there's been an incident, here at my home."

"What kind of incident? Are Gina and the baby okay?"

"Yes, they're fine, thanks, but he's been here, in the house, earlier. Ryan Jacks."

"*What?* Why? How?"

"Passed himself off as a window cleaner, I wasn't here, obviously, Gina had apparently been thinking of getting a window cleaner so it was a lucky hit. He cleverly acquired her phone number by saying he'd ring her back after checking his weekly schedule for the area. She didn't suspect a thing."

"You were going to tell her, though, Andy, about your history with Jacks. We had a long discussion about it last week. *Didn't you do that?*"

Andrew bit his lip and blew a heavy sigh before answering. "No, I – I just hadn't found the right words, but she knows now. I've told her absolutely everything."

"Right, well, what's done is done. I think you've learnt a big lesson today, lad. If she'd been in the loop, a) Jacks wouldn't now have her phone number, and b) he probably wouldn't even have got into the house."

There was a brief silence as Harry let Andrew have a moment to think about what he'd done, or rather *hadn't* done, before continuing. "I'm going to ensure Gabe Downs pays him a visit, make certain he's aware he must stay away from you and your family because there's a child living in the house. Gabe doesn't need to know about your past connection, so don't worry about that. If Jacks doesn't comply, we'll get a restraining order issued. He needs to be questioned about his call to the *Courier* anyway. Why would *he* know anything about these cold cases and the possibility of bodies out there in Kirkdale Woods?"

"Exactly what I was thinking, Guv."

There was a knock on the door and Harry looked up to see Suzanne Moorcroft through the glass… "Look, Andrew, I've got to go. I'll get Downs to see what he can find out."

"Okay, boss, I'll see you in the briefing room tomorrow."

"You will – and Gale?"

"Yes, boss?"

"Boss is also good."

He put the phone down and waved Suzanne into the room. She was carrying a notebook and displaying an excited expression.

"Just got this in from Kelly Novak – it's about the skeleton."

Harry held his hand out. "That must be the DNA results; she told me she'd get them to me this week. You'll need to run them against the National DNA Database? With a bit of luck—"

She passed over her notebook. "It is, and I've already run the checks. I discovered the NDNAD was established in 1995 but didn't need to go back that far. In fact, what turned up as a match came from someone much closer to the present."

Harry's mouth dropped open as he read what Suzanne had written. He looked back up at her and she nodded.

"I double-checked with the niece's DNA as well."

"Who'd have thought they were running a drugs nest up here back in the nineties. I knew they were down south but…"

"Raiffe Zandini's father and Zoe Zandini's great uncle …" Suzanne stood tall, arms crossed, looking mighty pleased with herself.

"The not-so-invincible head of the family – *Sergé Zandini*…"

TWENTY-SEVEN

CLAYTON HOUSE GRAMMAR SCHOOL KIRKDALE CUMBRIA

WEDNESDAY 18TH SEPTEMBER 1991

Charlotte and Emily were sitting on the bench. It was morning break and as usual they both had crisps, cheese and onion, naturally. Emily was looking thoughtful…

"Charlie … I've been wondering something, about Mrs Lewis."

"Oh my God, she's not been snorting coke in *lessons*, has she?"

"Noooo … *course* not! No, I was looking over at the arches just now, and wondering about what happened the other week when she came marching out from them looking like thunder and swinging that dead crow."

"Oh yeah, that was super weird," laughed Charlotte. "Even cookie Karen Lewis hasn't done *that* before."

"So what I was wondering," continued Emily, "was why? *Why* would somebody have sent her a *dead crow*?"

"Husband's a bit of a nutter by all accounts, shoots them with an air rifle if he gets bored with used beer cans. No doubt someone thought that wasn't very nice and wanted to make a point."

"Jeez. They're a right pair, aren't they." Emily screwed up her empty crisp packet, aimed it at the bin and missed. As she went to pick it up and place it inside, she saw something lying flat at its edge, something that looked as though it didn't belong in there. It was clean and white, not a piece of rubbish at all. Inside, the bin wasn't too messy, mainly crisp packets and chocolate bar wrappers, so she slipped her hand down the side and pulled out a long slim envelope.

"What you doing, Em? Rummaging in a bin is so *not* cool."

"Look at this." Emily walked back to the bench with the sealed envelope and sat down. It was bulging slightly in the middle, not a lot, just enough to show there was something inside it, and there was no writing front or back. She handed it over to Charlotte, who already had her hand out.

"*Weird...*" She turned it over and back again and then, after first glancing around to make sure there was nobody within close vicinity, carefully opened it along its length. Her eyes popped and then grew wider still when she saw what was inside.

"What on earth are *they*?" asked Emily, peering at six little silver packets now in Charlotte's lap.

"I think they're *drugs*," she whispered back, as if

someone would overhear them. "I've seen stuff like this on TV, all wrapped up in silver paper; they're literally called wraps. They can get left in secret places by a dealer to be picked up later by the user. Maybe both know when our bins will be emptied so assumed they'll be picked up before bin day."

"*Blimey*. What are you going to do with them, then? You can't *keep* them."

"Well, I certainly can't *tell* anyone, *can* I? Not with what we know about Miss Dean, old Fishy Phillips and cookie Karen Lewis. If they thought I actually knew anything for sure about their drugs business, I'd be in even *more* danger." She put the silver wraps back in the envelope, folded it up and shoved it deep into her book bag.

Emily looked concerned and placed a hand on Charlotte's arm. "Well, you'd better hide them well, Charlie, because if they get found in your stuff…"

"Oh I'll—" At that moment the bell went for end of break and both girls got up to make their way to their different classrooms. Emily's tummy worrying about her friend all the way to French, and Charlotte's heart beating a little faster than it had at the end of the previous lesson…

* * *

The moon was bright and full. It was just past 2.00 a.m. as she watched her PE teacher, Felicia Phillips, move around the playground frantically checking various waste bins.

Charlotte had put her trainers on knowing they were the softest and quietest to help keep her out of earshot. She followed her teacher around, carefully ensuring the moon didn't reveal her mobile hiding places as she hid in the shadows.

Fishy couldn't find them. She'd checked every bin in both the senior and junior playgrounds and they weren't there. Of course they weren't. Charlotte knew she wouldn't find them, not the ones Emily had discovered anyway. They were well hidden, safe and secure, in the darkness under her mattress.

There had been a clanging noise that had woken her at about 1.45 a.m. She'd been sleeping very lightly since the chloroform incident at Clayton Hall, too scared to let herself go into a deep and relaxing sleep in case Fishy Phillips repeated the abuse. Slipping on her dressing gown and gym shoes, she'd left her room and walked the corridor of the boarders' lodge, glancing out of the windows as she went. Overlooking the senior playground, she saw someone who didn't live on-site digging around in one of the bins. With her tall, lean figure and closely layered shoulder-length hairstyle, it wasn't difficult to spot Fishy Phillips looking for something. Something she couldn't find by all accounts. Several cans lay around the bin's base which must have been the clanging sound that woke her up. Then she heard something else entirely…

"Shit, shit, *shit*! *One* mistake and I'm totally fucked! Where the *hell* is it?"

Oooh... naughty, naughty!! Shouldn't be swearing on school property, Miss Phillips... thought Charlotte, giggling, and then immediately clamped both hands over her mouth and held her breath as Fishy swung round to look in her direction. She shrank back even further into the shadows, pressing herself flat against the wall in between the pillars of the language lab.

Fishy stood absolutely still, listening intently. There was literally nothing to hear except a light breeze on the air, and the rustle of autumn leaves that had just begun falling. Charlotte took her hands away from her mouth, let her breath go very slowly, and then with alarming realisation she was about to hiccough, slammed them back over her mouth again. Unfortunately, despite a double-handed stifling attempt, a squeaky one burst out, and Fishy's head spun both ways! She began walking quickly towards the familiar noise that had catapulted through the night's silence. The shock of that stopped Charlotte's hiccoughs dead in their tracks, too late, though, from a non-discovery point of view. It was fight or flight. She hadn't come off well the first time around, so it was now or never, dart or die! She decided to get the hell out of there before the chloroform queen did her worst, but Fishy was marching quickly towards her, advancing at a rate of knots. She may have been a daily chimney for Benson & Hedges the last thirty odd years, but was an ex-county-runner in her youth and could still move at pace on the flat if she wanted to.

Charlotte took off at speed along one side of the language lab, at that moment no longer worrying about hiding in shadows, no longer thinking about Fishy's drug searching, and certainly with no thoughts of being quiet. Her gym teacher was surprisingly fast and with legs like Cindy Crawford, but Charlotte was younger, lighter, fitter, more flexible, could dodge in and out of doorways when she got too close – *and she didn't smoke.*

She flew round the corner at the end of the long language lab and stopped for a moment. It was one of the more modern parts of the school, all windows and new brickwork. The entrance drive and bike sheds were within sight – that's where she was heading – thank goodness for trainers and jimjams, thank goodness for warm September nights.

The moon had slid behind a cloud and it was now really dark with the street lamps being further out. Clayton House was set away from main roads, away from the hubbub of the village, and as she looked up at the sky, all she could see was inky black. Luckily, Charlotte knew the school layout like the back of her hand and was soon across the drive and behind the end wall of the bike shed. She sat on the floor with her back to it for a moment, to catch her breath and plan her next move.

Suddenly there was a faint aroma of smoked haddock … or maybe she was just imagining it? The answer to that soon became apparent. She wasn't. The sound of footsteps and panting was close – too close. Charlotte couldn't believe Fishy had found her, and although the woman couldn't *know* it was her, as she'd definitely not seen her face, Charlotte knew she needed to make a decision – and *fast.* The drive stretched all the way down to the road but it was completely in the open, she'd be seen immediately if she went for it.

"Whoever you are, I know you're there and I'm going to find you in the next two minutes. So make it easy on yourself and come out – *now!*"

Charlotte stood up, took a deep breath, fixed her eyes on the end of the school drive ... *and started running for her life!* She could hear Fishy behind her, pounding the tarmac, calling after her in stilted panting, aggressive rants, gaining on her rapidly, closing the gap between them with each determined stride!

"You ... you *won't* get away from me! Don't think ... don't think you *will* you ... you *interfering ... little ... bitch!*"

Charlotte wanted to cry. It was a first – she never cried – but right then she wanted nothing more than her mother's arms around her, and a good bawl. But she didn't, she kept running and running and running....

Suddenly, Charlotte couldn't see the drive anymore. She was in a long tunnel she didn't recognise at all. *Is this part of an underground road system below the school? If so, how did I get here? And where's that music coming from?* Charlotte looked behind her, screwed up her eyes in the darkness but couldn't see Fishy anywhere. She began to slow down, rechecked Fishy definitely wasn't still chasing her, and smacked a hand on the side of her head to stop the music, but the song lyric wouldn't go away... 'Wake up it's a beautiful morn – ing, the sun shining for your eyes...' *I love pop but I've never heard that one before.* The chorus kept playing on a refrain as Charlotte reduced to a slow jog through the endlessly long black tunnel. She had no idea where the sound was coming from, and no idea where she was going, but desperately wished Emily was with her, and light, more than anything now, she just wished there was light...

TWENTY-EIGHT

ICU BASSETLAW HOSPITAL
KILTON HILL - WORKSOP
MONDAY 24TH MAY 2021

It had not been a good start to the day. The previous evening Sofia had discovered some personal female items in Mike's bathroom, and although their relationship was still very new, she nevertheless felt a mixture of emotions – top of which was being totally pissed at him for not telling her he was seeing someone else.

It was only a few things, a lipstick, tinted moisturiser, an obvious woman's shower gel, and one or two other bits, but they were clearly not his mother's. Not that she'd ever *met* his mother, and probably never would now, but that wasn't the point. On finding them, after they'd eaten a takeaway and watched a film, she'd decided not to stay the night, made an excuse she was tired and had some things to do at home, and went back to her flat. It was fair to say Mike was a bit confused at her sudden coolness, and obviously disappointed at her not staying over.

On arriving at work and walking along the ICU corridor, Sofia was surprised to see an officer in full uniform standing formally outside Charlotte's room. She hadn't thought Mike was actually *serious* about security for Charlotte Peterson – between all the nursing staff they could ensure nobody was injecting propofol or anything else into her, couldn't they? Unless … she stopped by the drinks machine to mull it over, and pushed the button for a strong black coffee to help her think. Her gaze was still with the uniform outside Charlotte's room as the paper cup dropped at an awkward angle and the black liquid started spurting out all over the grating instead of inside the cup. It poured down the machine front and onto her shoes as she instinctively jumped back to avoid any splashing across her scrubs.

"*Bloody* thing's always doing that to me!" She fished out a couple of tissues, bent down to wipe her shoes, then cleaning up the machine as best she could, dumped the used tissues into the bin alongside. When she finally looked back up, the officer was gone. She dismissed the idea of getting coffee and continued up the corridor to Charlotte's room. It was empty, but the hospital radio had been turned on, and a rather incongruous chorus of 'Wake up it's a beautiful morning' was playing. She'd only vaguely heard of it, but thought it *was* quite catchy and the DJ mentioned it was a hit in 1995 for a group called The Boo Radleys – *cute name*! She was only four in '95, so not surprisingly it wasn't on her radar, *but Charlotte Peterson would've been a teenager around then*, she thought – *shame she couldn't enjoy it.*

APPLE TREE COTTAGE - APPLETHWAITE

DC Ricky Thompson pulled the black vintage doorbell and waited. Through the mottled square glass panes, he could clearly hear its coiled bell jangling noisily on the other side. It reminded him of his parents' cottage. He looked up at the white uneven stone walls with white Georgian barred windows sitting in black frames. They had definitely seen better days. A little metal lamp hung from the centre of the peaked porch, and baskets full of colourful blooms dangled one on each side from the top of the porch struts. All black, apart from the flowers. There was even a little round table and two chairs, *black of course*, in front of the window to the left of the glazed Georgian-style door. However, as yet, no one had answered that bell.

His boots lightly scrunched on what was left of the sparse gravel as he walked around the table and chairs. Holding his hand to his forehead to shield the sun, he peered through the square panes into the room beyond. The furniture inside was dated, but the room was clean and tidy, and he could see part of a paperback on a table next to an armchair. Moving to the next window, head at an angle, he was just trying to see if he could make out the title, when he felt a tap on his shoulder. Rick twisted round sharply, on full alert, to be met with a shortish frosty-haired elderly lady, wearing blue dungarees and carrying a trowel.

"Sorry, I was in the back garden. Pansies won't plant themselves, you know. I take it you're the policeman?"

Ricky, hesitated, instinctively feeling for some unexplainable reason he ought to stand to attention... "Yes, ma'am, I'm DC Thompson, the officer who emailed you about your piece in the *Herald* in 1995, the one about the disappearance of Clayton House pupils Jackie Squires and Denise Fraser? I'm hoping you're Ms Roberta Phillips?"

"You did, and I am. Follow me, I'll put the kettle on."

He did as he was told. As he walked behind her, a flash of red on the right-hand side of the property caught his eye. He craned his neck past the wall to see the rear end of a bright cherry-coloured sports car tucked down the drive and made a quick note of the plate. What was even *more* surprising was the back of Roberta's hair matched its paintwork! Feisty *and* fun, he thought, smiling, as he shut the cottage door behind him.

Inside, the decor struck him as comforting, which was a strange word to use to describe a property, but it was neither very old-fashioned nor very modern. He decided the word comforting felt right because it was so much like his parents' place. Lots of peach and cream walls and fabrics, dark brown leather sofas, absolutely no modern duck-egg blue or grey shades anywhere, but neither were there any heavily textured ceilings and walls or those hideous seventies brown and gold swirly carpets.

Yes, comforting was definitely the right word, probably because he felt as if his childhood was all around him.

Roberta ushered him into the lounge, and ten minutes later brought in two mugs of coffee on a tray, with a biscuit barrel, two spoons and a bowl of sugar. Once the serving and receiving had been carried out, Ricky posed his first question...

"Thank you, this is lovely, you're very kind..." He took out his pocketbook and pen. "So, Ms Phillips, you mentioned in your reply email to me this morning that in 1995 you were friendly with a teacher at Clayton House School, a Karen *Lewis*? Are you still in contact with her?" Ricky knew Karen Lewis was the missing teacher, one of the three cold cases the team were investigating, but wanted to see how Roberta would react to his question. She hesitated before answering, her eyes flickering in all directions before looking back at him. Sighing heavily, she looked down into her lap before raising her head to speak.

"I haven't seen Karen since the year everything happened, officer. She simply disappeared, like those two unfortunate girls."

"She didn't contact you at *all*; you didn't try to contact *her*?"

"Of course I did, she was my closest friend, but it was like she'd been abducted by aliens – there was simply no trace of her. She had a bad marriage you see, no children, renting, living a nightmare, and if I'm honest, it was probably her bastard of a husband that sent her over the edge. Anyone else would've drunk through their misery, but not Karen. Cocaine became her new best friend."

Ricky jotted it all down before continuing. At least she'd confirmed what little they already knew about the missing teacher, although aliens probably hadn't featured... "If you don't mind me asking, can you tell me why you've decided *now's* the time to speak to police about the events of the two missing girls in your *Herald* article."

"Well, to be honest, Detective Thompson, I've had some very bad news recently and—" Roberta's mug shook, and she put it down to begin fiddling with a silver cross hanging around her neck. "I have a brain tumour. They can't do anything, and I don't want to meet my maker with what I know hanging over me."

Ricky blanched. "I'm sincerely sorry to hear that, Ms Phillips, *really* I am."

"Thank you. It does take some getting used to. Still, it wasn't *just* my friendship with Karen I needed to explain about, *or* the missing girls. And just to be clear, there were actually *two* articles. One in July '95 when Denise disappeared, and the second in the November after Jackie went missing. Oh, and in case you were wondering, Karen's disappearance wasn't in either one because she was still here in the August, and I was away in Scotland on a break."

Ricky tried to write everything down as quickly as Roberta was delivering it, wishing he'd got the shorthand skills his mother had acquired decades ago.

She began re-stirring her coffee and staring intently at the spoon as it went round and round. "Felicia, my sister, she …" Her head turned to a dresser standing against the wall where a photo of a middle-aged woman stood in an ornate silver frame. "They used to call her Fishy, you know – the girls at Clayton House. She wasn't that popular, you see."

"She was a teacher there, I understand," chipped in Ricky, as he reached into the barrel for a Hobnob.

"Yes, PE teacher, gymnastics, cross-country, that sort of thing. Her partner Phil was a fishmonger, dead now, but the kids used to make out there was a bit of an odour around her. There wasn't, of course, not really, it was just cheek, but she was overly strict and with everything that was going on …"

"What, Ms Phillips? What was going on?" asked Ricky gently. Roberta began fiddling with her cross again and he wasn't sure if it was out of guilt, comfort, or both.

"She made me keep quiet for over twenty-five years, but at the end of the day, I felt I *had* to anyway – she was my sister. I'd split up with my husband that year you see, 1995, Felicia gave me a home here with her and Phil, literally put a roof over my head. I moved in and reverted to my maiden name. It was only meant to be temporary till I got back on my feet but—"

"What did she make you keep quiet about, Roberta?"

She took a deep breath and looked up. "Clayton House was haemorrhaging money. The headmistress, Veronica Dean, and her sister, Patricia, who ran the school, were under *huge* pressure, barely able to pay staff salaries, and the canteen food was dire by all accounts. The Ofsted reports had only just been launched in 1992, so if they had a school check they made sure all the stops were pulled out for that one day."

"Even so, it couldn't have been easy if funds were *that* low?" asked Ricky, availing himself of another biscuit.

Roberta didn't notice. She was now looking somewhere over his right shoulder... "Felicia's partner, Phil, knew some dodgy people back then, and I mean *really* dodgy. She knew the problems Veronica was having, and long story short, put her in touch with someone Phil knew from some kind of drug gang, to put in place what they called a 'financial plan'. I don't know the proper terms for these things, to be honest – they had a funny gang name, too."

"That's okay, you're doing fine. Do you remember the name of this gang?"

"Zindy ... or ... Zandy ... or ... *Zendy*? Something like that?"

Ricky's hand dropped back from its third trip to the biscuit barrel. "Was it *Zandini*, by any chance?"

"That's the one. So, basically, the Deans began buying and selling drugs. I know this to be true, not just because one night Felicia came home in a terrible state and spilt the whole sorry tale, but because Karen Lewis was my friend, and I knew she had a *serious* cocaine habit. God knows how she managed to teach those kids. Felicia would have been selling to her for Veronica, and knowing my sister, taking a cut off the top while she was at it."

Ricky Thompson was still having difficulty connecting the word *Zandini* with what he reckoned to be, *despite the flash of red hair and sports car in the drive*, a lady of at least seventy years old. "Are you *sure* the name of the drug gang your sister's partner was involved with was *Zandini*, Ms Phillips?"

"Yes, definitely. Once you said it, I was instantly back there, well, here actually. It was in this very room that Felicia told me everything. In fact, she was sitting right where you are now."

Ricky shifted uncomfortably, aware he hadn't asked the obvious question as yet. He needed to – and *now*. "Where is your sister at the moment, ma'am? Is she still…"

"Kirkdale Nursing Home, detective, Alzheimer's is a wicked, *wicked* disease, and her heart's none too clever either. Try as I might, I just can't cope, not with … Anyway, that's where she is. Where *was* I?"

"Felicia was facilitating a connection between the Zandinis and Veronica Dean, through her partner, Phil."

"Ah yes, yes … that's right. Well, Felicia literally made the connections between the Zandinis and Veronica Dean. Phone calls, dates, pickups, drop-offs payments and so on. One night she came home extremely late, scared, agitated and dishevelled."

"When was that?"

"It was the summer of '95 – Monday June 5th. I remember because it was my birthday and we were supposed to be going out."

"On a *school* night?" He winked.

Roberta smiled. "We had this thing in our family, always went out on our actual birthdays if we possibly could. Silly really, but it was one of our quirks."

Ricky reverted to interview mode. "Why was she in such a state, though, and do you remember the time she returned from school?"

"It was late, *really* late. I remember she had to take a detention class for one of the other teachers, but that would have finished about 5.00 p.m. She never turned up here till nearly midnight – and when I say turned up, I mean *flew through the door*." Roberta took a deep breath and reached behind her cushion. She brought out a silver flask, unscrewed the lid and added a slug of something to her coffee. Glancing up at Thompson, she mumbled quietly, "Whisky. Guilty pleasure, don't do it that often. Would you … no. Duty and whisky don't mix."

Ricky nodded, a light smile playing on his lips. *Red sports car, matching hair, hidden whisky flasks – there was a lot more to come from this lady…* "What happened next?"

"She was shaking, sobbing; hair all over the place like she'd been dragged through a hedge, couldn't get anything out of her at first, and Phil was away on some golfing trip, so he was no use. Finally, she stopped hyperventilating and started breathing more normally. I poured her a stiff drink and made her tell me why she was so upset. What unfolded that night absolutely horrified me, and we were up till two in the morning discussing what to do for the best."

Ricky leant forward for another Hobnob, praying his pocketbook wouldn't run out, as he tended to write everything in *explicit* detail. He also hoped there was a second biscuit barrel.

"Someone got shot."

"What? Who? *Who got shot?*" He pulled his hand out of the barrel so fast it fell on its side and knocked his mug over. Luckily, it was still on the tray and with very little coffee left.

"I'll make some more, *and* refill the barrel – somebody needs to be feeding you properly, young man."

Ricky blushed and mumbled his thanks at further refreshments. This was proving to be the most interesting interview of his career so far, and when Roberta returned and set the tray down, their conversation resumed immediately...

"There was a groundsman at the school, or caretaker, whatever he called himself. Stevens, I think his name was. *He* was involved for sure because Felicia said he'd found a gun a few weeks before when police had come out to the school. An armed man had broken in and threatened to kill the head and her sister if they didn't hand over money they owed for some drugs. They lived on-site, you see. It was assumed one of the officers had dropped his gun and lost it when scouring the woods for him. Ron Stevens found it quite by chance and had hung on to it just in case of a repeat incident."

"Was he caught?"

"Not sure, but there *was* a repeat incident, and someone different turned up at the school threatening God knows what the night Felicia came home late. Ron

Stevens shot *that* man, and they buried him near the woods."

"*They?*"

"Ron, Felicia and the Dean sisters – Karen didn't live on-site, but Felicia had taken the detention class and later been in a meeting with Veronica about the drug money still owed to the Zandinis, so she was there. Felicia said they'd never be connected to it because Ron had thrown the gun in the grave after he'd shot the guy, and worn gloves the entire time."

"I take it you've seen the recent news about the skeleton that's been found in the Clayton House School grounds?"

"Yes, that was the main reason for my responding to your email. I knew about that man's death. However, all these years I've been wondering if those two girls are out there somewhere, too. I nearly rang Stella over at the *Courier* when I saw her piece in the paper. We used to work together at the *Herald*, you know, back in the nineties, then she went on to marry Peter Gray and they started the *Courier* together."

"*Really?* No, I didn't know that." Ricky began tapping his pen thoughtfully on a fresh page. "Surely there was no reason for the caretaker to kill Jackie and Denise, though?"

"No, well … not unless they heard or saw something, of course?"

It was then Ricky remembered something else about the skeleton site. It had been reported in the paper so there was no reason he couldn't mention it. "There was a bag of five pence coins in that grave did your sister tell you anything about those?"

Blood drained rapidly from Roberta's face as her hand crept up to grasp the cross once more. "No … not a thing."

"Are you absolutely—"

"But I will say this." *She looked behind her to the hall, and out of the lounge window as if there was someone hiding, listening, preparing…* "After being a crime reporter for forty-odd years, I still keep up with everything crime related in the news, on TV, in the papers – even online. That business last year with the officer being sent down for arson and murder of police colleagues? He wasn't acting alone. There was someone higher up co-ordinating all of that, *much* higher up. I strongly believe they're still doing so, I can feel it in my water…"

Ricky's guts clenched, and inside, adrenaline was teeming at warp speed.

TWENTY-NINE

UNIVERSITY HOSPITAL NORTH DURHAM

10.00 A.M. TUESDAY 25TH MAY 2021

Terry Hackett had enjoyed having a cell to himself for a few days since Dave Cookson's admittance to hospital following his 'nut allergy incident' courtesy of Tony Marcetti. It was massively unusual to be sharing anyway, but considering the current and phenomenal overcrowding, there'd been no choice. He was down for a move given prison rule seven stating anyone on remand shouldn't be made to share with a convicted prisoner, but as yet it hadn't happened. However, Cookson had now been back for six days and things were tense, to say the least. Terry hadn't forgotten his *Dave the Blade* nickname. He'd been treading on eggshells ever since the man had barged back through the cell doorway, eyes like lasers and wearing the expression of a bulldog.

Nothing specific had happened for a week, not since his brief, Rebecca Weston, had come in to see him the day before Dave had returned. He hadn't heard anything from her since then, and amazingly, not been attacked (or worse), in the showers, his cell, or been poisoned at meals. That *was*, of course, until just before breakfast that morning. He'd been keeping himself very much to himself, well, as best as he could given he was sharing a small square box with a crazed killer. Shortly before nine, one by one, four of Cookson's muppets arrived, admittedly muppets who spent a lot of time in the gym… Three came in and one stood on watch outside. Terry began to sweat profusely and the knot in his throat prevented him from saying anything coherently, not that speaking would have helped much. It was explained to him in simple detail as each fist made contact with his face, and each foot with his torso and bollocks, that he hadn't carried out Cookson's orders regarding Tony Marcetti. Dave the Blade wasn't a happy bunny at all. As he saw it, had Terry despatched Tony as instructed, which was basically any way he liked, as long as it was *quickly*, Dave wouldn't have nearly choked to death at the hand of Marcetti's minder. Within two minutes Hackett had found himself underneath all three of them receiving a damn good beating and there was fuck all he could do about it. Hence he was now in a private room at North Durham's University Hospital, with security posted at his door and a prison officer cuffed to his left wrist. Not much fun for either of them, but at least for a week or so he again had a room without a bastard psycho in it.

Two weeks later and Terry Hackett was no longer in that room. He wasn't back in Frankland either. He'd been due a transfer out of the shared cell, but now he wasn't in Durham, the county … or even the UK. The transfer he'd been given was a bit further out, quite a *bit* further out, in fact. Not that he was complaining, even though his ribs were still killing him, his jaw felt worse than his ribs and *that* was still mending. Despite *all* that, all things considered, he knew he'd won, and won big. But what was really bugging him was why? *Why* would du Guarde go to these lengths to protect him?

He reached for the cold beer that sat on the table next to his lounger and kept turning it over in his mind. As he carefully sipped it through the straw, the sun tanned his bruised torso all the way down to the garish pink and green flamingo shorts that had been laid out to greet him in the bedroom. She'd thought of everything at her villa in Dominicalito – clothes, food, books, various IT devices, a stocked bar, personal bathroom items, even private nursing staff. It had been explained to him shortly after his arrival in Costa Rica that in order to get him out of Frankland, the attack had unfortunately been necessary. As a category 'A' prison, the chances of escape were less than zero – they *had* to get him in genuine need of high-level hospitalisation. His solicitor was of course as bent as a corkscrew, and had merely held a meeting with him in order to keep everything looking normal. She'd just told him what he'd want to hear, because enlightening him with the truth of what was shortly going to happen was unlikely to have him react naturally on D-day. The security detail that went with him *was* of course, also planted.

Wearing a cream Fedora, he was staring out beyond the pool to the Pacific Ocean, beer in hand, brand new laptop and phone lying on the table, when he suddenly realised the likely reason Dominique du Guarde couldn't possibly allow his case to get to court. If he fell apart on the stand, or was feeling in any way resentful, which, let's face it, was entirely possible, he could drop her, the Chief Constable of Cumbria, deep in the brown stuff. Costa Rica had no extradition agreement with the UK, and because of her *intimately* close connections with the Zandinis, she owned several very nice luxury properties due to their seriously lucrative business operation. She would not allow *anyone* … or *anything* to destroy that.

He placed his glass back on the table, wrapped his hands behind his head, smiling, and stretched out *very* gently. It was certainly a damned sight better life than he'd had at home before everything had gone tits up. Yes, Tacky Terry Hackett, ex-Cumbrian-DC from Kirkdale was definitely on the way up. He tipped his straw hat down over his eyes and was still grinning beneath it when the bullet seared through his skull.

11.30 A.M. INCIDENT ROOM
KIRKDALE POLICE STATION - CUMBRIA UK

Gabe Downs had just finished giving a quick résumé on a conversation he'd had with Ryan Jacks, asking him to stay away from Andrew Gale's home and family following his visit there the previous day. There was no general knowledge in the station about his connection to Andrew and what had taken place between them at the care home, only Harry, Suzanne and Joe Walker officially knew about that. Andrew had always assumed Jacks had never seen who'd attacked him that night twenty years ago, so in theory there was no reason for the man to threaten him and his family. Gabe had just been instructed to keep an eye on Jacks due to the nature of the crimes he'd served time for, and his recent release into the area. It was reasonable for a family with a child or children to request that a known paedophile, someone on the sex offenders register, did not approach them or their home, especially if there had been any type of connection between them.

Now Ricky Thompson was standing and had the room's full attention. Following his interview with Roberta Phillips, he was about to report on the information he'd received, which was quite a lot and pretty detailed. *Very* detailed given his style of intricate note-taking. Most of the team were present apart from new trainee Hannah Carlin, and Harry and Suzanne were out front hoping for some good news. Before he started, Harry had some important information to impart...

"If you can just hold fire a minute, Ricky, I've had some crucial confirmation in from forensics regarding the skeleton at Clayton House School." Ricky sat back down and everyone else sat up straight. A few '*sounds interesting*' murmurs and raised eyebrows passed around the room… "It appears the skeleton at Clayton House was definitely that of Sergé Zandini. At the time, he was the head of the Zandini family." A few jaws dropped and heads turned at this announcement, plus low mumblings that required quietening… "Exactly … we had no idea the Zandinis were operating in the North West twenty-five years ago, so this has been a surprise to say the least. I was aware of them running drug rings and money laundering in London and the South East when I was in the Met., but at the time there was certainly no intel of them spreading this far up."

"How do we know it's definitely a Zandini?" This from Gabe Downs, now sitting arms crossed and brow furrowed.

"The DNA markers came back as a match with Raiffe Zandini who was found with a bullet through his head last year and dumped in a farmer's silo. We had both of them in the national database, together with his niece Zoe Zandini, also murdered, whilst sectioned at Rampton Hospital in Nottingham."

"Unlucky family, then, by all accounts," replied Gabe after whistling through his teeth.

Harry paused for a second. It was a trite remark that didn't quite fit with the general mood of the room. However, Gabe had come over from Ireland so hadn't necessarily been aware of the recent Zandini murders the year before. He moved on quickly. "Okay, DC Thompson, can we have your report on your interview with Roberta Phillips now, please?" Ricky stood up again, and addressed the room…

"I've been trying to track down the two teachers from the nineties who taught at Clayton House, and mentioned to DS Walker there was a possible long shot from a journalist in 1995 who'd written two articles about the missing girls Jackie Squires and Denise Fraser. That journalist turned out to be the younger sister of one of those teachers, and yesterday she replied to my email. Ms Roberta Phillips is in her early seventies, and lives in Applethwaite. Her sister is Felicia Phillips, known back in '95 as 'Fishy' Phillips, the gym teacher, who I now know is residing in a nursing home, suffering from Alzheimer's and a heart condition. I doubt there'd be any point in interviewing her, but that's down to the Guv."

"We might still need to try, Ricky, but what did you get from Ms Phillips?" asked Harry.

"A good deal as it turned out, boss, she made it very clear she wanted to get it all off her chest, so to speak. She's a complex lady, appears very religious judging by a silver cross round her neck that she kept touching, but also quite funky in her outlook. She's got a broad section of red hair across the back of her head and drives a matching-coloured sports car."

"You got the make and plate number, I take it?" asked Suzanne, wondering if this was going to be as long a description as the actual interview.

"Yes, not likely to forget that one in a hurry. It was an old MGB convertible, with a personalised plate, 'Hot Rob 1'! Told you she was complex!" A few engine-revving vocals immediately hit the room, silenced equally fast by Suzanne, although she did think it was quite funny.

"Why did Ms Phillips reply to your email and agree to see you if her sister is implicated in these cold cases?" she asked.

"Sadly, this lady's been diagnosed with a brain tumour and the prognosis doesn't sound good, said she wanted to meet her maker with a clean slate." There were some sympathetic faces at this remark, and one or two understanding nods. "Anyway, Roberta was very friendly with Karen Lewis, the other teacher from the nineties. We learnt from current head and ex-pupil Sandra Wainright, when she told the Sarge, that Karen was involved in a drugs ring. Roberta says she knew she was a right coke … had a serious cocaine habit. The school was apparently drowning in debt despite charging high fees, and the head teachers at the time…" he whipped out his pocketbook for the names… "Veronica Dean, and her sister, Patricia, were literally crippled by the lack of funds." He kept the book open… "Roberta's sister had a partner, Phil, now deceased, who had some dodgy contacts, and set up the whole drug-selling arrangement. The Dean sisters knew they were treading a thin line, but presumably didn't want to lose the school, so grabbed it as a lifeline. Unfortunately, they got behind with their instalments … and get this, it was the *Zandinis* they were buying the coke from, which earned them an armed break-in by one of their men demanding payment, and a police response team scouring the site for him, *one* of which lost their gun on the night! Stevens the caretaker found it and held on to it in case of a second attack."

"Well, if they were the supplier … *that* fits in with the skeleton's DNA being Sergé Zandini," added Gabe.

Harry started shifting uncomfortably as he and Suzanne engaged in brief eye contact. He knew exactly where this was going and had still to speak to Chris Hitchings about the forensic reports on his gun from that night, and all it entailed. However, he also knew they had to let Thompson finish his report or it would look odd. It would also be highly irregular to shut down a colleague with vital case information. He began to feel in dire need of a barley sugar … or better still, a double whisky. And thinking of whisky, it suddenly hit him. *Molly's vision a few days ago of a red car face down in the water …*

Suzanne tried to deflect it a little… "Did you ask Ms Phillips why she never spoke out before now about what she knew? And *how* exactly she came by all this information?"

"Well, that's the key part, Sarge," continued Ricky. "One evening, around midnight in June '95, her sister came home from school in a hell of a state, said a man had been shot and killed and they'd all helped to bury him – Felicia, the Dean sisters and Ron Stevens, the caretaker. Karen Lewis didn't live on-site so wasn't there. I did ask her if she was still in contact with Mrs Lewis as they were such close friends, and we know she was the missing teacher, but she said she never heard from her after the summer of '95. Karen had been trapped in a bad marriage and Roberta attributed her cocaine habit down to her husband's aggression towards her." Ricky then switched to the two girls…

"Ms Phillips also suspects the two missing girls, Jackie and Denise, may be buried out in the woods, but doesn't know why or believe Ron Stevens had anything to do with that. Well, not unless they saw something of course…"

"No wonder Stevens disappeared then if he shot Sergé Zandini and possibly two school pupils as well!" piped up Gabe Downs. He'd discovered the previous week from a Clayton House admin whose mother had run the local newsagent in the nineties that the caretaker, a daily customer, had done an overnight disappearing act. There were nods and mumblings of agreement at his comment.

Andrew then added, "I don't know if it makes any difference or adds to anything, but do you remember Hannah mentioning at the excavation site about the perimeter of the field possibly being different if the skeleton had been hundreds of years old? She said the woods could have been further forward then, but as we now know it's only twenty-five years old, maybe it's been cleared along that line since to make room for a big sports field for the school? That would make sense for the body not appearing to be buried in woodland, because surely nobody would've buried someone in an adjacent open field? Even under the cover of darkness? They'd have gone deep into the woods. If that's the case, it was only trees that were cleared from the surface, rather than a major deep dig, because the skeleton was only recently found. If anyone *else* was buried out in the woods, they wouldn't have been found with only a surface tree clearance. Those girls *and* their teacher, Karen Lewis, could be out there."

"I *do* remember Hannah saying that, although that part of the field wasn't exactly flat when we visited the crime scene, so maybe funds hadn't been available to complete the job?" suggested Suzanne. A few 'that's true' and 'good point' comments were made. "However, in view of Ricky's interview with Roberta Phillips, I think a major deep dig might be in order," continued Suzanne, looking questioningly at Harry. "Do you think we could warrant it now, Guv?"

Harry nodded his head slowly, thoughtfully. An awful lot of what Ricky had been told by Roberta Phillips matched up with what Sandra Wainright had divulged to Suzanne when she'd gone to interview her five days ago. All in all, it had pushed the investigation forward considerably, or at the very least given them valid reasons for taking decisive action.

"Yes, I think we should get those woods initially searched. Suze, if you can arrange for the dog squad to do their stuff? If nothing comes from that, which is likely given the passage of time, I'll speak to Chief Superintendent Hitchings about a full-scale bone-detection search with ground-penetrating radar before engaging diggers. If Jackie and Denise *are* out there, and possibly Karen Lewis as well, we're going to do our damndest to find them."

"Yes, Guv – on it," replied Suzanne, pulling out her mobile preparing to message the dog unit.

"You haven't heard the best bit yet," added Ricky

folding his arms and pulling himself up to his full height, "Roberta's *insisting* there's a bent copper in our police force, really high up, co-ordinating the whole drugs thing. She's apparently kept up with all things crime over the years given her previous occupation, and mentioned Terry Hackett's involvement with Big Mac's murder last year." That certainly got the room buzzing, and neither Harry nor Suzanne shushed them down.

Harry's mind was tumbling with all that was being said. Roberta Phillips certainly appeared to have a nose for uncovering information, but then a good crime journalist usually did. If she was right about a rogue senior officer running things from inside the constabulary, then given what he now knew about Hitchings re the loss of his gun in '95, it looked like that accusation could be pointing directly at *him*. Other than anything happening to Fran or baby Jamie, the possibility of what he was thinking now would be his worst nightmare ever. His gut instincts told him Chris Hitchings *wasn't* rogue – so if it wasn't him....

THIRTY

CH. SUPERINTENDENT CHRIS HITCHINGS' OFFICE KIRKDALE POLICE STATION
9.00 A.M. WEDNESDAY 26TH MAY 2021

Harry knocked on the door. He'd never felt so nervous since his transfer from London, didn't even know how to open the conversation, let alone how his boss would take it and what the next move would be. He'd had the information for five days and couldn't put this off any longer.

"Yes – come in, Longbridge."

Harry took a deep breath, opened the door and walked into the hardest and most outlandish discussion he would never have expected to happen in his entire career. Inside, Hitchings was sitting bolt upright, hands clasped on his desk, ready to speak to him, something that almost never happened given he was usually shuffling paperwork or staring at a screen. He looked ten years older, and there was an extra tenseness around his eyes, his jaw...

"Sit down, Harry."

He did so, mind jumbling. This was not how he saw this playing out at all.

Chris stared at his clasped hands on the desk, thumbs incessantly rolling over one another before he looked up at his DCI. "I know why you wanted to see me, Harry, so don't look so anxious."

"Sir?" He feigned puzzlement for a second as Hitchings' tense gaze searched his face, then quickly continued. "I thought I'd just bring you up to date on the Skeleton Case at Clayton House, we've had quite a few develop—"

"I *know* about the developments, Longbridge, so don't worry, I'll make it easy for you." Harry eyed his boss suspiciously now. Hitchings was suddenly looking and sounding like an entirely different man. He felt as though a rug had been pulled out from under him.

"How did you …" *His boss waited for the penny to drop.* Harry blew a long understanding sigh… "Gabe Downs. Of course, that's why—"

"Yes, I'm afraid so. I'm sorry, Harry, but once that skeleton was dug up and my gun found, I had to have someone close in the team informing me how certain things were progressing."

"But only DS Moorcroft and I know about the serial number being police issue; and because of forensics, it must have been signed out to you that night before—"

"Let me tell you what happened, and then we can have a conversation about correct procedure – for me at least."

Harry nodded … and waited. He felt as if he was in a particularly corrupt Dirty Harry movie.

"We got called out to the school one night. It was the end of May '95 and I was a newly promoted DI. The caretaker rang. He lived in the grounds, was the only adult there that had seen a light on really late inside the school, and had heard shouts and some screaming. After following the noise to the head's study, he overheard a man threatening to use a gun which is why I ended up leading an armed unit and attending the scene. During the rescue of the head and her sister, Veronica and Patricia Dean, and the chase and hunt of the perpetrator for several hours, I lost my gun. It was a crazy, *horrible* night that started off with a light drizzle, and ended up with thunder and lightning. The rain was absolutely torrential, we could hardly see in front of us and it got mighty slippy out there in the woods once we'd chased him across the school field. That man should have tried out for the Olympics – we just couldn't catch the bastard. Anyway … I panicked, Harry. It was stupid, *I* was stupid. I know that, I should have just held my hands up to losing my firearm. The officer who'd signed that gun out to me—"

"Who *was* that," interrupted Harry, "we can't find hide nor hair of who signed that gun out."

"It was a young DS called Dominique." He saw Harry's brain ticking over, and not for very long. When his eyebrows flew up, Chris knew he'd clicked. "Got it in one."

"Not? Nooo … *surely not*?!"

"Yes, Longbridge, our very own Chief Constable Dominique du Guarde. She was a twenty-five-year-old firearms officer back then, determined to get on – and *fast*. We'd worked together as sergeants, and she saw helping her new DI as a route to getting what she wanted. We were both DSs waiting for promotion and there was only one vacancy. I got it. Dom said she'd cover my back, destroyed the signing in and out records for the gun she'd issued to me, and nobody was any the wiser. That wasn't easy, believe me. Not with the checks and balances going on, but with some senior help, she managed it. A few months later Dom moved to Dublin when a DI vacancy came up, applied for and got it. No internal transfers to ROI, as you know."

Harry nodded. "But what about the OB (Occurrence Book) and your chief super at the time? He'd have been checking it daily, so how the hell did—"

"As I said, she had some senior help. Chap called Henderson, and in answer to your question, I have absolutely no idea how, or why, he agreed. What I *do* know is he transferred to the Met. shortly after that … and blew his brains out within a week."

"*Henderson*, you say? I *remember* that incident! I was twenty-five and only been in the job seven years – shocked the hell out of me, but dear *God*, man – apart from the massive irregularity, and that's putting it *mildly*, your decision to allow du Guarde to cover everything up for you, put you in her *debt – forever!*" Harry was beside himself that anyone, but *especially* his whiter than white boss, could have been so bloody idiotic. His superior rank had just instantly dissolved.

Hitchings didn't even flinch at the disrespect. "Don't you think I *know* that, Harry? I've spent the last twenty-five years with this hanging over my head, and having to doff my hat to du Guarde when she returned to Cumbria ten years later and sailed past me up the ladder to chief constable!" He got up abruptly and started to pace the room, finally ending up staring out of the window to the town of Kirkdale below. Harry remained quiet for a moment, allowing his boss some thinking time before quietly returning to the information he needed to tell him.

"DS Moorcroft dealt with forensics and they told her they didn't bother to try and get prints off the gun because of the mess it makes for ballistics later. They got DNA though. Moorcroft ran checks on the PED (Police Elimination Database) and the CED (Contamination Elimination Database) and, well … your details came up."

Eyes now downcast, Hitchings held the bridge of his nose, and sighing heavily, slowly brought his hand down his face. Looking through the window again, he looked across his town and replied somewhat resignedly. "Gabe filled me in yesterday on DC Thompson's report regarding what Ms Roberta Phillips told him in interview. Particularly about the caretaker, Stevens, finding my gun at the May incident and using it to kill Sergé Zandini a week later."

"Which means," cut in Harry, icily, "that either you cough to the loss of your weapon and the cover up of the signing in and out, or …"

Chris turned round to face him… "Or I go down for murder. Trouble is, that means admitting Dominique and I collaborated in a criminal offence."

"Did Gabe Downs tell you *everything* in Ricky Thompson's report on the Phillips interview?" asked Harry tentatively, knowing the biggest problem had yet to come out.

"Well, quite a lot, about her sister Felicia's involvement, the Zandinis, the drug ring at the school, most of it, I think. I've not got a copy of Thompson's report yet, which, incidentally, I think I *should* have."

"Obviously Gabe missed out the most worrying part, then," replied Harry as he prepared to deliver possibly the worst news Chris was yet to hear. "Given the events of last year with DC Hackett murdering PC McPhail and his wife by setting fire to their house, plus killing others, and his admitted employment by the Zandinis, Roberta's utterly convinced there's someone extremely senior in our force co-ordinating the whole drugs thing from within." The two men stared hard at each other, Chris still standing, hands now on his hips.

"I hope you're not suggesting what I *think* you're suggesting, Harry, because if you are …"

Harry had no intention of holding anything back. It was futile, Chris was finished anyway. "It *does* point to her, sir, if it's not the chief constable, the assistant, or deputy chief constables, and I can't see Raymond Greaves or Tim Casey being involved, can you? Who the hell else is there that's *extremely* senior? Considering Greaves spends most of his time outside the job singing with his church choir, and Tim Casey's anti anything intoxicating outside of coffee and fruit-flavoured vapes, I don't see there's anyone else that could fit the bill, do you?" Hitchings had grown horribly pale and was now gripping the back of his chair for support. Harry continued…

"Our Chief Constable Dominique du Guarde has always had something … *uncomfortable* about her, Chris – *you* know that. I seem to remember you telling me last year if I even *thought* like Gene Hunt, she'd have your balls hanging from the rear-view mirror of her turquoise Bentley. *Now we know why.*"

Hitchings moved his hands slowly round the top of his chair and eased himself gently back down onto it. Not only was he finished, career gone, reputation shredded, pension up in smoke … it was seriously appearing as though he'd collaborated with an officer who'd been doing a lot more than fiddling the books. *He would almost certainly go down for that.*

Harry had no idea what to suggest to him. The way Chris was looking right now, knowing what they both knew and the unspoken possibility their chief constable was in fact a *Zandini*, he was seriously concerned for his mental health. He decided there was only one rational thing he could suggest… "Chris, listen to me. Give me your mobile, I'll text you my number, just in case you need a friendly face to talk to." Hitchings looked momentarily surprised before handing it over. Harry found his details and connected their phones before handing it back. "You need to speak to someone official, and *fast*. Never having been in this situation before, as I see it, you only have one of three choices. The Assistant Chief Constable Raymond Greaves, the Deputy Chief Constable Tim Casey, or go straight to the IOPC (Independent Office for Police Conduct). In view of Greaves and Casey working so closely with Dominique, I would recommend the IOPC – they will at least be impartial – *hopefully*. And of course you'll need to see the fed rep."

He didn't reply. The current Chief Superintendent, Christopher Hitchings, barely nodded in silent accord. He wasn't sure any of those people were going to be required. Not today, not tomorrow, not ever. *Not even Harry…*

THIRTY-ONE

CLAYTON HOUSE GRAMMAR SCHOOL KIRKDALE CUMBRIA

7.30. A.M. TUESDAY 18TH APRIL 1995
SIXTH FORM (YEAR 12)

Charlotte's radio alarm was blaring out The Boo Radleys latest hit – a song about waking up because it's a beautiful morning. She liked it a lot but was half asleep and had no desire to wake up, let alone *get* up. At sixteen, a lie in was infinitely preferable to a school day, especially when you've been used to a two-week Easter break. She'd actually spent ten of the fourteen days at home as her parents weren't travelling, not that it had been much cop with her dad working the stock market in his study, and her mother running around town organising all her charity events. If she hadn't been able to bus it over to Emily's, the break would have been a disaster. At least that Ros Lisle lived on the other side of town so wasn't hanging round Em for the holidays. Now she was back in her school bedroom on the first day of term, staring at the ceiling, definitely *not* wanting to get up.

She let the song finish, stretched a hand out to hit the flat, square power button on the top of the radio and dragged herself out of bed. If it kept playing she'd be there all day listening and drinking coffee, and there'd be no chance of her making it to last lesson, let alone assembly. Double swimming was definitely out that morning anyway, given the building it was housed in had mysteriously burnt down two weeks before end of term. *Very* convenient, she'd thought. It had become increasingly clear her school was struggling for money and the Dean sisters were now digging deep trying to increase finances any which way they could. Burning down the swimming pool complex was dangerously imaginative, but these events were also becoming glaringly obvious and hugely embarrassing.

She quickly showered and dressed, tied her hair back in a *very* loose ponytail, as there'd been so many teacher moans about long hair and safety (*especially in Home Economics which she hated anyway*), and made her way to the sixth-form social room's kitchen to grab some toast.

She made 9.00 a.m. assembly by the skin of her teeth, and brushing crumbs from her jumper, slid quietly into her row near the back of the hall. As she picked up her hymn book she could see Emily a couple of rows down on the other side, and irritatingly saw Ros Lisle was sat next to her with a tissue under nose as usual. For four years that girl had been a thorn in Charlotte's side, four years of simpering and clinging to her best friend, and she'd just had to put up with it. Em was far too nice to say anything, although recently, she'd seen some quite hot-headedness from her, mainly directed at rules and teachers she didn't like, even taken up smoking to help calm herself down. Smoking was not something Charlotte was interested in at all, and since achieving great GCSE results in English, biology, physics, chemistry and maths, was now taking these at A level with a view to studying medicine at University Medical College. She knew she was exceptionally academic with a quick bright mind, and had no intention of bunging up her lungs with tar or smelling like a bonfire. Emily, on the other hand, was all English language, literature, French, history and art, loved old sixties films with the likes of Natalie Wood, Brigitte Bardot, Sophia Loren and Mia Farrow etc., and thought smoking was quite sassy and chic. She also did *not* like tying up her long red hair any more than Charlotte did, and it had to be said, after four years at Clayton House, had changed enormously. Charlotte rather liked the fact that as *she'd* grown cooler, Emily had morphed into quite a fiery character. *Just goes to show how opposites attract and how personalities can reverse*, she thought as her fingers pulled at the hair band to loosen her ponytail further. But Em was still giving Rosalyn Lisle plenty of rope in the irritation stakes. One of these days there'd be enough of it to ha—

A dig in the ribs from one of her hangers-on stopped her train of thought… "Charlotte, *look – look at her face!*"

Donna King hissed, pointing to the back of the room where history teacher Karen Lewis was sitting.

"What? What am I looking at?" Charlotte whispered behind her hymn book, having turned to see what Donna was on about, as Miss Dean the younger struck the first chords of 'Morning Has Broken' on her well-used, now slightly out-of-tune piano.

Donna had 20/20 vision so was pretty sure Miss Lewis had a bruised cheekbone under a whole pile of makeup. *That* meant it must be black under there… "Can't you see it? Karen's had a whack! Reckon that husband of hers got a bit overly tactile with his fists. And she's barely singing."

Charlotte turned round again to where the history teacher was sitting and screwed her eyes up to see if squinting would help. It didn't… *It wasn't the first time she'd wished her eyesight was as excellent as Donna's, it would have helped considerably a few years ago when she'd been looking out the window at Fishy Phillips the night she'd been rummaging bins for a drug drop-off… It had been a huge relief she hadn't had the woman as her PE teacher since that awful second year…* "Well, if he did give her a smacking, I, for one, feel sincerely sorry for her. She may be a mega coke head, but nobody deserves *that!*"

Donna nodded. Then, holding her hymn book and looking straight ahead as if she was singing, said in a low voice… "It's interesting though, isn't it? I mean, it's common knowledge the man shoots at crows with an air rifle for fun – at least, we *assume* it's an air rifle, and now he's knocking his wife about."

"Hmm… might need to keep an eye on our Mrs Lewis," replied Charlotte, "in a caring way, obviously." Donna smiled slowly, pleased she'd been able to tip off Charlotte with something she'd like to know about, which in turn would be ten virtual team points for her.

At the same time whilst neatly picking up the refrain of 'Morning Has Broken', Charlotte looked over at Ros Lisle to see her looking adoringly at Emily. *Well, well, well. I think the little Lisle girl's got a mini crush. In fact, I think it could be far more than that…*

Sitting in biology, Charlotte watched her pen as she spun it over and under her fingers, her mind not on what Mrs Dennison was saying as the teacher busily chalked her way across the blackboard. Her thoughts were back in assembly that morning, on Ros Lisle, on the way she was looking at Emily … her best friend.

"… and so what would the blood-flow result be like if I chopped off Becky's head right now, Charlotte?" Eva Dennison stood with her arms crossed, waiting impatiently for an answer. "Charlotte Krane, are you *list*—"

"Sorry. What?" Charlotte looked up from her hands as her pen dropped onto the desk, rattling its way to the edge before rolling off and bouncing onto the floor. She bent down to pick it up and managed a weak smile that was not entirely meeting her eyes, and where a nervous tic had begun an irritating twitch.

"I *said* … what would the blood-flow result be like if I chopped off Becky's head?"

Charlotte looked shocked and glanced over at Becky Wright, who was full-on grinning… "I, er … the result would be … it would … well, she'd be totally dead, Miss!" The class erupted in laughter, and luckily, the bell went for morning break as the teacher rolled her eyes, quickly gave out homework instructions and wiped the board clean. Everyone filed out, and Charlotte was still gathering her stuff when Eva Dennison called her to the front.

"I expect more from you, Charlotte. You have potential, *real* potential, don't blow it. Whatever you're daydreaming about, it's really not worth it. You have every chance of straight As in *all* your sciences, not just biology – *so think on*."

"Sorry, Mrs Dennison, it was just a blip." She felt her eyes on the back of her head as she left the class, sure that staffroom conversations over the years would have proven many times it wasn't a blip at all. Charlotte was often 'daydreaming', although her thoughts were becoming less 'dreamy' and more uncomfortable in nature. In fact, just lately they'd been getting worse. She'd been shrugging them off, refusing to let them take root, but ever since Fishy Phillips had drugged her at Clayton Hall four years earlier, and her need to ensure she was never alone with the mad witch, a kind of self-preservation and cool facade had embedded into her psyche.

As she sauntered back up the outside steps to the sixth-form social room to grab a coffee and slump onto a sofa, she saw Emily with Ros Lisle under the arches laughing and queuing for crisps from the tuck shop. A sharp intake of breath and ridiculous pang of loss struck in that moment. She winced. The twitch in her right eye had begun to be more regular just lately, and it started right then. She swiped at her face, feeling intensely irritated by it. *For God's sake, get a grip, it's only bloody crisps!* But the memories of putting their school world to rights, stuffing themselves with bags of cheese and onion crisps at break times on the playground bench, (especially Emily's first year at Clayton with herself in the second), and initially *no Ros Lisle* ... it was haunting her. She wanted that back. She wanted it *all* back. She wanted to return to those early school days when it was just them, when she was Emily's early school guide and protector. But more than that, she wanted something extra, something *special*, something *dark* and *secret*, something that would bind them together forever, stronger than they were now, *stronger, harder* and for *always. Always and forever.* And there was only one thing that would ensure that...

THIRTY-TWO

ICU BASSETLAW HOSPITAL
KILTON HILL - WORKSOP
11.30 A.M. WEDNESDAY 26TH MAY 2021

After Sunday night's discovery of a woman's personal effects at Mike's flat, Sofia had tried her level best to avoid him. He'd repeatedly phoned her but she'd cut his calls dead when his number flashed up, and walked in the opposite direction or jumped into a lift at work so she didn't have to have 'the conversation'. It was fair to say she was hurt and confused, but more than that, couldn't understand why he hadn't been honest with her. If there was one thing that really made her angry, it was lies and deceit. Experiencing a good share of that over the years was one of the reasons she'd held back a little when Mike had first asked her out. Now, however, there was no avoiding him. He was standing outside the ICU, talking to the new security officer.

Mike briefly glanced at her through the window before saying something else to the officer, who then walked off down the corridor. Sofia moved to Charlotte's bedside to imply the checking of her monitoring equipment, although she *was* actually studying that as well. In the last few days all her responses had stopped completely and she was concerned, not just for Charlotte, but about having to explain that to her consultant, Mr Shepherd.

Mike now had his hand on the door handle and she instantly felt tense, knowing she was going to have to explain her behaviour and would probably end up accusing him of seeing another woman – or *women*. With a stern face, he marched into the room and closed the door behind him.

She looked up… "Mike I—"

"What's going on, Sophia?" He moved to the opposite side of Charlotte's bed, palms upward and arms out wide. "You've not returned my calls, of which there've been *many*, and you pretty much ran out on me Sunday night. I think you owe me an—"

"Who *is* she, Mike?" Sophia hissed under her breath, across the noise of bleeping monitors and the stillness of Charlotte's form. "I think you owe *me* an explanation – *actually.*"

"What? I don't know what you're talking about, what do—"

"The lipstick? The moisturiser? The shower gel? They're not *mine*." Her voice had raised high enough to cause concerned passing staff to slow down and look through the window – she waved them on with a nervous 'everything's okay' smile.

283

Mike smiled himself then, and began to stifle a laugh…

"*Don't you laugh at me it's not—*"

"She's my sis—"

"I've put up with this before and—"

"Sofia she's my—"

"—I'm not putting up with it any … *what* did you say?"

"I *said* … Hanny is my sister, my *sis*–ter. She's staying over at mine for a few days, that's all."

"Your, your … she's your *sister*?" He nodded slowly as a creeping, dawning flush crept up Sofia's neck and lit up both cheeks. She rippled her shoulders and then dropped her head to look at her feet for a few seconds, before hearing the laughter he could no longer suppress. Mike walked round the bed to where she was standing, tipped up her chin and planted a kiss on her forehead.

"I forgot to mention it because she'd turned up out of the blue early on Sunday morning after a major row with her boyfriend, and did what she always does – kips at her big brother's place for a bit. I'm sorry I never said anything; she'd gone out with a friend Sunday so I wasn't thinking about her. Not when I had *you* snuggled up beside me on the couch."

Sofia smiled weakly, now feeling a complete idiot. An apology was clearly in order… "I'm sorry, it's just that—"

"No apology necessary. It's entirely my fault, I should have said. Now … will you come over tonight? Hanny's with her friend again – we can make up properly then?"

He turned to her patient on the bed. "Without an audience…"

"Yes, of course … I'd love to. Whilst you're here though, I've been meaning to ask you about the security off—" But Mike was already at the door…

"I'll see you later – don't worry about the security, it's all in hand." With that, he was gone. At least, gone from Sofia's presence…

Outside the lifts at the end of the corridor, the 'security officer' was waiting for him.

"Everything okay?" she asked.

"It's fine, she doesn't suspect at thing. Well, not *now*, anyway but you'll have to be out tonight though, Hannah. We don't want any awkward questions – *especially about our parentage…*"

1.00 P.M. BELLA'S CAFÉ - KESWICK

Harry walked into Bella's holding his mobile to his ear trying to listen to the estate agent above the general hum of customers chatting and laughing and ordering their food, toddlers protesting loudly for the right *kind* of chips, and babies crying seemingly in contest with the chip-designing toddlers. Not *his* baby, though, who was lying contentedly in his ridiculously expensive navy Bugaboo 'travel system' that, at well over a grand and a half, had cost more than his first car. Still, he had to admit that so far it appeared to be proving effective, and Fran had said it was the best by a mile, so that had pretty much clinched it.

On reaching her table… *which he noted was in a corner farthest from the entrance, because as she often reminded him, it was nearest the loo and therefore more practical, especially since Jamie's arrival…* he sat down and turned the volume up on his phone. Mouthing 'estate agent' in an exaggerated manner, and pointing to his mobile, he automatically kissed the fingers on his spare hand and brushed them gently across Jamie's head before speaking into the phone. Meanwhile, Fran went to the counter to order coffees and custard doughnuts.

"Sorry about that," said Harry to his caller, "just walked into a café as you rang. Do you have some news for me?"

"Yes, Mr Longbridge. Just to confirm, it's Dave Barrett from Symonds, Barrett & Hughes. We wondered how you'd feel about an open day this Saturday for your sale, rather than individual viewings. It would be less time-consuming and we could take care of it all for you. You wouldn't even need to be there."

Harry paused for a moment, imagining Baxter doing a very good job of showing everyone round himself, and with a great deal of enthusiasm too, bless him. In reality, he'd be taking him to the park, and then leaving him at Kate's. She loved having him to stay, as did her two young lads, and he was working Saturday, anyway, so… "Sounds like a good idea. If you can make it for midday that would be best, and then I can leave the keys with my next-door neighbour, Kate Hoffman, at number thirty-two."

"Right, that's great, leave it with me, I'll sort the details and be in touch, bye for now."

Harry responded and ended the call, to see Fran had sat back down, with her face now buried in *her* phone. An increasingly larger, more incredulous expression was growing by the second, and just as Harry was going to ask her what was so intriguing, she looked up and slowly turned her phone round. He took it, to see an international news report from Costa Rica…

On Remand British Police Officer Found Dead

Escaped Ex-Cumbrian-Police-Officer Terence Hackett shot dead in private Dominicalito villa – Costa Rica

Ex-police-officer Terence Hackett was recovering in Durham's University Hospital following a violent attack whilst on remand in HMP Frankland. An audacious escape that is believed to have been aided and abetted by the prison officer who accompanied him, plus one other, followed a two-week hospital recuperation. British authorities have admitted they had no idea how or where he'd gone, until the Costa Rican police contacted New Scotland Yard today…

DEAN ROGERS – CRIME REPORTER SKY NEWS
PUBLISHED 25 MAY 2021

"Jesus Christ!! How the *hell* did *tha*—"
"*Harry!* Take it *down* a notch! Fran whispered harshly,

looking around her and checking the baby, who'd begun to stir at the sound of his father's excitable and overly loud voice. A few people at nearby tables were also looking their way, wondering what the outburst was.

"Sorry, but I'm just so … I didn't even know he'd *escaped*, let alone got out of the country. Honestly Fran, I don't know what the hell's going on lately, it's all kicking off our end as well."

"Oh, really, what's happening?" She automatically leant back and thanked the waitress as she placed the coffees and doughnuts on the table.

Harry now lowered his voice considerably… "The Clayton House, Skeleton Case. Forensics on the gun in the grave came back – *with Hitchings' DNA on it.*"

"*What?* But *how*? Hitchings is so damned clean he'd have to bathe in *olive oil* to stop squeaking when he walked!"

"*Ha ha* – very good!" He plopped three sugar cubes into his coffee and stirred. Fran raised an eyebrow and made the shape of a 'D' with her fingers indicating his diabetes, but he waved her concern aside.

"Once in a blue moon won't hurt, listen, Chris is—"

"You've got a custard doughnut in front of you Harry, that's—"

"Fran, just forget the big 'D' for a minute, *okay*? Chris Hitchings is in a massively serious situation. I had a long chat with him first thing this morning and quite frankly this is going to have to go to the IOPC. He's finished, Fran, and I'm *really* concerned. He told me the whole damning story of his involvement at an emergency call-out to Clayton House twenty-five years ago. He looked absolutely *terrible*. But there's more to it than that, much more…"

She lifted her doughnut off the plate, and before going in, said … "*Tell me everything…*"

2.30 P.M. RAMPTON HIGH SECURITY HOSPITAL NOTTINGHAMSHIRE

Miles was feeling guilty. This was not an unusual feeling for him, since it had been an almost daily occurrence whilst married to Charlotte. However, that was connected with his many extra-marital affairs – *this* feeling of guilt was quite, *quite* different.

Having gone through all the checks, and the locking and unlocking of doors from the hospital's entrance to the chair he was now sitting in, he was waiting in the visitors' lounge for Annie to be brought down from her room. Anxious, and with his tea untouched, his mouth was dry, his shirt damp, and he couldn't stop licking his lips or fiddling with his hands. There was no doubt about it – *Miles Peterson was shitting himself.*

And then suddenly, there she was. For a moment he thought he saw hope in her eyes as she stood at the lounge entrance, or at least something that looked like hope, only to be replaced by suspicion when she saw his own flick away and back again – *when she saw the guilty red flush light up his neck.* The seconds between leaving the doorway and reaching him felt like hours. The steely stare that now replaced the initial hopeful, and then suspicious, carried an unmistakable threat. He'd been used to similar looks, the steely stares, and evil glares that preceded so much that lay behind them. And this was exactly why he was going to be ending his relationship with her today. Their meetings over the last eight months had gradually increased in tension and decreased in number. He swallowed deeply, sweat beads popping across his forehead as she stood silently before him, expecting a kiss. *How on earth had she morphed into Charlotte so easily, and in such a short space of time?* He pushed himself up on the arms of the chair and stood up slowly, leaning forward, he avoided her lips to kiss her lightly on the cheek. She raised an eyebrow very slowly, displaying an unblinking, icy and threatening expression.

"What is it, Miles? There's clearly something bothering you." She sat down, her back ramrod straight; legs elegantly crossed, and flicked her now untreated two-toned blonde waves over one shoulder. Lifting her chin in defiant readiness – *she waited…*

"Annie, I've come to see you regularly since … since everything happened, and—"

"Well, you *are* my partner, Miles. Surely it's reasonable for you to do that, and for me to expect it?"

"Yes, yes, of course, it's just that, well, you *know* that I've been … I *am* trying to form a healthy and permanent relationship with Gina, and with Andrew now being a police off—"

"And working – *with – my – husband*…" she finished for him, icily.

He sighed… "Yes, and I'm a grandfather too, now, I don't want to miss out on that." He paused. "Look … it's never going to work, Annie, it could *never* have worked – not really. I think you know that deep down."

She nodded slowly, understanding *exactly* where she stood and what he was saying. Yet again a betrayal, and from someone she thought might have been by her side for the rest of her life. First Harry had finally left for that tramp, Fran Taylor, after she'd followed them up to Cumbria, and then even her long-lost son Michael hadn't responded to her visiting requests. *That* had hurt – *really* hurt. She looked down at his full cup of tea stewing on the table, and then back up at him.

"Drink up, darling … it'll get cold…"

THIRTY-THREE

CLAYTON HOUSE GRAMMAR SCHOOL THE OLD DUNGEON DINING ROOM

AFTER SCHOOL - 5.30 P.M. THURSDAY 11TH MAY 1995

Charlotte had become increasingly agitated with Ros Lisle. It had to be said, she'd noticed even Emily was now losing her rag from time to time because the girl was practically Velcroed to her side wherever she went. After four years, and a good deal of coercing and constant pressure from Charlotte, Emily Rowlands had finally decided enough was enough. It was why they now found themselves in the school dining room, *the dungeons*, waiting for Ros to meet them.

To be fair to her, Charlotte had noticed Emily's attempts to extricate herself from the girl's limpet-like behaviour for months, if not the past couple of years. In her view she'd just not been firm enough, which is why she'd had to gently *persuade* her to pull back, by about a million miles… Now at last, Em was seeing things from *her* perspective, which is why she'd agreed to this little after-school scare set up in the kitchens of the dungeon dining room.

It had all been arranged between them the previous afternoon on the Wednesday. Emily had told Charlotte that Ros had a dental appointment so wouldn't be at afternoon break. This had given them a rare chance to chat properly and make a plan for Ros to meet Em after school today, Thursday, before Emily went home, as Ros was a boarder. In their last lesson, Emily told Ros she wanted to share a really big secret with her, and wide-eyed and almost apoplectic with gratitude and anticipation, the poor girl had lapped up the lie. Charlotte could tell Em felt a little guilty about it, but with Ros just not taking the hint that she basically needed to breathe for herself, Emily had reached the end of her tether, too, and just wanted 'it' *done*.

They had only intended to scare her…

All the lights were off, with the one at the top of the steps now covered in thick, wide tape. In the darkness, the room was large, dingy and airless, so different from the busy chatter and lit-up lunchtimes. The boarders were in their rooms or the library, and everyone else had gone home.

They didn't speak as they heard the door creak open at the top of the stone steps. In the silence, ancient, whispered voices could be imagined bouncing off the roughly hewn walls echoing through the darkness, past meals clinging to all its uneven surfaces. Oh yes … *it was a whole world away from lunchtime.* At first, they thought she might turn back – unfortunately for Ros, she chose not to.

"*Emily?* Emily, are you there?" *Silence…* "Where *are* you?" She whispered urgently, patting the wall to her right for the switch but unable to find it… "I can't see a thing, the light's not working. It doesn't feel right, sort of lumpy. Are you here yet?" She took a few tentative steps down the stone stairs, holding on to the heavy rope handle attached to the wall.

Charlotte sensed Emily was about to call out and clamped a hand over her mouth. They were hiding in the kitchen entrance, just behind the serving tables on the dining-room floor.

"*Emily*, what's going on, where *are* you?" She took another couple of steps down… "I'm not staying any longer if …"

Charlotte removed her hand, switched a small light on to her left, and then just placed an upright forefinger on Emily's lips.

"… Oh, a light's just appeared. Is that you?"

Emily dug Charlotte in the ribs and whispered, "*We'd better make our move or she'll be off!*" Charlotte nodded in agreement, stabbing a finger towards the area of the stone steps and back to their position, indicating the need to get Ros into the kitchen. Emily swallowed, running her tongue over dry, tense lips. She took a deep breath before speaking…

"I'm just over here, Ros. Come down the steps to the serving tables."

"I can barely *see*, even with that small light you must have put on. Where's the main one?"

Emily thought for a moment… "The fuse must have gone, I think, just hold the rope handle and take each step carefully, I'm in the kitchen, there's a small battery light in here for emergencies like this."

Ros trod slowly down each step, holding tightly on to the rope as she went, itself a little wobbly when compared to a long wooden bar handle Miss Dean had promised to have installed, but so far hadn't. One by one she went, partly anxious about the dark, and possibly falling, but mainly excited that Emily had wanted to confide in her. She'd said it was something secret and *very* important, and she'd chosen *her* to share it with. On the fifth step, her foot slid forward, and although her right hand was gripping the rope, she put her left down to stop herself tumbling the rest of the way. She managed it, but let out a little cry of fright into the shadowy blackness that engulfed her.

"Are you okay, Ros?" called Emily in a low voice, conscious Miss Dean's office and the staffroom above were both close to the dining room. Most teachers would have gone home by now, but Miss Dean, her sister and one or two could still be working.

"*Ye-es*, just *ab-ou-t*," she called back weakly, "my foot slipped, I nearly fell but I'm okay." They could hear the grittiness of the stone beneath her shoes as she continued gingerly down the steps.

Emily winced. This was starting to feel horribly uncomfortable. She looked imploringly at Charlotte, who immediately shook her head, and, using a finger, made a slicing motion from left to right across her neck. Emily sighed, rolling her eyes and nodded reluctantly.

Finally, it sounded like Ros had safely reached the ground floor. This was confirmed when they heard her walking slowing across the flagstones, patting various tabletops to feel her way with only the tiny glow from the kitchen to aid her.

Charlotte silently pointed out the giant walk-in fridge to Emily, a sly grin on her face. She'd already found the key to the padlock in a kitchen drawer, and it was now unlocked. She sensed Ros was about to enter the room and ducked down in the corner beside the huge double range cooker, shadows hiding her form. Emily turned from watching her hide, to the door where Ros was creeping in…

"Well, that was a bit of a performance, wasn't it?" stated Emily, as a small figure appeared, squinting at the poor light to see her 'friend' leaning up against one of the huge wooden tables running centrally down the kitchen.

"So, what was it you wanted to talk to me about?" she asked, smiling tentatively, "it sounded very important."

"*Well* …" Emily started to walk slowly towards the huge fridge, head slightly bowed and hands clasped in front of her, elbows out, as if she was thinking carefully… "The thing is, Ros, I need to …" on reaching the fridge, she opened the door, the light came on and she peered inside at the shelves as if they were super interesting…

"Ooh, look! They've got huge blocks of that lovely strong cheese! Shall we have some? We could make a sandwich!"

"What? Aren't we a bit old for midnight feasts?" replied Ros, sounding confused now. "And it's not even *midnight*!"

"No, I know, but I absolutely *love* this cheese and they never serve it up to *us*." She stood back from the fridge and made a big thing of looking up and down the countertop as if searching for something. "I've just spotted a knife block down the end…" She walked towards it and called over her shoulder…. "Get the cheese can you, Ros? It's right in front of you on that middle shelf a few feet in."

Charlotte stood up from where she was crouched in the shadows beside the cooker, being careful to remain in the dark as Ros walked straight towards the cheese shelf inside the huge fridge. When she was far enough in, Charlotte shot out from her hiding place and slammed the door behind her! The two girls' voices egging each other on to be quick with the padlock and key were almost drowned out by the screaming and hammering from the other side of the fridge door where Ros Lisle was absolutely hysterical, her fear unmistakable, *the sound of their giggling and shrieking, the cruellest, most terrifying thing she'd ever experienced…*

ONE HOUR LATER …

The banging and screaming had eventually dissipated. Initially, it had been replaced by loud, guttural heaving sobs, intermittent with her begging to be let out. Emily and Charlotte were astounded nobody had heard the din she was making, but with the kitchen door shut and sat below surface level in a stone-walled dungeon, walls that were several feet thick, it had clearly kept them soundproofed. Eventually, it was only quiet whimpering that came from the other side of that fridge door, until even that stopped.

They hadn't left, not for a moment. They weren't so stupid as to do that. They knew it was imperative she wasn't in that fridge for too long, and never intended for…

"Okay, that's enough, it's been over an hour. We need to let her out," said Emily, who was now feeling anxious and somewhat guilty.

"Do we *have* to?" groaned Charlotte, exploring cupboards and enjoying the situation far too much for her friend's liking.

Emily shot her a 'be reasonable' stare, grabbed the key and jumped down from the wooden table she'd been sitting on.

"Don't worry, she'll be *fine*. I swear I can still hear her whining," said Charlotte, walking slowly back to lean casually against the table, arms crossed, although not looking *quite* as confident as she sounded.

Emily pulled the door open and *gasped*! Hand flying to her mouth, she twisted round to see Charlotte's hanging open, then back to see Ros Lisle lying slumped on the floor, not moving, barely appearing to be breathing, and *terrifyingly quiet*.

"Oh – my – *God*! What have we *done*?" Emily was now leaning over Ros, shaking her shoulders. "Ros, Ros, wake up! Wake *up*!"

"But, but, she was ... she was only talking a litt—"

"Well, she's not *fucking* talking *now*, *is* she?!"

Charlotte started walking slowly and then more quickly towards the lifeless body of Ros Lisle inside the fridge, the actually now noticeably very cold, and as had become apparent, oxygen-reduced fridge. "It must be faulty. I've seen TV dramas where people were fine for *hours* inside a fridge! This can't be bloody happening – for *fuck's sake*!"

Emily turned Ros over on to her back. Her lips were grey, and limbs limp, but then, thankfully, before she started trying CPR, she heard a tiny gasp. "Oh, Christ, thank *God*! *Thank you, thank you, thank you, God!!* Help me sit her up and get her out of this damned fridge, we need to get some warmth into her."

They dragged her out of the gigantic cold box and into the kitchen. Emily ran to the wall and hit the switch – light bulbs popped all along the ceiling, flooding the room with light. She spun the hot tap round till the water fell steaming into the sink and slapped tea towels in the warm water, soaking them, ringing them out and then pressed them around Ros's face and neck. The girl started to mumble a bit, but there were no coats or blankets in the kitchen, and they weren't wearing anything that could help, either.

"We've got to get her out of here and back to her bedroom – *now*!" said Emily as she dabbed the hot towels around Ros's head, arms and hands, replacing them each time they cooled off. She was beginning to move her limbs slightly and open her eyes, but when she saw them looking down, her face broke into a terrified expression and her mouth opened to scream. Charlotte put her hand across it and pressed down.

"*Don't* do that, Ros … it's really *not* a good idea."

"Charlie, what are we going to do? She's not going to keep quiet about this, an hour was too long. We shouldn't have left her more than five minutes. We shouldn't have done it at *all*…"

"Ros . . ? I'm going to take my hand away now and we're going to get you to your bedroom, *okay*?" The girl nodded – eyes wide with fright.

"You *sure* . . ?" She nodded again. Charlotte slowly peeled her hand away from her mouth, watching her all the time.

"I'm *so* sorry, Ros," Emily choked back tears, "I just wanted to reduce your clinginess; it was beginning to get suffocating. I have *tried* over the years, but you just wouldn't take the hint. I thought … I *hoped* you might at least go off me after this, but I *never* meant for—"

"That's enough, Em. She's not in any fit state for a conversation at the moment. Let's just get her up to her room – preferably without being seen and asked any awkward questions."

* * *

300

The evening before hadn't been easy, but they'd managed to get Ros back to her bedroom, put to bed with a hot water bottle, and found an extra couple of blankets to cover her duvet. She'd complained of a terrible headache and the start of a migraine, so they'd given her some paracetamol and left the packet on her cabinet plus a glass of water, in case she'd needed them later. It was gone 6.30 p.m. by the time they'd left her room, both apologising and praying she wouldn't say anything. Emily went home, and Charlotte had gone back to the sixth-form kitchen, in theory, to microwave herself a ready meal.

There had been several others in the social room where she'd taken her dinner on a tray to eat on one of the sofas, but she'd barely touched it. A strange atmosphere had hovered in the air that night. The social room was shared with the post-sixth-form college as well, and yet nobody was talking. It felt like they were all looking at *her* – including Jackie Squires. If that had made her feel uncomfortable given she was Sandi Lisle's best friend, and Sandi was Ros's older sister, it was nothing compared to what happened the following morning in assembly when the fire alarm had sounded. That was because at 9.15 a.m. precisely ... Rosalyn Jane Lisle was found in the music room – *hanging from a beam.*

THIRTY-FOUR

INCIDENT ROOM
KIRKDALE POLICE STATION
9.00 A.M. THURSDAY 27TH MAY 2021

There had been rumblings about the forensic reports on the gun found in the skeleton grave. Everyone was tense, disbelieving of what they'd heard about the DNA results – but DNA rarely lied, although every officer in that building was praying this time it was skewed. Harry had no intention of bringing the subject up, but was acutely aware gossip was already spreading throughout the station, although hadn't a clue who'd started it. Given that Gabe was Hitchings' brother-in-law, he couldn't see it being him. Officially, Hitchings was taking some time off, a long holiday due to stress… However, everyone knew their chief super had already been suspended, following, as yet, inconclusive evidence.

There was also, of course, the news of Terry Hackett being busted out of the University Hospital of North Durham and his escape to, and murder in, Costa Rica of all places. This shock had been a useful distraction, however, from the even heavier bombshell of Chris Hitchings' apparent involvement with their Skeleton Case. Although Harry, of course, knew the finer details pointed to otherwise.

As various points were discussed on the cold cases, one was raised by Suzanne about one of the missing girls, Denise Fraser…

"We still haven't uncovered anything through contacting old pupils and teachers where we could locate them, or her family. I don't know why, but I feel I should go back and speak to Clayton House's headmistress, Sandra Wainright, see if she can tell me anything more about her. Last time I felt I was being hurried a bit, she kept looking at the clock and now I think about it, was a bit edgy, too. I can't quite put my finger on it but—" An incoming call had Gabe Downs getting up and going to his desk…

"DC Downs. Yes … yeah, we did, hold on …" he got a pen and paper in front of him. "Go on … red MGB convertible … plate? … Hotel – Oscar – Tango – Romeo – Oscar – Bravo – 1. Are you absolutely sure about the driver being …? No chance of … no, no, I understand, okay. No, no, that's fine, I'll relay that, thanks for letting us know. Bye." He put the phone down and rejoined the meeting.

"Gabe? Anything?" asked Harry impatiently. His thoughts now switching to Molly's red car boot water vision, giving it star billing and the realisation he'd yet to mention it to Suzanne.

"That was Andrew. He's out in the area car with uniform for some basics and they took an emergency traffic incident twenty minutes ago. Roberta Phillips' MGB has just been pulled out of Lake Buttermere, looks like she came off the B5289 just outside the village. She was still in it, confirmed dead at the scene."

Rick's face was crestfallen. He'd really liked Roberta… "What *exactly* did he tell you, Gabe? Were there any notable skid marks, is the car damaged from behind to indicate being rammed?"

"Didn't say, mate, the crane had just pulled the car out and she was still strapped in behind the wheel. Till forensics and pathology do their stuff…" He hunched his shoulders and held palms upward to indicate due process was needed to discover the details.

"*And* the recovery garage's report, of course," added Rick, looking at him pointedly.

"Of course, naturally the garage needs to give it the once over, too," replied Gabe, holding his eyeline.

Harry and Suzanne exchanged glances from either side of the whiteboard at the front of the room. There was definitely an electric current running between those two – they'd both instantly felt it. "It'll be thoroughly examined, Rick. I'll make absolutely sure of that," said Harry. He also made a mental note to mention Molly's water vision to Suzanne, and also the second one about the possible body in a well out at Clayton Hall. Maybe he'd be able to convince her of Molly's … *abilities*.

Suzanne drew a black cross on Roberta's whiteboard

photo, and decided to change the subject before the atmosphere became too uncomfortable. She pointed to another photo on the board – that of the woods bordering Clayton House School field – and tapped it with her hand.

"I organised a dog search of the woods yesterday regarding a possibility that either or both Jacqueline Squires and Denise Fraser are out there. Karen Lewis as well, come to that. However, they didn't turn up anything. If there *are* any bodies deep down, we're going to need ground-penetrating radar first to try and detect them before engaging the diggers."

"There was Stevens, the caretaker-cum-groundsman who disappeared as well, Sarge," said Gabe, only raising his hand *after* speaking.

Suzanne let the discourtesy go… "There was no missing persons report filed for Ron Stevens, and as we've ascertained, the skeleton is Sergé Zandini, I think any search for Stevens should be with regard to his connection to the murder of Sergé following intel from the now sadly deceased Roberta Phillips. She had no reason to lie about him being an accessory, so where he's concerned, I think we should concentrate on carrying out a search for a live person, for now."

Harry nodded in agreement. "I'll ask for clearance on the GPR and the excavators if necessary. Before we finish, there's something else I feel hasn't been investigated yet, and that's concerning the bag of thirty five pence coins found with the skeleton. It's been reported from various officers that when this bag has been mentioned, the implication has been one of betrayal. The head of Clayton House and Roberta Phillips both referred to 'thirty pieces of silver', yet we still don't know what that connection is."

Joe Walker raised a hand… "Clearly sounds like Sergé Zandini let someone down, Guv, and I reckon we should start with those who saw him last. According to Ricky's report from Ms Phillips on Monday, that was her sister Felicia Phillips, Ron Stevens, and the Dean sisters Veronica and Patricia, who ran the school."

"Has anyone had any luck in locating either of the Dean sisters?" asked Suzanne. "I've not heard a peep of information about those two as yet."

Everyone looked at each other, shrugging and shaking their heads with some calling out, "No, nothing, Sarge," in response.

"Well, I think it's time we paid Kirkdale Nursing Home a visit, then," said Harry. "Felicia Phillips may have Alzheimer's, but from what I understand of the disease, sufferers can have lucid moments, and she may just be willing and able to help us. Maybe more than we realise. Other than Sandra Wainright, without locating Karen Lewis and the Dean sisters, Felicia's our only available and direct link to that time."

Ricky raised a hand… "Roberta did imply her sister was very seriously affected with Alzheimer's, so not sure how much she'd be able to help. It sounded really bad because I think she would have kept her at home if she could."

Harry narrowed his eyes and paused for a moment. He knew that what people *said*, even good people for good reasons, and what was actually *true*, could either be two completely different things, or at the very least, exaggerated… "I still think it's worth a try. Can you get over there today, Rick, given you interviewed her sister?

"Yes, Guv, I'll get over there this afternoon."

"I'll give them a ring to let them know you're coming. Someone's got to tell her about Roberta as well, but make sure you've got a member of staff with you, and that they've cleared it with her doctor she's not too mentally fragile to receive the news. Okay, that's all for now, I'll leave you to it."

As everyone returned to their desks, Harry turned to Suzanne and said, "Can you wait behind for a few minutes? I need to share some classified information from our Miss Fields…."

11.45 A.M. KIRKDALE NURSING HOME CHESTNUT COURT, KIRKDALE

He got out of his car and stood looking up at the large grey and white expanse that crossed in front of him. It was long, with three gables and lots of little lead-lined glass windows that clearly needed updating or at least repairing. There were several bushes and small trees to break up the dark dominant slate, but a beautiful red Acer stood proud, its branches spreading out and upwards to greet an overcast sky.

Closing the door without turning, he held the key behind him, hearing the bleep as he walked purposefully towards the entrance. Inside, he followed the signs to the reception area where a dark-haired thirties-something woman dressed in a navy trouser suit sat busily typing into a screen behind a rounded oak desk. Her name badge read Ella Barton. With absolutely nobody else in the vicinity, she looked up as he approached.

"Good morning, can I help you?"

"Yes, hello, I'm here to see Miss Felicia Phillips. DCI Longbridge from Kirkdale Police Station has made the arrangements."

Ella returned to her computer and tapped across the keyboard several times before looking back at the man in front of her.

"DC Ricky Thompson?"

He leant on the reception top and checked out her ID badge. "That's me … Miss … umm … Barton?" He flashed his warrant and a big smile before pocketing the card.

Ella forced herself not to fall for the obvious flirty pass, and trying not to smile too broadly, replied… "Miss Phillips is on floor one, which is down there to the left and up the stairs, or you can take one of the lifts which are opposite the staircase. Room number seventeen. She may have a nurse with her at the moment, though, it's nearly lunchtime and she'll need to get her ready, so you might have to wait." She held out a security lanyard with his name and temporary-pass details, which he took and placed around his neck.

"Thank you – *Ella*. Nice name, by the way," and with that, he winked and moved quickly through the hallway to the lifts, pressed a call button and waited – *impatiently*…

Suzanne had just put the phone down as Joe walked through the door. It was about noon and he was in dire need of coffee and something chocolatey. When he saw the shock on her face, though, he immediately went to her desk.

"Suze?"

"That was the recovery garage, where Roberta Phillips' car was taken."

"Yes, and? What did they find?"

"They found a gold bracelet with a loose clasp."

"So? I expect it came off on impact when she hit the wa—"

"They also found cut brakes."

"Ah – not good. Do you want me to let the Guv know, or …"

"And the engraving on the bracelet says, 'To Gabe – Much Love – Denise.'"

"You – *are* – fucking – *joking* me?!"

Suzanne didn't know whether she was more shocked Joe had dropped an F-bomb, or that it looked like Gabe had deliberately sabotaged Roberta's car. Come to that, was it just coincidence the other name on it, *clearly the person who'd gifted it to him*, was someone called Denise? Could it be the missing Clayton House girl, Denise Fraser, or was she just jumping to conclusions? After all,

Gabe had been a Garda in Ireland until six months ago, so ... *surely* not?

"*Where is he now?*" stated Joe, interrupting her thoughts whilst steadily punching in Harry's internal number on the desk phone.

"I've got a horrible feeling he's driven over to Kirkdale Nursing Home." Rick had left an early lunch pasty on his desk and had now joined them, appetite suddenly vanished. "There's something horribly twisted about all this, isn't there." It was a statement, not a question. "He knew I was going to interview her this afternoon, he's obviously slipped out and—"

"721 to control, 721 to control, are you receiving?"

"Control to 721, yes, yes, go ahead."

"*Urgent! All available units to Kirkdale Nursing Home –* so far?" Suzanne spoke with levelled clarity into her radio and turning to him said, "Rick – *address?*"

"Yes – so far ..." replied Control, relaying an understanding of the need to await further information.

Rick pulled out his pocketbook and flipped it open.... "Hold on ... yep ... got it. Chestnut Court, CA12 4LS."

"*Repeating* – all available units to Kirkdale Nursing Home, Chestnut Court, CA12 4LS, that's *Charlie – Alpha – One Two – Four – Lima – Sierra.* Wait at location for back up – thank you, over."

"Received 721 – over."

"Thank you, over and out."

She clicked the radio off and turned to Joe, who'd been talking to Harry... "What did he say?"

"I've briefed him on what's happened and he's—"

"Joe, Ricky, with me – *now!*" barked Harry, who'd already been on his way down whilst talking to Joe, and was now at the office door. "Suzanne, I want you here for when Andy gets back – see if he's got any other info from the crash scene, and ring the nursing home, tell 'em we're on our way but not to approach Downs. Right, let's go – *and pray to God Gabe hasn't finished off the older sister as well.*"

THIRTY-FIVE

12.15 P.M. KIRKDALE NURSING HOME

CHESTNUT COURT, KIRKDALE

As Gabe Downs left the lift on the first floor, his mobile rang. When he saw who it was, he told them to hold on, realising the need to find somewhere private to take the call. Looking up and down the corridor, he smiled at a cleaner who was hoovering disinterestedly, and mouthed '*Gents?*' She pointed to the top of the corridor and he smiled, gave her thumbs up and walked quickly to the end, found it and slipped inside. After checking the cubicles were empty, he remained in the washroom area and picked up the call…

"Right, I can talk now, but don't know for how long."

"You know what you have to do, don't you? We can't risk this woman giving any details that could lead back to me, either. We don't know if she has anything definitive, but she *did* have an affair with my father-in-law, and her sister has already muddied the waters."

"Don't worry, ma'am, it'll be done, one way or another."

"Good. Ring me tonight when you're off duty. Now – *go*."

Gabe shut the call off and walked smartly out into the corridor. Next, he just had to find number seventeen which couldn't be difficult because he was already on the correct floor. The hard part was to avoid being encountered by anyone particularly observant and/or holding a senior position. He did at least have a security lanyard, but still didn't want his face to be memorable.

The room was a few doors down and Gabe was just about to knock when he heard talking inside. Two voices, one younger than the other. It was clear both ways, so he pressed his ear against the door.

"Is Sergé coming to see me today? I haven't seen him for *such* a long time…"

That's an older voice – must be Felicia, he thought.

"No, not today, Felicia, lean forward a little and I'll plump your pillows up for you."

Obviously the nurse, Ella said she'd probably be with the old bint…

"But … he said he'd *always* be there for me, *always*, and yet he hasn't visited at all, why? Have *you* stopped him? Has *Karen* stopped him?"

"*Noooo* … no, of *course* not. Maybe Roberta will visit today? She usually does Thursdays doesn't she, that'll be nice won't it?"

*Don't think so somehow, she's a bit on the wet side, and very cold…*Gabe grinned callously, still keeping an eye on the corridor. The next bit from inside that room, however, grabbed his attention big time…

Sitting in the corner chair and getting her phone out for a flip through social media, the nurse knew Felicia was about to start reminiscing. She always did if she mentioned that Sergé bloke, so barely listened to her then. Having heard the story *so* many times before, she could reel it off herself, but this time decided to tape it. The police officer booked in to speak to her today still hadn't turned up, and it was quite likely by the time he did, her patient would revert to being muddled and vague again.

Felicia had now fallen back onto newly plumped pillows … and into the past. It wasn't exactly difficult, because that's where she lived most of the time, and it was when she was at her most lucid, even if she was only talking to herself…

"Sergé said he loved me, said he'd always be there for me; take me away from my humdrum life at that bloody school, and living with Phil, the most boring man on the planet. We were together for six years, six years, till that woman betrayed my friendship. Well, maybe not friendship exactly, but it was me who kept Karen Lewis supplied with the white stuff she needed. I was mad as hell with Sergé too, of course, but never dared to show it. I wasn't about to ruin my only chance at escape, and wealth, all that wealth… So, I took my misery out on her … and all those bloody affluent yuppies. God, how I hated those snotty, overindulged little rich girls. Especially Krane … that bitch Charlotte Krane was my nemesis."

The nurse briefly looked up from her phone…. "Oh, I knowww, it must have been so *horrible* for you Felicia, I completely understand, I really *do* get it…."

Felicia remained glassy-eyed, staring at the wall in front of her, hearing nothing and only seeing the past. The nurse's attention had already returned to her newsfeed…

On the other side of the door, Gabe Downs was torn between what he was hearing and the need to have that nurse leave ASAP. His luck of no footfall in the corridor was not going to hold out much longer, but Felicia's memory rant was definitely compelling…

"I was so angry that first time in 1991, two years after we were an item. I knew she'd been with him. I just knew *it! I could tell just by looking at her, that's why I delivered the dead crow to her house the following day. Everyone thought it was an upset pupil because of her husband's nasty little bird-shooting habit. No.* (Sniggering laughter.) *That … was me.*

The bag of five pence coins, those thirty pieces of silver? They should have been left on her desk the day Sergé died. I didn't get a chance, though, so I threw it in his grave after the caretaker shot him that night he'd barged his way into Veronica Dean's house in the grounds. I'd loved him, but at the end of the day, Sergé Zandini betrayed me, and doubly so because Karen Lewis was taken into the Zandini family like she was one of their own. Her vicious husband never knew where she'd gone, and neither did anyone else. Only me. Only me…"

The nurse knew she'd finished because that's where Felicia *always* finished. She stopped recording, snapped her phone shut and stood up. "Are you ready for your lunch now, Felicia? I think you've got Spaghetti Bolognese today."

Gabe heard her walk towards the door, and decided, after the length of time from his arriving in reception and being seen by her now, it might be prudent not to wait for her to walk through it – even if he *was* there as Ricky Thompson. He dashed to the end of the corridor, hid round the corner and when he heard the door of room seventeen open and close, carefully leant his head forward to see the nurse walking away towards the lifts. Now. *It was now or never.*

Ricky and Joe held on to the door handles as Harry broke every speed limit on the way over to the nursing home. It was naturally done with great skill – he had after all been trained as an advanced driver in the Met., but nevertheless, it was a first for both of them to be narrowly missing vehicles and flying round corners with sheer … *wizardry* was the only way they could describe it.

"Boss, I know it's an urgent run, but I'd still like to keep my breakfast down." Joe was in the back seat holding the door handle – riding there hadn't been a good idea to begin with, his stomach never agreed with it.

Harry looked up in the rear-view mirror. "If you think *this* is fast, don't ever get in a vehicle with DI Taylor. Fran used to be my driver in the Met. and thinks she's her Formula 1 wannabe brother most of the time, and she hasn't even got an advance driver's ticket, *plus* … I've got no intention of letting Felicia Phillips die, particularly at the hands of one of my officers!"

As they got closer to the nursing home at Chestnut Court, multiple sirens could be heard in the distance. Harry tipped his left wrist to check the time – 12.20 p.m. They weren't far away, but uniform could get there first.

They pulled into the car park just as two patrol cars and an ambulance turned up with full blues and twos blaring. Harry rolled his eyes. They could have done without giving Gabe Downs a warning of their arrival, and Suzanne should've told their guys no sirens. He pulled on the brake and once all three of them were out of the car, sent two uniforms to the rear of the nursing home, left two on the door, and was about to take another two inside with them, when receptionist Ella Barton came running out. Harry's heart lurched at the expression on the young girl's face, praying they weren't already too late.

"Thank God you're here! He's got Miss Phillips in her room and—"

"Which floor, which room?"

"First floor, room seventeen – the lifts are at the end of the hall," replied Ella, eyes wide and breathing shakily, with one hand on her stomach.

"Ricky, with me, Joe, you stay with Miss …"

"Barton – Ella Barton."

Speaking to Joe, Harry tipped his head towards Ella. "Stay with Miss Barton, see if she needs anything for shock from the paramedics, organise some uniform inside the social areas of the home and then wait for me to radio you."

"Guv." Joe escorted Ella to one of the waiting paramedics. Harry and Rick walked into the building and turned down the hall to the lifts.

Felicia Phillips sat up and stared hard at the man standing at the end of her bed. He looked vaguely familiar, but then all men reminded her of him these days…

"Sergé, you *came*! I've been waiting for so *long*!"

Gabe was taken off guard for a moment. He wasn't expecting her to speak first, or at all, really. This wasn't going to be easy. He was hoping she'd have dropped off after her earlier rant, but clearly not. His heart was thumping as he walked towards the bed.

"Come and give your Felicia a big hug and a kiss, it's been too damn long," she chided, holding her arms out to him.

Placing a pillow over the head of someone already asleep was bad enough. Trying to suffocate an old lady suffering from Alzheimer's who was missing a past lover and holding her arms out for an embrace was quite another. His hesitation was all it needed for him to be far, *far* too late – for completing Madam du Guarde's orders, and probably for his own safety, both from her *and* the law. He'd already thought there were sirens close by, although they could be anywhere in the vicinity, but …

She continued to hold her arms out as he stood there. Gabe simply couldn't do it. He walked over to the bed, and smiling, kissed her on the forehead then patted her shoulder before turning back for the door. After checking the corridor, he slipped out of the room. *Now to find a discreet exit...* he thought. Stopping for a minute, he rationalised his situation. *Hold on, I've not actually done anything wrong here. All that's happened is that I've signed in to interview an old lady, a constabulary-arranged visit with the home. Admittedly, it should have been Ricky's call, but I can say I was free to do it sooner than he was, so came along, that should hopefully quash any 'reception deception'. The old girl's in perfectly good health, and although I got my information through the door whilst waiting for the nurse to finish with her, I can say she told me that herself. The nurse wasn't there when I knocked. Nobody can link me to Roberta's brakes being cut, so if there is any police presence outside, I can still walk straight out the front door. No shit – no problem.* He took a deep breath, walked to the lifts, and with one arriving immediately, stepped inside and pressed 'G'. *The lift doors closed.*

The lift doors opened.

Harry and Rick flew down the first-floor corridor to find Felicia Phillips' room. With two of them checking both sides of the hallway, it took less than a minute. There was no sign of Downs. Harry was about to barge in to room seventeen through sheer anguish, as nobody had seen Gabe since he'd arrived earlier, but it was very quiet on the other side of that door. If the lady was okay, to go bursting in would be very upsetting and unsettling, shocking, probably. He knocked twice, sighing impatiently and shuffling his feet. Rick was itching to get in there just as much as his boss – both were twitchy, and just as Harry was about to enter the room, the nurse who'd been with Felicia earlier came hurrying up the corridor.

"Wait – let me go in first, I know what's going on, that other officer, Joe somebody who's with Ella, he told me. Didn't want me coming up here but I told him I had to. She'll be scared if two burly police officers go charging in."

Ricky stifled a smile, even in that tense moment. At a slight five ten with sandy hair and a zero six-pack, if there was one thing he definitely couldn't be described as – it was burly.

The nurse let herself into the room and immediately went to Felicia's bedside. She was lying on her back, with her mouth open, and appeared to be sleeping. She leant over her frowning, picked up her wrist, then swung round to Harry and Rick who were right behind her, anxiety and distress flooding her face.

"Oh my God … she's dead!"

The lift doors opened.

Gabe Downs walked out onto the ground-floor corridor and into a barrage of blue where he was surprised to be instantly apprehended. He made it clear vocally and physically he hadn't done anything wrong, questioning their actions, pulling his arms away from being restricted, and suddenly aware his banging heart was threatening to burst through his chest. He was immediately hauled off down to the reception area and held there.

Joe immediately radioed Harry, who'd just got into the other lift on the above floor with Ricky and the nurse. When it arrived, Harry marched angrily down the corridor to reception looking seriously grim. On reaching Joe and the group of officers holding Gabe, he stood, seething, directly in front of Downs. Gabe immediately stopped struggling against the handcuffs and the two men eyed each other. The younger one spoke…

"What's going *on*, Guv? I don't get it, I've not—"

"You've not *what*, Gabe? Not *done* anything?"

Gabe squinted involuntarily, trying to think fast, brain teeming then freezing… *What does he know? What – the – hell – could he know?*

Harry kept staring into his eyes whilst telling one of the officers to uncuff him. They looked uncertain but followed his order. Gabe brought his hands forward and began rubbing his wrists.

"Thanks, Guv, I—" the sick realisation he wasn't wearing his ID bracelet and where it must have slipped off was painfully instant. He looked at the paler skin on his arm, the gap where the sun couldn't normally reach, the gap where that bracelet should be right now.

Harry dropped his gaze to Gabe's right hand and then flashed it straight back up. "*Missing* something, Downs?"

Gabe looked up and immediately tried to make a break for it, but was held fast by officers either side of him.

"Re-cuff him," said Harry, voice like granite. "Gabriel

Downs, you are under arrest for the murder of Ms Roberta Phillips, and the suspected murder of Miss Felicia Phillips."

Gabe's mouth dropped open… "*But … but she—*" he looked behind him towards the lifts.

"You do not have to say anything. But it may harm your defence if you do not mention when questioned something which you later rely on in court. Anything you do say may be given in evidence…. *Get him out of my sight.*"

THIRTY-SIX

2.30 P.M. HEADMISTRESS SANDRA WAINRIGHT'S OFFICE
CLAYTON HOUSE SCHOOL

Sandra's hand hovered near the handle for a few seconds before slowly pulling, until it sat there, gaping, like a large square open mouth – one she knew was holding an unexploded bomb. She gingerly reached into the drawer until her hand hit the back. Bringing out the piece, and laying it face up across her palm, the watch looked up at her, time stuck for over two decades. It really didn't look anything like a bomb, so delicate was it, that silver filigree band, she could easily turn it over with one finger to read the inscription on the back of the oblong casing.

To Denise on your 15th birthday 1995
Love Mum & Dad xxx

When Suzanne had rung half an hour earlier to say she wanted to speak with her again, this time in more detail about Denise Fraser, Sandra knew there was going to be a lot of digging, and not just metaphorically. *She was arriving in less than ten minutes.*

Sandra rolled the watch over and over through her fingers, not even looking at it. If there was a pound for the number of times that inscription had glared up at her, she'd be a rich woman by now. She didn't even know why she'd kept the damned thing, not really. It was sheer madness and she shouldn't have, but at eighteen the silver filigree had seemed so pretty, so exquisitely pretty. It seemed a shame to never see it again. Still, if she'd been thinking straight at the time, just had a bit of common sense, *it would be lying at the bottom of that well with its owner.*

She put Denise's watch down, took her own off and laid it on her desk, then placed the silver filigree band around her own wrist. She fixed the clasp. The sun was streaming through her window and the watch caught it, sending little lights dancing across the walls and ceiling. Sandra held her arm up to admire it. She'd always loved that watch when Denise had worn it at school all those years ago, always wished it was hers. Well, now it was, but of course she could never—

"DC Moorcroft to see you, Mrs Wainright." The knock on the door had clearly not been loud enough; either that or she'd been lost in another world entirely, more likely another *decade*. Sandra snatched her arm down from the air to behind her back, away from where her gaze had been lost in its sparkling entrancement, away from DC Moorcroft's now suspicious eyes…

"Oh, I, Suzanne … yes, of course. Please … sit down." Sandra sat back down in her leather swing chair, carefully keeping her hand below the desk, but Suzanne's instincts were clearly aroused. She didn't sit down. She remained standing, looking at the leather-strapped watch lying redundant on her old head's desk. Sandra followed her eyeline and without thinking brought her hand up to remove it, then a sharp intake of breath escaped from her as Denise's watch was in full view of them both.

"You seem uptight, Mrs Wainright, upset even. Can I see that watch, please?" With Gabe Downs' recent ID bracelet now being a piece of major evidence in Roberta's murder inquiry, jewellery was at the forefront of her mind and Sandra was behaving extremely oddly.

"I – it's …"

Suzanne held a hand out across the desk – her expression stern. "*Please?*"

Sandra's face had drained of colour the moment the office door had opened but she was now looking increasingly grey, adrenaline swamped her blood, her throat dried, and no matter how much she swallowed no moisture returned. *This was it then. Finally.* Shaking, she released the clasp and let the silver filigree watch slip onto the desk, falling face down, inscription on the back plate plain to see. It seemed to happen in slow motion, pictures of the past flashing through her mind.

Suzanne fished a packet of blue latex gloves and an evidence bag from her jacket pocket, opened the gloves and put them on before picking up the silver watch.

Sandra was looking as guilty as hell, but as yet, Suzanne didn't know why. After reading the words, she took out her mobile and photographed the inscription on the back, turned it over in her hand and did the same with the front, before placing the watch in the evidence bag and into her pocket. Sandra sat motionless.

"Is this Denise *Fraser's* watch?"

She remained silent. The woman who was her headmistress less than ten years ago now represented something else entirely. No longer was she someone she'd admired and respected, although plenty of her contemporaries hadn't, the ones who had no real academic interest and were only there because of their parents' ability to pay. No, Mrs Wainright had suddenly become someone else altogether. It was as if all Suzanne's years at Clayton were an illusion, which felt really quite surreal, but also felt really sad...

"Mrs Wainright, when I came to see you a week ago regarding the skeleton found in the school grounds, the missing teacher and two missing girls from 1995, you implied you barely knew Denise Fraser. You couldn't even remember her name at first. Why are you now in possession of a watch engraved as a gift from parents to a fifteen-year-old girl called Denise, dated that very year?"

Sandra opened her mouth as if she were about to say something but then changed her mind and closed it again. She leant forward onto her desk, face in her hands.

"Sandra Wainright, you are under arrest for the suspected disappearance and murder of—"

"She *never* stuck up for her – for my sister, *never*! Ros was … needy, delicate. She just wanted to be liked, loved really. When Ros got obsessed with Emily Rowlands, Denise hated being dropped. They'd originally been best friends, and then that, that *bitch* Charlotte Krane—"

"Please stop there, Mrs Wainright, I *have* to caution you – we need to move this discussion to the station and conduct a formal interview." Sandra nodded, looking totally washed out and replacing her own watch back on her wrist, winced at Suzanne's words as she began again…

"Sandra Wainright, you are under arrest for the suspected disappearance and murder of Denise Fraser in 1995, you do not have to say anything, but it may harm your defence if you do not mention when questioned something which you later rely on in court. Anything you do say may be given in evidence. Do you understand?"

She looked up and in a quiet voice, said, "Yes, I understand." Truth was, she more than understood. Sandra Wainright, formerly Sandi Lisle in 1995, was fully aware of what was coming her way, and had been ever since that year nine's metal detector had gone off over the skeleton grave. When the bag of thirty five pence coins had been discovered, she hadn't been surprised in the slightest. She didn't know who'd thrown them in there, but they were a good analogical representation of thirty pieces of silver. She wished she'd thought of it herself, for the well … for Denise. Back then, one way or another, so many people had felt betrayed …

* * *

KIRKDALE POLICE STATION
INCIDENT ROOM
9.15 A.M. FRIDAY 28TH MAY

In the last twenty-four hours everything had been kicking off pretty spectacularly, which meant that everyone was stressed. The room was buzzing when Harry walked back in, giving his standard visual sweep. The meeting had started at 9.00 a.m. where Gabriel Down's arrest and charges had been raised, and the disgust of his colleagues palpable. Sandra Wainright had also been in custody since the previous afternoon, and was being questioned regarding the disappearance of Denise Fraser in 1995 – that at least was a win, from the point of view of detection.

Harry had needed to leave briefly to take a call, but had now returned to the front of the room. The stress of his officers was obvious, but given the levels of police criminality, both current and historic, he could also sense how unsettled his team had become.

Ricky Thompson surreptitiously slid a pasty and a pack of cards back into a desk drawer without taking his eyes off the boss, and shut down YouTube's 'Poker Tips for Kings' whilst he was at it. He'd not even looked at the video since logging on, anyway. The channel would usually grab his attention, but not today, not since the station rumour mill had been flowing non-stop. Obviously, he knew about Gabe Downs, but not—

"Where's Carlin?" barked Harry. "Surely, she's not still off? We're down a man as it is!"

"Here, sir!" Hannah Carlin entered the room through the door behind him – *late*. "Sorry I'm slightly late, I'm on a three to—"

"*Trainee* Carlin ... you are fif – *teen* minutes late. Please don't repeat that error!"

Hannah's cheeks flushed as she walked up the room and slid behind her desk into her chair. It was her first reprimand and she didn't like it, especially the sarcastic 'trainee' comment, even if it was true. But she wasn't going to respond negatively. Instead, a false, polite smile became tightly fixed on her face as she waited for the meeting to restart.

Harry was looking very serious, which was probably why he'd ticked Hannah off so strongly. He stood at the front of the room with Suzanne Moorcroft to his left, Ricky in his usual back-of-the-room position, Hannah mid-way, Joe and Andrew at the front. *Gabe Downs' new position was in a cell...*

"I've just had phone confirmation that newly promoted Chief Superintendent Judd will be temporarily transferring from Penrith next week, whilst our Chief Superintendent Hitchings has some time off." It was obvious to Harry nobody was buying the 'time off'. He and Suzanne exchanged knowing glances, Joe raised a hand and Harry indicated for him to speak.

"Sir, it's common knowledge the chief super's been linked to the gun in the Skeleton Case because of forensic reports. Rumour mill says he's been suspended, but there's also been some talk about the chief constable."

Harry thought for a moment. If what he'd just been told about Dominique du Guarde was the same intel, things really *were* in the brown stuff... "So ... what's the rumour mill churning out on Chief Constable du Guarde, Joe?"

Joe looked around the room – you could cut the air with the proverbial knife. "They're saying there's a warrant out for her arrest, Guv, that she's skipped the country ... to *Costa Rica*."

Andy turned round to get Hannah's reaction. They'd both met the chief constable during their first training day at Carleton Hall. Her fixed smile had completely vanished – she looked shockingly pale, more so than anyone else. He was wondering why as he turned back, trying to recall anything specific at Carleton Hall that might shed some light on that.

Ricky stood up. "Costa *Rica*? Isn't that where Terry Hackett was found dead in a villa after being smuggled out of the country?"

Harry knew there was nothing to be gained by trying to stall things completely. "There's a great deal to be sorted out, that's all I can tell you, but ... yes, it appears to be true, as is the chief super's suspension. But again, there's a great deal to sort out there, too, and it's above my pay grade to divulge any more detail on either case. I will just say one thing regarding Chris Hitchings ... he made a massively bad paperwork omission as a young DI in 1995, which has resulted in certain forensic results appearing a certain way in the Skeleton Case. However, do *not*, I repeat, do *not*, jump to any conclusions."

There was a good deal of shuffling and murmuring following Harry's response to Joe's question, not least Andrew's instincts that were shouting at him. He could almost *feel* the fear and heat coming off in waves from behind him. Hannah Carlin's breathing was anything but relaxed.

THIRTY-SEVEN

CLAYTON HOUSE GRAMMAR SCHOOL KIRKDALE CUMBRIA

2.00 A.M. WEDNESDAY 30TH OCT 1995

Charlotte's deep, dark secret to bind her and Emily together forever had not gone entirely as planned. Five months ago she hadn't realised Ros Lisle had been so depressed and anxious, but now it was obvious. It was the reason she'd been clinging to Emily so much, but Charlotte had never picked up on that, just found her exceptionally bloody annoying for the past four years. All this had culminated in Ros hanging herself after the fridge incident in May. Now here they both were, Charlotte and Emily, on the eve of Halloween, digging a grave in the thickly wooded grounds of Clayton Hall for the person who'd threatened to blab. The person who'd seen them half walk, half drag Ros back to her bedroom that regretful night. Unfortunately for that person, they'd decided it would be a good idea to use that knowledge for a little blackmailing project, and that dirty money-making scheme had been persecuting them both for the last five months. *Jackie Squires really shouldn't have done that.*

This seemed fitting then, given that Jackie, and Ros's older sister, Sandi Lisle, had seen her four years earlier, being carried out of Clayton Hall drugged and unconscious by Fishy Phillips and Karen Lewis, *but done absolutely fuck all to help*. Karma, Charlotte was discovering, could be very satisfying – if somewhat scary.

They'd spent what felt like hours digging in the cold and dark. There was barely a moon that night, hiding as it was behind unseen clouds, and all they had was a small torch. It had been a mammoth effort getting her there in the first place. Emily having secretly borrowed her parents' car (*illegally, as she was underage so hadn't passed her test*), meeting Charlotte in the sixth-form social room, carrying the body down the steps and laying it in the boot. Her dad's heavy-duty folding trolley cart had been an absolute godsend in the woods, especially with the necessary two shovels as well.

Earlier that night, Jackie had tried to blackmail Charlotte once too often. Their usual monthly midnight meet in the social room had not gone quite as she'd planned, well, not for Jackie Squires, anyway. Like everyone, Jackie knew Charlotte's parents, the Kranes, were notoriously wealthy, and so Charlotte always had access to money. As Jackie pocketed the hundred pounds and turned to go, Charlotte picked up a Le Creuset frying pan, and her blackmailer's lights quite literally – *went out*.

They rolled Jackie's tied and sheeted body into the makeshift grave, hearing the muffled thud as it landed on the soil below. Suddenly, it felt as though someone was watching them. Whether it was guilt or reality they didn't know – until, of course, the twig snapped. Their backs, legs and arms felt wobbly, and were aching like crazy from hours of digging, especially as they were shit scared already, not helped by body-coursing adrenaline turning their muscles to jelly.

"What the *fuck?*" Emily hissed, whirling round, eyes squinting in the dark, flashing in all directions.

"Calm *down*, Em. Stay still for a minute – *listen*," whispered Charlotte, not feeling calm at all, but emphatically determined to imply she was.

It was a cold night, but the digging had kept them both warm. Emily pulled a hand across her slick forehead and undid the buttons of her jacket, not noticing a loose one that was no longer hanging on its thread. She listened intently, eyes locked on Charlotte's. All was quiet now. Deadly quiet.

"Okay … it's okay, must've been an animal," said Charlotte from the other side of the hole. "We need to fill it in now, and quickly. Hopefully it's deep enough not to be dug up by dogs, foxes, badgers or whatever." They began shovelling the earth back into Jackie's grave, every load feeling heavier than the last, every pile landing with grim finality on top of her body, defining a secret bond inextricably linking them, cementing them together – *forever.* Half an hour later they were exhausted but done. *And then the dog barked…*

They both grabbed at each other. Two male voices hit the air at the same time as they saw a torch beam switching through the trees. They weren't too far away either. One voice they recognised, he worked at their school…

"Ryan? Where's that bloody dog gone now? He's always off somewhere he shouldn't be – *Jazz, here, boy!"*

"God knows, Dad. Mum's always saying the same when she walks him near the home – says that's a springer for you, always on the hunt!"

"Well, we'd better find him, or she's gonna go nuts and not let you night walk him again. I enjoy our late runs without all the other walkers around." Ron flicked the torch on to double full beam.

"Dad, she doesn't even know I'm *here*, you know that, neither does that crap stepfather of mine, *Toby.* I have to slip out the back door with that dog every time. *Jazz! Jazzy, where are you? Come here!"*

"Hmmm… she had no right making you take that man's name, son. I'll not forgive her for that, not ever. You're a *Stevens* – not a bloody Jacks!"

Charlotte and Emily had barely breathed since hearing their school caretaker speak. *Had he seen them?* From their nearby hiding place inside a den of thick bracken and branches that thankfully some kids must have been playing around with, they could hear every word. Not that they wanted to, they'd only just remembered to bring the cart and shovels and it was horrible in there. Emily was convinced she had a spider in her bra… Peeping through the gaps in the greenery, they saw Ron Stevens and his son, Ryan Jacks, standing beside the patted-down earth that covered Jackie Squires' body. Ron was holding the torch and sweeping the ground slowly, still calling for the dog. Suddenly, Ryan grabbed his arm.

"What's that?" He pointed to the long shape of newly turned earth at their feet, and taking the torch from his dad, aimed it more closely at the area directly in front of them.

"If that's what I think it is, we should get out of here – and *fast*!"

Ryan bent down and picked up something small, turning it over and over in his gloved hand. "We will, Dad, we will, just wondering what this is, that's all."

Ron looked at the button lying on his son's glove and gasped. The unmistakably distinctive and entwined C and H that decorated all Clayton House coat buttons looked up at him. His jaw dropped. "I've had enough trouble with that school this year, drugs, guns, murder, police crawling all over the place, and now *this*? Christ knows who's in *that* one. It's time for me to move on, son."

"Yeah, it's definitely a Clayton House button, and what looks suspiciously like a grave." He flashed the torch all over the freshly dug soil. "Might just keep a hold of this, though, Dad, never know when a bit of evidence might come in useful." Ryan pocketed the button and then smiled as an excitable young spaniel came running out of the trees. "Well, well, well, you little *bugger*! Come on, you're going on your lead till I get us back to the car."

Charlotte and Emily waited until they could no longer see the torch beam or hear Stevens' and Jacks' voices before emerging from the kids' den. And it wasn't easy to wait. They were desperate to brush off their hair and clothes from spiders, their webs, and all sorts of other ghastly creepy crawlies. Finally, when they were sure the men had gone, they came out and shook themselves all over. Charlotte immediately flicked the torch up and down her own coat and then Emily's.

"That button they found, it's off your coat, *look*!" She pointed to the loose thread where the bottom button had been.

"Damn! I've been meaning to fix that for ages. I should have worn one of my own jackets, but my school one was hanging up in the hall and it was quicker to just grab it and go."

"Well, hopefully it won't come to anything. Stevens hasn't taken it, his son has for some weird reason. People are so odd, they'll hold on to all sorts."

"As long as he doesn't pay a visit to the local police station, Charlie, my *prints* will be on that."

As they laid the shovels in the trolley cart and took it in turns to pull it back to the car, they continued their conversation...

"Stevens looked dumbstruck when he saw your button, though, didn't he? And all that stuff he said about drugs, murder and police at the school! Reckon he was heavily involved in all of that with coke-head Lewis and old Fishy Phillips."

"I'm bloody sure of it, always thought he doubled for Uncle Fester anyway – *creepy as hell.*"

Once they'd got back to the rough parking area, collapsed the cart down and lifted it into the boot with the shovels, both hugely relieved at being all in one piece, they finally got in and locked all the doors. *It was a little after 4.30 a.m.*

"I'm totally and utterly shattered. I could sleep for a month," said Emily, leaning back on the driver's headrest.

"Snap. And I know food's the last thing I should be thinking of, but for some reason I'm absolutely bloody starving!"

Em turned her head sideways and pointed to the glove compartment. Charlotte looked at her. "You haven't…"

"Go on, open it."

Charlotte pushed the button to release the catch, and when the door fell down, two packets of cheese and onion crisps sat there waiting. A smile spread across her face as she handed one to Emily. "You're unbelievable, Em, you really are *bloody* unbelievable."

"I know you too well, Charlie. I know *us.* Any kind of stress, and out come the cheese and onion, there's some more in the back." She pulled open her packet and got stuck in. Charlotte did the same as they both stared out through the window.

"It's been a helluva year, Em. Not sure how we got here to be honest but I can't go through any of that again. After two burglaries in June, one week after the other – at least, that's what we were *told* they were by Miss Dean Senior, clearly after Ron Steven's comment, they were a lot more than that. Police sirens and helicopters everywhere, bloody great big search lights over the woods, and I swear I heard a gun going off one night."

Emily's hand hovered by her mouth before shovelling in some more crisps. "A gunshot certainly fits in with what Stevens said. It's at times like that I'm glad I don't board, Charlie."

Charlotte turned to her, "I know, but I still wish you did. Better not come in tomorrow, though, take a sickie – I'll do the same."

CLAYTON HOUSE GRAMMAR SCHOOL
KIRKDALE CUMBRIA
THURSDAY 31ST OCTOBER 1995 -
HALLOWEEN...

For the third time that year, the fire alarm was screeching at full throttle, echoing ear-piercingly loud through the classrooms, ancient halls and corridors of Clayton House. However, it wasn't because of any fire. Nor had a drill been planned for that morning or the caretaker's cat become stranded high in the boughs of the larger of the two oaks flanking the entrance gates. No. For the third time in a few months, something very serious had happened at the once-prestigious school. One pupil had already been found hanging in the music room five months ago, and a teacher had completely vanished the month before. Now the rumour was a second girl was missing. Nobody knew how, and nobody knew why. For the second time, they didn't know when, where or how long she'd been gone. At least, no one was *admitting* to knowing anything about the current whereabouts and health status of the Clayton House pupil, or even if *this* one was still alive.

Beneath the sound of the screaming siren, girls began quickly forming orderly queues outside their classrooms under direction of their teachers. Everyone from year seven up moved methodically and autonomously through the building; a low buzz emitting from most; all meeting outside at designated areas of several large playgrounds. Everyone that was, *apart from seventeen-year-old Charlotte Krane and sixteen-year-old Emily Rowlands ...*

THIRTY-EIGHT

ICU BASSETLAW HOSPITAL
KILTON HILL - WORKSOP
10.00 A.M. MONDAY 31ST MAY 2021

Charlotte's arms began jumping. Then both started repeatedly brushing down her chest. There was nothing there, but whether there was or not was hardly the point – she was moving her arms, and above waist level!

Sophia was shocked because nothing like this had happened before. She knew she needed to record it on the GCS sheet immediately, and call in Mr Shepherd as well as the full healthcare team to help with analysis. It could be time for extubation or at least the beginnings of gradually reducing the drugs altogether. Recent blood tests before the weekend had indicated a drop in the Propofol that had mysteriously and stubbornly remained at high levels, keeping her patient very heavily sedated and not responding to anything much. It was amazing she'd not succumbed to bed sores, urinary tract infections, aspiration pneumonia, or blood clots. Any of these could happen to a coma patient, but Sophia and her colleagues had done everything physically possible to avoid any secondary health issues.

Standing over her now, Sophia saw Charlotte's eyelids flickering, which meant her eyes were moving quickly beneath them, but her arms had become calmer and had now returned to her sides. Sophia looked up at the readings. Her body temperature and blood oxygen were normal, but pulse, respiration and blood pressure were all slightly raised. This wasn't necessarily a concern, sometimes it could happen for a short while depending on what the patient was experiencing in a deep dream state. Fear or some other intense feeling in a dream may well have an effect on their body's vital signs and show up on the monitor.

She reached round the back of the bed and picked up the OBS chart from a hidden shelf. Storing it there since the last time the GCS report was removed had been a good idea. Taking a pen from her top pocket, she recorded the arm movements as a two, which was the highest she could give. She was so pleased at what she'd seen she wanted to write *ten* in the motor-response column. She filled in the other parts of the GCS and was just about to clip it to the OBS chart when there was a cough. Charlotte actually coughed. There was nowhere on the GCS report for that, but she wrote it on the blank paper she'd clipped to it. This was hopefully progress and not a chest infection. Either way – *it needed reporting*.

11.00 A.M. KIRKDALE POLICE STATION
KIRKDALE - KESWICK

Andrew thought about it long and hard before calling her over, and finally decided he had no choice. This was too big to be kept hidden.

"Sarge, I think you should see this." Suzanne stopped what she was doing and went over to Andrew's desk. She was surprised to see he was looking more than a little apprehensive.

"You okay? You look a little peaky. What you got?"

Andrew turned the monitor to face her so she could read the email that had just come in.

From: Undisclosed Sender
Sent: 31st May 2021 10.47 a.m.
Re: Clayton House School Missing Persons – 1995
To: TDC Andrew Gale
    andrew.gale @cumbriapolice.uk
Cc: DCI Harry Longbridge
    harry.longbridge@cumbriapolice.uk
Img.Att:

Guess what I've got, Mr Gale?

Well, actually you won't have to – just open the attached image and you'll find out.

I have reason to believe it belonged to your wife's estranged mother, and found it in 1995 beside a newly dug grave in Kirkdale Woods.

Newly dug as in minutes before I arrived on the scene, which is why I notified the *Courier* when I read the piece on the skeleton – that was a different body in a different place, of course.

Interesting evidence though, I think.

I may not be able to get you for what you did to me, but I can certainly cause some heartache none the less.

At least – I hope so.

He opened the image again for Suzanne to see an enlarged photo of a coat button with two letters entwined on it, sat inside a Ziplock bag.

Suzanne raised an eyebrow and blew a rushed sigh… "C and H – could it be Clayton House? We never had engraved buttons when I was there, but whoever sent that email is suggesting that button belongs to your Gina's mum, Emily Stone, and we already know she was at Clayton in the nineties."

Andrew shifted uncomfortably. He really didn't want his past involvement with Ryan Jacks being spread to the whole team, but it looked like he wasn't going to have much choice.

Suzanne waited, hoping Andrew would speak but he didn't, so she carried on. "Any idea who the sender is, given they're making an accusation towards you and the email addy is anonymous? He's also sent a copy to Longbridge, so if you've anything to say, now might be a good time to … wait a minute, that's not from—"

Andrew opened his mouth to speak as Suzanne's mobile rang. It was Harry.

"Guv?" She continued to look at Andrew whilst nodding to what Harry was saying on the other end. "Okay, yes, see you in five." She pocketed her phone. "*Is that from Ryan Jacks?*"

Andrew looked around the room. Everyone appeared to be getting on with their own stuff. He lowered his voice… "It's got to be him, it *must* be, but I don't want to have to go through it all to—" He gestured with his hand indicating the office, and Suzanne nodded.

"Yes, of course, the picture of the button though, and the fact that Jacks has it … that's not good for Gina if it has her mother's prints on it. It would, however, give us a good reason to get the diggers in those woods. The dogs never found anything and we didn't expect them to, but now we can bring in Ryan Jacks and hopefully get him to show us where he found that button. Vegetation will have changed dramatically in twenty-five years so it won't be easy, but ground-penetrating radar will help if we can establish a rough area, and I think we'll get the go-ahead for that now."

"So do I, Moorcroft," said Harry, having entered the office. "And I've just been to see Chief Superintendent Judd. He started today, and amazingly has agreed to my GPR request first time. It won't specifically detect bones, but it *will* show solid matter, and if there's been any soil disturbances. Bring Jacks in with this button of his. *Let's get this show on the road!*"

After Suzanne had arranged for Ryan Jacks to be brought in with his button evidence so he could take them to where he'd found it, or as close as possible given the time lapse, she had to book the GPR survey. Whenever that could be done, it would need to coincide with Jacks' presence. Clearly, Andrew could not be around when he *did* come in, and Jacks' email may even be considered a criminal offence, although that could open a whole other can of worms regarding Andy's past, so Harry would probably let that slide…

A quick check online had shown the bespoke Clayton House buttons were discontinued in 1996, so that at least alluded to the fact it was unlikely to have been dropped post 2001. Any pupil joining the school from September 1996 would have had plain buttons on their blazers and coats. And Jacks had implied he *knew* it had belonged to Emily Stone (*formerly Rowlands*).

The previous Friday, after Suzanne had arrested Sandra Wainright at Clayton House School for the suspected murder of Denise Fraser in 1995, her old headmistress had remained in custody for three days. It was decided Suzanne should not be one of the interviewing officers considering her previous school relationship, and to be honest, she didn't want to be. It had been a massive shock to discover someone she'd looked up to and spent her entire secondary school education with, as her headmistress, had killed a pupil in her teens, and at the very same school. Under questioning by Harry and Ricky, she'd finally admitted to and been charged with the involuntary manslaughter of Denise in July 1995, two months after her younger sister Ros had hung herself in the music room.

Sandra's statement had continued with the information she'd begun to relate to Suzanne in her office four days earlier, and, despite not wanting to interview her, she still wanted to read her statement... Basically, Denise Fraser, Sandra's sister Ros Lisle, and Emily Rowlands had all been in the same class and originally good friends, then Ros had become totally enamoured with Emily and the whole dynamic shifted dangerously off-kilter. Although Emily was kind to Ros for several years, her best friend, Charlotte Krane, definitely *wasn't*. Denise had done nothing to support Ros against Charlotte, mainly because she was hopping mad Ros had, in *Denise's* mind, dumped her for someone who wasn't interested … every day, for four whole years. It all sounded so stupid and childish a quarter of a century later, but at the time, and to those teenage girls, *the bond of friendship was the most important thing in their world.*

Ros had always been needy and lacking in confidence, and Sandra had always protected her sister, right from primary school. Her health hadn't been that great either and she'd regularly fallen prey to viruses which had made her appear weak and vulnerable. It was why, when Denise had let her down so badly and so repeatedly, Sandra Wainright, known as Sandi Lisle in 1995, intended to have it out with her once and for all. *Meanwhile, she would also blame Charlotte Krane for absolutely anything and everything she could that related to her sister.*

Denise Fraser had no clue she was attracting Sandra's contempt. She was far too engaged with the fact Ros no longer wanted to hang out with her – in school or out. So when Sandra approached Denise at a lunchtime break, asking to speak to her privately in the now burnt-out swimming pool building with a view to helping her get back on track with Ros, Denise jumped at the chance. However, once inside the disused and charred remains, Sandra's attitude instantly changed and she delivered a tirade of angry accusations at the bewildered girl, advancing on her swiftly as she retreated backwards. Open-mouthed and in shock, her balance wavered, until finally her feet disappeared from under her, tripping on some broken pool handrails from abandoned repairs years earlier.

It was an accident. At least, Sandra swore in her statement that it was, and there were no witnesses to disprove otherwise. Until they found the body and had a forensic pathologist examine it, they only had her version of events to go on.

Denise Fraser had apparently fallen backwards onto the stone floor, head cracking hard on impact. According to Sandra, she'd died instantly, what she *hadn't* done without help from Sandra … was to completely vanish from a ruined pool building thoroughly searched by officers at the time. There couldn't have been much blood to clear up, because even tiny traces would have been discovered. It may not have even been checked for blood, with no reason to think any crime had been committed there.

When Suzanne came to the last few lines of Sandra's statement, she clamped a hand over her gaping mouth as her eyes popped. In 1995 Sandra was nineteen and in the post-sixth-form college. She had her own car. The reason Denise's body was never found by police in the old pool building was because later that night she'd been bundled into the boot of a vehicle already parked nearby. Sandra then drove over to Manor Lane, through the huge gated entrance of Clayton Hall, up the drive and round to the back where an overgrown graveyard lay. There, in the darkness, save for a cloudy moon, she pushed Denise Fraser over the edge and into the depths of a very deep, very musty, and very narrow ancient well. But not before she'd removed her beautiful silver filigree wristwatch…

Suzanne let out the breath she'd been unaware her lungs had desperately needed to release, and forced her eyes up from Sandra's statement. *So … Molly Fields, local psychic barmaid – you're not so damned kooky after all…*

THIRTY-NINE

KIRKDALE WOODS
11.30 A.M. WEDNESDAY 2ND JUNE 2021

Two days earlier, on the Monday morning, Sandra Wainright had been released on bail. The judge had considered her no further risk to the public, and although it was rare given the charge, it had only been granted because of no previous convictions, plus she was required to be tagged, report to police at regular intervals and surrender her passport. She also had a disabled mother at home with no other carer available, and this may have influenced him in making that decision, but only because of no other criminal activity during her life before or since that date. She had also made a complete confession and been cooperative, which, with everything else going on, was a relief for Harry. Judging by Sandra's demeanour, it was also a relief for her that bearing a crushingly guilty secret of twenty-plus years was finally over. An appearance in Crown Court for sentencing would follow in due course.

Now, though, Kirkdale Woods was a hive of activity. Harry, Suzanne, the coroner and the GPR company, along with Ryan Jacks, who'd been brought in for location details and the surrender of his 'historic coat button', were waiting for the penetrating radar work to begin. Given that Sandra had stated Denise's body was at the bottom of a disused well in the Clayton Hall graveyard, the body Harry was expecting to find, if *any*, would be that of the second nineties Clayton House pupil, Jackie Squires.

On the one hand, Jacks had been quietly smirking because he knew he was right about the grave, even if it *had* taken him a couple of hours to find the correct spot given the intervening decades, but on the other, a little anxious he could be in trouble for not reporting his suspicions twenty-five years ago. However, it had been made very clear to him by the DCI in charge there would be no questioning on that score, providing the threatening implications in his email to DC Gale were as of that moment withdrawn, dead and buried. The irony was not lost on him considering their present location, and he quickly agreed.

It didn't take long for a shout to go up from the radar operator to say there was a solid shape about ten feet below the surface, and diggers were then brought in having already been booked on the strength of Molly's insistence that a young woman was definitely buried out there. In the normal order of things, sheer cost would have meant a delay on the digger until there'd been a definitive radar result, but Harry's shaky belief in what he called Molly Fields' 'abilities' was, despite his resistance, now heading towards concrete. Consequently, he'd told Suzanne to book them both together.

Less than an hour later, the mini JCB had uncovered a skeleton. Harry and Suzanne exchanged raised eyebrows – Suzanne's in disbelief and, it had to be said, a pang of overwhelming sadness, and Harry's in full and final acceptance. He may not *like* it, *but Molly was the real deal.*

On return to the station a couple of hours later, Harry and Suzanne were about to find Ricky Thompson had received news of Felicia Phillips' autopsy. Having interviewed the old lady's nurse at the weekend and listened to her phone recording of Felicia's 'memory rant', he'd now finished typing it up. It contained much of the 1995 events at Clayton House he'd wanted to ask Felicia about before Gabe Downs had got there first, and had matched up with what Gabe had said he'd heard through the door. Gabe still maintained he was waiting to go in and interview her himself because he wasn't as busy as Rick that day... As it turned out, the autopsy showed she'd died of natural causes, ischemic heart disease, and there were no signs of foul play. He was, however, still charged for her sister Roberta's murder, having partially cut her brake cables, causing them to finally perish, and sending her off the road into Lake Buttermere.

Joe had just entered the office, and as usual was getting his coffee fix at the machine behind Ricky's desk. Turning round, mug in hand, he grinned as Ricky surreptitiously slid a half-eaten pasty behind his monitor just before Harry and Suzanne approached them.

"DC Thompson, I don't know why you keep hiding your bloody pasties – for God's sake, man, just finish the damned things!"

"Sorry, Guv, didn't want to put you under any pressure, what with your diab … you know, you're not supposed to have—"

"Just *eat* it, lad, and stop worrying about my … *pressures*. Right now, I just want to know what's come in and what you've done about it since I've been out there in the woods digging bodies up."

Joe and Suzanne winced at their DCI's blunt description of his morning, and at exactly that moment, the printer churned out Ricky's report on the Felicia Phillips voice recording. He reached over, picked it off the tray and handed it to Harry.

"Pretty much covers everything that was going on at Clayton House in the nineties, Guv. Seems Felicia Phillips *and* the missing teacher, Karen Lewis, were having an affair with Sergé Zandini, and in anger, Felicia had chucked the bag of thirty five pence coins into the grave after Ron Stevens had shot him."

"Our thirty pieces of silver then?" said Harry, blowing a sigh as he read the report.

"Yep, and the Zandinis took Karen Lewis into their organisation, according to Felicia. Nurse said the only time she was lucid was when she went into a memory rant. Only taped it that day 'cos she thought it unlikely she'd repeat it a second time, and guessed I'd be relying on that information for when I went in to interview her."

"Matches up with Gabe's statement of what he said he heard through the door, then?" added Joe.

"Yes, it does, and Felicia's autopsy report came back today, too, natural causes. Heart, apparently. So, Gabe won't be getting charged with *her* death."

"Well, he'll be going down for the sister Roberta's murder," said Suzanne firmly. "That ID bracelet found in her car was definitely his, no question. Forensics can still get DNA and fingerprints on metal despite being in the water."

And right on cue, Ricky's phone rang. When he came off, he had the definitive evidence from forensics on Gabe's bracelet. He may have worn gloves when he tampered with the MGB's brakes, but his jewellery had quite literally *sold him down the river.*

* * *

3.15 P.M. CLAYTON HALL ESTATE GRAVEYARD MANOR LANE - KIRKDALE

Literally everything had been kicking off for the team that day. It was all coming in at once, but that was often the way at the end of an investigation. Now that Sandra Wainright had been interviewed, given and signed a statement admitting the unlawful killing and disposal of Denise Fraser, there was no reason not to immediately set up recovery of the teenager's remains. Then, of course, there would be the need to forensically identify them in order to make the extremely difficult and harrowing visit to Denise's parents. In some ways, it would bring them closure, but they all knew most parents, if not all, would hang on to everlasting hope that one day their missing child would walk through the front door. The same, of course, would be true for Jackie Squires' parents.

This had meant the day was turning into an exceptionally busy and quite difficult one for Harry and Suzanne. Suzanne especially had found it stressful to think of the three past girls from her own school as having such a terrible end to their lives. Initially, they hadn't even known about Ros Lisle because in 1995 her suicide had been examined and dealt with by police at the time. Nobody discovered that Denise's disappearance had been connected to Ros, and Suzanne found it incredible Sandra Wainright had managed to live with what she'd done for twenty-six years and keep it a secret.

The yellow and black tape around the Clayton Hall well was strangely still. There was no breeze in that graveyard, and the air felt somehow different from air everywhere else. It wasn't, of course, but the lack of natural movement had everyone speaking in even lower, more respectful tones than usual. The second forensic tent of the day stood empty … and waiting.

Just like the burial site in Kirkdale Woods, they had very

little to do other than observe and let the recovery specialists, and eventually the coroner, do their jobs. It was a tense wait to see if there was indeed a body at the bottom of that well. It wasn't likely the search would be futile, though, not unless Sandra Wainright was seriously unhinged, or someone else had removed Denise's remains. However, there was nothing to suggest either of those outcomes would be the case.

It wasn't long before a sad bundle of tattered cloth and bones was retrieved from the tightly enclosed, dark and musty walled depths – *just as Molly Fields had predicted…* Suzanne blinked a tear away until several more took its place, and Harry hesitated, worried as usual about being overly tactile or patronising, before awkwardly patting her on the shoulder. She pulled a tissue from her pocket. Quickly making use of it as their eyes met, she cleared her throat to resume a steady breathing pattern whilst barely managing a weak smile.

"Sorry, Guv. That wasn't very professional."

"Maybe not, Moorcroft, but I'd far rather have a loyal officer with genuine feelings than a rogue one without – so don't you give it another thought."

"Thanks – I guess that's a good point. It's just that … when you've gone through an important part of your life such as school years, sitting in rooms where all three girls had lessons, walked the corridors and playgrounds they would have …" Suzanne looked away, trying to swallow the lump in her throat…

"And your headmistress was someone you liked and looked up to as well?" asked Harry.

"*Exactly* that. I had really liked her, didn't know anyone in my year or out of it that didn't. It messes with your head, Guv – a *lot*."

Harry nodded and stood silently now as Denise Fraser's remains were carefully and respectfully removed to the forensic tent. He noticed Suzanne's breathing was still a bit shaky.

"Why don't you go back to the car, I just want to ask the CSI if there's anything obvious that determines it *is* actually Denise."

Suzanne gave a wan smile. "No, it's okay, I'll stay. I feel a friendly someone from her school should be here, another pupil, even if we weren't at Clayton together."

It would never cease to amaze him how this young sergeant would quickly resume her composure, even in distressing circumstances. She was only twenty-six, young enough to be his daughter, and Harry would have been super proud of her if she were. He *was* super proud. "Okay, well, I'll just go and ask Rob Davidson if he's found anything obvious, like a fracture on the back of the skull that would correspond with Sandra Wainright's statement. I noticed him arrive just now before he suited and masked up, then we'll go back to the station."

Suzanne waited whilst Harry spoke to Rob, and tried to console herself with the fact no wild animals could have got to Denise's body due to its position. Then suddenly the thought of rats occurred to her as she knew they could very easily climb walls and could quite possibly have found … "*Shit!*" Her eyes blurred over again as she cursed

angrily under her breath, "*Shit! Shit! Shit!*" then shivered
– *as if an icy wind had shot down her spine…*

When they got back to the nick, it was 4.30 p.m. Harry
called Joe over to Suzanne's desk where she'd got a coffee
on the go, and Ricky offered up a pasty owing to her
looking a bit washed out. She declined. It was true she'd
not had lunch, but she just couldn't stomach anything.
Harry, though … *he wanted that pasty.*

"DC Thompson, as you have a pasty going spare
behind your monitor, please chuck it this way, I'm bloody
starving. I'm also your Guv, so if you want to earn some
team points …"

Rick looked questioningly at Suzanne as if she was the
pasty police, and all things knowledgeable in the diabetic
dietary sense, but she merely shrugged. As Harry was
beckoning him to hurry up, Rick chucked the bag over
and Harry caught it one-handed. He immediately began
working his way through it with a look of pure heaven on
his face.

Joe grinned, although a little concerned Suzanne was
so quiet. She was the sensible one and would usually be
the first to make a comment about Harry's lack of diabetic
compliance.

Not many minutes later, Harry screwed up the bag,
binned it, and addressed the two officers he needed for
a special job. "Rob Davidson was able to tell me that the
skeleton in the well at Clayton Hall cemetery, although in
… erm …" he glanced at Suzanne, who was still looking

downcast … "in disarray, was definitely that of a young female. He said he's going to try and get the forensic dentist to carry out a detailed analysis tomorrow and let us know categorically through dental records, pulp DNA, and one or two other specialist methods, if it's definitely Denise. Same for Jackie Squires buried out in Kirkdale Woods. Until we get definitive answers, we can't go to the parents and tell them for certain their daughter's remains have been found. We *can*, however, let them know of our findings and that there is a *presumption* of death. They've all been waiting for over two decades to hear what's happened, and that's why I'm specifically talking to you two." He looked from Joe to Suzanne and back again. "If you feel up to it, I want you both to do the death notifications together." Suzanne immediately sat up straighter and looked as though she was about to say something but didn't. Joe wasn't all that surprised as he'd been asked before.

"Your ecclesiastical background with your father being in the church has given you a calm quality, Joe, and I believe you've had some experience with this." Joe nodded both in acknowledgement of the experience and acceptance of the job. Harry turned to Suzanne, whose face was surprised but calm.

"Yes, I'll do it. It's the least I can do for them, for my fellow Clayton House pupils. *I want do it – for both of them.*"

"Good decision – I hoped you'd say that."

* * *

Two days later, forensics on Denise's skeleton had shown her skull had one fracture at the back, crossing the occipital and parietal bones, which corroborated Sandra's statement that she tripped and fell, rather than being repeatedly hit with a blunt instrument or attacked from the front. Dental records cross-checked with the forensic dentistry exam showed several fillings that matched exactly.

Jackie Squires had similar dental findings and also head trauma, although she'd suffered two parietal fractures. Of course, they had nobody for *her* death … *yet*. As always, though, Charlotte Peterson's name hammered inside his head like a demented woodpecker. They knew Emily Stone was at Clayton House in the nineties because of Andrew's family connection. With the myriad of events over the previous few weeks, and Charlotte being in a coma, they'd yet to find out if *she'd* been a pupil at Clayton House, too. One of the team had discovered *a* Charlotte Krane had been found on an old year photo in the school's records, so it was quite likely, but with no known family to corroborate, it was still not definitive.

Harry had just finished a call with Suzanne about those forensic results, as he wasn't going in till later that day. Now he finally picked up his toast and was just about to bite into it when Baxter's hopeful eyes appeared just above the table's edge…

"You have *had* your breakfast this morning, Bax, you

do know that, don't you? It was a big stack of meat and biscuit in a blue bowl with your name on it." Baxter's eyes flicked to the toast and marmalade and back to Harry's on repeat, following it up with a lift of the head and a little whine. "It was your favourite chicken variety," he pleaded. Baxter's eyes now concentrated on the toast alone… Harry looked at his watch. "Oh, go on then." He passed it over the table and could've sworn the Lab smiled before opening his mouth to bite into his second breakfast that morning. "I'll get something later, you cheeky git. Now don't eat it all at …"

FORTY

UNIVERSITY OF CUMBRIA STUDENT HALLS - FUSEHILL STREET - CARLISLE

11.45 P.M. SATURDAY 14TH FEB 1998

"God, I shouldn't be here, you shouldn't be … we … this is all *wrong*, it's *all* fucking *wrong*!"

"*All?* Surely you don't mean *all?* I think it's been pretty damned amazing actually, best Valentine's party I've been to in a long time."

"That's not bloody funny, Miles, and you *know* it!" Emily began pulling on her sparkly silver party top, now missing a few sequins in its earlier throws of frantic removal. "Charlotte does not forgive lightly, and *this*—" she gestured his bed area with both arms, "*this*, is never, *ever* going to get *either* of us forgiven!"

Miles lay back on his pillows, relaxed and with zero qualms of having just been fully unfaithful to his fiancée … at least twice. "Calm down, sweet pea, Charlie's never going to find out – not tonight, not ever. We've just had some fun post-Valentine's dance, it's no big deal, and she's been in the sick bay for two days so—"

"Just had some *fun*? Well, thanks for that! God, why do I give in to tequila shots every bloody *time*?" She hastily pulled up her shiny pink wide-legged cargos and buttoned them with one hand whilst grabbing her jacket off the end of the bed with the other. Running a hand through her hair, she was just about to open the door when she stopped, thinking she'd heard something, or rather some*one*, on the other side. *Shit! How long had they been there?*

"What's up, Em? Decided to stay for round three?" Miles laughed lightly at his crass joke and reached for a cigarette. The lid snap of his new Zippo lighter gifted by Charlotte at Christmas just gone punctuated the air.

"No, she *hasn't* – and as you can see, I'm no longer sick!" The door suddenly swung open, nearly hitting Emily square in the face as she automatically jumped back. Charlotte wasted no time in expressing her feelings as Emily reeled sideways from an instantly delivered violent slap, and her now *ex*-best friend flew towards her to grab handfuls of wavy hair as Miles jumped off the bed, pinning Charlotte's arms to her sides to prevent any further damage.

"Let *go* of me, you fucking *bastard*! I'll *never* forgive you, *never*! You can both rot in *hell*!" She scraped a heel down his calf, wrenching herself free from his grasp, white with anger, as Miles swore loudly in pain, "And *you* …" Charlotte now rigid with fury, pointed an outstretched arm at Emily, a long red nail on her forefinger seemingly going on forever, and a face twisted in a snarl so evil, in all the years they'd been friends, Emily had never seen… "*You* … you'd better get out of here now before I kill you. And I *will* kill you one day, Emily Rowlands, be sure of that. You are *dead* to me. *Dead. Our – bond – is – broken…*"

FORTY-ONE

ICU BASSETLAW HOSPITAL KILTON HILL - WORKSOP
MIDNIGHT THURSDAY 2ND SEPTEMBER 2021

Sofia could barely stop Charlotte's body from thrashing about. Her head was twisting left and right on the pillow and her arms were all over the place. When she lifted her right arm to point directly at her, lips curling around the endotracheal tube, Sofia pressed the alarm. It wasn't strictly a code blue because Charlotte was breathing and obviously responsive, but Sofia needed assistance. She wanted a doctor, preferably, to witness her patient's behaviour, so used the call system. Mike had the day off, so knew he wouldn't be responding, but ideally she wanted to see someone more senior. Mr Shepherd, the consultant, would not routinely be in, but she knew he could be called in an emergency.

"Okay, it's okay …" The monitor was bleeping loudly at her changing vital signs as Sofia stood close to the bed, holding Charlotte's hand. Her heart rate, respiration and blood pressure were all going up, with oxygen saturation dropping through obvious stress. The call light outside her room was now flashing and there were three nurses in the corridor running towards it. Sofia beckoned them in through the glass just as Charlotte had begun to reduce her excessive body movements. She spoke to them as a group...

"She's been doing this ever since she came into ICU, much less dramatic than now, but regularly all the same. In the five minutes before you arrived, she was thrashing about and her face was contorted. These are strong dream state reactions, but I'm wondering if she should have her endotracheal tube removed now so we can wean her off ventilation."

The door opened and, behind the nurses, a man had entered the room...

"I agree, Nurse Torres. We should wean her off the sedative drugs over the next few days if possible, and try to extubate her."

"Mr Shepherd, I thought you were—"

"I was. I got called in an hour ago for an emergency in cardiology, heard your request on the call system and guessed your patient has radically altered her responses. I wanted to come and see for myself. Look ... ideally, she needs a GCS scale of at least eight, but if she has a good cough and gag reflex we may still be able to extubate and let her come round on less than that. We're all acutely aware that the longer a patient is ventilated, the more likelihood there is of bacterial lung infection."

There was a general murmur of consensus, and now

Charlotte was calm again with all vital signs returned to normal and a consultant was present, those who'd responded to the call system now left and returned to their wards.

"I'll get her healthcare team together in the morning and we'll go from there, then, Mr Shepherd."

"Yes, I think it's time. Clearly the propofol levels haven't soared again, very strange that business... Anyway, this is likely why she's more active in her movements and responses, so let's give it a try. It's been four months now. Keep me informed."

Sofia wondered if there was more to it than just a reduction in Propofol. She would dearly love to know just exactly what kind of dreams or memories her patient was experiencing. But she didn't say *any* of that. Mr Shepherd already had his hand on the door, his mind having leapt to the next emergency of the night, or maybe something to settle his ulcer... Instead, she replied – "Yes, sir, of *course*."

That night shift was a long one. Sofia was watching Charlotte very carefully for any signs of movement or distress, but all was calm. Tired but wired, it was now 10.00 a.m. and she should have gone off at six but didn't want to leave. Arrangements had been made to reduce the Propofol in the next hour, with a view to removal altogether over the next forty-eight hours. Sofia wanted to be present.

She stayed for a further couple of hours before deciding to go home for a sleep. Charlotte had remained the same in that time, which wasn't unusual as it could take a few days for her to wake up. Raya had never had the chance of being weaned off a ventilator, and Sofia couldn't be there for her sister as she wasn't a nurse back then, so now she wanted to be there for her patient … *despite that patient's history.*

* * *

The shower felt absolutely glorious. Hot water rained onto her skin as she lifted her face to meet it and rinse the shampoo from her hair, finally squeezing out the water and turning the dial off. Opening the door, she stepped onto the bathmat, and reached round to the radiator for a huge towel, luxuriating in its soft and heavy warmth as she snuggled into it. Mike always had such beautiful top of the range towels, always white, always huge, but then a third-year doctor's pay allowed for that kind of expenditure, *that* and beautiful sheets…

As she walked through to the bedroom, rough drying her hair, Sofia could hear muffled sounds from downstairs. It was just gone 1.00 p.m. and all she really wanted to do was flop into bed after her night shift, but hunger dictated a bowl of cereal first.

Her arms slipped easily into Mike's black and gold dressing gown, which obviously drowned her petite figure, but she loved wearing it because of the scent of his Invictus cologne, and, like the towels, it was incredibly soft and snuggly.

At the top of the stairs she heard voices. It sounded

like Mike was on the phone in the living room, but he was agitated, and whoever was on the other end must have been speaking loudly because, despite not being able to make out the words, she could hear their voice. A woman's voice. He'd already explained the makeup items she'd found belonged to his sister who'd recently visited, so she wasn't going to jump to conclusions again. But why did the person he was speaking to sound so stressed out? And why was Mike's voice matching hers?

"Let her wake *up*? Are you *insane*? *Why*, Hannah?"

Mumbled agitated voice....

"But Charlotte Peterson owes our family thousands *and* she murdered Zoe in Rampton, *our sister, Zoe*, or have you forgotten that? Why is mu—"

Mumbled agitated voice......

"She's *what*?!!"

Sofia couldn't stay at the top of the stairs any longer. Once she'd heard Mike mention Charlotte's name, she knew something was horribly wrong. She wanted to get dressed and get out, but first needed to find out what he was talking about and who he was talking about it with. She crept down the stairs till she could hear the voice on the other end of the call, very aware of the danger she could be in if she couldn't fake ignorance over his conversation.

"She's been outed, Mike, something to do with her deliberately losing the paperwork on the signing back in of a police-issue gun in the nineties. Our chief superintendent was DI at the time, it was *his* gun, and it's all connected to three cold cases we're working on."

"So what's the instruction, Han? What do we do now?"

"Mum got out of the country before it all kicked off. She's at the villa in Costa Rica and there's no extradition to the UK so she'll be safe with the—"

"Yes, yes, I get that, and thank God she's safe, but what are *we* supposed to do? Who's running the business in the UK?"

"We are, bro. *We're the only Zandinis at the head of the family here.*"

"You *are* fucking kidding me? That's not good, Han, that's seriously *not fucking good.*"

"I suggest you don't let the family know you're thinking that – there are plenty who'd like that position."

"They can *have* it, I don't want it! Working at the extremities is one thing, stepping up to take the position of UK don is something else altogether."

"It's not a choice, Mykhailo – you *know* that, it's a law. There are many. Uncle Raiffe learnt that to his cost, as I'm sure you remember."

"But—"

"*There – are – no – buts.*"

The phone clicked off and there was silence. *Sofia could barely breathe.* There was no sound from the living room, but she imagined her crashing heart palpitations were about to give her away at any moment. Her head was teeming with questions. *What the hell was Mike involved in? Why did the woman call him by a foreign name? Who* was *he and what had she got herself involved with? More importantly,*

370

what should she do now? Sofia turned round shakily and silently re-climbed the stairs, remembering to avoid the one below the top that always creaked. Back in the bedroom she got dressed faster than a vitals crash. It was as she was buttoning her trousers she heard the creak…

"Sof … ? Sofia, are you th … where *are* you?" Mike walked into his now empty bedroom.

"I'm in the en suite. I'll be down in a minute."

"You need to get some shut eye, Sof – have you eaten yet?"

"No, not yet, I'll grab a bowl of cereal shortly and then get my head down."

"Okay, I'll see you downstairs then. I'm off today so not rushing out anywhere."

"Yes … won't be long."

Sofia's eyes were glued to her terrified reflection in the bathroom mirror. Her fingers, almost white now, were gripping the edge of the flamboyantly shaped basin as her brain spun trying to decide what to do for the best. She couldn't believe he'd got the day off and had no memory of him mentioning it.

Her boots, jacket and bag were in the hall near the door. The lounge was on the left at the bottom of the stairs when going down. If Mike was in the kitchen at the end of the hall past the stairs, he would definitely see her running to get her things because the kitchen door was always open. If he was in the lounge and she could be ultra quiet, the door would shield her from where he always sat because of the way it was hung.

A couple of minutes after Mike left the bedroom, Sofia heard him go back down. She came out of the en suite, walked to the top of the stairs again and listened. The TV was now on and she recognised the theme tune of a film he'd recorded a few days ago. He'd been really looking forward to seeing it so was probably well settled. With her body filled with adrenaline, she stepped over the creaky stair and crept down one level at a time, praying the volume level of the TV would hide any slight sounds she was making, and the film was as good as he'd expected.

At the bottom, outside the lounge, her heart was literally hammering against her ribs. She felt desperately sick but carried on tiptoeing down the hall to her things. Luckily, there was carpet underneath her feet, and her boots were easy to slip into and quickly pull on. She picked up her bag, put the strap over her head and reached up to the hook for her jacket. *And then she smelt it … the Invictus cologne…*

FORTY-TWO

FRIDAY 3RD SEPTEMBER 2021

"Where are you going, Sofia?"

Mike stood a couple of feet from her, looking genuinely puzzled. In that flash of a second, Sofia realised he hadn't cottoned on she'd overheard his conversation with Hannah. It was also suddenly clear his sister Hannah was the security officer he'd brought in for Charlotte's room recently. No doubt she'd been injecting her with Propofol and God knows what else.

"I – I got a call. From my—"

Mike's own phone rang again. He wriggled it awkwardly from his pocket as it was a slightly tight fit and his hands were large. He swiped and glanced at the screen. That brief distraction gave Sofia enough time to spin the lock, yank on the door handle and be down the drive to where her car was parked opposite the house, before he could stop her. She could hear him yelling her name – pounding the drive after her as she frantically rummaged her bag for her keys as she ran, but she couldn't find them! *Then from nowhere it felt like they were pushed directly into her hand*.... Sofia pulled the fob out of her bag, pointed her arm at the car and pressed the auto button as she flew out of the open gate and across the road. With his tall frame Mike was gaining quickly and the look she saw on his face over the roof of the Fiesta told her that *now* he *knew* she knew – *knew* she'd overheard him talking to his sister and learnt enough to make her run.

Open – in – close – lock – it was even faster than she'd dressed as she fired the engine and screeched away from the kerb, too scared to cry, too terrified to breathe – she pointed the car towards the hospital, changing up quickly through the gears, losing the back end on every corner, not caring if she was speeding but praying she wouldn't crash. Praying Raya was watching over her... She *had* to get there, she *had* to – *work was now the only safe place to be!*

Within minutes, Mike's Ford Puma had shot into view in her rear-view mirror. Sofia cursed in desperation, smashing her hand on the wheel and ramming the gear back down to third as she screamed up High Hoe Road till it crossed at Kilton Road, and then gasped as she barely made it across to the B6041 roaring up a low-rise Kilton Hill. Mike was still there behind her, she pressed down harder on the accelerator, nearly flooring it as she flew the Fiesta under the bridge by the lights and up the hill. Sofia was going so fast now she was shaking, the *car* was shaking, it wasn't *built* for speed, but she knew the hospital was almost within sight, it was so close, *safety* was almost within reach, but Mike just *wouldn't* give up. The nose of the Puma's white bonnet was now showing up in her driver's wing mirror as Mike sped up Kilton Hill, trying to overtake and cut her off before she reached the hospital entrance coming up on the left. Sofia now floored the accelerator as one final push came from Mike just before a pelican crossing to bring him alongside and force the Fiesta to career left into a side road. Skidding and screeching at eighty before flipping across the carriageway, she smashed through the wall of a corner property's garden – *the car landing on its roof...*

Continuing on past Shepherd's Avenue where Sofia's mangled car now lay amongst a pile of bricks, steam coming from the radiator and oil dripping from the engine, Mike Leyland watched in his rear-view mirror all the way to the turning, but didn't hang around to check out the grisly truth. As the Ford Puma indicated next right into Plantation Hill he was already planning to report it stolen. The police would find it burnt out in the next twenty-four hours, miles away somewhere. It wouldn't matter where. Any guilt he'd felt over Sofia Torres had already been blocked – he had to let it go or it would crush him. *Mike just hoped she was well on her way to finding Raya...*

* * *

ICU BASSETLAW HOSPITAL
10.00 A.M. SUNDAY 5TH SEPTEMBER 2021

When Sofia didn't turn up for work two days later to start her day shift, nobody asked any questions. Not one person. The reason for the apparent lack of curiosity was because they had no need to ask. *Sofia Torres was lying in the ICU – broken.* She had broken arms, a broken right leg, three broken ribs, severe concussion, suspected brain damage, and several nasty facial lacerations. Not to mention whiplash and four fractured vertebrae. She was a total mess – but a mess that could still talk – *just.* It was because she could still talk that a couple of police officers had been sent to Mike Leyland's house for a detailed chat. There had also been three eyewitness accounts phoned into Worksop Police Station on the day Sofia had been forced off Kilton Hill into Shepherd's Avenue at high speed by a man driving a white Ford Puma. It was a car with a private plate – ML18 ZZZ – which meant it was easy for Joe Public to remember. It was also unusual, even for a private plate, and that car was not in Mike's drive, nor the police discovered, was it in his garage.

"I reported it stolen three days ago." They were all seated in Mike's living room. The young PC's eyes roamed the decor, noticing it was very black and white, very male; very minimal. The older officer, a sergeant, was asking the questions.

"Yes, so we understand, sir. Tell me … your missing car, a white Ford Puma. It has a private plate, ML18 ZZZ."

"That's right."

"Quite unique wouldn't you say, even for a private plate?"

"Well, I would have thought that was the idea, Sergeant. Can't drive about with non-unique ones, it would get—"

"Why *Z Z Z*, Mr Leyland? What does it mean, if *anything?*"

Mike sighed and crossed his arms, "I'm a doctor. I work at Bassetlaw Hospital – as an *anaesthetist*. So it's *ZZZ* as in going to sleep – get it?"

The PC stopped roaming the one white, one black curtain and following the crack along the coving, and brought his eyes back to their suspect. His sergeant thought about Mike's answer before 'getting it', looked at his PC and waited. There was silence for a few seconds before the younger man realised he was supposed to be asking a question… "Where were you on Friday the third of September at approximately one thirty-five to one forty-five in the afternoon – sir?"

"I was here. On account of the fact I've got no car because some bastard's stolen it and it also was my day off. As was yesterday *and* today, so have you actually got anyone out there looking for it or am I going to have to bus it in on Monday?"

"So when did you last use it and where was it when you last saw it?" asked the sergeant, noting his sarcasm and ignoring both questions.

Mike was beginning to feel uncomfortable, but

breathed steadily and kept his cool. "I drove home from work on Wednesday evening the first of September and parked it on the road. I don't usually do this, I normally leave it on the drive, but intended to cut the grass, including the strip between the paving slabs, so left it on the road. Clearly, someone stole it somewhere between Wednesday evening and Friday lunchtime, because it was gone when I went to use it Friday afternoon to go shopping. Why all these questions anyway? I reported it missing Friday afternoon and your station sergeant's got all this info already."

"Trouble is, Mr Leyland, we have two witnesses to say they saw you get in your car that was parked outside this house Friday afternoon about one fifteen. You then chased a Ford Fiesta down your road at speed, where, after following the route to Bassetlaw Hospital, *three other* witnesses say you forced that car off Kilton Hill into Shepherd's Avenue where it lost control and flipped onto its roof."

"What the . . ? Who the *fuck* said that?! *Who?* I *told* you my car was stolen! If that happened, it was the bloody thief who killed her not *me!*"

"Killed *who*, sir? I never mentioned a female driver or anyone dying."

"I – er – I ..."

"Mr Michael Leyland, you do not have to say anything, but it may harm your defence if you do not mention when questioned something which you later rely on in court. Anything you do say may be given in evidence. John – *cuff* him."

The young PC already positioned by the lounge door blocking any escape to the hall, now came forward. Mike sank into the sofa cushions – he knew when he was beaten. He also realised that judging by what the sergeant had said, Sofia was still alive, and that was seriously bad news. Unless their mother, Dominique du Guarde, could get her out of the country, from now on, his sister Hannah Carlin was on her own. But then, knowing Hannah – *she was almost certainly preparing to step into their mother's shoes…*

FORTY-THREE

SATURDAY 4TH SEPTEMBER 2021
NEW BEGINNINGS

Harry could hear banging outside again – only this time he knew the likely reason. The open-day house viewing his estate agents arranged in May had gone even better than any of them had hoped, and a good offer had come in quickly, which he'd accepted. Now the sold sign was presumably being hammered into his flower bed, probably crushing the last of the pansies…

Fran's flat, which had luckily found a new owner in July, was proceeding, and they'd had an offer accepted on a four-bed detached in Newton Reigny in Penrith the same month. Everything appeared to be going through okay, thank God, because Harry really didn't have the time or inclination to do the solicitor's work for them.

It was a lovely modern place, with good-sized bright rooms and very little work to do, which, given their jobs and a nine-month-old baby, suited them both. It also had a reasonable-sized garden for Baxter to have a romp in now and little Jamie Ross when he found his legs in a few months. At the end of that thought, he had the good grace to acknowledge an Annie-shaped twinge of guilt which always seemed to accompany any pleasant plans and dreams. He'd tried his damndest not to fall in love with Fran, in fact, he'd tried several times over the years not to fall in love with her, both in London and since she'd moved up to Keswick, but nothing had worked. He'd had to leave London because Annie had felt uncomfortable about his partnering Fran at work, in fact, she'd insisted on it, and so he'd gone along with basically being put out to grass in the Lake District. But if he was honest, Fran had always been there at the back of his mind, and despite a last half-hearted attempt at patching up his marriage, trying to encourage Annie to get help with her past demons, *or more specifically, teenage demon rapist and more recent abductor, Kenny Drew,* he knew they'd grown too far apart for sticking plaster repairs. The New York trip eighteen months ago to bring Charlotte back after her escape had basically sealed the fate of his marriage, especially after Jamie had been conceived out there.

He was just about to make himself a second coffee when his phone rang. It was Fran – she didn't wait for him to say hello…

"Harry, I'm on my way to the pub to drop Jamie off with Molly and Gina. They're at the leisure centre with the children at the moment but will be back by the time I get there. Don't be late picking me up, will you?"

"No, of course—"

"By the way, Gina's told me she's thinking of running a crèche and that could be really handy for when I go back to work, which, *much* as I adore our son, I *am* missing the chall—"

"You *do* remember we're moving to Penrith in the next few weeks, don't you? Wouldn't it be easier to find someone closer to the new place?"

"*Absolutely not*, Gina's a perfect choice and I know I can trust her. I'll have to drive back to Kirkdale, anyway, unless they transfer me to Penrith, of course. Not sure how long we'll get away with both of us at the same station now everyone knows we're officially a thing."

"A – *thing?*"

"You know what I mean. Look, you need to get going, we don't want to be late for his big day."

"Absolutely – I'm on my way, just got to drop Bax off next door with Kate, and I'll be with you."

2.30 P.M. KESWICK LEISURE CENTRE
STATION ROAD KESWICK

Molly and Gina were juggling coffees, cakes and babies in the café area of the leisure centre, having spent an hour in a softball play session with the girls. Now they were trying to enjoy a well-earned cappuccino and large slice of chocolate cake. Gina had Ellie in the crook of her left arm on her lap and was lifting a piece up whilst Ellie repeatedly grabbed the fork and tried to direct it into *her* mouth. Gina put the fork down and cut a small piece off with her coffee spoon to let Ellie taste some. Flying arms, excited rocking and a huge grin told her it was a big hit!

"This one's definitely taking after me, I'm going to have to watch that or she's going to be a little barrel!" She leant forward to fork some cake into her own mouth then looked up to see Molly doing the same. They both grinned, followed by their eye-raising heavenly expressions only reserved for favourite cakes! It appeared Molly's Christie loved it too, after she'd popped a little piece in her open and demanding mouth.

"By the way, did I tell you I was thinking of opening a crèche? I mentioned it to Fran the other day and she seemed really keen for when she goes back to work, after they move. Andy thinks it's a good idea as long as I keep it to a small group. What do you think?

"Sounds brilliant – are you thinking of running it from home?"

"Well, no offence, but the authorities probably wouldn't think a pub was ideal!"

Molly laughed, drained her cup and lifted Christie off her lap to place her, resisting noisily, back into her buggy. "I guess not, although I'm sure Mum wouldn't mind, our private lounge is huge!"

"Oh, and big news this, Miles told me he's finally pulled out of his relationship with Annie Longbridge," said Gina, offering Ellie her baby juice cup which she grabbed with both hands. "I'm relieved to be honest."

"I'm really not surprised, Gee. He's a grandfather now and despite his past icky behaviour with women, I think he genuinely wants a good relationship with you and Ellie-Ro."

"Yes, I think so too, and with Andy working with Harry it was inevitable, really. At the end of the day, she committed a murder and an attempted murder, and although he'd clearly been besotted with her before he knew what she'd done, I think his feelings cooled considerably after that."

A few heads turned and mouths dropped at that sentence, so after checking her watch, Gina quickly finished the last of her cake and cappuccino, and strapped Ellie into her pushchair, too.

"I think we'd better make tracks, Molls, Fran's bringing Jamie over to us at the pub soon because of the award ceremony."

As if on cue, her phone bleeped a notification and Gina reached round to pick it up from the table to see Andrew had messaged her. She read out the gist of it as she pulled on her jacket. "Celebrations are going to be at the pub later for those who couldn't go because of number restrictions. He's said for me to meet him there instead of going home."

"We'd better get back, then, I'm sure Mum could do with some help, she'll want to lay on a big spread."

"Absolutely, and much as I love 'em … *I don't think Maisie's spicy shepherd's pies will really cut it tonight!*"

3.30 P.M. CARLETON HALL - PENRITH BRAVERY AWARDS CEREMONY

Joe Walker still couldn't believe it was happening yet felt extremely proud, but also humble, that it was. When Assistant Chief Constable Raymond Greaves pinned the George Medal to his chest and turned him round to face his applause, Joe initially dropped his head in slight embarrassment – he just wasn't a guy used to basking in the limelight. That was until he saw his mother holding a tissue to her eyes, his father beaming from ear to ear, and Harry wildly clapping for all he was worth – *only just held back by Fran's hand on his arm from using his ear-piercing dog whistle in wholehearted appreciation...*

"Spoilsport – lad deserves a bloody good riotous applause. Saved my life and I'll never forget it, I'll never be able to repay him – *never...*"

"I know, I know..." she stroked his arm and squeezed his hand... "I'll never be able to either, but let's save the noisy celebrations for the pub later, shall we? I don't think the assistant chief constable would appreciate dog whistles reminiscent of a football match – do you?"

Harry harrumphed. He knew she was right but hated all the stuffiness, even more so because of the type of award his sergeant had won, and why. It doesn't get much braver than taking a bullet for a colleague, and because of his heroism he'd naturally got a soft spot for Joe – *he was practically family now.*

When Raymond Greaves had given his speech and

the official duties had been discharged, there was a room everyone drifted through to where light refreshments had been laid on for all officers and their families who'd proudly come along to support them. In the normal run of events, a medal of such distinction as Joe's would have been awarded at a big ceremony in London, with the prime minister, the Met. commissioner and Home Secretary present. However, Joe had requested to receive his medal at Carleton Hall where he'd done his training, and where fellow officers from Penrith and Carlisle were receiving bravery honours, too. One had saved a child from drowning, another, an elderly man from a house fire, and a third had talked down a depressed teenager from jumping off a motorway bridge. All very worthy awards, *and all four of them had trained together.*

The doors of the reception room opened out onto a terrace, and with the summer still hanging on, there was only a slight breeze accompanying the sunshine.

"Lovely sunny day," said Fran, trying to balance a plate of tiny sandwiches plus a cup and saucer and eat at the same time. "But then they do say the sun shines on the righteous."

"They do, indeed. Look, there's a table – let's offload," replied Harry also doing the buffet juggle, only he had *two* plates of food with his cup and saucer. They sank into comfy leather chairs and relieved themselves of all their china.

"I've been thinking. Joe's been a DS for … what? Eighteen months? He could be an inspector by this time next year."

"Are you trying to give my job away, Harry?"

"You arrived in the Lakes already a DI, Fran – it's time you thought about promotion. I obviously won't be going any further, not as an officially retired DCI. Don't forget I've only been here as an advisor because of the Peterson case, and then you being on maternity leave."

"I know. I do forget that sometimes, it's just so natural, us working together as we did in London."

Harry smiled, a little misty-eyed remembering their time at the end of the nineties to 2013 in the heart of the City, Fran a sergeant and he her DI. "You're only forty-four, you could get to chief super before you finish if it's what you want, *definitely* DCI."

"Maybe, as you say, definitely DCI. Talking of superior ranks, have you heard anything about Chief Superintendent Hitchings?"

"No, I was thinking of giving him a call, actually. Caroline must be worried sick for both Chris *and* her sister, what with Gabe being charged with Roberta Phillips' murder as well, and the whole Zandini connection."

"Life can just change in an instant, can't it? One minute you're on course for normality, happiness even, and the next, the entire sky falls in."

"That's very deep, DI Taylor, everything okay?"

She laughed, then. It sounded funny, him calling her by her official title since they'd become an item, but now it was more of a pet name than anything else. Yes, things had certainly changed… "It's all good, Longbridge, all good."

Harry looked around the room. Joe and his parents were balancing their own cups and plates now, whilst in conversation with Assistant Chief Constable Greaves, probably soon to be *chief* constable now there was a warrant out for Dominique du Guarde's arrest. He decided to take the opportunity to ring Chris Hitchings, to see how he was coping with his suspension, explained to Fran what he was going to do, and took a walk across the terrace to a bench on the adjoining lawn.

He pulled up Hitchings' number, something he wouldn't normally have, but had since his and Chris's in-depth talk on the DNA report, and Chris's gun being found in the skeleton grave. The line only rang twice before he heard a very quiet voice on the other end…

"Hello …"

"Mrs Hitchings?"

"Speaking…"

"It's DCI Longbridge, Mrs Hitchings – *Harry*. Is Chris—"

"He won't speak to you, Mr Longbridge. He won't speak to anyone. He's barely speaking to *me*."

Harry winced. "I've been wondering how he is, and if that might be the situation. He wasn't in a good place when we last spoke at work."

"This has knocked the stuffing out of him, Harry; he's a completely different man. I've got my sister Denise here, too. She's fallen apart at the seams since Gabe's arrest; we just can't believe what he's been involved with and I'm not sure what to do to be honest – it feels like our lives have fallen apart overnight."

Gabe's ID bracelet instantly came to mind, then, the one

found in Roberta Phillips' car inscribed 'To Gabe Much Love Denise'. Unlikely to be from a teenage Denise Fraser to a teenage Gabe Downs, but they'd all wondered, and even if it was, Sandra Wainright had already coughed to her manslaughter. Even so…

"Mrs Hitch—"

"Caroline – please…"

"Caroline. Did your sister give Gabe an ID bracelet with her name on it by any chance?"

"Yes, she did. A few Christmases ago, I believe, why?"

"No matter, just that the same name came up in a case we were working on. All sorted now."

"Thank God. I don't think Denise could have coped with any more."

"Look … Caroline, Chris and I have had a somewhat up and down relationship since I transferred from London, but recent—"

"Harry, listen to me. Chris may have seemed offhand with you at times, but I can promise you this. *You* were his mainstay. *The* senior officer he depended on more than *any* other. It's why you were called back in, *both* times, not just because of Fran Taylor's request. He may not have told you very often, Harry, *if at all*, but he told *me*."

Harry tried to reply but it appeared his mouth had forgotten how to work.

"Are you still …"

"Yes, yes, I'm still here, just a bit … *shocked*, to be honest. Nice shocked, obviously."

"Well, it's the truth. Now though … now he's lost. A shadow of his former self and I just can't reach him."

"Caroline – please tell Chris if he'd like to chat … offload … *anything*, tell him to ring me. *Anytime* – I mean that."

"I will. Thank you, Harry. I'd better go now, see if he wants anything. Try and get him to eat."

"Yes, of course, and, I meant what I said. Bye for now."

"Goodbye, and thank you again."

Harry disconnected the call and sat quietly with the phone in his lap. He thought back to the day his home was turned over after Annie's arrest for the murder of Christopher Mogg. *That* was bad enough. It was actually hell. But *this* … the situation his chief super was going through … that was more than hell. *And long term it sounded like it was going to be more than Chris could cope with.*

8.15 P.M. CARPENTERS ARMS - KIRKDALE

The second celebration, and therefore second buffet of the day, was in full swing. Molly and her parents, Ron and Maisie Fields, running the pub of course, most of Kirkdale Station was able to be present, Ricky Thompson, Suzanne Moorcroft, Andrew and Gina, some of the secretarial staff and front desk officers (*only Hannah Carlin was mysteriously absent…*) and of course Joe's parents, Alan and Nicky Walker, were there too. All of them had given him congratulatory cards and insisted over and over again what a hero he was. His parents had taken photos at the medal ceremony at Carleton Hall, and the whole day's attention and importance had been quite overwhelming for Joe, who was really quite a quiet soul. But he didn't shy away from a photo with his mentor and senior officer, the man who because of him, was alive today. The picture with Harry's arm around Joe's shoulders, beaming with pride and thanks, would definitely be taking pride of place on his mother's mantelpiece, with of course, a copy on his own...

After the photos, Harry took an opportunity to slip away to the private lounge, where between the three of them, Gina, Molly and her mum, Maisie, had been taking it in turns to be with the babies. Christie would normally have been in her cot upstairs, but they'd all been together for the afternoon and crashed after their tea. Being the earth mother she was, and guessing Ellie and Jamie might be there on occasion, Maisie had bought two extra travel cots precisely for times like this.

Harry tiptoed into the room where Maisie was sitting on the couch, reading. She looked up when he came in, and putting her magazine down, whispered quietly to indicate she was popping out for a moment and would be back shortly. He nodded and walked over to the cot Jamie was sleeping in, sitting down in the chair next to it. His nine-months-old son lay on his back, mouth slightly open, little arms high above his head, with one hand's fingers rippling slightly as he stirred, and a mop of dark brown hair sweeping across his forehead just like his mother's. Harry sat forward, chin leaning on clasped hands, gazing at him and listening to his rhythmic breathing. The emotion caught in his throat as it always did when he watched him sleep, when he saw him smile, when he was basically just in the same room. He still couldn't believe after all these years he was finally a father, and the love that filled his heart, his soul, every part of him, had grown since his birth with every passing day. He knew without a shadow of a doubt he'd protect him with his life, *for the whole of his life…*

"You know, Jamie, lad, one day we'll tell you, your mother and I, when you're old enough and can understand properly. We'll tell you all about your twin brother, who grew alongside you before you were born, but wasn't quite strong enough to make it all the way to live in the outside world and share a life with you. But he will always be close, Jamie, don't ever forget that. Your brother, Taybridge, is still here, all around us and he always will be." Jamie slept on soundly, and as he leant over the cot to stroke his hair, Harry heard the slightest click of a door. He turned to see Fran, her eyes glazed, looking dumbstruck that a big hairy copper could deliver such tender words, and with such heartfelt meaning. And if you could ask them – *they'd swear blind they just heard the sound of a baby's laughter…*

EPILOGUE

ICU BASSETLAW HOSPITAL
MONDAY 6TH SEPTEMBER 2021

It hadn't been possible to get into her room quite as often over the last few months, which meant the propofol to keep her sedated had been delivered less regularly than was ideally required. It had still worked, *just*, there'd been some ups and downs, but once the coma team had decided it was time to try and let Charlotte wake up naturally, remove the endotracheal tube to see if she could breathe on her own … well … *that had to be prevented*. Thwarting it had been extremely satisfying, dangerous and frustrating, but satisfying – *for both of them…*

Passing yourself off as one of Bassetlaw's doctors had not been *that* difficult, it was a very big and busy place, although there'd been one or two occasions where thinking on one's feet had become necessary. There was clearly still a risk, even though this wasn't a solo vendetta. Today, though, reaching her room fairly quickly and without incident had been a relief. The coma nurse in the corridor on previous days wasn't there, which was good. Familiarity was clearly not helpful, but the huge window meant it was easy to see who was in the room. Then of course it was just a matter of waiting for the current nurse to leave for a few minutes. *And of course she did ... eventually.*

As always, it was important to wait until medical traffic in the corridor was low, to avoid conversation when opening the door and slipping quietly inside. The capped syringe sat deep in the pocket of the now regularly worn white coat, lying snugly between several tissues – ironically, a favoured killing method of the woman lying in the coma. The content was meticulously measured to avoid death, but would ensure her deep 'sleep' continued. Researching it a million times to be certain had been paramount, and it had worked just fine this past fortnight. Now prayers were needed that any earlier absence would not have ruined all their hard work.

Now standing by her bedside, observing the IV line that ran into the back of her left hand and sifting through the tissue to locate the wrapped syringe, it was carefully lifted out, cap removed and a test amount squirted in mid-air. For a second there, it looked as though she shivered, just briefly, when full attention was on the syringe. No. Must have imagined it, although when studying the drug dosage, the research had revealed it wasn't impossible. Picking up her hand, the IV stopper cap was pulled out, a deep breath taken, and the syringe lifted, ready to insert. Wait. Was that someone talking outside? Turning to check the window, anxiety caused an increased heartbeat, but nobody had stopped in the corridor to enter the room, just a couple of medics exchanging conversation before going on their way – one of which was a friend. *Miles Peterson smiled knowingly over his shoulder and continued walking.*

Turning back, just for a moment there was a thought of – what if? Then, bending down, whispered words were delivered into her ear … "What if next time I actually *did* give you an overdose, Charlie, finished this completely, once and for all? Isn't it time to end all these years of regret, the breaking of bonds, the betrayal on both sides? You nearly finished me off completely in New York, maybe it's time now? Time to finish this whole damned—"

Suddenly a hand slapped on her wrist, gripping like a vice, her eyes wide open – cold as ice.

"I hate to freeze your fire – *Emily … but guess who's back?* And yes, it is time. Time for **Retribution**…"

* * *

I hope you enjoyed *Fire & Ice* as much as the first three books in the DCI Harry Longbridge series. I wanted to thank you all for your continued support – it's so much appreciated, especially with the long waits you have in between my books.

I will always be grateful.

Ali xxx

ACKNOWLEDGEMENTS
HUGE THANKS MUST GO TO...

Andrew Barrett – Senior CSI (Crime Scenes Investigator) with West Yorkshire Police

For digging me out of a seriously worrying hole on ballistics and correct forensic detail that I simply couldn't find online – literally a *massive* thank you! Andrew also writes crime thrillers set in his home county, one series from a CSI's point of view. If you enjoy dark and gritty – you might like to look him up!

Nick Burrows – My long-suffering IT guy

For maintaining my laptop, keeping me connected to the internet and generally helping me not go into meltdown – I literally couldn't write any of my books without you!

Dawn Wood (Dawnie) – A dear friend, past colleague and long-time diabetic

For all the detailed information you gave me with regard to diabetes, which helped considerably in being accurate when referring to my character DCI Harry Longbridge's own condition.

Jo Moss – My dear author friend and 'booky' companion!

For literally nagging me to dig *Blood List* out of my laptop in early 2018 after letting it 'sleep' for ten years, bring it up to date and finish it. Without you, *Blood List*, *Dead Girls Don't Cry*, *The Delegate* and *Fire & Ice* would not be in anyone's hands right now…

Everyone at Troubador/Matador – For simply being the best!

Grateful thanks for running the most professional publishing set up in the business, giving authors worldwide choice and control over their work.

Bruce – For his belief in me

And, of course, not forgetting my husband, Bruce, who does a lot of cooking (actually *all* of it!), and has to spend an awful lot of time living with someone who creates murder and mayhem! Also, for driving me to and setting up the book stand at all my events. He is literally my roadie!

AUTHOR'S LICENCE

Whilst trying to be as realistic as possible, in order to write an enjoyable *fictional* story, and despite documentary research, the specific layouts, security, daily routines and methods of working in the ICU at Bassetlaw Hospital, Worksop; Rampton High Security Psychiatric Hospital, Nottinghamshire; and HMP Frankland, County Durham; are unlikely to be accurate. I hope this fact won't have spoiled the story for anyone having links with Bassetlaw, Rampton and/or HMP Frankland at any time.